ERIC VAN LUSTBADER

THE KOBALT DOSSIER

HEAD
of
ZEUS

An Aries Book

First published in the USA in 2021 by Forge Books,
an imprint of Tom Doherty Associates

First published in the UK in 2021 by Head of Zeus Ltd
This paperback edition first published in the UK in 2022 by Head of Zeus Ltd,
part of Bloomsbury Publishing Plc

9 7 5 3 1 2 4 6 8

A catalogue record for this book is available from
the British Library.

ISBN (PB): 9781800243156
ISBN (E): 9781800243163

Typeset by Divaddict Publishing Solutions Ltd

Printed and bound in Great Britain by
CPI Group (UK) Ltd, Croydon CR0 4YY

Head of Zeus Ltd
5–8 Hardwick Street
London EC1R 4RG

WWW.HEADOFZEUS.COM

For Victoria, my one and only, my everything.

Revenge has become our way of life.
Now we enter the darkness.

—LYUDMILA ALEXEYEVNA SHOKOVA

Prologue

THREE AND A HALF YEARS AGO

"The obliteration of the face," Anouk said, "is essential." She regarded Bobbi Fisher with her gray-flannel eyes. "This point cannot be stressed enough. Without complete obliteration it may be possible to forensically retrieve the teeth." She lifted a long forefinger. "Even one tooth can be enough for identification, and you will be undone. Exfiltration cannot be accomplished."

She paused, a broad-shouldered woman with muscular arms, thick legs, and features as blunt as a weapon. Bobbi had turned her head to check the closed door to the square room—a kitchen that had been turned into an ad hoc classroom. Bobbi sat on a high stool at the central polished concrete island. By her right hand was a pitcher of ice water and a glass tumbler. Fists of rain beat against the streaked windows, blurring the restless trees that separated this two-story house from the identical ones around it. The rain-swept streets were as clean and clear as one would expect in a new development in Virginia, suburban sprawl of DC.

"Bobbi." Anouk's voice was as sharp as a knife blade. "What are you looking at? You are required to pay strict attention."

"Where is Leda?" Bobbi said without looking back.

"I am here now, Bobbi." Anouk, standing beside the refrigerator, arms at her side, hands half-curled, stood as straight as a sentry. "It is to me that you report."

Bobbi's head snapped around. "My condition when I was recruited was that Leda—and only Leda—would be my handler."

Anouk's smile bared her small white teeth. "That was some years ago," she said. "Leda has moved on."

"Then I should have moved on with her."

Anouk pursed her lips in distaste. "You had an affair with Leda, didn't you?"

"That's none of your business."

"Everything about you is my business, Bobbi. You should know that." When no reply was forthcoming, Anouk went on: "It was quite torrid, from the reports I've read."

"Damn you."

"Ah." Anouk grinned like a crocodile. "At last I have your undivided attention."

"Indeed, you do."

"Well, then, you should know that Leda is dead."

"Dead? No."

"Purged." Anouk sneered. "And I can easily arrange for you to follow her."

Bobbi rose from the stool. "Is that a threat?"

Anouk shrugged. "You'd better get used to it; it's my method."

Grasping the tumbler Bobbi drained it of water. "I want something else," she said. "Something sweeter." She walked the length of the counter, to where Anouk stood. "Excuse me." Anouk moved just enough so Bobbi could reach down for the handle of the half-refrigerator tucked beneath the counter.

As she opened the refrigerator door, she smashed the tumbler against the edge of the counter. Anouk's arm was coming but, anticipating, Bobbi grabbed her wrist, controlling it. Anouk was stronger than Bobbi, but Bobbi had the leverage, and, in any case, she only needed a split second to drive a knife-like shard into Anouk's left eye. Anouk jumped as if electrified. Bobbi kept tight hold of the bottom of the tumbler, ground it farther and farther, until the tip of the shard pierced Anouk's brain.

She stepped smartly back, avoiding both the corpse's collapse and the last spurts of blood. The kitchen's door opened. She turned to see Leda step smartly inside, close the door behind her.

Leda smiled. Everything about her was medium: height, weight, features, and yet there was something about her, something magnetic that was almost a physical thing. You might not recall her if she passed you on the street, but if you sat down opposite her in a bar or restaurant for drinks, you'd be hard-pressed to pull away.

She didn't even bother checking out the sprawled body, merely stepped over it as she crossed the large square room. "You haven't lost your reflexes, I see," she said.

"Or my rage."

The two women embraced.

"Fisher. I never could get used to your married name."

Bobbi shrugged. "What's in a name?"

Leda chuckled. "It's been a long time since we've seen each other."

Bobbi nodded, a smile wreathing her face. "Too long. Texts are no substitute for the real thing."

They kissed, then broke away. Though it was a businesslike kiss, their eyes were shining, a remnant of what once was.

A man and a woman in boilersuits and latex gloves entered, but Leda bade them wait with a commanding wave of her hand. Now she crouched down, examining Anouk's corpse with the thoroughness of a forensic pathologist. When she rose, she said, "*Idem.*" *Come on.*

Leda led her through the sparsely furnished living room and

into a space that would someday be a den or a media room, leaving the suited and gloved pair to clean up the blood and get rid of the remains.

Bobbi's eyes narrowed. "She knew about our affair."

"Did she?"

"She said she read about it in reports."

"That was an out-and-out lie."

"Really?" Bobbi cocked her head. "But isn't that your job: to recruit through seduction?"

"Seduction is only part of my job description. A small part—or, more accurately, a *selective* part. I'm much more elevated than a sparrow, else I wouldn't be here now, with you. I am your handler."

"But you have seduced others."

Leda's expression turned enigmatic, as if two or more thoughts had occurred to her at once. "You're jealous."

"Of your time, not of your charms."

"Perhaps," Leda said. "Listen to me, Bobbi. I did seduce you. Yes, I did. Without question. But let's not mince words: you wanted to be seduced."

Bobbi thought about this, thought about how right Leda was. She *did* want to be seduced. Badly. Perhaps desperately. Was that need a weakness in her? If so, she would do well to eradicate it. On the other hand, she was where she wanted to be, so why should she care about the rest? And yet, she did. She had an innate abhorrence of weakness in any form. With an almost physical wrench, she returned her thoughts to the present. "You didn't answer my question: how did Anouk know about our affair?"

"Well, now," Leda said with a twinkle in her eye, "that's an excellent question."

A silence yawned between them. Behind the kitchen door scuffling, muted sounds of the cleanup in progress. Otherwise the house, being new, was very still.

4

Then Bobbi had it. "*You* told her."

Leda laughed softly. "It did get your blood up, her knowing, didn't it?"

All at once, it seemed obvious. "So this was a test." It wasn't a question.

"Oh, it was more than that."

"Seriously?"

"You were always meant for greater things, Bobbi. I hand chose you. I didn't seduce you on a whim or because I detected a weakness. You did not hold a position advantageous to us."

"No." A slow smile. "Evan is like an impenetrable vault."

"Well," Leda said, "we'll see about that."

Bobbi frowned. "Meaning?'

"You will see." Leda went back into the kitchen and returned with an ice-rimed bottle of vodka, two spotted water glasses, and a manila envelope, also ice-rimed, tucked firmly under her arm. She poured triple shots into both water glasses and handed one to Bobbi. Leda lifted her glass high and Bobbi followed suit. They drank in the Russian fashion, all in one. They were clearly toasting something, Bobbi's graduation? Anouk's death? Bobbi had no idea what.

Leda set aside her glass. "Anouk was your final exam," she said as if reading Bobbi's mind. "Your schooling has been long, I know. And now you have graduated summa cum laude. As a consequence, two weeks from now Bobbi Ryder Fisher will cease to exist. She will die. And from then on you will be known only by a new operational name I will give you when you leave here."

"A new life." Her eyes flicked to the envelope, but she said nothing. She knew to wait.

Leda nodded. "It's what we promised you. It's what you wanted above all else. Is that still true?"

Bobbi was incredulous. "Of course!" She had married knowing what would happen someday. Paul had insisted on kids and, frankly, when consulted Leda was all for it, wisely saying that it would only deepen Bobbi's cover. "*But there's a risk*," she had warned. "*A mother's love can—*" "*I have no trace of a maternal instinct*," Bobbi had interrupted. "*I don't see the point of children, not in this day and age.*" And Leda had been satisfied.

"Nothing whatsoever has changed since I was read the terms of my recruitment."

"Then to your first—and last—assignment in DC." Leda opened the envelope and removed a 5x7 photo, which she handed to Bobbi. It was a head-and-shoulders shot, the image lacking vivid color, flattened due to the long-lens surveillance camera with which it had been taken. "You know this woman, yes?"

"Of course," Bobbi said. "It's Benjamin Butler's wife, Lila."

"She's a friend of yours," Leda said, "yes?"

"You want me to go to Berlin?"

"Mrs. Butler arrived here this morning," Leda said. "Her father isn't well."

Bobbi considered this for a moment. "It was you who made him unwell, wasn't it?"

"Well, not me personally," Leda said, half-offended. "But, yes, it was achieved on my order."

"So the end could come here, where I am."

Leda's smile spread slowly, like butter in sunlight. "You are my best pupil, Bobbi. I knew it the first time I laid eyes on you, in Copenhagen when you were seventeen. We're like family now."

"How?" Bobbi said. "How could you know I'd be your best pupil?"

"Between you and your sister you were the one having fun."

"I was enjoying life."

"No," Leda said. "You were devouring it."

★★★

Forty-eight hours later and after a brief respite the rain had persevered, though reduced to a drizzle. The residents inside the Beltway, umbrellas unfurled, hurried along slick sidewalks. Those bravely, or foolishly, without sprinted toward crowded doorways or shimmering awnings.

Bobbi saw Lila Butler before Lila saw her. She had texted Lila the day before, made a date for a shopping expedition and lunch, "to take your mind off your father," she'd said. Lila had been openly grateful for both the break and the company of an old friend, giving Bobbi the sense that living in Berlin was starting to grate on Lila. Bobbi had a remedy for that.

She looked both ways, waited several moments, checking her wristwatch for the time. Her heart rate picked up as she crossed the street against the light to intercept Lila before she turned in to the department store where they'd arranged to meet.

Beneath Lila's umbrella, they embraced. Lila had always been birdlike, but now she was thinner, paler, and the wetness on her cheeks was tears, not raindrops. Bobbi's hunch had been right: Berlin did not agree with her.

Bobbi first asked after Lila's father's health. It was failing, quickly. Bobbi wondered what Leda's people had given him. Only then did she ask about Berlin.

Lila sighed deeply. "Berlin is so gray," she said. "And the people . . ." Lila shivered. "They're friendly on the surface. Maybe too friendly. Underneath there seems a darkness—the river Styx running through them. And now the immigrant issue has given a fervent raison d'être to the neo-Nazi movement."

They were standing at the curb in order to avoid the crowds of foot traffic along the sidewalk, shoulders touching beneath Lila's umbrella. Bobbi placed a gentle hand on Lila's arm, bony as a sparrow's wing.

"I'm sorry you're unhappy," Bobbi said with one eye on the oncoming traffic. "How about Zoe. How's she doing?"

"Unlike me, Zoe loves it over there. But then again she's four so her world is as small as any four-year-old's."

"Be sure to give her my love, though I doubt she remembers me."

"Of course she remembers you," Lila exclaimed. "She remembers everything and everyone."

Bobbi smiled. She saw the SUV. Its rain-streaked tinted windows reflected the buildings and the low sky as if in a fun house mirror. "When do you think you might all come home?"

Lila shrugged. "I don't know. Ben's still got business over there."

"Of course. So, how long will you be in DC now?"

"That will depend on my father's condition. But I already miss Zoe."

"Your father's health aside, and even missing Zoe," Bobbi said, "I think the trip back here will be good for you, even if it's only for a few days. Berlin is so gloomy, isn't it?"

"*So* gloomy." Lila smiled. Bobbi had forgotten how the space around her lit up when she smiled. "I'm so glad you contacted me." Lila gave Bobbi's arm a brief squeeze. "I can't tell you how good it feels to see a friendly face. Things are pretty grim at my parents' place." And she leaned in to give Bobbi a peck on the cheek.

Which was when Bobbi appeared to stumble off the curb. She swung Lila around. Off-balance, Lila's umbrella tilted, shielding them from the eyes of the bustling crowd on the sidewalk. Bobbi let go of her elbow and hip-bumped her, hard, directly into the path of the SUV, now speeding toward them.

Bobbi had started moving away even before the sound reached her ears, the *thunk*, heavy, wet, ominous. She eeled her way through the crowd at precisely the same pace as those around her. Behind her came the squeal of tires, screams, shouts, and the crowd began to press toward the curb, attracted to the scene like mice to cheese. The approaching wail of sirens found her on the fourth floor of the department store, shielded by a forest of expensive designer dresses, heading toward the escalator down to the entrance on the far side of the store.

PART ONE

PART ONE

1

WASHINGTON, DC
PRESENT DAY

Benjamin Butler had made a mistake. A grave mistake. By Zoe's determination, anyway. His daughter, eight years old going on sixteen, had made him promise that there would always be Oreos in the house. Because they just returned from a week at the Atlantis in Paradise Island, celebrating her eighth birthday, tonight there weren't any, which was why Ben was trolling down the wide aisles of the Costco on Market Street NE, in DC with an impatient Zoe on his heels. It was almost 8 P.M.; they had just over thirty minutes to find and purchase the Oreos before the store closed for the night. He should have known where they were; he'd bought them often enough. But Costco had this annoying habit of moving displays around.

At last, after long minutes of hunting, Zoe spotted them midway down the snacks aisle.

"There, Dad! There they are!"

He pushed his cart after his sprinting daughter and caught up with her in front of a massive stack of the oversized blue boxes filled with thirty six-packs of the cookies Zoe loved so much. He grabbed one, looked at her happy hungry face, and decided to make it two, so he wouldn't have to think about buying them for weeks. As he turned to head for the register lines, he saw a suit standing at the end of the aisle. Looking back over his shoulder, he saw the suit's twin—or near enough. Ben had been in the business of espionage long enough to recognize government bodyguards with a single glance. He could smell them too—a combination of cheap aftershave, cheap fabric, and sweat. No one was in the aisle save himself and Zoe. He prudently decided to shelter in place and let the situation reveal itself. He stood with his hands on the bar of his shopping cart, Zoe in front of him cradled between his arms, and waited.

A few seconds later, a new actor emerged from behind a display of M&M boxes the size of his chest. The no-neck monster Ben knew as General Ryan Aristides, his boss at DOD, who had proved himself a gutless wonder when Ben's job and reputation were on the line several months ago. Instead of coming to Ben's defense against Brady Thompson, the Secretary of Defense, he had stepped away, keeping himself clear of whatever fallout would ensue from Brady coming down on Ben's head and on Ben's clandestine shop. As it turned out Ben and Evan Ryder had been able to neutralize Thompson, uncovering evidence that he had been working for the Russians and turning him. As a double agent, he now delivered vital intel to Aristides while feeding disinformation to his erstwhile Russian masters.

The general's big square face looked pale beneath the harsh blue-white overheads. He walked with a rolling gait, slightly bowlegged, result of his time aboard ships.

"Quite a sweet tooth you have there, Ben," he said, pointing at the Oreos.

Ben. Aristides always called him Benjamin. Something was up. It was only then, as the general approached, that Ben realized Aristides was out of regs: he was in a shiny suit he might have worn to his daughter's wedding.

"Zoe," Ben said.

"Ah, yes, the lovely Zoe."

The general should have been smiling, but he wasn't. Anyone else would have said hello to the girl, asked how she was, but Aristides was busy looking at a display of gummy bears. "I hated these when I was a kid," he said, his voice a basso rumble. "Disgusting stuff, don't you think? All that sugar, just rots you from the inside out." But it was clear he didn't expect or want an answer. In fact, it wasn't altogether clear whether he was speaking about gummy bears at all.

The general sighed, turned back to Ben. "I think it would be best if Zoe took a stroll around with Wilson here." One of the suits stepped forward. He was young, fresh-faced, and, unlike his boss, was smiling at Zoe.

Ben took a short moment for a sit rep. Evaluating the situation wasn't difficult; Aristides had given him little choice. He leaned over and put his mouth to Zoe's ear. "How about it, kiddo? The general and I need to have a bit of a chin-wag." He couched the request in as unintimidating terms as he could.

Zoe, who was both smart and used to the secretiveness of her father's job, nodded. "Okey-doke.

"I'm not a child," she said, slipping out from between her father and the shopping cart, ignoring Wilson's extended hand, fixing him with her disconcertingly direct stare.

"My mistake." Wilson scarcely missed a beat.

When the two of them were out of sight, Aristides cleared his throat. "Ben, I'm afraid I have bad news."

Ben's stomach dropped, as if he were in a fast descending elevator. "Let's have it," he said.

The general picked up an enormous bag of miniature Snickers, regarded it as if it were a crystal ball, then, almost angrily, shoved it back with its brethren. When he turned to Ben, his gaze was concentrated on a spot in the middle of Ben's forehead.

He can't look me in the eye, Ben thought, and braced himself as best he could.

Aristides heaved a sigh. His neck was bulging, threatening to burst out of its collar. "As of today, your shop is out of business."

"Wait. What?" Ben couldn't believe what he just heard. "You can't be serious."

"Everyone but Evan has already been reassigned."

"After we delivered Thompson as a double agent? The Secretary of Defense? The biggest espionage coup in . . ." Ben shook his head. "How is this possible?"

"You delivered Thompson to me, personally. No one else knows we compromised him and to protect him that's the way it needs to remain."

"I understand. Of course I do. But still—"

"Listen to me, Ben. First, POTUS doesn't care for your agents being female." Aristides began to count on his fingers. "Second, you lost control of one of them, Brenda Myers. She went rogue and killed a civilian. Third, your shop's incursion on foreign soil and its messy aftermath have made you and Ryder some extremely dangerous enemies here at home—billionaires with the wherewithal and power to influence POTUS."

Ben grunted in disgust. "General, with all due respect, you still need me, need my shop. These people aren't done. Samuel Wainwright Wells is right at the heart of the same evangelical conservative cabal that's been funding Nemesis's neo-Nazi arm here in America. That's the right wing's plan, meld their brand of conservatism with white supremacy. He's their top dog. I've got my eye on him, with his people spewing their evangelical racism through the TV and radio stations he owns."

"Undoubtedly. Nevertheless, Ben, these evangelical conservatives have POTUS's ear. Wells's Super PAC played a major role in his election. Ever since Wells married his third wife, the former Lucinda Horvat, just over a year ago, he's been even more seriously into the evangelicals."

Ben shook his head. "Right. They had a low-key wedding at the DC hotel owned by one of POTUS's companies. I heard he offered the hotel gratis—as a wedding present."

Aristides nodded. "Tight guest list—an echelon of his compadres, but none of her family; they're all dead. Probably because Lucinda is in her late twenties, the marriage caused something of a ripple in the mainstream press."

"Which set off the usual backlash in the right-wing media. And even they weren't allowed to take photos."

The general nodded. "Wells is notoriously reclusive, so there wasn't much of a story for the press to latch onto. And, of course, Wells's own virulently right-wing media network ignored the age difference altogether. In any event, it took the new Mrs. Wells no time to climb into the Wellsian life. By all accounts he's content to have her be his mouthpiece. And POTUS seems enamored of her. She often leads his private prayer group. Word is, she also appears to be taking a more active role in Wells's business affairs. She's seen more often at high-level corporation meetings than he is."

"Well, there you go. Their involvement in Nemesis is a logical conclusion, General. Even you can see that."

Aristides's expression did not change. "All circumstantial, all conjecture. You have no proof, Ben. As far as we are concerned, the Wellses' hands are clean."

"Their hands are as dirty as they come." Ben shook his head. "This is insane, General. I know it and you know it." Ben realized that unconsciously he'd taken up a defensive stance: feet at hip's width, arms hanging at his sides, hands slightly curled. But it was no use—Aristides had already attacked him. He was rocked back on his heels. The ground had been scooped out from under him, and he was falling into an abyss.

"I wish it were, Ben, but facts are facts. This cabal of ultra-wealthy conservatives, whoever they are—"

"Who, not incidentally, are raping this country, following the game plan of the robber barons of the early 1900s."

"Irrelevant to this discussion. What is relevant is that you thwarted them when you took down Nemesis," Aristides continued, ignoring Ben's furious outburst. "They're not likely to forget that. They're not used to losing."

And this is the thanks I get, Ben thought. *I get fucked while they get away scot-free.* But he didn't say it. Self-pity was not a trait Aristides could abide. Nevertheless, Ben felt the rage rise in him like bile, burning his stomach and throat, momentarily muting him.

He'd spent a decade in the field, facing innumerable forms of peril that placed him so close to death he could feel its icy heartbeat. He'd deliberately wrenched himself out of the field—a place he had come to view as home—in order to work himself up the intelligence ladder, and at last he'd been delivered his reward: his own black ops shop.

Now it was gone, vaporized with a cynical and self-serving command.

"I've pulled some strings, dodged a couple of regs, to get you an extremely generous severance package."

Ben's lip curled. "Am I supposed to thank you for that?"

Aristides's meaty shoulders rose, fell. "Either way, the money is yours. It's in your account."

"And that's it?" Ben said with pointed belligerence.

"It's a shitload of money," Aristides said with equanimity.

"What about Evan?"

"She has a choice. Either accept a reassignment to the Department of Energy or take severance."

"The Department of fucking Energy? You must be joking. What is she going to do there?"

The general shrugged. "Politics, Ben."

"You already know what her choice will be, General."

Aristides nodded. "Money will hit her account tomorrow morning."

Aristides took another step closer. "A word of warning. These people, they'll never forget what you and Ryder did," Aristides said in a raspy whisper. "They'll never forget."

Ben passed a hand across his forehead; it came away damp and clammy. He was grateful that Zoe couldn't see him in this state. The general had done one thing, at least, to ease Ben's pain—and it was no small thing.

"*But—*" Aristides's voice returned to its normal level. "Lemons, lemonade."

Ben's eyes narrowed. This was no time for word games. "Please."

The general's expression softened like taffy. Ben recognized genuine compassion in his eyes.

"Seen in a new light," Aristides said, "this turn of events can be fortuitous."

Ben goggled at him. A bitter laugh exploded out of his mouth. "In what multiverse?" He was incredulous.

"Yours." Aristides spread his hands. "New start, new opportunities. You were always a wizard at those."

Aristides's face was sallow, unhealthy-looking in the overhead illumination. Briefly, Ben wondered whether he looked as bad.

General Aristides glanced at his watch; their time was up. "Evan Ryder is the only one of your field assets currently out of the country," he said. "Yes?"

Ben nodded.

"For her sake and yours get her the hell back here ASAP."

2

EN ROUTE
THREE DAYS LATER

At thirty-five thousand feet aloft, the Pacific was a sheet of beaten brass. Not long into the flight, however, clouds raced in, hurrying to unknown destinations, and the view out the window turned white as a desert sky at noon.

Evan Ryder, strapped into her seat, slid the plastic screen down over the window, sat back, and closed her eyes. Thinking of Lyudmila, their many weeks together in Sumatra, their last goodbye for what might be many months before Evan had stepped onto the ferry to Bali.

Lyudmila Alexeyevna Shokova, one of only two female apparatchiks in the Politburo, had managed to amass so much power that the Russian sovereign had ordered her purged. Her contacts had not failed her, flying her out of Moscow in a crate on a private flight, then secreting her aboard a freighter out of Odessa, crossing the Black Sea to Istanbul, where she vanished into the incessant crowds.

Lyudmila had told Evan that Bobbi, Evan's younger sister, had been a sleeper agent for a highly secretive arm of Russian intelligence.

"*What?*" Evan had blanched. "*I don't . . . I can't fathom how that's possible.*"

But the dossier Lyudmila had shown her proved the truth of what Lyudmila had said. The Kobalt Dossier, for that was her traitorous sister's operational name. Kobalt. "*We're going to find out how this is possible,*" Lyudmila had told her. "*You're going to need my help. Bobbi was part of Directorate 52123, we think within the SVR.*"

"*But there is no Directorate 52123 within either the SVR or the FSB, so far as I know.*"

"*Which is why we're not sure Directorate 52123 is part of the SVR. In fact, it's so secretive no one I've contacted has ever heard of it or can find any trace of it. The sole evidence of Directorate 52123's existence is in this dossier, buried soul-deep in the SVR server.*"

"*I can't go on not knowing how she was recruited. And why.*"

"*Your dismay is my pain, pchelka. So. Revenge has become our way of life. Now we enter the darkness.*"

Evan stared out the Perspex window at the whiteness of nothing at all.

If not for Ben's summons, she would still be with Lyudmila. They had been preparing to move on, to wend a circuitous route to wherever it was that Lyudmila had set up her independent shop.

Evan closed her eyes. She tried not to wonder what was behind Ben's signal that had appeared on her mobile. She longed to be with Lyudmila, for them to journey together into the dark enigma of Bobbi's betrayal. How could her sister possibly . . . ? It was unthinkable, unspeakable. Evan shifted, feeling the presence of the icicle that had been thrust into her when she had begun to read the dossier on her sister that Lyudmila had shared with her.

But what if . . .

What if the intel in the dossier was disinformation? It was

possible; the Russians were expert at *dezinformatsiya*, a dark art that had its origins in Stalin's KGB black propaganda directorate.

The only problem with that theory was she couldn't for the life of her fathom why they would bother. What was Bobbi to them, except her sister? Her little sister, who had died in a hit-and-run incident on the streets of DC a little over three years before, ten days after the similar death of Lila, Ben's wife. Evan and Ben had always believed that the two deaths were linked—murders—retribution for the havoc they had wreaked on the Russians during their last field assignment together. What would this bit of *dezinformatsiya*, even if it found its way to Evan, gain the Russians?

So, probably not.

Turning her mind away from her attempt to absolve her sister, she drew her handbag onto her lap, plucked out the presents she had bought at the Pasar Atas market in Bukittinggi: for Zoe, Ben's daughter, a clutch of old hotel room keys—some purportedly from hotels that were occupied by spirits. Zoe had moved on from her obsession with dinosaurs, which she now saw as too babyish, to researching hotel hauntings—ghosts of those who had been murdered or terribly wronged. This led her to collect hotel room keys. From knowing the names of every dinosaur that ever roamed the earth, she now knew the provenance of every key in her possession, which numbered in the hundreds, meticulously tagged and cataloged. For her niece and nephew: a batik scarf for Wendy and a "Save the Sumatran Tiger" T-shirt for Michael. Wendy was eleven, Michael, nine. They were growing up so fast. She closed her eyes, asked herself the question that often tugged at her: What if she had chosen Bobbi's lifestyle—marriage, kids, a suburban home, two cars, maybe a dog? The same day-after-day drudgery. She had never understood why Bobbi had opted for such a boring life, let alone how she'd managed to bear it.

Now, of course, she realized that Bobbi hadn't opted for the boring life after all. She had chosen a double life—married mother of two, a husband who ran a conservative Super PAC for candidates backed by Samuel Wells, and a life of secrets, shadows, living in the interstices between things, where no one looked. What ate at Evan was how her sister could have chosen the other side? What had made Russia so tempting for her? These unanswerable questions pinballed around Evan's mind. But with Bobbi dead, the questions would remain unanswered. The finality of that made Evan's anger at her sister all the more galling.

With no little deliberation, she replaced the presents in her handbag. Of course, she had forgotten to buy something for Paul. He was always an afterthought, if she thought about him at all. She could never fathom Bobbi's attraction to him. The fact was Evan couldn't stand him; she found him condescending on a good day, dismissive on a bad one. He once told her to cut out the abrasive and combative attitude, clearly preferring how Bobbi seemed to roll over every time he put his foot down. The less contact she had with him the better. When she would visit the kids after Bobbi was gone, she was always cordial to Paul for the sake of Wendy and Michael, but their interactions were abrupt and chilly. She suspected that Paul disliked her as much as she disliked him. And in time it seemed to her that he came to resent her being around the kids so much. Not that he spent much time with them, so far as Even could tell. But still, as he so bluntly put it, "I don't like you rubbing your scent all over this house."

Paul didn't matter, though. She missed the kids: Wendy's bright blue eyes, her winning smile, the way her thick blond hair smelled of lemongrass; Michael's serious expression, his clever, curious mind, the way he wrapped his arms around her neck when he buried his face in the hollow of her shoulder; the way the siblings finished each other's thoughts, as if they were twins, rather than Wendy being her brother's senior by two years. Ever since Bobbi's murder, she had made it a point to spend time with them and with Zoe, whenever she was back in DC. Sometimes she brought Zoe along. The two girls, especially, got along and, God bless them, they had an unspoken understanding not to leave Michael out of their time together. None of this, however, stopped her from feeling she never spent enough time with them. The truth was she hated DC, tried to stay away as much as possible. If it weren't for the children, she'd probably take her new remits from Ben remotely.

At length, with thoughts of the three kids dancing like sugarplums in her head, she drifted off.

From twenty rows behind her, a man—nondescript, inoffensive, so completely unremarkable even those sitting in his row were scarcely aware of his presence—stared at the top of her head so intently it was as if he were memorizing each strand of her hair. Every time a flight attendant or a passenger moved up or down the aisle, obscuring his view, he closed his eyes, as if trying to imprint what he had seen on the inside of his eyelids.

Distanced from sleep by a tingling that rose from the base of her neck all the way to the crown of her head, Evan's eyes popped open. Already fully awake, she turned in her seat. Scanning the rows behind her, she saw no one looking her way. Nevertheless, she rose, headed for the toilets at the rear of the plane. She passed a young woman reading the current issue of *Vogue*, a man in a corporate-style suit engrossed in the screen of his laptop, a kid playing with his Nintendo, a young couple holding hands, whispering to each other, a thin man reading an old hardcover of *The Ugly American*. The novel caused a sensation when it was published in 1958, detailing as it did the corruption and incompetence of U.S. foreign policy in Southeast Asia. No one and nothing seemed out of the ordinary, nothing to have caused the tingling. And yet it persisted, as she stood in back, waiting for a toilet to be free. She stared back down the length of the plane, taking in every detail, every movement of head or hand, but could find nothing untoward or out of place.

A flight attendant smiled at her, indicated the toilet on her right. "It's free now," she said.

Before her flight from Singapore had taken off she had fired up her mobile, scrolled through her list of specially curated images, sent the image for Singapore Airlines, followed by the flight number, to Benjamin Butler, for the past several years her boss at an unnamed intelligence shop funded by the DOD.

Upon arrival at Dulled, she passed quickly through customs and while she waited by the carousel for her suitcase, she turned on her mobile. Ben had sent his reply while she was still in the air: a clock without either hour or minute hands. The service used images with prearranged meanings so that even if the mobile was hacked, the "conversation" would be meaningless. But to Evan and Ben it meant:

RDV at 1

All service mobiles were deemed secure, the software updated bi-weekly, but in these days of constantly evolving hacking by bad actors in China, North Korea, Russia, Kazakhstan, Iran, even Israel, it paid to be paranoid.

She grabbed her suitcase and threaded her way through the crowd to the exit. Once outside, she took a deep breath of the balmy mid-May air. It was overcast, dampness in the air, but it felt almost cool and dry compared to the heat and humidity of Sumatra into which she had sunk so deeply for two months. Packs of other newly arrived travelers milled around her, pushing and shoving to get to their taxis, Ubers, shuttle buses.

Evan paused, forcing herself to casually look around, as if she were meeting someone. The tingling in the back of her head had returned, stronger than ever. But all she saw above the heads of the milling throng was the DC night sky, and the branches of recently leafed-out trees swaying in the slight breeze.

She had left her car at a hotel lot in Herndon, which offered long-term parking rates one-third the cost of the lots at Dulles. With a wheeze of brakes and the sigh of doors opening, the shuttle arrived, and her exhaustion after the long series of flights mixing with her anxiety over Ben's sudden recall signal impelled her onto the vehicle. Taking a seat across from the folding doors, she watched every person who boarded. Her sister was again very much on her mind, arising like a dark shadow the moment Evan had stepped outside the terminal. Her betrayal of Evan and the ideals of her country were unspeakable. Evan's feelings were in no way mitigated by Bobbi being dead for over three years. Why hadn't she seen what Bobbi had become? The answer to that was, of course, obvious. She was too close to the subject; sibling clashes had blinded her to the larger truth.

The driver was reaching for the lever to close the doors when she saw Ben. He was outside the terminal, his back to her, craning his neck, presumably looking for her. She knew it was him—without question it was Ben.

"Hold on!" she called, rising from her seat. "I've got to get off."

She swung off the shuttle, reached Ben just as he was turning around.

"Ben, what are you doing here, breaking protocol?"

"Thank God I've found you." He took her elbow, steered her away from the curb, into a pocket of space away from anyone else.

"Listen, Ben, I have news that's been eating at me all the way back from Sumatra."

"Whatever it is can wait." He cleared his throat. His eyes caught hers as if with a hook. "We've got to find your niece and nephew."

"What?" Her heart lurched, began beating so hard and fast she felt it in her throat. "What did you say?"

"Wendy and Michael are missing."

She blinked heavily. Her lips trembled as she felt an icy quiver run through her. "I don't understand—"

"Neither does anyone else," he said. "Not even the FBI suits who've been assigned to the case. They're gone as if they never existed."

"But that's impossible. What about Paul?"

"Paul Fisher is MIA. No one in his workplace knows where he is. They haven't heard from him and neither has anyone else, including their babysitter. And before you ask, Fisher has either turned off his mobile or destroyed it. No signal, no GPS, nothing."

"How long?" Her eyes were shining, enlarged with incipient tears.

"It's Monday night . . . so it could have been anytime from Friday night until today, when the kids failed to show up to school."

"I want to go to their home. Right now."

He nodded. "Come on. I'll drive you."

"I have my car in a lot in Herndon. I don't want to leave it there."

"Let's go then."

They crossed to the center median where his car was parked, its emergency lights blinking. They got in and Ben pulled out into the slowly moving traffic flow.

Evan was aware of his warmth, his solidity as she sat beside him. She hadn't thought about Ben the entire time she'd been away, but now that she was back inside the Beltway, all the memories of their time together in the field rushed back to her, as if they were a pack of needles penetrating her flesh, particularly the mistake they had made on their last assignment together.

Fifteen minutes later, they pulled up at the entrance to the parking lot.

"I'll wait for you here, then we'll caravan over."

She nodded numbly, her mind whirling. What could have happened to Wendy and Michael? Had Paul taken them? But why? And where on earth would he take them?

At the edge of the lot she paused, trying to clear her mind. Her keen training kicked in as she made a close observation of the geometrical rows of cars, taking inventory. A family of four banged out of the hotel's side door, laden down, barking at each other as they made their way to their Ford Explorer. A businessman swung his briefcase into his Audi, climbed in after it.

No one else was about. She could see the twin beams of Ben's car as he waited for her.

She unlocked her matte-black 2013 Dodge Charger SRT8, swung in behind the wheel, thinking inanely, *I've got to get that taillight fixed*. The Charger might look like crap from the outside, but that was just camouflage. Inside, it was tricked out with a new turbo-charged 650-horsepower engine, the latest three-point seatbelts and airbags, plus a clutch of other goodies. She strapped in, then slipped the key into the ignition. In that instant, as she leaned forward slightly, she sensed a shadow out of the corner of her left eye, emerging out of the darkness. It moved fast, and so did she. But she was not fast enough. She was half-turned out of her seat when she found herself confronting the muzzle of a Sig Sauer P320 Compact semi-auto pistol aimed at the center of her forehead.

She tried to look up at who was holding the pistol, but he was making sure she couldn't see past his chest.

"Unlock the rear doors," he said in a smoker's phlegmy voice.

She did as she was told. Her body was rigid, her muscles tense, even though she did her best to relax. She was not in the field, not in a blood zone. Half of her mind was on her niece and nephew and Ben, the other half still back with Lyudmila on the sun-splashed beach carved into the shoreline of Sumatra. She cursed herself for not being more vigilant.

"Hands on the wheel," he said. "Ten and two." He settled himself in the backseat directly behind her, not bothering to use the seatbelt. People most often didn't when they were in the backseat of a vehicle, and he, especially, wouldn't want to hinder his own movements.

A glance in the rearview mirror proved fruitless; he'd pulled a woolen balaclava over his head. All she could see of his face were his eyes and mouth, neither of which gave away anything.

"Let's go," came the directive from the backseat.

"And then?"

"You'll know soon enough." A harsh laugh. "Turn by turn."

Her mind was reeling, as if she had stepped onto a Tilt-A-Whirl going full speed. How had she missed his approach? She thought she had covered all quadrants of the parking lot. Her exhaustion, the time change, the shock of Ben's news all had contributed to her lapse. But they shouldn't have.

"Now!"

She felt the muzzle of the Sig cold as an icicle at the back of her neck. "Or what? You'll kill me?" She forced out a metallic laugh. "If that was your purpose, I'd already have a bullet in the back of my head."

"How's this?" He growled and slammed the barrel of the pistol into the side of her head just behind her ear.

Her torso recoiled sideways, and she bit off a yelp as pain shot through her like an electric shock.

"Liking that, are you?"

She tried to speak, but only a gasp emerged from between her lips.

"Okay, then. Get going."

She put the Charger in gear, pulled out of her space. All of a sudden, it began to rain, water quickly slicking the road, blurring her windshield. She flicked on her wipers, had to turn them to fast.

"That's right," her captor growled. "Take the east exit out of here."

As she drove out of the parking lot, Ben's car pulled out ahead of her. Her captor didn't notice; he was wholly fixated on her and completing his assignment. He told her to make a left. The filthy weather made oncoming traffic difficult to make out clearly, the expanding lights smeared against her windshield. The road ran straight ahead for as far as she could see, which wasn't far at all. Rain thundered onto the roof.

Just then she heard her mobile sound. Ben!

"Don't even think about it." And the muzzle dug painfully into the base of her skull, grinding away. She winced, and was immediately angry at herself all over again, for letting the pain get to her. At the same time, she knew she had to stop blaming herself, but her mind felt unfamiliar, sticky as melted taffy. *I've got to think clearly*, she said to herself. *Think quickly and strategically, or this will end in tears for me.*

One minute she was in his rearview mirror, the next she wasn't. *What the hell*, Ben thought. He punched her number into his mobile, but when she didn't answer, he made a frighteningly quick U-turn. Brakes screeched, horns blared, and drivers hurled epithets silent against their windows. Ignoring it all, he returned to the intersection where he'd lost her. He looked left, then right, immediately saw the Charger with the busted taillight, and gunned the car after it, fishtailing on the wet road as he made the turn. He righted the car, got it under control, and sped off.

* * *

Vehicles passed her, drivers and passengers alike oblivious to the mortal danger she was in.

"What do you want from me?" she said. The best thing—the only thing—she could do now was to keep him talking. Maybe he would inadvertently reveal something important.

"Keep driving."

"Where are we going?"

"Where you need to be," he said with a deep chuckle, "and from what I hear you'll wish I had kept you driving."

Something: a tiny ray of light. "You could, you know."

"What?"

"Keep me driving," she said. "We could go—"

"Huh. We couldn't go anywhere where they wouldn't find us."

They. So she was right. There was a "they."

"Who are these people who want me so badly?"

"Don't know, don't care."

He directed her to head north.

"One thing's for sure though, they're gonna have you killed in a very unpleasant way. A terribly slow and painful way. They hate you." He tapped her on the left shoulder with the barrel of the Sig. "Bear right at that fork. Then a right at the first signal."

"Why do they hate me? What do they know about me?"

"Everything." He laughed again. "Every-fucking-thing."

Could that be true, or just what he was told? A shiver ran down her spine. She needed another ray of light in this deepening darkness. "Like what exactly?"

She saw the signal up ahead, one of those new steel ones with LED lights.

Her eyes flicked to her side mirror in one last desperate hope that Ben was behind her. But she saw no headlights. She was alone with a gun at the back of her head and the knowledge of nothing but a sure and exceedingly agonizing death ahead of her.

Her gaze switched to the rearview mirror, locating her captor's precise position in her mind. She tried as best she could to calculate the vectors of speed, his weight, and centrifugal force. She counted off the seconds, terrified out of her mind.

"Everything you've ever done from the cradle till earlier this morning." Finally answering her question.

Her blood seemed to congeal in her veins. "How?" she managed to get out through a thick and furry tongue.

It was now or never, she thought.

"They're fucking magicians, that's h—"

He would have finished the sentence but Evan, accelerating, turned the wheel hard as she could to the left. The Charger slewed wildly on the rain-slick road. She'd judged it just right. She rammed the right rear side of the Charger into the steel signal post at such speed the rear side door staved in. The car jolted, shuddering and screaming like a beast in its death throes. Glass and twisted metal flew across the backseat. Spears, arrows, and edged weapons impaled her captor in thighs, groin, belly, and chest. The Sig discharged as, in galvanic response, his forefinger pulled the trigger. The bullet tore through the agitated air. A spray of hot blood, sweetly copper, and then the pain shot through her.

Dimly, she could smell smoke, the heat as of a fire somewhere behind her. She tried to turn her head, but her seatbelt and the airbag gripped her too tightly, locking her in place. She tried harder and—

Everything vanished into a vast black whirlpool.

3

MOSCOW, RUSSIAN FEDERATION

Half a world away, it was sleeting. The ice piled into corners, stairways, rooftops, and doorways, before slowly melting, blueish in the illusory light of a false dawn. Spring in Moscow could be magnificent or tainted with the last claws of the long winter.

Inside the private suites of the Kremlin, where she stared at herself in a floor-length mirror, it was warm as toast. The Sovereign himself saw to that. She stared at her face first, making sure her makeup was neither too little nor too much. No eyeshadow, but definitely lash thickener. Her green eyes stared back at her, implacable, impenetrable.

Her hair she had dyed blond upon her extraction and, liking it, had kept it, and had it cut into a bob that reached just above her shoulders. No matronly drawn-back-into-a-bun hairstyle for her.

She wondered, not for the first time, who she was, and when, precisely, she had stepped out of one world into another. Or perhaps she had always been in this world because three and a half years in Moscow had not changed her. It had occurred to her more than once that she had been born with Moscow in her blood buried deep like a seed awaiting its time in Russia's watery sun. And now, in just a few moments, it would be her moment to shine, to become her own sun, burning brightly beneath the vaulted and gilded ceiling of Russia's palace of power. It had taken her less than thirty minutes to feel comfortable in the baroque excessiveness of these interiors, so at odds with the drab utilitarian streets beyond the square.

"You look magnificent!"

Her gaze shifted from her own reflection to that of Dima Nikolaevich Tokmakov, a man with an outsized personality. Despite being in his middle years, he was as slender as he had been in his youth. He was good-looking and knew it. His full beard and hair, both thick as hedgerows, were shot through with silver streaks.

She smiled, turned to him, twirling like a runway model.

"I'm proud of you," Dima said. "You have become everything Leda promised you would."

"And more," she said, without a trace of boastfulness.

Dima took her hand, laughing. "We shall see, *moya malen'kaya osa*." *My little wasp*, his private name for her. No one called her by the name her parents had given her. Outside the confines of work, she was known by any number of aliases OT Directorate cooked up for her. Within the directorates, she was known only by her operational name. But Dima called her anything he wanted, depending on his mood.

"There's nothing little about my sting," she said. Then with perfect seriousness, "I won't disappoint you, Dima. Whatever you ask of me will be done."

His dark eyes gleamed like black opals. "Anything?"

She nodded, matching his expression. She was terrifying when she adopted this particular façade. "Anything and everything."

His eyes narrowed. "Leda warned me. She thought you had a death wish."

"And yet," she riposted, "it's Leda who is dead, not me."

Dima grunted. "You dispatched her in extremely imaginative fashion."

"Her end was ruled 'death by misadventure.'"

"Well, you saw to that," Dima smirked. "You two went rock climbing. Her ankle got caught in a rope, she stumbled and slipped off the rock face." If he was expecting her to give him a clue as to her feelings, he was disappointed. He heaved a sigh; it did not become him. "Leda was one of my most capable operatives. I will miss her."

"Oh, bullshit, Dima. Who gave me the order to terminate her with extreme prejudice?"

"It was going to be you or her. I found the outcome enlightening as well as edifying."

She paused for a moment, staring at him fixedly. "You bet against me. How much did you lose?"

"Don't be absurd," he scoffed.

She took a step toward him. "I hope it was a shitload, Dima." Her eyes never left his. "I hope you were duly *edified*."

He gave out with a laugh, but it was an uneasy one, laced with an undercurrent of foreboding only she could discern. She could push him only so far, she knew. She might have come close to crossing the line with him. That would be bad for her, considering her ambitions here in the heart of Mother Russia.

She was about to utter a roundabout apology but decided to let the matter die of its own accord.

The door to the anteroom swung inward, and one of Dima's underlings appeared. "It is time, Comrade Director." Tokmakov was head of Zaslon, housed deep within the operations directorate of the SVR, the foreign operations arm of the Russian security services. Officially Zaslon did not exist, either inside Russia or without. Even in the rare existing documents it was referred to as Directorate 52123. Zaslon was the almost legendary and most feared black ops organization on the planet, or so the Comrade Director would have his people believe. She had already inured herself to the Russian administration's triple-speak. You needed to develop a sixth sense to smell out the truth amid the thicket of exaggerations, deliberate disinformation, and outright lies ricocheting around the Kremlin and its environs.

Dima looked up from glancing at his wristwatch. "Ah, so it is." He offered her a grin. "Showtime!"

As they were about to pass through the door, the underling held out a slip of paper folded in the middle and sealed. "But first," he said, "there is this."

"Bah!" Dima almost batted the paper away. "Your timing couldn't be worse, Feliks. Later perhaps, when—"

"It's from Operations Directorate." Feliks held it up. "It's marked U and A." Urgent and Actionable.

Dima snorted. "All right, all right." He snapped his fingers. "Hand it over, if you must."

"Apologies, Comrade Director." Feliks's face was white as a sheet now. His hand trembled. "The U and A is addressed to Kobalt."

Dima looked at her, his face dark with barely suppressed anger. "Go on, then, Kobalt." He nodded to her. "See what all this fuss is about."

Kobalt, his little wasp, took the message and, once Feliks had scurried from the room and closed the door behind him, slit it open, and read. Its contents, like all such U&As, was terse and to the point.

She read it twice before she could get her mind around the intel. Then, like a hammer coming down, it sunk in all at once. She showed it to Dima.

"What do you intend to do?" he said.

"The Omega remit you gave me ended in my being found out."

Dima clicked his tongue. "You were assigned to infiltrate the Odessa compound of this mysterious group, find out what form of threat they presented to the Federation, inventory their leaders. You failed."

"I was burned," she said. "I made no mistake within the compound."

Dima waved away her words. "You failed to return with the requisite intel."

"Omega came to our attention because they were recruiting Russian citizens off the street," Kobalt said levelly, "sometimes against their will."

"Abducting Russian citizens cannot be tolerated," Dima needlessly elaborated just to make his point.

"I did find out that Omega is not, so far as I could tell, a terrorist group. They're a religious cult. A fanatic one, at that."

"Just as dangerous," Dima grunted. "In some ways even more so."

"They also harbor secrets I was working out how to get my hands on when I was burned," she persisted. "Point being, I brought home vital pieces of intel."

"With your tail between your legs. That's a failure, Kobalt. Period, full stop."

"Which my new plan I was going to present to Director General Baev would rectify." She pointed to the sheet containing the U&A Feliks had brought her. "Omega is behind this, I know it."

"Evidence?"

"My gut. This is payback for my getting as far into them as I did. They have no way of knowing what secrets I came away with before I fled. If I were them, I'd suspect the worst. That's the only logical conclusion to take."

"So you conclude . . ."

"I have been given a second chance at them, Dima," she told

him. "A chance to discover who their leader is, where their home base is. That's my conclusion."

"You seem certain of the linkage of what just happened and your infiltration of Omega."

"Nothing else makes sense."

"I'm not sure. You've been back two months now."

"Their operation took time to plan and execute." Her eyes sparked with her need. "Dima, you have to trust me on this."

"Watch yourself, Kobalt," he snapped, "I don't have to do a damn thing."

She had become inured to his mercurial changes of mood, especially when it came to her. She, probably correctly, put them down to sexual frustration. She had lost count of the number of times she had rebuffed his advances. He, like every other man inside the FSB, wasn't used to being told no by a female subordinate. She knew it rankled him, fostered it, knowing it mitigated her feeling of helplessness being in a male-dominated environment, an organization that furthermore denigrated women every chance it got.

Dima was across the room, having stalked away from her. He stood hands clasped behind his back, staring out the windows. Indigo twilight had settled over the onion domes and, beyond them, the bleak brutalist buildings of Moscow. Yea or nay, which choice would benefit him the most? The Omega remit was a blot on her records and, therefore, on his. He needed that erased, the sooner the better. Her new plan was a good one, but this divine intervention might just be better.

His expression did not change when he returned to where she was standing, but she saw something shift behind his eyes. "Then this is your new remit. It supersedes all others."

Kobalt nodded. "And the meeting with Director General Baev—"

"You will meet the head of the SVR another day, this I

promise," Dima said. "I'll smooth it over with him." He put a hand on her shoulder. "If you are correct, you will complete your original remit using the opening Omega has provided." His fingers gripped her shoulder. "Go, my little wasp. Go now."

4

WASHINGTON, DC

Ben's entire body contracted, muscles like steel bars.

"What the hell?" he shouted into the interior of his car. "What the hell does she think she's doing?"

He saw Evan's Charger slew its back end directly into the steel light post, almost as if it was a designed maneuver. He saw the offside rear door staved in as if by a giant fist, saw the Charger shudder and squeal like a stuck pig. The car's front end, with Evan in it, stuck out into the road at an almost forty-five-degree angle. But she couldn't—she wouldn't—attempt such a thing.

He was running toward the wreck, having braked wildly, thrown his car into park, and hurtled himself the intervening twenty yards. The Charger's rear left-side passenger door had burst open, a figure impaled so many times Ben could scarcely count the projectiles half-out, spine bent viciously backward, arms dragging on the ground, blood staining the street black, glistening like oil in the sodium lights. Flames danced across the backseat.

In his haste to reach Evan, he stumbled over one of the man's arms, kicking something forward—his gun, maybe. But there was no time to look, no time to waste. He hauled on the driver's door, but it was locked. He'd had to do this many times before, from Berlin to Bratislava. Pulling out his utility knife, he swung its blunt butt end to smash the safety glass. Pebbled shards showered down outside and inside the Charger. He pulled the latch, swung the door open. The heat from the flames hit him then as they moved faster, reaching the impaled man, greedily eating through his skin, fat, and muscle. It sounded like the fire was smacking its lips. The stench was revolting.

Evan was unconscious. Blood oozed from a wound along the left side of her skull. That told him it wasn't deep. Her skull hadn't been pierced. He fumbled with the seatbelt buckle but couldn't get it to unsnap. Evan was locked in. The rear of the car was on fire. Perhaps the spreading black pool he'd seen on the ground was actually a mixture of blood and oil. In that case, the wreck could go up in a fireball at any moment.

He squatted down in order to get a better angle on the buckle. That's when he saw the object he had kicked when he'd stumbled over the man's arm. It wasn't his gun after all. It was something small and smooth, glinting in the murky dark as if it were metallic. Something dangled from it. Dimly, he heard sirens wailing in the distance. Without giving the object a closer look, he picked it up and put it in his pocket. Now, from this lower angle he was able to slide the seatbelt's obstinate metal piece out of the holster. Quickly now, he unstrapped Evan. Scooping her up, he ran with her back toward his car.

"Evan," he said, and more urgently, "Evan!"

Her eyelids fluttered open, her eyes trying to focus on him. "Ben?"

"I'm here. I've got you."

Almost to the car.

"Where . . ." She paused, her tongue emerging to lick her lips. "Where were you?"

"Behind you."

"I looked for you . . . I looked but I didn't see you. Otherwise, I wouldn't have . . ." But her voice was fading. Her lids at half-mast.

"Evan, Evan! Stay awake!" He was terrified that she'd sustained a concussion.

He reached the car, managed to grab the door handle, maneuvered her gently into the backseat. The sirens were wailing wildly, only a couple of blocks away now.

"Evan!" Her eyes were closed. He slapped her cheek. "Wake up! Look at me." He nodded, smiling through gritted teeth. "Try to stay awake, okay?"

She mumbled something he couldn't make out.

He leaned in over her. "It's important you stay awake, yeah?"

Slamming the door shut, he raced around and slid into the driver's seat. Throwing the car into gear, he took off in a spray of filthy rainwater.

They were nowhere in sight when the first responders turned the corner and came upon the bloody scene. All there was left to see was the Charger going up in a ball of smoke and flame.

5

KUBINKA, MOSCOW

The rain had abated, replaced by a wind that cut through every layer of clothing like a knife through cheese. May was a capricious month in Moscow. Kobalt hurried across the tarmac at Kubinka military air base. The SVR jet Dima had had prepared for this occasion was fueled and ready. Her heavily armored staff car had completed the approximately forty-three-mile journey in gloaming as the sun struggled to open its bleary eyes and rise amid the city's blocky high-rises.

A pair of SVR drones were already on hand, standing to either side of the plane's mobile Jetway. When one of them made to help her, she swatted his hand away. The other drone, his face trying its best to be impassive, handed her a hard-sided briefcase. It was made of titanium and was lead-lined to stop X-rays from penetrating its secrets.

Once inside the plane, Kobalt took a seat at a work desk as the Jetway folded up into the fuselage. There were no other passengers. The pilot and navigator had already been given their instructions and worked out their flight plan.

Kobalt placed the briefcase on her lap. She coded in the

release mechanism on the digital lock, snapped open the lid. Inside, set into gray foam, was a 9mm GSh-18 handgun with an eighteen-round magazine and bullets that could pierce body armor. Three knives—a larger one with a serrated blade, a medium-sized dagger, and a small knife that fit in a sheath that strapped around her ankle. Two coils placed one on top of the other, each two feet in length. The first was made of nylon monofilament; the second was a bit thicker and made of steel, twisted into a spiral. Both had small wooden handles at each end.

In a folder set within a snap pouch on the inside of the lid were all the papers needed for her new legend: passports and driver's licenses for Russia, Turkey, Germany, and America all bore her face and her name: Karin Wagner. She was variously a cultural attaché, an importer-exporter, and a sales rep for a digital marketing firm. Should anyone check, the two businesses had websites, made to look alive and active. Emails, texts, and phone queries would go directly to OT Directorate, who created the docs for her. Keeping the folder out, she closed and locked the case, set it on the seat next to her. Then she set about memorizing Karin Wagner's bio and CV.

The engines revved up and the jet rolled along the taxiway to the foot of the runway. But abruptly it stopped, the engines powering down. Kobalt—Karin—looked up, saw the flight attendant unsealing the door, then looked out to see the Jetway being redeployed. Moments later, someone carrying a black case ran up the steps and entered the plane.

Anton Antonovich Zherov.

Smiling like a lithe cat who had swallowed an obstreperous canary, he sauntered down the aisle toward her. He was tall and slender, moved with a dancer's stealth and grace, and possessed a mind like a steel trap. He forgot nothing, thus held grudges until the end of time or got his own back from those who he felt had wronged him. He was a dangerously loose cannon who had never met an order he didn't disagree with, so much so that *spetsnaz* had bounced him. The only place for him to wash up was Zaslon, where Dima, indulging his constant shenanigans, took advantage of his adored mentor's status with Zherov to wring the best out of him.

"So, Natasha"—he never referred to her operational name, preferring to think of her as Natasha Fatale, partner of Boris Badenov in the American cartoon series *The Rocky and Bullwinkle Show*—"what are we up to?"

"My current legend is Karin. Karin Wagner," she said coolly as he sat down in the seat opposite her.

"To reiterate, what are we up to, *Karin*?" he enunciated with the exaggerated precision of an elocution teacher.

"Better buckle up, Anton," she said, as the engines revved up again. And when he had complied: "You mean you haven't been briefed."

He shook his head. "Dima said there wasn't time."

The jet's engines rose to a scream as the plane raced down the runway and, lifting off, vanished into a sky thick as cotton wool.

"I take it this brief is highly personal," Anton said, as he crossed one leg over the other, brushed imaginary lint off his trousers.

"It is." Kobalt stared at him. "So what the fuck are you doing here?"

"Dima's orders, Natasha." He smiled his maddeningly skin-deep smile, opaque as porcelain.

"I need you like I need a third tit. We'll drop you off in Istanbul. You can find your way home from there."

Instead of answering her, Anton hoisted the case he'd brought onto his lap, opened it, swiveled it around for her to see. The interior looked much like hers, with its dark gray foam bed. But instead of small arms, Anton's case cradled a Scorpion EVO

3 submachine gun. It fired 9x19mm Parabellum ammunition, with two thirty-round magazines clamped together for faster loading. The stock was currently in a separate bed. It was lightweight, as some of the parts were made of a polymer material. It was a fine concealed carry weapon, lethal as hell, firing in semi-auto, three-round bursts, or full-auto modes.

"Oh, you'll need me, Natasha." His grin was as hungry as a tiger's. It was rumored that Anton Zherov had developed a keen taste for blood. "Indeed you will."

"Listen, Anton, we need to come to some sort of détente," she said as she returned from the lavatory. "I have enough on my mind without worrying about you slipping a knife between my ribs."

He looked up at her. As she sat back down, he said, "This was neither my idea nor an assignment I would have volunteered for." His steely gaze seemed to track the movement of her eyes. "I don't like you. You can change your name as many times as you want. I don't like you; I don't trust you. You're the product of a recruitment program the parameters of which are no longer in existence, thankfully, since so many of you people blew up in our faces. In fact, you're the last of your line, the only living proof that the program ever existed."

She was careful to keep her rage out of her eyes. "So I'm an embarrassment to you."

"No, not an embarrassment. You're a clear and present danger—to me and to everyone else in the SVR. You may have Dima hypnotized, but rest assured that'll never happen with me, no matter how wide you spread your legs."

The words were no sooner out of his mouth than, in a blur, she leaned across the table and slapped him hard enough to make his head turn. A white flower, quickly turning red, bloomed on his cheek. He made no move to counter, said not a word, but rose and stalked to the rear of the plane.

To her horror, she noticed her hand trembling. She felt the sting where it had impacted his cheek all the way up her arm or imagined she did anyway. Her pulse galloped along at its own pace, and her thoughts squirmed away from her like fish frightened by the emergence of a shark. She bit her lower lip, dug her fingernails into the palm of her idle hand. When she smelled the blood welling, she brought it up to her face and licked, the coppery taste a reminder of who she was and what she must do to keep ahead of the pack of vindictive males snapping at her heels.

6

WASHINGTON, DC

The three-story cream stone and butterscotch stucco Italianate mansion stood near the corner of California Street NW and Massachusetts Avenue, two or so blocks from Rock Creek Park. A passerby might mistake it for the embassy of a foreign nation. It was nothing of the kind. A small courtyard paved with octagonal tiles was guarded by a pair of stone urns, each filled with a holly bush, their winter ruby-colored berries now gone, but their glossy dark-green foliage full and lush. Eight-foot evergreen hedges guarded the front of the building.

This was the home of Isobel Lowe. And it was to Isobel that Ben now carried Evan. Isobel and Ben had met in Israel, more than ten years ago. He'd been a field agent then, and she worked for Mossad. This was before he and Evan had even met. Eventually, Isobel became disenchanted with the current Israeli government, quit Mossad, and moved to DC. Her distrust and hatred of Russia never wavered, however, aligning with Ben's own antipathy. Now she worked for one of those Silicon Valley companies that had amassed more personal data on more people worldwide than the NSA and the DOD combined. She and Ben were closer now than they had been in Haifa.

He had texted Isobel on his way from Herndon. She was watching for them at the side door and swung it open as Ben took the steps two at a time with Evan in his arms. Security dictated he not approach from the front, which was lit up with security lights.

"I'll take her from here," Isobel said, and Ben who would in normal circumstances tell her he was fine to carry Evan into the house and upstairs, acquiesced without a fight. The truth was, he was shattered, emotionally and physically and every other way he couldn't for the moment think of.

As he followed Isobel and Evan through the kitchen, past the pantry, down the long, pecan wood–paneled hallway, gleaming and immaculate, into the spacious front entryway, he felt a heaviness of spirit.

Shock was finally setting in—the twin traumas of losing his beloved shop and seeing Evan slewing at speed into the light pole, almost dying. An unnatural cold penetrated his flesh to settle in his bones. The fear of losing Evan, the acknowledgment of what she meant to him, how he felt about her, had undone him. The deep-seated emotion had finally sunk its claws into him, and he knew he'd never be the same.

He paused, watching Izzy carry her up. His heart flipped over, and he hurried to follow them into one of Isobel's spare bedrooms, where she tenderly laid Evan onto a bed. There was already someone else in the room. By the professional manner with which he examined Evan's wound, Ben knew he must be a doctor. A hospital had been out of the question. That was the one thing he was sure about as he drove away from the fireball that had been Evan's Charger. Too many questions for which he had no answers, and a bullet would automatically be reported to the police. These days, Isobel, with their history, her contacts, and her competence, was the only one outside of Evan he could trust.

After a few moments, Isobel turned away from the doctor and his patient, undoubtedly to ask Ben what the hell happened, and finally noticed his extreme pallor. She led him across the hall to her own bedroom, she sat him down in an oversized upholstered chair, brought him a double shot of bourbon poured from a decanter on the mahogany sideboard, placed his fingers around the glass.

"Drink," she ordered. "She's in good hands." Then she left him alone.

Ben sipped the bourbon without tasting it. Eventually, though, the liquor's warmth ran through his body. He realized he was gripping the arm of the chair with his free hand so hard his knuckles stood out, white and skeletal.

Taking out his mobile phone, he sent off a text to Zoe. She was staying at her best friend Rose's house, five blocks from Ben's own house in Georgetown. Rose's mom, Mae Rand, was always willing to take Zoe in when he wasn't around. The girls loved being together. The arrangement was convenient for everyone. It was late, so Ben didn't expect a reply until morning, but he wanted Zoe to know he was okay as soon as she awoke.

He stowed his mobile away, put his head back, and closed his eyes.

Fully half the time he'd been a field agent Evan had been his partner in wet work. They had spent many sleepless nights on surveillance—a mind-numbing job if ever there was one, but necessary all the same. They had been in firefights, been wounded, had clung to each other for solace in the most godforsaken places, and, once, had spent the darkness making ferocious love again and again. Well. The way of the world—the world of evil, lies, and treachery in which he and Evan had chosen to live.

"*Never again, Evan. I've already betrayed my vows to Lila for this one night, I can't betray my love for Zoe.*"

She held his hands in hers. "*It's* our *betrayal; I'm as guilty as you are.*"

And how much more deeply did their guilt eviscerate them when Lila was killed. He had never told her their secret, had been unable to confess to the woman he loved. He and Evan were saucers full of secrets. What was another one to either of them? Their burdens were already too heavy to measure.

And yet it was everything.

When General Aristides had given him his own black ops shop Evan had been the first field agent he recruited. Predictably, Aristides wasn't happy about the hire. "*You two have a history together,*" the general had complained. "*You can't be in the least objective when it comes to her.*" Which was all too true. Not that Ben gave a shit. Evan was the best field operative he'd ever worked with. Her record was impeccable. When she was given a brief, she completed it, come hell or high water. Sometimes, to be sure, he suspected she had a death wish lurking somewhere in the back of her psyche. Maybe because of her sister. Evan and Bobbi had had a distinct sibling rivalry before their parents were killed, before Evan was forced into the role of Bobbi's sister, mother, and father rolled into one.

Ben looked at his watch, scrubbed a hand across his face. Evan had caused so many complications in his life, had raised a ridge of guilt in him that could never be worn smooth. And yet, he wouldn't have missed a second of their time together.

The truth was he was still as ignorant of the flame that drove her as he had been the day they first met. She remained a complete enigma. For him, who spent his entire adult life solving the riddles of human motivation, treachery, weakness, and greed, she was a vault without a key code, an irresistible nymph in the deepest forest of the night.

Aristides's prophetic words swirled through his mind now: "*You can't be in the least objective when it comes to her.*"

No, he couldn't, not in any way, shape, or form. In those horrific moments as he saw her Charger nearly folded in two, when he bolted out of his car, running so fast he thought his heart might explode out of his chest, when, terrified that she had been mortally wounded or already dead, he finally understood why. He understood why he had taken the unspeakable risk of making love to her, betraying Lila and Zoe, the loves of his life.

His eyes opened, barely registering where he was. He was trained to keep his emotions under control, to be stoic in the face of the most grotesque and stomach-churning situations.

But this was different.

This was Evan.

With a groan that emanated from deep in his belly, he hurled the empty glass across the room, where it shattered against the tropical flowers and birds wallpaper.

That sound of the glass shattering brought Isobel. She looked at the mess he'd made and, crossing to him, she said in her husky voice, "I see you're coming back to yourself."

Looking up at this willowy woman with wide-apart devilish tawny eyes and an enigmatic smile, so familiar, so welcoming, he knew he had made the right choice bringing Evan here.

"Sorry," he said, giving her a watery smile.

"Don't be." She tossed her head with its thick cascade of dark hair. "Dr. Braun would like a word."

He sprang up, a pang of anxiety returning. Isobel immediately reassured him. "She's fine. Just resting quietly. You can talk to her after Dr. Braun leaves."

Instead of leading him across the hall, they turned right, heading through a pair of polished mahogany doors with brass knockers in the shape of closed fists, into the large study that Isobel had used for her nightly poker games, where she hosted the Beltway's elite in high-stakes rounds. She had stopped the games several months ago, and now the study was as it had been before, with a mahogany desk facing a pair of leather sofas and two matching easy chairs, a wet bar along a side wall, and books in orderly rows on shelves built into the back wall.

Dr. Braun was standing by the desk, his medical bag beside him on the gleaming wooden surface. Ben, at last regaining a sense of himself, crossed the room, shaking the doctor's hand as he introduced himself. "Thank you for coming."

Dr. Braun waved away his words. "Any friend of Isobel's . . ." He was a short, compact man. If Ben squinted, he could pass for a middle-aged Mel Brooks. His eyes sparkled and there were deep laugh lines scored on either side of his mouth.

"I'll make this short and sweet," he said, as Isobel came to stand beside Ben. "First, your friend is in no danger; she did not suffer a serious head wound, or a concussion. Second, I have cleaned and disinfected the wound. I have also applied a liquid bandage. It contains an antibiotic and is waterproof. " He shifted from one foot to the other, and now his voice lowered, taking on a warning tone. "Third, all that said, she was exceedingly fortunate. If that bullet had done anything more than take the first two layers of epidermis off her skull, we'd be having a completely different conversation. Oh, and don't worry about the contusion behind her left ear. It will subside within a few days." He dug in his old-school physician's pigskin bag and handed Ben two plastic phials. "The same antibiotic that's in the liquid skin." He tapped the phials with his forefinger. "I doubt she'll need it, but my training compels me to err on the side of caution." He touched the second phial. "Analgesics. She's going to have one killer headache for the next twenty-four to forty-eight hours, so only light activity and plenty of rest." He snapped his bag closed. "Well, that's about it." He turned to go. "Isobel, if you need me . . ."

"Thank you, Stephen," she said as they all stepped into the hallway. "Let me show you out."

He shook his head. "I'll see myself out, Izzy. You have better things to do."

Which left Ben and Isobel standing face-to-face.

Ben's face had regained much of its color, now he knew Evan wasn't seriously injured. "Listen—"

"I know what you're going to say. No need to thank me."

He gave her a serious look. "Well, okay, then I'll thank you on Evan's behalf."

She nodded. "Best she and I don't meet, Ben. She was already here once for that ill-fated poker game. I've no idea what she thinks of me and now's not the time to try and explain."

He nodded. "Agreed. No reason for her to know about our association. But there may come a time."

"I understand."

"Okay then." They kissed on both cheeks, in the European manner. It seemed to him a solemn goodbye.

Ben was left alone for only a moment before he went softly down the hall and into the room where Evan lay.

She heard voices, far away and sounding like the brook she and Bobbi used to push each other into when they were young girls. Even then, there had been a dark edge to their shoving, needle points to their laughter. They were more than sibling rivals. There was always something between them, a darkness, a shadow that she couldn't understand then and which, later on when she was obliged to take care of her sister after their parents were killed, she dismissed as a fancy of childhood.

Through a red haze, she sees herself running down the steep slope to the bank of the brook. Bobbi is right behind her when it happens. Later, Bobbi claimed she'd tripped over a tree root, stumbled and pitched into Evan, knocking Evan head over tail into the brook. It is spring laden with bouts of heavy rains, and the brook is in full spate. She is pitched in headfirst, gasping, gulps water, starts to choke as she flails her arms uselessly. The water smashes into her, allowing her feet no purchase on the stony brook bed. She tries to get to the bank but has lost all sense of direction. Every time she strikes out with her arms and legs the current slaps her in the face and she goes under again. What would have happened if Bobbi's arm hadn't wound around her waist, hauling her up into the sunlit air. She will never know. She lies on the bank, feet still in the water, gasping and choking until Bobbi turns her on her side, and she vomits up the water she has taken in through her nostrils, down her throat, into her lungs.

"There now," Bobbi says, sitting beside her. "There now."

The next afternoon, Bobbi is ahead of her as they run down the slope where no tree grows. Bobbi hadn't tripped after all.

Now Bobbi was dead. Now Bobbi was a traitor. Bobbi had been a Russian spy, a sleeper agent or a mole. What secrets had she gleaned or stolen from Paul's political work over the years? When had she been indoctrinated? How had she been indoctrinated? Who had lured her over to the enemy, and what had they used to entice her? What would make Bobbi keep lying to Evan, to her children, the people who loved her the most?

Evan ached all over, as if she had been pummeled by a heavyweight boxer. Her head felt as if it were splitting in two, the pain so bad she could scarcely think. She opened her eyes, saw Ben smiling down at her, but even in her pain-riddled state she could tell the smile was off—strained, marred by concern.

"Hey," he said.

She opened her mouth, meant to say "Hey," but what came out was, "My head."

"Right." He moved out of her view for a moment, returned with a glass of water and a bendy straw. "Open." He laid a pill on her tongue, placed the straw in her mouth. "Drink," he said. "Swallow." She did those things. Moments later the pain subsided to a dull roar.

"Ben," she said, wincing only slightly. "What happened?"

"The man in the backseat," he said, "that's what happened."

"He was holding a gun to the back of my head. He hit me with the butt. I . . . I needed to get away while there was only one person."

"Couldn't you have found something else less drastic than deliberately totaling your car?"

"It seemed like the only viable idea at the time." When he didn't even crack a smile, she said, "Fuck, I want to sit up."

He went to help her, but she batted his hands away. He put pillows behind her, instead, tried not to watch her struggling.

She had clearly heard the anxiety in his voice if not seen it in his face. Stoic Ben. Emotionless Ben. As always. "He jumped me in the parking lot as I got into my car, pointed a handgun at the back of my head and directed me to drive."

"Where?"

"No idea. We didn't get far after you lost us."

"I doubled back. I went as fast as I dared in the weather. I got there in time to see the crash, to get you out before the fireball."

"So no way to ID him from remains."

"Not unless you know a good necromancer."

"Google?" A bitter smile danced across her pallid face. Her hand reached up, touched the bandage. "The shot?"

"Just a scratch. Again, lucky."

"Luck didn't enter into the equation. It was because what

I did threw him off-balance. It was because his world was collapsing in on him."

Ben seemed to ignore this or dismiss it out of hand. Anger rushed through her, and she was back in the brook in full spate, gasping for air, for life.

"Did you see his face?" Ben asked. "Any distinguishing marks?"

"He wore a balaclava." Evan tried to set her anger aside, but it seemed to be growing exponentially.

"What about his voice? Anything there?"

She tried to think back; too many images crowding her mind like a panicked stadium full of people all rushing to get out at once. "American, through and through."

"Can you regionalize it?"

"It was more or less flat, but that's all."

Into her mind swam a bit of the conversation she'd had with him:

"Who are these people who want me so badly?"

"Don't know, don't care. One thing's for sure though, they're gonna have you killed in a very unpleasant way. A terribly slow and painful way."

"What do they know about me?"

"Every-fucking-thing."

When she repeated this to Ben he stiffened visibly. "If they know everything about you—I mean, we've by definition got to take whatever he said with a couple grains of salt. But even so, it's urgent we find out who this guy was working for."

"I don't give a shit who he was, or who he was working for."

"Well, you'll have to because that's our priority now. We're both in danger. Aristides warned me there are going to be repercussions to our dismantling Nemesis. Looks like the ringleader of the cabal of conservative billionaires who were funding them was Sam Wells. And possibly his third and current wife, Lucinda, is involved."

This was all it took for her to become well and truly pissed off. Her anger manifested like a demon in the night. "Don't care. All I'm concerned with is what happened to my niece and nephew."

"'They're gonna have you killed in a very unpleasant way. A terribly slow and painful way.' Was that or was that not what your assailant told you?"

She glared at him. "What we need to concentrate on is finding Wendy and Michael. Bobbi isn't here to protect them. Their father is MIA. Their welfare is my responsibility."

"I understand. We're on the same page, Evan."

She nodded, but there was more to tell him. "Listen, my trip to Sumatra wasn't all fun and games."

He frowned deeply. "I remember you saying you had news when I cut you off to tell you about the kids."

She took a deep shuddering breath, then let it out. "Bobbi was a sleeper for the SVR."

"What?" Only Ben's eyes moved, widening in stunned reaction, while his body tensed, as if preparing to combat an immediate threat. "No. It can't be true. Whatever you found must be Russian disinformation."

"I wish it were, Ben. But it's the truth." She sat up, rubbed the heels of her hand into her eye sockets. "I saw the dossier, I know the markings and frankings." Now she looked him straight in the eye, there was no other way to go on.

He let out a long breath that was almost a whistle. "I'm trying to get my head around this, so I can't even imagine what you must be feeling."

She shook her head. "I don't know. It's like a nettle that's digging into my insides, something I can't reach—something I'll never reach because Bobbi's dead."

"It's a real sucker punch." Ben leaned in. "My condolences. Again."

She nodded, not wanting for the moment to meet his eyes.

Nevertheless, she was grateful he hadn't said he was sorry. She didn't want anyone's pity, least of all his.

Ben understood this, for he hurried on. "We can speculate that for some reason her new masters found her wanting."

Evan nodded. "Maybe she realized she'd made a mistake, wanted out." A tiny hint of longing in her voice.

"Wishful thinking. It's far more likely she made a beginner spy mistake. Maybe Paul found out."

"No." She couldn't imagine such a thing. "Bobbi was meticulous about everything she did and said."

"But think about it, Evan, if Bobbi had a change of heart don't you think she would've come to you? You're the one person who would have given her protection, no questions asked."

Ben was right. Constant emotional clashing or no, Bobbi was the epitome of practicality. She would have come straight to Evan. But she hadn't.

Ben's expression mirrored the bleakness on her face. "And you're absolutely sure the dossier is genuine."

"Yes. Plus, it came from an unimpeachable source."

"And who might that be?"

"Sorry."

He reared back. "Seriously?"

"Ben, please, trust me."

The look in her eyes clearly swayed him. Plus, he did trust her. He'd trusted her with his life many times when they were in the field together.

"You know I do." He sighed. "It's just not like you to withhold something so vital."

"It's personal. Too many people would be put in danger if I said any more."

He held up his hands. "Okay, okay. What else was in this SVR dossier?"

"Here's the curious part. Bobbi belonged to Directorate 52123."

"Well, there you go. There's no such thing as Directorate 52123."

"That we know of," Evan said. "But there are so many things we don't know about the FSB, the SVR, *spetsnaz*. Or Zaslon. Does it even exist or not? What's its remit? I could go on, and so could you. Anyway, my contact assures me that this Directorate might not even be SVR, but part of some mysterious entity, perhaps Zaslon, again, if it even exists."

That's when the shock wave hit her full force, and she collapsed back onto her pillow, hands over her face. "My own sister. I mean, my God, Ben, we grew up together. I took care of her after Mom and Dad were killed. I was sister and mother to her. How could she ... I mean, this duplicity ... it's unspeakable, unfathomable." She stared at him. "I mean, why in the world would she ... What could they have offered her?"

"Evan," he said in as calm a voice as he could muster, "you know as well as I do there are only three reasons for what Bobbi did: money, sex, or ideology."

She nodded morosely, winced at the resulting pain. "I still can't get my head around it."

"Listen to me, Evan, the reason we've got to find out who ordered your death is that if my sneaking suspicion that it was Samuel Wainwright Wells, as retribution, is correct, then we have to consider also that Wells may have had Wendy and Michael abducted."

"What? Why?"

"To keep me—or me and you if the attempt on your life failed—running around in circles while they get on with whatever they're planning next without interference."

Evan made a little sound in the back of her throat. "There's a hole in your theory big enough to drive a semi through."

Ben stiffened. "And what would that be?"

"Paul. My brother-in-law. He's missing, too. Wells's Super

PAC is one of his main clients. Why would he cripple his best lobbyist by taking Paul out of the picture?"

"Who knows, but—" Ben stared at her, because she had thrown off the bedcovers and was swinging her legs over the side of the bed.

"What the hell d'you think you're doing?"

"What does it look like?"

He reached to stop her as she got unsteadily to her feet, and again she batted his hand away.

"Listen, Evan, Dr. Braun said you need to take it easy. Sleep. Rest."

"Stop treating me like a child."

"I've not been treating you like a child." It was an automatic response, a reflex meaning nothing, which he regretted the moment he said it.

She glared at him. "I took care of myself when my Charger was hijacked, I can take care of myself now."

"Really? You almost got yourself killed."

"Fuck you. I did what I had to do."

"Whatever." His hand cut through the air. "The reality is you're hurt."

"I'm just fine."

"You were shot."

"A scratch. You said so yourself." But she swayed a little even as she said this.

"Please just sit down for a minute at least. Give your body and brain time to process and get back in sync."

Swamped by a wave of vertigo, she knew it was a good idea, but she was goddamned if she'd admit that to him. She took a breath, perched on the edge of the bed as if at any moment she'd rocket off it.

"I know what you're feeling."

Her rage grew white-hot. "You haven't a clue what I'm feeling." The terror of being held at gunpoint, of almost dying, had ripped open the psychic wound she had so carefully bandaged when Lyudmila had shown her the SVR dossier on Bobbi. From that moment to this her anger had been festering beneath that bandage. The shocks she had been through had burst the wound open and now all the bile was spilling out.

She leapt off the bed, grabbed Ben by the shoulders, shaking him, "Don't you understand. Not only is Bobbi dead, but she never existed. She wasn't Bobbi at all—the girl I took care of, nurtured, tended to, cared for, and loved. She was a sham, a shell, a fucking legend!"

"You can't know that for certain," Ben said, his mouth working before his brain could catch up.

Evan struck him across the face. "Idiot! The reason I need to find Wendy and Michael is because they're the only family I have left, and I will not allow what was done to Bobbi to be done to them. I will not allow them to be turned."

Ben was so shocked by her behavior he didn't even think to raise a hand to his reddened cheek. "Turned? What the hell are you talking about?"

"*My* suspicion, Ben, is that they've been taken by the Russians. By the FSB. Which is why I'm not going to rely on the FBI to find them."

"What?" Ben looked like she'd struck him again. "Where does this theory come from?"

"Bobbi was one of theirs, indoctrinated to Mother Russia. She's gone now. Why not indoctrinate her children?"

Ben's eyes opened wide. "My God, Evan, they're only children!"

She let go of him before she did something she would surely regret. "Better to get them early, Ben. The indoctrination's all the easier."

He shook his head. "This is crazy talk. You're in shock. You're overwrought."

"This now?" Her rage had turned from black to red. "From

you, of all people?" She wanted to tear someone's eyes out and he was closest to hand. Her fingers curled into claws.

"Evan," he said, trying to keep his voice mild and level, "I'm still your boss." It was a sign of how desperate he'd become with her, how he kept crossing the line Aristides had warned him about. When it came to Evan, he was no longer objective. He was trying to keep order in a situation which the chaos of his own emotions had cracked open.

"Really? Then I quit."

"Come on. You don't mean that." He recognized a losing battle.

She took a step closer to him, and he backed away. His instincts warned him that he was facing an enraged tiger. "Don't you ever tell me what I mean and what I don't mean."

To his dismay, he realized in trying to maintain order he was saying all the wrong things. "You know I didn't—"

Her eyes flashed more warning signals. "I don't want you to help me find Wendy and Michael. I work alone, you know that well enough."

Ben looked lost at sea, an orphan clinging to a spar amid a storm he hadn't seen coming. "We worked together in the field."

"That was forever ago. I'm quits with rules and regs, anyway."

"That's a dangerous path to go down."

"So what else is new." She turned away. "I'm going to do what I'm going to do. Period."

"I didn't say I wouldn't help you."

"I don't want your help."

"Evan." His eyes were pleading even as his voice remained calm. "I know you can do this by yourself. You're the most resourceful agent I've ever known. But I'm the only one you can count on now."

"Really."

He nodded. "I've always had your back, Evan. That's never going to change."

Her lips pursed. "Prove it. In or out, Ben? Which is it?"

Ben took a breath, let it out. "Well, I mean, what about Paul? How does he fit into your theory?"

"He doesn't." She was moving away toward the chair where, by some miracle a new outfit was folded and waiting for her. "Whose house is this, anyway?" She looked around. "Something familiar about it."

He needed to get her back on track. "So Paul doesn't fit into your SVR theory?"

She gave him a brief querying look. "Whoever it is I owe them a huge thank-you."

"I've already passed that on." He gestured. "What about Paul?"

"If I'm right," she told him, "Paul is dead."

"That's one theory."

"So." She was still breathing hard, still running with excess adrenaline as she picked up and inspected each item of clothing. "Okay, Boy Blunder, let's find out."

7

ISTANBUL, TURKEY

Gauzy sunlight spread itself over the cobalt-and-umber Bosphorus, sending up dazzling scimitars in its wake. Heavily laden boats, wallowing ferries, and Bodrum-built gulets, their wooden hulls gleaming, passed back and forth from Asia to Europe and back again. In the distance vendors' cries rose like mist from a morning field.

All this and more came to Anton Zherov and Karin Wagner as they sat beneath a gaily striped awning on a wide, sun-splashed terrace on a promontory overlooking the water. Behind them, the restaurant was bustling with the morning breakfast hustle. Waiters, trays held high over their heads, were busy picking their way to and from tables. The soft clink of glassware and cutlery combined with the drone of conversations to create a calming lullaby.

Zherov shifted in his seat. "For the hundredth time, what are we doing here?"

Kobalt, deep into her new legend. "We're importing something or other and exporting something or other."

He glared at her with one eyebrow raised. "Really, Karin!"

"Patience, my pet."

"I'm not your pet!" A flush had bloomed on his cheeks, which he worked furiously to dissipate.

She was laughing silently. She wore black jeans, a white T-shirt over which she had donned a lightweight jacket of her own design that had more interior pockets than Batman's utility belt. For his part, Zherov was overdressed in a gunmetal sports jacket and a striped tie in two shades of gray. The waiter set down before her a large bowl of yellow yogurt and fresh yellow figs, neatly quartered. She picked up a spoon and took a bite. "Mm," she said, swallowing. "This is delicious. You really must try it." She raised a hand to summon the waiter back, and when he reappeared at their table, she continued. "There is nothing like fresh Turkish yogurt and ripe figs." She seemed to say this to no one in particular. Then she shifted her gaze to the waiter. "My partner will have the same."

"Right away, madam." The waiter gave a slight deferential nod before whisking himself away to the kitchen.

Zherov made a sound deep in his throat. "Cut the crap, will you."

She took another spoonful of her breakfast, chewed thoughtfully, head cocked as though toward the mournful hoot of a tanker as it passaged the Golden Horn. Setting her spoon down, she looked at Zherov across the table. "Listen closely because I'm only going to say this once. I didn't ask for you. I don't need you. You don't like my attitude, take a fucking hike; nothing would make me happier. Either stay and take whatever I dish out or be gone." Her eyes held his for an electric moment. "Are we clear?"

His jaw clenched so tightly his mandibular muscles bulged. He turned his gaze away.

"Are. We. Clear. Zherov."

His eyes swung back, smoldering with disgust and hate. "Clear."

Seemingly satisfied, she once more dipped her spoon into her breakfast and resumed eating as if nothing untoward had occurred. Zherov's breakfast came, along with a refill of her strong Turkish coffee. She pushed her cup over to him. "Drink up, Anton."

"I won't touch that muddy swill."

"Not a real man, huh?" She was about to take the cup back, when he snatched it away, downed the coffee in one. He swallowed and grimaced terribly.

She laughed. Her hand swept out to encompass their view. "Nearly four years ago, Istanbul was my first stop after I was exfiltrated from America. That's when I had my first cup of real Turkish coffee, right here in this restaurant. It's why I chose it now." She bared her teeth and called for another coffee. "I fell in love with it from the get-go." The problem with Zherov, she reflected, was that he was too clever for his own good. His successes in the field caused him to feel entitled. When he was home in Moscow he liked to be hailed as the conquering hero.

She looked him straight in the eye. "You resent strong women, don't you, Anton?"

"No." He shook his head. "I resent you."

Another silence, taut as a drawn bow, the arrow aimed—but at whom?

"Because I was born and raised in America."

"You've got America in your veins," he said with a note of disgust. "You're polluted, damaged beyond repair."

She snorted. "Anton Antonovich, I am entirely uninterested in your personal animus toward me. Remain professional— this is all that's required of you."

Zherov stiffened. She'd hit a nerve. "I am nothing if not professional." He snapped this off like a Red Army officer.

Her coffee came and she spooned in four cubes of sugar, stirred slowly and with precision, the spoon never scraping against the inside of the cup. She took a leisurely sip, then set the cup down, looked up at Zherov.

"I have your word?"

"I already gave it."

"Say it," she insisted, and he did, grudgingly, between gritted teeth.

At that moment, they both became aware of a portly individual wending his way toward them. He had a moon face, small, simian ears, and suspicious eyes the color of Kobalt's coffee. He was nattily dressed in a cream suit with very wide lapels and legs, as if he had appeared from an earlier age. He wore a sand silk shirt and a dove-gray knitted silk tie with an enormous knot that helped cover his double chin.

He came up to the table, looked at Kobalt, and gave the slightest bow. "Dearest lady, good morning to you." He had a deep foghorn sort of voice. He then turned his attention to Zherov. "You I don't know. But whatever I see I don't like."

"Good morning, Ermi," Kobalt said. "Here is Anton Zherov."

"Just consider me a fly on the wall," Zherov said, thinking himself a wit.

"More like a bug on the sole of my shoe." Ermi turned back to Kobalt. She did not ask him to sit and he did not seem inclined to want to.

"Where are they?" Kobalt said shortly.

Ermi spread his thick-fingered hands. "Alas, that I do not know, dearest lady."

Something changed behind Kobalt's eyes, something dark and restless stirring. "Yet you contacted me. Even so you are of no use this fine morning."

"Oh, but dearest lady, for you I always have a use. In the context you mention I have a close business acquaintance who may know their whereabouts." With this pronouncement, he set a folded slip of paper on the table beside her coffee cup.

Kobalt studied it for a moment as if trying to read the tea leaves or the bones thrown. Then she picked up the paper and read its contents. Without another word she reached into a pocket, drew out a number of bills, folded into a pack.

Ermi whisked it away as quickly and smoothly as a magician performing his vanishing coin trick.

"A pleasure, as always, dearest lady." He bowed slightly, backed away, then turned and with surprising agility and speed, disappeared off the terrace.

"Lovely fellow," Zherov said with a laugh as he glanced at the address written on the paper in Kobalt's hand. "Where is this, anyway?"

"Across town," she said, frowning. "We need to get out of here now." But their waiter was nowhere around.

While Zherov went to pay the bill, she turned her gaze back out to Istanbul, which had been much beloved by her. Now, the tenor of the times, the presidential strongman, the Islamic crackdowns, the tension and anxiety souring the air, made her feel sad.

The address Ermi had given her was a shop in the eastern quarter of the labyrinth of the city's famed Grand Bazaar. The sprawling market seemed even more jam-packed than the last time she had been here, if that was possible. As they negotiated the twisting, narrow lanes, merchants on either side beckoned, smiling, urging them to buy silks and broadcloths woven with gold and silver threads, felt and suede slippers with turned up toes and tassels at the heels, copper pots, bronze figurines, intricately filigreed hanging lamps, strings of beads of all kinds from cheap glass to semiprecious stones. They passed coffeehouses, where heavy-lidded men lolled drinking and chatting, shop fronts jammed with hookahs of all sizes and shapes from traditional to fanciful, and so many rug dealers they soon became impossible to count. Here and there, the wooden fretwork balconies of cafés and restaurants overhung the street under the canvas ceiling. And everywhere people teemed in an unending stream. Above all, the exotic scents of cinnamon, clove, allspice, myrrh, sage, cumin, sumac, and mint created a heady swirl, along with the multitude of raised voices enticing, cajoling, bargaining, and haggling vociferously but good-naturedly.

"Who is the 'they' who were the subject of your negotiation with that smarmy piece of—"

"Shut your piehole," she snapped.

"I'm not familiar with—"

She turned on him. "You like pies?"

"I do."

"Now you know what a piehole is," she said.

"Another of your stupid Americanisms," he muttered.

"Shut it and keep it shut until further notice."

He was about to respond, but the fiery look she threw him changed his mind in a hurry, and he shrugged instead, if only to save whatever face he had left.

Three-quarters of the way down their destination street, they came to a knife shop that displayed small bladed weapons made of Damascus steel, the kind from which Japanese katana were made. The method of layering stainless steel with carbon steel over and over gave those blades both strength and flexibility. The process, though refined to exquisite excess by the Japanese, originated in the Syrian city for which it was named.

Kobalt spent some time at the shop window, examining one blade after another. The shopkeeper, seeing her interest, stepped out and inquired whether she wished to buy some of his wares.

"Not any of these," she said. "I want to see what you have inside."

He gave her a penetrating look. He was a stone-faced man

with lifeless button eyes and buzz cut hair. His eyes roved over her. "Have I seen you before, madam?"

"I was in Istanbul four years ago."

"The weather was bad that year, if I remember correctly."

"It was too hot," she responded, the last part of the parole, the recognition exchange previously agreed upon.

The shopkeeper introduced himself as Ali Khan. Kobalt didn't bother to give him any name.

"Wait here," she told Zherov as he made to follow her and the shopkeeper.

The interior was narrow, dimly lit, and smelled of oiled metal and incense. Light was provided by a pair of shaded lamps hanging on either side wall. Tendrils of aromatic smoke spiraled from inside a squat worked brass burner sitting on one end of the counter. Motes of dust hung in the air, as sluggish as drunks in a bar.

Ali Khan stepped behind the counter. Snapped on a modern articulated lamp clamped to the center.

"Tell me what you know," she said. "But while you do, please show me your best straight-blade knives, not the crappy folders you sell to tourists."

If Ali Khan was insulted, he gave no sign of it, merely reached underneath the counter, producing a roll of felt. He unfurled it onto the polished wooden countertop revealing pockets, each with a knife tucked into it. That he hadn't offered her tea was the first sign that all was not as it should be.

The lamplight was a dazzling bluish oblong that illuminated the entire length of the felt. He slipped out one of the knives, held it under the light for her to examine. As he bent forward, she watched a bead of blood run down from behind his ear. This was the second sign. Looking down, she noticed the crescents of blood beneath his fingernails. *Three on a match*, she thought.

Keeping her voice calm and steady. "I'd like to hold the knife, check its balance."

"Of course, madam." But at that moment, he slapped at the drop of blood on his cheek as if it were a gnat.

"You're bleeding," Kobalt commented, as if annoyed at being distracted from her scrutiny of the knife.

"Forget it, it's nothing," he said forcefully.

But he was withdrawing the knife from the light. She snatched it from him, drove it down point first, impaling his hand, pinning it to the countertop. The eyes of the man who was clearly not Ali Khan opened wide. His mouth opened as well, but not a sound emerged. It looked like he was yawning.

"Who are you?" Kobalt said, as she rolled up the rest of the knives and moved them out of his reach. "What have you done with Ali Khan?"

The man stared at her with venom. But otherwise gave no sign he was listening.

"Anton Antonovich!" Kobalt called over her shoulder.

Zherov came at a trot. He took in the scene instantly. "Nicely done! What's going on?"

"This one isn't the shopkeeper," she said, moving around the end of the counter. "Watch him. Carefully. There's something weird about him."

"Weird how?" Zherov asked, but she was already through a beaded curtain into the back space.

The man was looking into the middle distance, ignoring Zherov completely. Leaning across the counter, Zherov slapped him across the face. No visible reaction.

Gripping the man's jaw, he turned his head so that the man could do nothing else but look at him. He studied the man's facial features for several minutes, and apparently recognized something there. "Who the fuck are you?"

When the man's lips curled upward, Zherov broke his nose with the heel of his hand. It happened so fast, the man's eyes briefly rolled up in his head. Blood squirted out as if from a squeeze bottle. He hated to admit it, but Kobalt was right. There was something weird about the guy. Either he was one of those people incapable of feeling pain, or his non-reaction was something else altogether. Something sinister.

"Hmm." Zherov came around the counter, took up a knife, slit the man's shirt, then ripped the shirt entirely off, baring him down to his waist.

The man stood immobile, as if he was inured to being stripped and searched.

"Tats," Zherov murmured to himself. "It's tats I'm looking for." But there was nothing on the guy's back or on his arms, though he searched every square inch, looking to see if a tattoo had been abraded with a brick or scraped off with a shard of glass.

While he was thus occupied, the man's free hand gripped the handle of the buried knife and with a mighty effort that spasmed the muscles in his arm and shoulder wrenched it free. He whirled, the bloody knife raised to strike at Zherov's heart, but Zherov's fist was already moving. It slammed into his throat, fracturing his windpipe. All the energy should have drained out of him as his body was deprived of oxygen, but the knife still followed its arc. Though Zherov was positioned differently it was too late to alter the path of the knife, which buried itself in the meat of Zherov's left biceps. Zherov snarled into eyes as flat and stony as discs. A punch to the man's heart finally stopped him. Zherov pulled the knife out of his arm, teeth bared as he grunted in pain. The man collapsed back onto the countertop, gasping like a landed fish, utterly spent.

That's when Zherov saw the tat. Through the blood from the man's broken nose, he found himself staring at a tattoo of a knife plunged through the man's neck: the hilt and part of the blade on the right side, the point of the blade on the left. It was a Russian prison tattoo, crude but effective, made with a mixture of rubber scorched in the kitchen ovens and urine. Each tattoo had a specific meaning and carried a heavy weight. This one marked the guy as someone who had killed an inmate in "the zone," as Russian prison was called, and who for the right price was available to kill again.

Clearly, he'd continued this profession when he'd been released from "the zone." Who had hired him to intercept Kobalt was unknown and now, because Zherov's interrogation of him had resulted in retaliation, it was no longer possible to retrieve that information. Ripping off a length of cloth from the man's shirt, Zherov fashioned a tourniquet, tied it tight above the wound on his own biceps with the help of his teeth.

The criminal assassin splayed out, sliding down off the countertop to crumple at Zherov's feet, as dead as everything else in the downtrodden knife shop of horrors.

Speaking of horrors, the real Ali Khan was waiting patiently for Kobalt.

A trap, she thought. *Fucking Ermi led us into a trap.*

He was sprawled on the floor of the back room, a space filled with shelves of finished blades and unfinished handles. Machines for grinding, sanding, and carving, as well as a thick-topped wooden worktable, took up most of the space. Judging by Ali Khan's ripped nails and knuckles he hadn't known the man in the front of the shop and had put up the best fight he knew how. But squatting down beside the mutilated corpse, she could tell that he'd had no chance. Whatever else that guy posing as Ali Khan was, he was most definitely a professional sadist.

Kobalt was well acquainted with the sadistic mind and the devastating abuse, both physical and emotional, it could inflict, since long before she was exfiltrated out of the United States. But this devastation was something else entirely. The unabashed delight with which this unspeakable horror had been inflicted spoke of a sadistic mind of a higher order. The man had been carved and gutted.

He was to all intents and purposes inside out.

8

MOSCOW, RUSSIAN FEDERATION

It was a fact, known throughout the vast and terrifying Lubyanka building, that Dima Tokmakov was possessed of a restless nature. It was also a known fact that once a week, without fail, through sunshine, rain, sleet, and snow, he would take a long lunch with his mistress du jour, a position that spun as often as the wheel in *Wheel of Fortune* and was currently occupied by a svelte blonde named Nadya.

Clad in his heavy overcoat, Tokmakov took the elevator down to the ground floor and made his way out of Lubyanka Square. He walked to the Lubyanka underground station. Approximately two minutes later, he boarded a train on the K line, exiting one stop later at Teatral'naya Square. He could have walked the distance, and in fine weather he was tempted to do so, but his security conscious mind would not allow that. It was far easier to check for tags and to melt into the crowds in the massive underground passageways and stations.

Nadya was waiting for him at their appointed time at the Christian Louboutin Petrovka Street boutique. She laughed when she saw him and kissed him boldly on the mouth in front of the browsing tourists, all of whom, men and women alike, felt pangs of jealousy like arrows through their hearts. And why not? Nadya was gorgeous, tall, lean, blond, and blue-eyed, with the figure of a pole dancer, which she, in fact, had been before she met Dima. Now through his influence she was a top model at a first-rank international modeling agency. This perfect specimen pointed out the shoes she coveted this week and he bought them for her, no questions asked.

Afterward, as was their weekly routine, they strolled arm in arm to the flat he rented for his rotating mistresses a block and a half from the Bolshoi Theater. Once inside, she turned on some sultry music, kicked off her shoes, slipped on the new Louboutin pumps, and began to slowly undress for him. Dima, still in his heavy overcoat, watched her with eyes gleaming with lust.

When she was naked, save for the Louboutins, she lowered herself to her hands and knees, crawled across the floor to where Dima stood, eyes riveted on her. Still on her knees, she rose until her torso was perfectly straight. She raised her hands to her breasts, offering them up to him.

There followed forty or so minutes of strenuous, not to say acrobatic, sex, integrating an astonishing array of erotic implements, that resulted in Dima lying flat on his back gasping for air while Nadya took a wet face towel to his red and sweating parts. This resulted in another erection, to which she attended as artfully as an ikebana *iemoto*—grand master.

Later, they shared ice-cold vodka, along with a light lunch, after which Dima left without a word or a backward glance at Nadya's gracefully sleeping form.

It was now precisely two in the afternoon. There was a seven-minute walk south awaiting him from Teatral'naya Square to Nikolskaya Street. He took a circuitous route, doubling back several times before entering the vast, humming post office. He crossed the echoing space to the bank of small brass lockboxes against the left-hand wall. Using a key, he opened his box, slid a neatly wrapped package approximately the size of two bricks laid one atop the other from within his voluminous overcoat, and locked the box back up.

Crossing to the other side of the room, he joined a queue for stamps. He waited patiently. From time to time, he graciously allowed someone to precede him so that he never came close to the bronze-framed window where the stamps were being sold.

At precisely 2:45 a uniformed courier entered the post office and, without looking around, proceeded directly to the bank of bronze-faced lockboxes. Using a key identical to Dima's he opened Dima's lockbox, took out the package, wrote on a receipt with the tracking number, placed that in the box, and locked it.

When he was gone, Dima left the queue, opened the box, slipped the receipt into the pocket of his overcoat. Eighteen minutes later, he was back at his desk in the Lubyanka, dealing with SIGINT—signals intelligence consisting mainly of electronic intel reporting, risk assessments on targets, and possible assignments in order of their importance.

He was thinking how easy it was these days to interrupt or even redirect electronic communication, which thankfully could not be done with a private courier service, when Feliks knocked on his door.

"Come."

Feliks set a pair of red-jacketed dossiers before Dima. "How was lunch?"

Dima picked up his faint snicker. "Better than yours, of that I am certain." He didn't look up or in any other way acknowledge Feliks's presence.

9

WASHINGTON, DC

"The fact is I'm actually no longer your boss."

"I already established that."

Ben and Evan were in his car, heading toward the Fisher house in the Cleveland Park area. Ben was driving, Evan in shotgun. She was staring fixedly ahead, as if she could already see Bobbi's house. She wore black stove-pipe jeans, a black T-shirt with THE WHO in white across the chest, and a great-looking three-quarter-length car coat with a stand-up collar, in a shade of jade green. It was the outfit that had been left carefully folded over the slat-backed chair in the room where she had recovered. Much to her surprise, every item fitted her perfectly, which meant they were picked out by Isobel, not Ben. Of course it was Isobel; she remembered the house from when she'd been there previously. It seemed strange to her that Ben hadn't mentioned Isobel by name. Was he trying to hide his relationship with her? And, come to think of it, what exactly was his relationship with her?

Ben shot her a quick look. "Yeah, but what I mean is we've been fired."

That got Evan's attention. "Come again?"

"They've closed down the shop. The others have been reassigned, probably as desk jockeys stashed somewhere in the bowels of NSA, filing briefs no one cares about." And he told her why POTUS had decided to ax his shop. "Partly, he hates women in any capacity of power, hated that I had as many women agents as men. It's also part of the systematic gutting of the intelligence sector. But also this is retribution for our dismantling Nemesis in the Bavarian Alps three months ago."

This news shook her out of her monomania, at least for the moment. "You must be devastated. I know how much the shop meant to you. You'd been working toward it for years."

He stopped at a light. It was so early in the morning— around 4 A.M.—there was hardly any traffic. "I really don't want to talk about it."

"Okay, sure." She turned away.

The light turned green and they took off.

Ben slowed the car as they approached their destination. "How's your head?"

"Never better." She heard her own words through incessant thunder. The analgesic she'd been given was wearing off and she wasn't about to screw with her reflexes by taking another one.

He pulled the car up to the curb and parked, bit off a harsh laugh. "I don't know why I bother."

"Clearly, you can't help yourself."

It was a cutting remark, certainly, one of many she had hurled at him after the accident. But this one was different; this one truly cut him. She could see it on his face, though he struggled mightily to keep it hidden. Something occurred to her then that should have registered long before. Ben was a master at keeping his emotions secret—save when it came to her. She felt something tap her heart, the tip of his finger maybe, the sense that perhaps she and Ben could be a field team again. This should have warmed her. Instead, it had the opposite effect: it incensed her. She felt vulnerable, naked to his gaze. She felt unaccountably violated.

She swung out of the car. It was raining again, but gently. Evan stood on the sidewalk in front of the Fisher house with legs slightly apart, the way a seaman might on the deck of a ship in rough water. The vertigo she'd experienced when exiting the car had passed. She breathed in deeply, filling her lungs until her head cleared fully.

Ben came up beside her. "Do you have a way to get into the house?"

"I do."

"Well, we'd better get going. But I can't imagine what we'll find. No doubt the FBI boys have been over every square inch of it already."

"I know the house better than they do." Evan still hadn't looked at him. She felt an electricity between them that was entirely new and not particularly pleasant. *After all we've been through*, she asked herself, *what is this now? And what do we do about it? Nothing*, the answer came back from the recesses of her mind. *Not a damn thing. Just put one foot in front of the other, head into the dark like always, and see where it leads*. But this dark led into Bobbi's house, where ghosts were interred, ghosts alien to her. Inimical. She felt a chill ripple along her bones. Her hands felt stiff, frozen despite the warmth of the spring night.

Ben gestured. "Shall we?"

She was on the verge of acquiescing when she saw the black Chevy Tahoe from out the corner of her eye. Both she and, she was sure, Ben knew who the occupants were. They quickly moved into deep shadow, concealing themselves.

She placed a hand on his forearm. "Let's surveille the competition first."

Two FBI suits appeared, checked their mobile phones, then started up the brick walkway to the Fisher house. One was taller, beefier, and older than the other. The younger one was slim but filled out his suit nicely. Evan was willing to bet the older one was ex-military and that he'd been the champion boxer of his unit in the heavyweight class. His face featured a jaw like the prow of a ship.

"Okay," Evan said as they disappeared through the front door. "Let's go."

Ben was nonplussed. "You want to go inside while they're there?"

"Do you have a better idea?"

"Yeah. Let's wait until they leave."

"And what if they're joined by another forensics crew? No, we've got to get in there and have a look around as quickly as possible."

She led him around the side of the house to the back, which was screened in from the neighbors on either side by an army of tall evergreens. Paul liked his privacy, so he had let the trees grow so tall he had started getting complaints from the neighbors, which he had ignored completely until they simply gave up and ceased to call.

The backyard was loosely divided between use for adults—nearer the house was a fire pit, picnic table, chairs, umbrella stands, and a brickwork outdoor barbecue. The back half was mostly taken up by a swing set, a complex jungle gym, a slide, and one of those moveable soccer goals. All along the periphery, Bobbi's neatly planted gardens—roses, azalea, mountain laurel, flowering quince, hardy hibiscus—were blooming with color. Three wide steps led up to a back porch that ran the length of the house, protected by a railing with fluted iron spindles.

Evan picked her way over to the barbecue, stuck her hand into one of the niches on the left side of the covered grill, pulled out a key.

She gestured toward the back door, and she and Ben mounted the stairs. She turned the key in the lock, and they slipped silently into the kitchen. For a moment, all was deathly still inside. The emptiness was absolute and, for Evan, heart-wrenching. After a short time, the ghosts manifested. The faint rise and fall of two voices in conversation. All the lights in the front rooms had been turned on. Evan led Ben through the kitchen. A box of take-out pizza lay crumpled in the garbage bin. No after odors of cooking. As they moved stealthily into the dining room, toward the hallway to the living room and den, the place seemed dead, no scent of Wendy's lemongrass shampoo, no echo of Michael's loud voice. The sadness—awfulness of their loss struck her all over again like a punch to the gut, redoubling her vow to find them. She examined everything with the minuteness of a Sherlock Holmes.

They heard the voices more clearly now, and Evan sang under her breath, "The Badger and the Ferret went to see in a big black SUV," to the rhythm of "The Owl and the Pussycat" nursery rhyme she used to recite to the kids when they were very young.

But the voices were coming their way, so they backtracked, turned to the right as they reentered the kitchen, took a narrow flight of back stairs to the upper floor. Three bedrooms, one each for the children and the master. They went through each one methodically, silently, but could find nothing of value.

"Not even a single photo," Evan said sadly. "They've stripped the corpse bare."

"Only what you'd expect from the FBI," Ben replied.

In Paul's home office they found an expensive desk, expensive task chair, expensive furniture—just the way Paul Fisher liked it. And on that expensive desk, only wires trailing on a surface completely devoid of any electronic equipment.

"So the Feds must have the laptop," Ben mused. "Their

cyber-forensics team is no doubt already scouring the hard drive, social media accounts, emails, and the like."

"Or whoever took the kids. Either way, it won't do them a bit of good." Evan peered inside the empty wastepaper basket. "I know Paul. He was deeply paranoid about his work, let alone what private life he's had since Bobbi was killed. He's too savvy to have left even a single breadcrumb."

Ben nodded. "It's helpful you know him, but I hoped maybe the people who took them might have inadvertently left a sliver of themselves behind."

"Not fingerprints. The place has been dusted. Anyway, they'd have worn gloves."

"Removable booties too."

She was on her hands and knees, checking the corners of the room. She turned on the flashlight feature of her cell. With her head near the floor, she turned it sideways to look under the leather sofa and chair. Not even a dust ball. But bending down like this was a mistake. Her head pounded worse than ever.

She rose, switched off her flashlight function. "Here we go."

Ben said, "Are you sure this is a good idea?" on the way down the stairs.

"We need to know what they've discovered."

They emerged from the gloom of the back staircase into the now-lit bright butter-yellow of the kitchen. Linebacker and Slim were in attendance, staring into the open refrigerator.

Evan chuckled grimly to herself. "If you're looking for a treat, gentlemen, you're bound to find Butter Brickle ice cream in the freezer."

At which, they both whirled. Slim's service Glock 9mm was drawn and aimed at the two intruders.

"Who the hell're you?" Linebacker said. "And may I ask what you're doing here?"

"This is an active FBI investigation scene." Slim had an unexpectedly deep voice. "You're trespassing and therefore subject to arrest." With his free hand, he swung out a pair of handcuffs.

"Hold on there." Ben showed them his ID. He asked for theirs and they offered them: Linebacker was Jon Tennyson, Slim Jason Leyland.

"Now." Tennyson's eyes narrowed. "I don't care what part of the federal alphabet soup you're from. Get out of my crime scene. I'll only ask this once."

"You're also part of the same federal alphabet soup," Evan pointed out, stepping toward him.

Tennyson peered at her. "Do I know you?"

"I doubt it. But why don't you take a look in the freezer, see if the Butter Brickle ice cream is there."

Leyland let out with a growl, but with the twitch of a meaty shoulder, hauled open the freezer. "Well, I'll be damned." Putting his gun and manacles away, he brought out two pint-sized containers.

"So?" Tennyson kept his eyes on the interlopers.

"Butter Brickle," Leyland reported. "Just like she said."

"I know this house. I've known Wendy and Michael since they were born. They're my niece and nephew."

Tennyson snapped his fingers. "That's it! You're the missing aunt. Evan Ryder."

"Hardly missing. I just returned from a long vacation in Sumatra."

"That must've been a helluva trip," Leyland opined, pointing at the wound in her skull.

"I was fighting with a Komodo dragon."

Leyland's brow furrowed. "What the hell is a Komodo dragon?"

"It's a lizard," Tennyson said. "The largest currently living, if I'm not mistaken."

"You're not," Evan said.

Leyland rolled his eyes. "She's pulling our leg."

"No kidding." Tennyson hooked a thumb over his shoulder. "Take another look in Mr. Fisher's study. Maybe forensics overlooked something."

"But—"

"Check for a loose floorboard."

"Right," Leyland said through gritted teeth.

"Okay, Ms. Ryder," Tennyson said as if he really meant it. He hooked a thumb over his shoulder. "Jason can be a bit abrasive but take my word for it he'll be a solid agent."

"Now you understand our interest here," Ben said.

Tennyson shook his head. "Your personal interest, yes, of course. But not you being here. Kidnapping is FBI territory. It would serve all of us well if you left us to it."

Evan stood hands on hips. "Not if a foreign hostile power is involved."

Tennyson blinked as if she had shone a bright light in his face. "I beg your pardon. This is a strictly domestic matter. Nine out of ten times the remaining parent takes off with the kids in tow."

Ben gestured. "Why would a man like Paul Fisher do something like that?"

"Gambling debts, coke habit running wild, a girl or two he's knocked up. Maybe a young man. All poison to a man of Paul Fisher's reputation." Tennyson shrugged. "Could be any or all of those things. The list is practically endless, but those are the most common."

Evan said, "I don't think they apply in this case."

"What have you got so far, Agent Tennyson?" Ben spoke at the same time.

Tennyson sighed, produced a notebook. "This is not a favor I bestow lightly." He flipped through several pages. "We've already spoken to the nanny, Dominica Sanchez. She's half out of her mind with worry. She has no idea where the father has taken them. He didn't leave her a note, hasn't been in contact with her, and his mobile phone is off. Her story checks out all the way down the line. We're monitoring Mr. Fisher's credit cards. His bank account remains untouched—no withdrawals in the last two weeks. We got an Amber Alert out immediately, of course, but to date no joy there either. Frankly, and it pains me to admit it, at the moment, we've hit a brick wall."

He pocketed the notebook. "By the way, there's no use you being here. You won't find anything. Our forensic team has gone over every room with a fine-tooth comb," he continued. "All the clothes are there. Ditto the suitcases. Plus, Mr. Fisher's car, which forensics also dissected. Mr. Fisher's laptop is, however, missing."

Ben and Evan exchanged a meaningful look. Paul's laptop was with the abductors.

Tennyson continued, "There's no safe, no hidden compartments we could find."

"So nothing," Evan said. "You have nothing."

"Not unless Jason finds a loose floorboard, but to be honest that's the stuff of movies and TV shows."

Evan continued. "Okay, well, answer me this. If Paul took off with his kids why would he leave his car here?"

Tennyson shrugged. "Maybe because his car'd be too easy to trace. And anticipating your next question, we're already canvassing the cab, Uber, and Lyft drivers to see if they had a pickup here anytime in the last three days."

He looked at them in turn. "Anything else?"

"Yes," Ben ventured, "Ms. Ryder has more experience in the field, in hostile territory, than you could imagine."

An uncomfortable silence arose like the drawbridge to a castle, everyone eyeing one another warily. Leyland strolled in on the scene and, oblivious to the tension in the atmosphere, said, "No joy. No loose floorboards in the study or anywhere else upstairs."

"Only to be expected," Tennyson said wearily. He gestured

with one hand. "What can you tell me about Mr. Fisher, Ms. Ryder?"

"Not that much. He and I got along about as well as oil and water."

Tennyson's detective's antennae were raised. "Why was that? You didn't like the way he was raising the kids, maybe?"

Evan gave him a thin smile. "I don't like his politics. He's a lobbyist for a select group of ultra-conservative interests backed by Samuel Wainwright Wells."

"The media baron. We're familiar with him." Tennyson's brow furrowed. "So maybe you think he's teaching his ideology to the kids?"

"What is it with you?" Ben said, his annoyance all too clear. "Evan has no connection—"

"Even though you were away," Tennyson said, cutting through him, "I assumed you were in contact with Michael and Wendy Fisher. What can you tell me—"

"Why d'you assume that?"

Tennyson's hands spread in front of him. "Butter Brickle ice cream?" He waited a beat. "Your only blood family since your sister was killed."

"There's nothing more I can tell you. I saw them occasionally. I love them. Of course I do. But I'm not in the habit of calling family and friends when I'm away. Wendy and Michael know that. They accept it."

Tennyson nodded. He looked from one to the other. "Let me be crystal clear. I don't like your kind. I especially don't like you being here at an FBI crime scene, and I sure as hell don't like you assuming you can hijack my case."

"So long, Tennyson," Evan said. "Meeting you has been about as much fun as a root canal."

As she and Ben headed for the back door, Tennyson's voice came to them. "Don't get in our way, you two."

"Is that a threat?" Ben said.

Tennyson shrugged. "Call it a warning shot across the bow. The next time my aim may be different."

Gathering her coat around her butt and thighs, Evan sat on the back steps of Bobbi's house. Dawn had begun to beat back the last vestiges of the night, still coiled around the boles of the pines and the bases of the Fishers' private playground.

Ben sat next to her. "What now? We have no clues as to where the kids are."

"I know where you took me," Evan said as if she hadn't heard him. "I know whose clothes I'm wearing."

"Oh?"

"Yeah. I recognized the house when we left. It belongs to Isobel Lowe. You picked me up there after that poker game I infiltrated went amok." She looked at him. "You never told me you knew her."

"Need to know."

"And now? Didn't I deserve to know now?"

"Maybe."

"Maybe. Uh-huh." She nodded, as if affirming something to herself.

They heard the door open behind them, turned to see Leyland emerge. He stopped, stiffened, clearly surprised to see them. Then he sat on the edge of a railing above them, shook out a cigarette, and lit up.

"Waiting for your limo?" He blew out a cloud of smoke above their heads. "Did you not hear what Special Agent Tennyson said?"

Evan contrived to ignore him. She was staring out at the backyard as more and more morning light illuminated it over the tops of the pines. "Okay, you've come for the kids—they're the ones you want. But their father is home. What d'you do with him?"

Ben was listening carefully but did not try to answer her. She was asking her own mind and he did not want to interrupt her train of thought. He'd seen this process play out plenty of times when they were in the field together—in the Caucasus, in Belgrade, on the outskirts of Kiev with the FSB hot on their trail. He cupped his chin in his hands and, looking out at the backyard, tried to see what she was seeing.

"Do you slit his throat on the spot? That'd spoil the mystery of whether he took them, and now that's precisely what the FBI think. You'd kill the wild-goose chase." She tapped a forefinger against her lips. "Do you take him with the kids? Too risky. The longer he's with you the more of a problem he becomes." She took a deep breath. "So." She looked around the backyard. "What d'you do with him?"

"Are you going to tell us?" Leyland was standing behind them, listening.

She gestured. "See these pines, Ben? See how tall they are, how they form a living wall on three sides?" She squinted. "Paul brought them in for privacy, yeah? Didn't want anyone to spy on his kids. Or on the guests he brought around for private meetings. Which makes this a perfect place for . . ."

She left the steps and got down on her hands and knees as she had in Paul's office, her head on the side so close to the ground the uncut lawn tickled her right cheek, like little spears on her skin. She began moving slowly across the grass, ignoring the throbbing beneath her wound.

"Ben." She rose, excitement in her voice. "The garage door code is 6163. Bobbi had a bunch of gardening tools. See if you can find a couple of trowels."

Leyland watched Ben as he vanished into the garage, but he remained silent. He had become an interested bystander.

Ben returned with a well-used garden trowel in each hand.

By that time, Evan was crouched down in front of the slide. "Look here." She pointed.

"Freshly turned earth."

"Right." Evan nodded. "Let's go."

Each with a trowel, they began to dig. Gingerly at first, then with more vigor.

Leyland had come down the steps, peering at them. "What are you doing?"

"Something here." Ben was using just the tip of the trowel now. They were barely a foot down, but the basic contours were appearing as if rising up from the underworld.

"Face-first." Evan used the edge of the trowel to peel away the last layers of dirt from each side of the head. She was about to use her fingertips when Ben stopped her.

"Here." He handed her a pair of physician's gloves, put his on as she did.

"Where did you get these?" Evan asked.

"Stephen Braun, the doctor who treated you."

Evan nodded. She delicately brushed away what was left covering the face.

She hunched over farther. "It's Paul."

"You were right."

She took no pleasure in that. Then she uncovered his hands. Dirt under his nails and something beneath the dirt, something darker.

Ben sucked in a breath. "Why are his eyes open?"

"So is his mouth," Evan said as she cleared off the last of the specks of dirt. "There's something in it."

"What the hell is going on over there?" Leyland took several tentative steps in their direction. He seemed caught between coming over and turning back to get his boss.

"Don't let him near us." Evan's fingers were slowly teasing out whatever it was that was filling Paul Fisher's mouth. "Not yet anyway."

Ben rose, turning. "You'd better fetch Tennyson."

Leyland's brow furrowed like a field ready for planting. "He's on the horn with HQ. What've you found?"

Ben rose. "Just go fetch him, would you?"

As soon as he saw the agent turn and lope back toward the house, Ben returned to Evan.

She had a sphere of balled-up newspaper in the palm of her hand. "We're going to need their forensics. Time of death will tell us when the abduction occurred."

"Judging by the body's condition it can't be more than a day or two, at most." Ben gestured with his head. "What the hell is this?"

Evan looked up from her work. Her gaze was bleak. "Paul Fisher was very neatly beheaded."

PART TWO

10

WENDY

I am dreaming of flying with Peter Pan to Neverland, just like the Wendy I was named for. "Second star to the right, then straight on till morning." The trouble is this night is never-ending. Dawn seems far away, out of reach. My mind is so fuzzy. I wake, or what seems like waking to me, into another dream. A steady thrumming beneath me, like a big car's engine, and cold air, so dry I automatically think of *Lawrence of Arabia*, which I saw just last week. So I'm in a desert—deserts, I read, are very cold at night (weird!)—or am I flying with Peter? Oh, oh, I so want to be flying with Peter because then Michael will be with me. If I'm in the desert, Lawrence of Arabia's desert, Michael will be elsewhere because he's too young to understand the film. I'm already eleven, so I understand it.

Wasn't I with Mikey just a moment ago? Hadn't I heard Paul yelling? Hadn't I heard unfamiliar men's voices speaking to each other? Was the TV on? I can't remember the TV being on. Maybe Mikey turned it on, certainly not Paul. But for sure I remember Mikey crying.

I say something now, calling for Mikey. It may only have been a murmur, like I'm still in a dream, but is that even possible? I am scared, I know I'm scared, but I've got to be brave for Mikey; he's the real scaredy-cat. But I can't help wishing Aunt Evan were here. If she was, she'd know right away what to do and how to get us out. She's also better at consoling Mikey than I am. I guess I get kinda fed up, which, right now, makes me feel just awful.

Right then I feel a presence somewhere over my head. I try to see who it is, but my vision is all smeary. Maybe I *am* still dreaming. Is that you, Peter? Where are you, Mikey? I mutter groggily. I've got to make sure Mikey isn't lost. He's my responsibility. But, try as I may, I can't see him in the darkness of the night. Where is the moon? Where are the stars? If I can't see the stars how will we find our way to Neverland?

Then I feel a tiny prick, as if a mosquito has bitten me. I try to swat it away, but my arms won't move. They seem to have been dipped in cement. I can't move at all and I'm really scared and the fear grows like a fireball heading my way. But in a moment a peculiar warmth seeps through me, as if I've put my whole hand into one of Winnie-the-Pooh's hunny pots. Though I haven't visited Pooh Bear for the longest time. I hope he won't be angry with me.

Anger. That's what I couldn't remember before, but now it's suddenly pushing through my foggy mind . . .

Mom and Paul are fighting. Again. Paul's always wanted us to call him Paul. Not that he had to—I never think of him as Daddy. He never spent time with either me or Mikey, hardly even spoke to us except to scold us about the TV being too loud, or me wandering into his office, where we never, ever should be. I was such a little girl then. I should've been asleep. Maybe I am asleep, and their fighting wakes me up. Not the words but the anger, which races through the house like a mounted Ringwraith.

Yes, the anger was what woke me. As I totter to the head

of the stairs, I hear Mom and Paul more clearly. Mainly Paul. Holding tight to the bannister, because Mom told me to hold tight and never let go until I reached the bottom, and because I'm a good girl, I sort of slide down on my fanny, my legs dropped over each riser.

"Why the hell did you even marry me?" Paul says in that awful voice of his. "You don't love me."

"That's a laugh." Mom's reply is somehow sweet and tart at the same time (mysterious!). "You don't know the meaning of love."

"I know you're not living up to your end of love."

Mom laughs, again the sweet tart that I can't understand. "And what would that be?"

"For one thing, hosting parties for my friends."

"You don't have any friends, Paul. You have donors to the Wellses' Super PAC who need to be stroked, and you want me to stroke them."

"Damn right I do!" Paul thunders.

"No matter what I do, how big an effort I make, it's never enough."

Paul's voice slows down, as if he's scolding her. "Because, Bobbi, they're the most important people in my life, which means they should be the most important people in yours."

"You couldn't care less about the kids."

"And you don't have to. I provide you with nannies to look after the kids. And are you grateful? Far from it."

"Maybe I would be grateful if you weren't fucking them one by one."

That's when I hear the thwack, like the time Paul dropped a whole melon onto the concrete out the back of the house. I cringe. I hear Mom's grunt. It's the sound an animal makes when it's in pain. I cringe again. My eyes are blurry, my mouth is full of tears.

Then Mikey is beside me, fists rubbing his eyes. He mumbles

something but I can't make it out. He's only three. He's crying. How long has he been there, how much of the fight has he heard? Has he heard Paul hit Mom? Gathering him in my arms, I kiss the top of his head, damp with sleep, his wet and salty cheeks. I take him up, one step at a time, and put him to bed. I kiss him good night, but he holds out his arms to me, and I crawl into bed next to him. With my body against his, it doesn't take long for him to fall back to sleep.

But I'm not yet ready. I'm too angry and upset and frightened. The word "anger" echoes in my mind, pinballing, stirring up echoes and shadows. Anger is also stirred up when Aunt Evan comes to visit. Mom and Aunt Evan love each other, I'm sure of that, almost, because that's the way it has to be—Mom and Paul don't love each other so Mom and Aunt Evan must, they just must! But there's also something underneath like an icy river that makes me shiver and turn away when they yell at each other. Their anger is different from the one between Mom and Paul. It's like a spiderweb, built slowly and painstakingly, one strand at a time, silken but strong.

I remember watching a spiderweb strung from one tree to its neighbor at the edge of our property. The strands looked so thin, so delicate as they swayed in the wind. But that day I learned how strong they were. An unsuspecting fly is caught in the web. The harder it struggles the more fiercely it's held in place. I watch with keen fascination as the fly's struggles reach a fitful frenzy and then stop—just stop. I wonder whether the fly ran out of energy or is dead. The fly doesn't move for the longest time, and then the spider, which has been crouched at the corner of its web, unfolds its legs, and delicately works its way toward the fly. The first to go are the fly's wings. They are so insubstantial I wonder whether they taste like cotton candy. The spider eats and then returns to its corner, folding its legs up like Mom's bridge table. Over the next several days, the spider returns, eating its fill, then retreating until, at last, there is nothing left.

I'm reminded of the spider and the fly whenever Aunt Evan comes over, when she and Mom stand face-to-face in the kitchen or out in the backyard. Whatever is between them is built strand by strand over a long time, and like the spider, they keep coming back at each other in a way that makes me very sad. Sometimes I cry, especially on the days I overhear them.

"You know what happened to our parents," Aunt Evan says, trying her best to keep her voice down.

"I don't," Mom says. "You're making up stories, as usual."

"You didn't tell me in the cave," Aunt Evan tells her. Her voice sounds like an iron bar—cold, hard, unbreakable.

"I was just egging you on. I didn't know a thing."

"You're a liar!"

"I can't have this same argument every time I see you," Mom says. "You're trying to undermine my confidence."

"Why would I do that?"

"I have the perfect life. The life you want to lead. Instead you have nothing. No husband, no children, no home. No love."

"What a hypocrite you are," Aunt Evan says, her voice an even darker iron. "You know what I think?"

"I don't care what you think."

"I think you hate this life. I think Paul hits you. I think you're living a lie. I think you need to get out . . ."

Mom's dead now, of course, but I still have these memories. They're all the same inasmuch as they're bad memories. Do I have one good one of her? Sometimes I try to find one, but all I get is a headache. But then again, we were so young when she died, especially Mikey. I don't think he even remembers her. Maybe that's just as well. Sometimes I wish I didn't either.

11

WASHINGTON, DC

Of all the neon glows in and around Washington, DC, the most iconic, though perhaps only to a small coterie of habitués, was the Art Deco sign for Lethe, a sixty-odd-year-old motel off the interstate on the outskirts of the capital. It had been in business more or less continuously since it opened. Though it had passed through a number of owners and several renovations, the essence of the place remained, which was precisely what its clients wanted. It was frequented by businessmen and pols with their assignation partners of either sex, traveling salesmen rest-stopping for an hour or two of out-call service, and assorted and sundry drunks escaping from their wives and AA sponsors. The one hard and fast rule of the house: no hard drugs allowed. Ever.

The rooms in the long two-story building were dimly lit but impeccably clean, filled with shabby-chic mid-century furniture. The floors were polished wooden boards, instead of the grimy industrial wall-to-wall in other such low-rent motels. The beds, which had always been another featured attraction of Lethe, were like clouds, perfect for making love and, afterward, exhausted sleep.

From the front window of their second-floor room, Evan and Ben could see the blue and green sign, apt colors for the underworld's river of forgetting that was the motel's namesake.

At the moment, however, Ben was off getting them some food, and Evan was on her mobile, texting Lyudmila to tell her about the abduction of her niece and nephew and their father's murder, along with the latest photos of Wendy and Michael she had. The communication was absolutely secure because it was sandboxed, which meant it was securitized, cut off from anything else on her phone. On Lyudmila's end as well, full end-to-end encryption that changed every twenty seconds.

Finished, she stowed her mobile away and turned her attention to the tightly packed ball of torn newspaper she had plucked out of Paul Fisher's mouth. She had just managed to secret it before Tennyson rumbled out of the back door, came charging across the lawn, trying to take command and to maintain order at the same time.

Ben had quickly cut through his bluster. "Evan was right, Tennyson. As you can plainly see Paul Fisher didn't abduct his children. He's right here, where Evan found him, beheaded, to boot. This isn't your routine case, Tennyson, and if Evan is right again and a hostile foreign power is involved, you and your pal are out."

Tennyson returned a glower of monumental proportions. He looked as if at any moment he would be struck down by an aneurysm. He had run his arm across his sweating forehead and said, his voice dripping contempt, "Just in case you're wrong, buster, we're going to search archives for serial killers with the same MO. *If* you don't mind, that is."

Now, perched on the edge of a wooden chair she had drawn up to the desk against the wall opposite the two double beds, she adjusted a goose-neck lamp to shine directly onto the sphere. It had almost completely dried out, and she began to carefully unwrap each ragged strip of newspaper, careful not to cause a tear. She laid them out one beneath the other on the left side of the desktop.

When she was halfway through Ben returned with burgers, fries, and drinks. She paid him no mind as he set the bags down on the desktop, began to unpack them.

"I don't know about you, but I'm starving." He laid out the food, the packets of ketchup and the large containers of soda. Their smell was overpowering, and he glommed onto one of the burgers, jammed as much as he could into his mouth. "Eat," he said. "Then we both need to get a bit of rest."

When she didn't answer him, didn't stop her slow and methodical unwinding, he moved around behind her to peer at the tiers of newspaper strips. As he chewed, he bent over to see them more closely.

"Hey," he said, pointing to one. "I remember this story. It was in the Sunday edition of the *Post*."

Evan immediately stopped what she was doing, took up the strip in question, examined it. "Are you sure? Then we've got the start of our timeline. We know Wendy and Michael were abducted on Sunday." Evan picked up her burger and bit into it without tasting it. It was fuel, nothing more. "I still think the FSB is our prime suspect."

"Maybe. Yes. But there's still also a chance that Sam Wells and his people are behind this."

Evan looked up. "Ben, we've been through this. Why would Wells get rid of Paul? Where's your conviction about this coming from?"

"Two unimpeachable sources: General Aristides and you." He took up a couple more fries. "Getting rid of Paul could just be a red herring—an inconvenient bit of collateral damage, yes, but lobbyists aren't exactly hard to replace in this town. I told you Aristides warned me about the American cabal behind Nemesis. They were the ones who got my shop closed down. He said they had long memories, that they'd never forget what we did. And believe me, it was not a casual warning, he was sweaty and deadly serious. Then, you yourself told me what your would-be abductor said about 'they.' They wanted you to die a slow and agonizing death. They know everything about you. That doesn't sound like a hostile foreign power—not anyone we're aware of anyway. It does sound a lot like Nemesis. So maybe it was this cabal led by Sam Wells that ordered your abduction. This could be another part of their scheme to punish us."

"I suppose . . . I mean, anything's possible at this point."

Ben shrugged. "Either way. Trouble is we don't have enough information to formulate our next step."

Evan had stopped unrolling the newspaper sphere while she tried to eat. Now, she set her burger down; she'd only taken a bite or two. Her vision was pulsing, and pain wound its tentacles around her head, not only from the wound but from the contusion behind her ear. Colors started to pop, as if she were on acid.

Seeing her wobble as she sat, Ben reached out for her so quickly he knocked over one of the containers of fries. A chain reaction ensued, as the first container hit the second one, which tipped over, fries spilling across the tabletop. A couple of them struck the newspaper sphere hard enough to set it rolling across the table. It dropped off the edge and hit the floor with an audible clunk. They froze, one of Ben's arms across her shoulders.

"You okay?"

"You heard that."

Ben nodded. "I did."

Evan turned her head slowly, slowly. "Let's find out what made that noise."

Ben held her closer. "Let's make sure you're all right. The sphere isn't going anywhere."

She placed her hands over her eyes. "Just give me a minute."

Releasing her, Ben stooped down, plucked the sphere off the floor. That's when he felt the hard object he'd taken from Evan's would-be abductor and unthinkingly shoved into the pocket of his pants. It had been an automatic response; his mind had been filled with Evan and only Evan, getting her out of her smoking Charger.

He rose and placed the sphere onto the table beside Evan's elbow. Then he extracted the object from the bottom of his pocket and looked at it for the first time. It was a blue plastic hexagon, inscribed with the number 512. Attached to it was a key. A hotel room key, surely. Except what hotel these days still used a key instead of a magnetic key card? Even Lethe now used key cards, though, according to the receptionist, some of the motel's oldest regulars had complained, until he'd explained the key card's added security. No one could duplicate one of those.

So what hotel had Evan's would-be abductor been staying at? He turned the blue hexagon over and over between his fingers, but there was nothing except the room number. Never mind, he happened to know someone who might be able to give him the answer. He took a close-up photo of it with his mobile.

He glanced at Evan, who had not budged from her position. Her breathing was deep and steady. Reassured, he retreated to the bed farthest from her, punched in a number on his speed dial.

"Hold on, Dad. I'm in class." He held while Zoe excused herself and apparently went into the deserted hallway. This was not an unusual occurrence, for once Ben had explained a heavily expurgated version of his situation to her teachers, she was free to take his calls, unless she was taking an exam. Happily, she wasn't this morning.

"Hi, honey, how are you?"

"Everything's cool. Did Aunt Evan get back?" She'd been

asking this same question practically every day since Evan left for Sumatra.

"I'm with her now."

"Cool. Let me speak with her."

"At the moment, we have a pressing problem I need your help with."

"Really?"

How disappointment and excitement could be expressed in a single word was a mystery to him. "Did you get the photo I WhatsApped you?"

"Just a sec. . . . Got it."

"We need your expertise. We found this last night. We know it's a hotel, of course. Probably a fleabag. But it's got to be local."

"It might be haunted, too."

"Always possible." Ben tried not to laugh. His daughter's current obsession was serious—at least to her.

"Huh." Silence for several moments.

"Zoe?"

"I think . . . hmmm. I think it's from either the Sans Serif or the Majestic. They're sister hotels . . . wait a sec. Both in Anacostia." She read off their addresses, presumably from her Google Maps app.

"I don't know, Zoe. How d'you do it?"

"What can I tell you, Dad." She laughed. "It's a gift, though what I'll do with it I have no idea."

"Thanks, honey. You're a life saver."

She laughed again, a golden, rolling chuckle he adored. "Anything for king and country, Dad. Love you forever."

"Love you forever."

He was reluctant to disconnect, but he knew she had to get back to her lessons. The mobile was warm against his palm. It took him a moment to put it away.

"Evan?" He rose, crossed to where she still sat.

She was slowly draining one of the containers of soda, sipping through a straw. "Just dehydrated." She turned, giving him a watery smile "What did my lovely bonbon have to say?"

"Well, first off she asked for the millionth time whether you were back, and then she wanted to speak to you."

"I would've liked to hear her voice right about now."

"I know, but I pulled her out of class."

Evan's brows knit together. "What for?"

"This." He plunked down the hotel key. "From your murderous friend. It was thrown clear in the crash. I nearly stumbled over it getting to you."

"Huh, his hotel key. Ancient of days."

"According to Zoe, it's from the Majestic Hotel or the Sans Serif, in Anacostia. She gave me the addresses."

Ben drove them over to Anacostia in the poorer, borderline dangerous southeast quadrant of DC. Strips of newspaper littered the well of the floor around Evan's boots. She had reached the center of the sphere. As the noise it made when it hit the motel room floor presaged, there was a hard core.

"This last slip of paper. Ben. It's not newspaper." She unfolded it. "It has Fisher's name typed on it." She peered at it more closely: FISHER "Made with an old-school manual."

"Clearly a man or men with a plan," Ben said.

Her fingers had turned cold. She pocketed the slip, turned her attention to what was underneath.

"So what is that?" Ben could only risk quick glances that told him nothing.

"Not a clue. It's black, metallic, about the size of a poker chip with the same vertical grooves along the edge, but it's thicker—about three times thicker, slightly rounded on one side, flat on the other."

The rain had passed. The low ominous clouds had been

replaced by streamers of cirrus, high up, translucent in spots. The sunlight had felt good as they left the gloom of Lethe behind them.

"No markings of any kind."

"Nope. Completely blank."

He stopped for a light, took it to have a better look. "Mysterious. It must mean something."

"But what?"

The light changed, and they took off. They were in the Anacostia area. Ben had inputted the address for the Sans Serif Hotel Zoe had given him into his mobile. Security dictated that he never use the car's GPS system.

He made a right turn. "We're about six blocks away."

Evan turned the disk on end, leaning to her right, holding it up to the sunlight streaming through the rolled-down window. She kept turning it slowly between her hands. "You know," she said, after a time, "I think there's a line, thin as a hair, running all along the circumference."

Ben pulled over and stopped the car. He handed her his knife, a very useful multi-bladed gadget. She chose the smallest blade and pulled it to the open position. Inserting the point into the hairline, she twisted the blade. Nothing happened. Tried again with a bit more force.

The two halves opened like a clamshell.

Ben leaned closer. "What the hell?"

Inside, nestled into a bed of black foam formed expressly to fit it, was a letter made of what appeared to be gold. It was an incomplete circle with two feet.

"It's the Greek letter for—"

"Omega," Ben finished for her. He couldn't help himself. "The end of all things."

12

ISTANBUL, TURKEY

Ermi Çelik's workplace looked more like a London gentlemen's club than a Turkish lawyer's offices: large rooms, plushly furnished with expensive pieces imported from England and France. The walls were covered in trellises of climbing roses and ivy courtesy of fine English fabrics, the desk in the main room was of polished mahogany, large enough for an elephant to stand on. Floor lamps, shaded and fringed, bathed it all in soft light. Kobalt switched them on when Zherov broke into the second-floor suite. The last one she turned on was on Ermi's desk, an old nickel and glass banker's lamp with a long base, grooved to hold pens. It cast its rectangular light over the mocha desk pad.

It was after hours and the offices were empty. This was slightly disappointing as Kobalt had hoped to find Ermi still at work. She didn't think he was one to burn the midnight oil, but it would have been sloppy not to check.

"As long as we're here," Kobalt said, "let's see if Ermi's business has anything to tell us that he was unwilling to give up himself."

"Like who paid him for selling you out."

Kobalt shot him a wicked glance. "As if you never had a Boris turn on you." Boris was the generic term for a clandestine contact.

Zherov grunted. "But yours almost got me killed."

Kobalt shook her head. The man was an incorrigible egotist. Everything revolved around him. Ignoring him, she looked through the files piled on Ermi's desk, then the drawers, one after another. The last one on the left held a humidor and a bottle of single malt scotch lying on its side. Naturally, in a country that was 98 percent Muslim, the consuming of alcohol was prohibited. Ermi wouldn't take the chance of offending any of his clients by keeping his liquor visible. She flipped open the humidor. Cigars were lined up like fat little soldiers. She started to shut the drawer, when she noticed how shallow the interior was compared to the outside.

Her removing the humidor and the bottle caught Zherov's attention, and he drifted over. "Found something?"

Digging her fingernails into the seam between the bottom and the side, she levered the bottom up. Underneath was a rather large manila envelope. With mounting excitement, she undid the cord and reached in.

Zherov leaned forward. "What is it?"

"Looks like a ledger." She read page after page, dizzied, then fascinated. "Well, well, well, it looks like Ermi was doing business with Dima."

"What?" Zherov was at her side in an instant. "That's impossible!"

Of course it would be written down. Ermi was too smart to risk an efile that could be hacked, especially one that contained such explosive data. "Here, take a look yourself." She handed him the folder. "The boss you idolize—"

"He's your boss, too," Zherov snapped.

"But I don't idolize him." She watched the blood drain from

Zherov's face. A better just reward for this imperious prick she couldn't imagine. "Dima is shoveling ill-gotten gains out of Russia through Ermi, who's stowing them in a secure vault in Credit Cypriot. And not only that. Look where the IGG is coming from."

"Skimmed from FSB operational services." Zherov could hardly get the words out; his tongue wanted to cleave to the roof of his mouth.

"Oh, but that's not all, Anton. Turn the page." She pointed. "I'll say this for Ermi. He keeps meticulous books, most likely to use as leverage when he needs money or when he wants to retire to a life of leisure aboard his boat." She stood, the better to judge Zherov's expression. "Remember the missions outside St. Petersburg, Berlin, Kiev, and Aleppo that blew up in SVR's collective face? All in the last decade. Dima's doing. Check the entries under the misleading title 'Misc. Trans.' The dates correspond exactly with the fiery ends of those missions." She gave a mirthless laugh. "Dima had me crosscheck all the mission personnel, trying to find a leak. Fifteen of your comrades, all told. Dima was the leak, Anton. Our dear Dima is as corrupt as they come, making money off the deaths of his fellow Russians."

Zherov, who seemed lost in the numbers, dates, and times, ran fingers through his hair. They came away damp. He sat down so hard he almost fell back into the cushy upholstered chair. He read and reread the pages of dates and figures as if they might change to Dima's benefit, or weren't detailing Dima's traitorous dealings, but someone else's.

Kobalt could have pitied him or felt a surge of triumph, even contempt, but she felt none of those things, though any or all would have been appropriate. Anyone who kept up such a rock-hard façade was bound to be brittle underneath. In fact, brittleness was the very reason for the façade. Zherov was hiding out behind the guise of the tough, fearless assassin. This was who Dima had sicced on her, this was who she had to deal with. She couldn't afford to feel anything toward him. He was a burden, a sleek beautiful mink she carried on her back, who, she knew, could sink its teeth into her neck at any moment.

There was an attempt anyway: "This is a lie," he grated. "All of it. It must be."

"Ah, no, Anton, you're not thinking clearly. Or not seeing clearly, to be more accurate. What you hold in your hands is the diary of a man in love with numbers, with accounts and balances, asset and debits. A man who sees the world in terms of mathematics. If Ermi listened to Western music he'd love Bach. This isn't the man I know, but he's revealed so little of himself to me. Now I know him down to his roots. Mathematics doesn't lie. It is hard-edged, clean, neat as a pin."

He was shaking his head, but whether in denial or in bewilderment she couldn't tell.

"You say the ledger is a lie. You believe your allegiance to Dima is commendable, and once it might have been. He was your mentor, after all. But it's put blinkers on you."

Up close his smell was harsh, rank as a zoo animal. "You think I don't know why you hate me? It isn't because I'm a woman. You think I don't know why you don't trust me? It isn't because I was born in the West, and it isn't that I've been infected with American decadence."

He twitched. "It's because Dima is in love with you. You have only to open your legs and his legendary carnal desires—"

"No, Anton. Why d'you insult me so?"

He had been half out of the chair, but now he subsided back into it, still edgy, still seething.

"Hear me, Anton. Dima is in love with the *idea* of me, what he's confident he's molding me into. But what matters to you is I have managed a bloodless coup. I have supplanted you. I am now his favorite. And I didn't have to open my legs. I wouldn't, anyway, even under pain of death. He creeps me out.

"But where does that leave you? Clinging to what once was, like a drowning man grasping a rotten spar. Keep that up and you'll both go under."

"Is that a threat?"

She shook her head. "Just a statement of fact, of an outcome if you keep going down this path." She smiled with her teeth. "But the truth is, unlike you, I am who I am—my own person. Dima doesn't own me, despite his delusion otherwise." She thrust her head forward. "Becoming your own man will give you choices."

He looked up at her with narrowed eyes. It was not a good look for him.

She gestured, and said almost gently, "Read the ledger again, Anton. This time with your eyes open."

Turning away, she crossed to the bookshelves, ran her finger along the tops until she came to *Jane Eyre*, which she had read many years before. Opening it, her gaze roved over the pages until she found the paragraph she remembered best: ". . . and I shall be called discontented. I could not help it: the restlessness was in my nature; it agitated me to pain sometimes . . ." And further down: "It is in vain to say human beings ought to be satisfied with tranquility: they must have action; and they will make it if they cannot find it. Millions are condemned to—"

She felt Zherov's looming presence just before he struck her from behind, and her instincts saved her from the full brunt of his assault. The blow glanced off the side of her head, knocking her against Ermi's massive desk. Her hip struck the edge, pain shooting up her side and down her leg.

Before she could draw another breath, Zherov was on her, hands at her throat. His eyes were wild, his beautiful lips pulled back in an animal snarl. She looked at him calmly.

"Anton, stop," she said, and then, as her windpipe was restricted, whispered it again. "Anton, stop."

But he gave no sign of stopping or even that he heard her,

so she raised her arms and slammed the heels of her hands against his ears. The pressure-pain was intense. His grip on her loosened, and she ripped his hands from her throat, slapped him hard across his cheek.

He blinked, and again. His eyes cleared. He was panting, his hands were trembling as he put them up, too late to protect his ears.

Her eyes engaged with his. "Will you stop now? Anton. Will. You. Stop."

For some time, he made no response. She waited, listening to his heavy breathing; seeing his tongue come out to wet his chapped lips. Her throat felt as if he'd sandpapered it from the inside and her contused hip felt hot and tight, but she was careful to keep her eyes calmly trained on his with no discomfort, let alone pain, visible in them.

After a long time, he disengaged his eyes, looked down at the ledger open on the floor, an indictment of his essential failing.

He scrubbed his face with his hands. "What now?" His voice sounded as if he were far away. He did not offer an apology; she hadn't expected one, not from a man like him, who found it so hard to admit his mistakes to himself he felt compelled to attack her instead.

Stooping over, she took the ledger, folded it lengthwise, stowed it carefully away in an inside pocket of her jacket. "Ermi's house is our next stop." She headed across the office. "You'll need to restrain yourself. Make sure you don't kill him before I squeeze every bit of information about his relationship with Dima out of him."

"I hope to Christ you're not making a joke at my expense," he grated.

"Frankly, it never occurred to me that you had a sense of humor."

13

WASHINGTON, DC

Sans Serif stood on a corner, next to a bodega. Not long ago someone had thrown a couple of missiles—bricks, beer bottles, who knew—through the bodega's front window. Accordion gates had been deployed, barring the entire place. The interior was dark and empty.

Sans Serif was no more inviting. It was narrow, mean, and filthy. The lobby, if you could call it that, reeked of stale beer, cat piss, and cigarette smoke. It was hotter than Hades on a summer afternoon. But as it turned out the Sans Serif wasn't their target. The clerk, a superannuated guy in a filthy wifebeater out of which gray hair sprouted every which way, showed them a room key. It was the same size and shape as the one Ben carried, but it was green, not blue. They couldn't get out of there fast enough.

A half mile away as the crow flies the Majestic announced itself with a vertical neon sign, dark now, probably forever. If not for its neighbors—a chop shop masquerading as a garage, and a clothing store specializing in Army-Navy surplus—it seemed likely it would have fallen down by now.

The front steps were crumbling and the interior, though less claustrophobic than that of its sister, was nearly as run-down. A pair of chairs with worn-out cushions flanked a potted palm, its leaves bowed by layers of dust, as if having absorbed all the sorrow that had flowed through the lobby, they had given up the ghost. So, it seemed, had the old man asleep or dead in one of the chairs. He might have been there for years.

"Guest isn't in Room 512," the corpulent woman behind the desk said without looking at them. She was of indeterminate age, with white skin, waved orange hair, and rouged cheeks and was clearly more interested in the show on the old portable TV than she was in them.

"We've got the key." Ben placed a twenty on the counter. "We're going up."

She waved a pudgy hand. "Like I give a shit." The twenty had already vanished.

They stepped out of the asthmatic elevator into a corridor that smelled strongly of grilled meat and rubbish. Room 512 was all the way at the end, where a grimy window overlooked a maze of scaffolding unfinished, perhaps abandoned when project money dried up, beyond which was the brickwork and papered-over windows of a building being rehabbed.

Ben inserted the key and they crossed the threshold into a small one-bedroom unit. The air was musty, static, flat. They snapped on their gloves. Evan crossed to a window, unlocked it, threw it open. Sooty wind stalked into the room, prowling, curious, but at least the air became breathable.

Evan took the bedroom while Ben hunted around the living room. Evan found the closet empty, ditto the drawers of the dresser. She pulled them all the way out, checking the undersides and the backs. A flight bag sat on the end of the rumpled bed. She opened it, found a single change of clothes, a bar of soap and a washcloth thin as a tissue, and a book. She pulled out the hardback copy of *The Ugly American*. Examining the labels on the change of clothes revealed they were anything but American—cheap Asian brands. But then he had no need for durability; he hadn't planned to stay long. Still, the most important item she'd hoped to find, his passport, was nowhere in evidence, though she checked all the seams of the flight bag. Tossing the rest of the room—mattress, box spring, checking for loose floorboards, shadowed corners—yielded nothing.

She heard Ben calling her name and returned to the living room. He was seated at the narrow desk, the drawer half out and his hand in the drawer.

"There's something in here, at the back, but it's stuck." His face showed the strain of concentration.

Evan stood just off his left shoulder. "While you winkle it out, I've got a news flash. This guy, whoever he was, followed me all the way from Singapore."

Ben glanced up at her, his eyes wide. "What did you find?"

"His flight bag. With a copy of *The Ugly American* in it. He was reading it, sitting near the rear of the plane that brought me home from Changi."

"You remember him?"

"I do, but I only saw him sitting down. His hair was short, dark. He had a small head, oval like a Persian melon. Small ears, like a monkey. I didn't get a look at his face, I only saw him from behind."

"The question is how'd he get onto you? Singapore was a transit for you."

"So was Denpasar in Bali."

"So, what? He was onto you in Sumatra?" Ben's brows furrowed. "How is that possible?"

"I don't know, Ben. I'm no more thrilled about this than you are, believe me. I'll worry about the how later, but like you, now my bet regarding the who is on the people who know everything there is to know about me. Nemesis. Wells." She paused. "But there's another side to this. If they're after me, they'll be after you, as well. We were both instrumental in taking Nemesis down."

At once, Ben pulled out his mobile, called Mae Rand, Rose's mother, at whose house Zoe was staying. He sketched out the broad outlines of what he wanted her to do: keep an eye out for strange faces or vehicles on her street, especially at night, make sure Zoe and Rose didn't go to any sleepovers, and would she pick them up from school? He reassured her these were just routine precautions.

When he disconnected, he went back to what he had been doing. Moments later he retrieved the stuck item.

Evan frowned. "A roll of electrician's tape?"

Ben shook his head. "Not what I was expecting, that's for sure."

She considered the roll of black tape. There was no dust on it; it was brand new. She snapped her fingers. "The bathroom."

They both headed into it. White walls, gray-and-white tiles, gone yellowish in the corners. Evan went straight to the toilet tank, felt behind it. Nothing. Ben was at the sink. On it was a stained toiletry kit containing a cheap plastic comb, a brush with some bristles missing, a folding toothbrush, a small tube of toothpaste, and a pack of unopened German Marlboro cigarettes.

"All the comforts of home," Evan said, eyeing a cigarette butt crushed out on the top of the sink.

Ben pulled out the stopper. "Clear," he said.

Evan stepped into the shower-tub, hunkered down over the drain. She pulled out the rubber stopper. "Clear."

Looking around the bathroom more closely, she noticed the flush lever on the toilet was down. Frowning, she straddled the seat, lifted off the top.

"Bingo!"

Setting the top aside, she fished out a double baggie that had been affixed to the inside with a length of the electrician's tape. Ripping off the tape, she toweled off the baggie, brought it back into the living room, set it on the desk.

The first item she pulled out was a passport. She opened it. "This is the guy on the plane, definitely. I can tell by the shape of his head, like I said, Persian melon. American passport. He was traveling under the name of William Onders—but I wouldn't bet on that being his real name."

There was also a driver's license, but it wasn't for William Onders.

"This guy looks tough and skinny as a twig, no Persian melon here."

"Jon Pine. So there are two of them. Onders and Pine." She considered a moment. "I'm thinking Pine was at the airport with a car for Onders. That's how he was able to follow me."

Ben peered over her shoulder. "And I'm thinking the driver's license is phony, too."

Ben gestured with his head. "What else is in the baggie?"

"Some money—U.S. dollars, euros, Indonesian rupiah—this." Her heart beat faster as she held up another sphere wrapped in strips of newspaper.

Ben's eyes narrowed. "Another death gag."

Evan took a breath, let it out. "Time to see who's behind door number two."

She took up the sphere but went still before she could start unwrapping it. "But wait a minute." She turned to him. "Like I said, old William and I were on the same flight."

"And?"

"So how did his belongings get here? Pine must've grabbed them from him when he gave Onders the car."

"So Pine's still out there, still dangerous." Ben pointed to the sphere. "And maybe Pine was given this death gag to use, not Onders."

"Onders made it clear he wasn't going to kill me. He was tasked with taking me somewhere where I would be killed. So yes, I agree, I think it's Pine's to use. After all, he left his driver's license here, which makes it likely he'll come back for it."

She placed the black metallic disk she had fished out of Paul Fisher's mouth on the desk next to the sphere, pried up the lid to expose the gold Omega.

Then she began to unravel the newspaper strips on the sphere they'd just found. "The text is English. *The Washington Post*."

"Hmm. It was fashioned here. But we found a pack of German cigarettes."

Evan nodded. "Odds are Pine was in Germany recently—maybe while Onders was in Sumatra surveilling me."

Ben frowned. "But who is this death gag meant for?"

Evan's fingers worked faster and faster until she was down to the last strip. As before, it wasn't newspaper. And beneath, another black metallic disk identical to the first one. Using Ben's knife, she pried it open.

"Another golden Omega." Ben stirred restlessly behind her. "Well, that's tacked 'conspiracy' at the top of our virtual wall."

Evan sat very still, but her heart was a triphammer, beating its too-fast tattoo against her rib cage. "How in the world could Wendy and Michael be at the center of a worldwide conspiracy?" Her whisper was as much to herself as it was to Ben. "I pulled a death gag out of Paul's mouth. Now this death gag in the hotel room of the man who abducted me and threatened to have me killed. Is this about me, Ben? Is this my fault? Have I put Wendy and Michael in harm's way?"

"One step at a time, Evan," Ben said softly. "Okay?"

She took a breath, nodded.

He reached around, picked up the last strip of paper at the center of the sphere. "This is going to give us the name of Pine's intended victim. Now we can get to him or her first before—"

Sunk in her own thoughts about her niece and nephew, it took a moment for Evan to register that Ben had stopped mid-sentence. Turning, she saw that he had gone perfectly still. He was staring down at the slip of paper.

"What? Who is the death gag intended for?"

When Ben failed to answer, she plucked the paper from between his fingers and looked at what was typewritten on it.

"Oh, God."

The paper fluttered to the desktop, where it sat uncertainly among the strips of newsprint.

"It's me." Ben's voice sounded hollow, grayed out.

And here was the proof of it, staring up at her.

BUTLER

14

ISTANBUL, TURKEY

Ermi's residence overlooked the West Istanbul Marina, which was convenient for him. His boat was docked at the marina. He had taken Kobalt out on it once, served her a lavish lunch, and then had attempted to jump her bones. A swift knee to his crotch had put a permanent end to those noxious exertions and had reset their relationship in the proper perspective.

Scimitars of villas in the rather ugly modern Turkish style knifed across the lowland topography. It was 9 P.M. by the time they arrived. Security was of the usual Turkish kind. A bit of baksheesh was all it took for the guard to stick his nose back into his phone and forget they ever existed.

The villa was all sandstone-colored concrete interspersed with tall windows. Sandstone pillars guarded the front. Though the grounds were lit up, the house itself was dark. No surprise then the front door was locked. Peering through the glass revealed starkly modern Italian furniture, low and sleek, more reminiscent of artwork than anything utile. The interior was the exact opposite of Ermi's office. From any angle they tried, there was nothing to see but inanimate objects. Around the back, the pool glowed aquamarine courtesy of underwater spots. A float meandered, turning, empty.

"Clearly not home." The first words Zherov had uttered since they left Ermi's office. His ears were still red, and she suspected his system might still be adjusting the pressure back to normal. Someone else might have felt remorse, but no such emotion existed for her. She had deliberately couched the truth in the harshest terms in order to test him, to see which buttons she could push in order to unearth his weaknesses. Now she knew she could goad him into fury, and she knew how. Valuable knowledge, especially when dealing with a treacherous prick.

She went up the low steps to the line of sliders, tried them one by one. The last one on the left opened. Glancing back at Zherov, she indicated with her head, crossed the threshold. She indicated for Zherov to take the first floor, while she went up the glass treads to the second floor. There, in Ermi's bedroom, she found drawers open, clothes sorted through, but all his large luggage was still stacked on a closet shelf, while a smaller space gaped like the hole vacated by a child's tooth.

Back downstairs, she said, "Packed."

He turned to her, disgusted. "He could be anywhere."

"No. He used his weekender." Kobalt was already hurrying to the open slider. "There's only one place now."

The West Istanbul Marina was vast, including slips along ten floating piers, boat repair and chandleries, hoists, lifts, and ramps, tennis courts, gym, and restaurant. Moonlight skittered along the water, highlighting its topography. Boats drowsed in their slips, sails furled, bare masts to the sky. There was scarcely a breath of wind. Ermi's boat was along the sixth pier, moored in a slip three-quarters of the way down.

"It's still there." Kobalt pointed as they fast walked toward it. Running would only make them more noticeable to the harbormaster. Overhead lights blazed as they passed beneath them. Near to midnight, there was no one else on the piers.

Ermi's sailboat was a fifty-foot cutter-rigged ketch. It had two masts and plenty of cabin space down below. The hull was painted red, the cabin white. Kobalt carefully stepped aboard, onto the polished teak deck, and stood unmoving, listening. One by one, the small sounds of the boat: the ring of rigging against the main mast, the soft slap of water against the hull, the ever so slight creaking endemic to every boat. She listened to the silence. The quality of it was strange, off-kilter, as if it had something to tell her. She recalled times with Evan, down by their local brook, crouched like frogs on the bank, heads cocked, ears open to the soughing of the wind through the treetops, sure that it was speaking to them of places near and far. She remembered one night in their bedroom, lights out, her sister asleep, when she whispered as the wind had whispered, and the next morning when Evan had told her excitedly about her dream of the wind speaking to just her, she laughed behind her hand at putting one over on her powerful sister. She resolved then and there to become even more powerful.

Brushing away the cobwebs of memory, Kobalt went to the offside rail, leaned against it with her forearms, hands clasped. She did not stop Zherov when he went below. Nosing around down there by himself would do him good. She stared out at the water between the piers, at the sleek boats contentedly rocking in their berths, dreaming of fair seas and following winds. Turning her head to the left, she looked along the curve of the hull to the prow, saw a metal cleat with a line tied to it. It could have been the anchor, but the boat was docked in its slip. There was no need for an anchor. She might have gone to take a look, but she didn't. Not for the moment, anyway. Instead, she waited.

When she heard her name being called, she went below, ducking down so as not to hit her head against the top of the hatch. The teak-walled cabin was surprisingly spacious, comfortably and expensively furnished, which was no surprise.

The door of the head was flung open wide. Zherov pointed inside. "Look what the cat dragged in."

Ermi was slumped atop the toilet. She could tell it was Ermi even though the corpse was headless and badly disfigured with suppurating blisters, flayed flesh, and empurpled bruises.

She took a breath, let it out slowly. "Goddammit."

"Now we know why he gave you up," Zherov said.

She nodded. "Tortured. He took quite a beating." Ermi's murder was the work of a dyed-in-the-wool sadist. And yet something didn't track. Judging by the consistency of the blood, it seemed to her that Ermi was likely killed at about the same time they were at the knife shop. There was a mystery here, an intersection where there should be no intersection, and until she had the answer, she would say nothing of it to Zherov.

"Check his pockets."

His eyes blazed. "I won't touch that piece of shit."

She pushed past him, went through Ermi's pockets, found the key to the boat on its plastic float ring, a thick wad of money, and that was it.

"Anything?" Zherov asked.

"Whoever killed him took his mobile. He was never without it." She dangled the key on one hand, while she pocketed the bills. "Want to buy a boat?"

"Fuck no." Zherov made a face. "Not this one."

"See, what did I tell you? No sense of humor."

He followed her back topside. "If you ever said something funny, I'd laugh just like anyone else."

"I doubt it."

She went back to the offside railing and moved along to the foredeck, to where the metal cleat rose, like the stub of a powerful arm. Kneeling, she grasped the line that had been tied to the cleat via a noose knot. Hand over hand, she pulled on it, until she came to the other end, which had been knotted around Ermi's neck with another noose.

Zherov's eyes opened wide. "Well, this is one for the books." He laughed. "On the other hand, he never looked so good."

Kobalt's lips curved upward for a moment. "I've been researching a mysterious group calling itself Omega. Beheading is part of the Omega ritual to deal with enemies of the cult, to make an unequivocal statement. That's why they're after me. I'm not so easy to get ahold of, so they've gone after . . . I have two children—"

"Wendy and Michael, I know," Zherov said. "Dima showed me your dossier."

Kobalt was both surprised and annoyed. But knowing Dima she shouldn't have been either. Then something occurred to her. "You must know something about Omega, too."

"Dima let me also read your debriefing report when he assigned me to you. You infiltrated their compound in Odessa, did a bit of digging, until you made a mistake."

"I did not."

"Then how?"

"Precisely, Anton. How?" She waved away the question. "In any event, Omega is using my children as a lure. I wasn't absolutely sure before, but I am now."

"So because of the beheading . . . Omega's responsible for Ermi's death."

"It would seem so." She looked closer. Ermi's mouth was half-open. She opened it wider, expecting to find the death gag that was another hallmark of Omega murders. Instead, she found nothing—at least nothing that should not have been there.

"Why were you looking in his mouth?" the ever observant Zherov asked.

"I check everything when it comes to murder," she said, keeping her questions to herself.

15

WASHINGTON, DC

Evan was at the hotel room desk, staring at the two gold Omegas when the call came in. She had taken them out of their cases, was turning them over and over between her fingers, failing to find a stamp of manufacture. Ben was at the window overlooking the front of the hotel, peering through the curtains. Her mind was still reeling from the knowledge that the death gag was meant for Ben, that both she and Ben were being targeted by what appeared to be Samuel Wells or one of his American Nemesis buddies. And when he made no indication that he'd heard her phone ring, she knew he was lost in similar thoughts.

She quietly stepped from the living area into the bedroom so as not to be overheard. She knew the call was from Lyudmila Shokova because it was sandboxed.

"I have news." Lyudmila's voice was like a breath of fresh air.

Her heart skipped a beat and hope rose in her. "About Wendy and Michael?"

"Not yet, no."

As quickly as it had lit up, hope was extinguished. Evan felt a hollowness inside.

"Listen," Lyudmila was saying, "it's about the black jacket dossier that came from the SVR central server. Directorate 52123 isn't SVR."

"We surmised that." Evan took a stab. "It's Zaslon, isn't it?"

"We were looking at it the wrong way around. There is no Directorate 52123, which was why we couldn't find a trace of it."

"Then what—?"

"Your instincts are as good as ever. Directorate 52123 is the name given to a closely guarded infiltration field ops run by Zaslon. Your sister was spearheading the operation."

Evan was for the moment speechless.

Lyudmila continued. "Zaslon exists as a wholly separate entity, with its own aims and initiatives, under the auspices of the SVR."

"And Bobbi was a member of it. Lyudmila, are you absolutely sure?"

"I'm afraid we are sure now, yes."

Evan forced herself to breathe. "Do you know anything about who her infiltration target was?"

"No. Only that the group apparently still exists. It's called Omega and is labeled by Zaslon Vragi Gosudarstva—Enemies of the State."

All the breath went out of Evan. "Omega is awfully similar to Nemesis's First Tribe."

"Could be just a coincidence."

"In our world there is no such thing as coincidence." Evan was gripping her mobile so tightly her fingers began to cramp.

"You're not wrong. Like the Hydra, Nemesis had many heads."

Evan felt chilled to the bone. "Maybe we only cut off one of them."

"As I said in Sumatra, we're in this together, Evan. All the way."

"Lyudmila . . ."

"I know, *dorogoy*. I'm doing everything I can to find the children."

Evan closed her eyes for a moment. "If Omega has them."

"I'm sure of it. The trouble is we can't find Omega's headquarters, don't even know what country it's in."

Evan's mind was firing on all cylinders now. "I'm beginning to think that Omega is in more than one country, and that there's a branch of Omega here in the U.S. According to the Kobalt dossier, Bobbi was assigned to find out about Omega, but as far as I ever knew, Bobbi never left America."

"Which means you must be correct," Lyudmila said, "a branch of Omega is there."

"Exactly." She considered a moment. "One thing doesn't track though."

"Tell me."

"If, in fact, Omega is an offshoot or a successor to Nemesis, why would the FSB be interested in them?"

"I would say to use Omega as they did Nemesis to continue to foment a cultural and religious divide in the American population."

Evan wasn't so sure but felt at this stage there was no point in mentioning her doubts to Lyudmila. Instead, she emphasized her overriding concern for her niece and nephew.

"We'll find them, I promise," Lyudmila said. "Now I must go."

The connection was severed. Evan tried calling her back but to no avail. She was about to try again when Ben called to her from the other room.

"Get over here!" His voice was hushed but urgent.

She rushed in, relieved to see that his back was still to the room. But she moved too quickly, and knocked *The Ugly*

American off the table as she passed. When it hit the floor it opened to where a card was stuck in as a bookmark.

"Evan!"

"Hush," she hissed. "I'm here. Wait."

Bending down, she pulled out the bookmark: a snapshot. She took it with her as she crossed to where Ben stood at the window, his attention still riveted to something outside, the curtain protecting him from being seen from the street below.

"There's a car just there, across and down to the right from where I parked," Ben whispered.

A black Chevy Tahoe crouched like a polecat. It had government plates. "Tennyson and Slim are tailing us."

"Those idiots are clueless," Ben said.

"Or else they think we're smarter than they are."

They both laughed at that.

"Look what Onders was using for a bookmark." She held out the snapshot.

A couple stood in a bucolic setting—in a small field dotted with mature trees—and off in the background stood a large low modern building, hazed, vague, indistinct, save for the outline. The man and woman had their arms around each other. The man was smiling into the camera, a goofy smile that hinted he'd just had a good laugh. The woman, several inches taller, had thick, wavy hair that came down to just below her chin, and she was wearing what appeared to be an unfashionable white smock that reached to just above her ankles. It was unbelted, so it gave no hint as to her figure.

Ben rubbed his chin. "The man is clearly Onders."

"In happier times." Evan tapped the photo with her fingernail. "And who is this with him? Wife? Girlfriend?"

"Mistress, maybe."

He might be right. She was classically beautiful—heart-shaped face, large eyes of an unusually deep blue, wide mouth—but also striking, which was not always true of the classical beautiful. There was something about the whole that was inescapably compelling. Evan could sense it even in the photo. Perhaps it was the size of her eyes, almost too big for her face, or her enigmatic expression. Whatever the case, hers was a face that the camera loved.

She gave him a quick look. "You can see why he was with her."

Ben worried his lower lip. "But why was she with him? I mean, he was a nasty bit of work, to say the least."

"Hmm." Idly, she turned the snapshot over. On the reverse a neat feminine hand had written: **To W. I love you, Ana.** It was dated the twenty-seventh of June two years ago. And then in smaller letters down in the lower right-hand corner: **countryside Koln: a breath of fresh air**

Evan frowned. "What was Onders doing in Germany two years ago?"

"If memory serves, Cologne is in Westphalia, the North Rhine region," Ben said. "A freaking big city."

Evan ignored his comment. "She's German. Köln. She used the German name for Cologne. And there's Pine's pack of German ciggies. Everything points to Germany." She tapped the snapshot. "We've got to find Ana."

"Really? She could be anywhere in Cologne. How can we find her? We don't even know her last name. And Ana is not exactly an uncommon name in Germany."

Evan took a photo of the snapshot, sent it off with a text. **Ana Onders (?) Köln next stop.** Then she did the same with the two gold Omegas, with the text **???**

Ben was staring at her closely. "Who did you send all that to?"

"The same person who showed me the SVR file in Sumatra. Someone who will help me."

"But no name."

"Need to know, Ben. Moscow Rules."

He grimaced. "So we start with Onders and go from there. But come on. That identity has got to have been whipped up by people in his service. Odds are the real William Onders has been six feet under for years. That's a favorite ploy of the back-room boys for creating legends."

"Listen." Evan waved the photo. "This is the first real lead we've found. We need to follow it. Do you have a better idea?"

Reluctantly, he shook his head.

Movement along the street returned their attention to the black Tahoe. As they watched, Leyland emerged from the shotgun seat, looked around, then glanced up at the hotel façade. Evan and Ben froze, but apparently, he didn't see them. He crossed the street, walked down to Ben's car. Again, he looked around, then squatted down, brought a small square out of his pocket, reached under the car.

"He's attaching a tracking device," Ben said. "Those sonsofbitches."

Trotting back to the government SUV, Leyland gave his boss a thumbs-up. Moments after he got in, the vehicle drove off at a sedate pace, no doubt to lay low at a discreet distance.

"Time to vacate the premises," Ben said.

Evan gathered up the Omegas, pocketing them along with the photo. She followed Ben out the door of the suite, but once in the hallway she stopped, put a firm hand on Ben's arm to keep him in place. He gave her a querying look. Her head was slightly cocked.

"Something's not right." He had to lean in to hear her whisper. "I can feel it in the silence."

"I don't hear anything," he whispered in a neutral voice.

Her head cocked farther. "It's on a waft of air coming up from the staircase." She shook her head. "Back up. Back up now!"

She pulled him back into the room, closed the door, double-locked it.

"What did you hear?" The question was genuine. He knew

better than to ignore her keen senses. They had saved the two of them more than once back in the day.

"Someone's coming."

"Not the FBI boys. They're gone."

"My guess is Onders's partner, Pine."

"We need to get out of here."

Evan nodded. "In a second." She darted into the bathroom.

"Evan! Now!"

But she was already back at his side. "Let's go. This way."

In the bedroom, the window looked out onto the same view as the grimy window at the end of the hallway. She unlocked it, opened it wide. In front of them was the alley filled with the maze of scaffolding between the hotel and the building ostensibly being rehabbed.

"Let's go." One foot on the sill, she swung out, grabbing onto the nearest vertical pipe, and from there onto a horizontal section on which a wooden board had been temporarily laid as a platform. A few paces ahead, she could see a welter of tools, carelessly left behind. A sudden lack of money will do that to workers who get paid by the hour or not at all.

Ben, crouched on the sill, suddenly turned his head and flinched. "The front door's being broken down."

As he turned awkwardly to close the window behind him, he lost his balance and had to grab onto the top of the window frame to steady himself.

"Ben. Ben! Get off there. Now!"

He swung onto the pipe she had vacated. As he did so, the glass in the hotel room window shattered outward in a hail of shards. Within the empty space, Evan saw a figure—Pine?— moving within the shadows of the room. He was screwing a noise suppressor onto the muzzle of his Glock. It was Pine, all right, with his close-cut hair, his thin reedy face set in an expression of absolute determination. Reaching out, she hooked her fingers around the handle of a hammer and, as the gunman leveled the Glock, she threw the hammer. She heard the skirl, followed by a grunt, and the open window was filled only with shadows and swirling drapes.

Ben was right behind her.

"Where the hell did you learn to throw a hammer?" His tone was both incredulous and approving. "Not at the Farm." The Farm was where they had both trained.

She picked up a screwdriver, stuck it in her back pocket. "Being in the field teaches you what the Farm instructors never even thought of."

The sketchy scaffolding swayed beneath them as they made their way through it toward the rehabbed building. Evan figured they could lose themselves in there. They kept moving from vertical to horizontal at what Evan, her senses heightened, thought a glacial pace. But trying to go any faster was too dangerous.

They had just come to the middle section of the scaffolding— the least secure part—when they heard movement down below. A heavy shudder ran through the scaffolding, causing them to grab hold of the nearest vertical pipe. Far below them, in the alleyway, Pine wielded the hammer Evan had thrown at him. With another heavy blow he sheared off the wing bolt at the bottom of one of the vertical pipes. The third blow was delivered to the inside of the pipe at the junction, causing the horizontal pipe to detach itself. He shook the scaffolding, and it listed like a ship in stormy seas.

"Come on down!" he called. He brandished the hammer. "I'm waiting for you!"

Another whack and the board they were on tilted and began to slide off the vertical bars on which it had been set. Tools and bits and pieces of detritus showered down into the alley, and Evan and Ben took advantage to swing across to the next-to-last vertical pipe before they could make the jump to the adjacent building.

But Pine was whacking away with the hammer, and now the entire structure was starting to come apart under the ceaseless blows. Vertical pipes dented, creased, then folded at the creases.

"It's just a matter of time!" Pine called. "There's nowhere to go!"

"He's right," Ben said. "We're going to fall."

Evan leapt to the last vertical pipe, but the horizontal bar Ben was on was falling away. Leaning out as far as she could, she grasped his extended arm, pulled. His weight almost pulled her arm from its socket. The shock caused her head pain to resurrect itself from the grave to which she'd consigned it. Grimacing, she held Ben up as his feet scrabbled for purchase before he managed to reach the last vertical.

But now the entire structure was undermined. Pieces flew off, slamming into the building walls, chipping off brickwork.

"You might as well give up!" Pine called. "I don't know how you evaded Will, but it hardly matters now I've got you both!"

Recklessly suspended five flights above street level, there was nowhere to go. Holding on to the scaffolding was no longer an option.

Ben grabbed her. "This way!" Five steps away, a bundle of cable TV wire hung down the side of the building from the roof where the equipment had been installed. The last horizontal pipe lurched from under them. Ben left his feet and lunged for the bundle of wires. He caught hold, but his weight ripped the rooftop equipment from its mooring, dragging it until it fetched up against the roof's parapet.

Ben had shot down a full floor, was hanging on four stories above the alley floor. Looking up at Evan, he called out to her, and she jumped just as what was left of the scaffolding collapsed. Grabbing onto the bundle of wires, she slammed against the brick siding, knocking all the breath from her.

The bundle slipped farther down. Their combined weight was threatening to pull the cable equipment over the parapet.

Placing her boot soles against the brickwork, Evan pushed upward, arcing back as she slid down so that on the inward arc her extended feet smashed through the old glass of a window. She was inside.

Turning, she saw Ben climbing hand over hand toward her. But for every foot he progressed, the bundle slipped a few inches down as the equipment began to roll onto the top of the parapet. A moment more, and it would come crashing down, along with the wires.

Ben got a hand onto the windowsill as the equipment came hurtling down. An edge of it scored along the left side of his back, just before Evan managed to haul him over the sill, into the interior of the building.

They heard sounds through the open door, echoing up the stairwell.

"No rest for the wicked," Ben said, gasping.

Evan drew him away from the splintered glass beneath the window. "No rest for the virtuous, either."

16

ISTANBUL, TURKEY

Kobalt leaned back, elbows on the railing, and looked up at the sky, paled out by the lights from the city. Suddenly, she wanted to be away from here—away from Ermi's boat, from Istanbul, from Omega's wanton disregard of life, but it seemed as if she could not outrun the feeling of being found wanting. For whatever reason she had failed in her mission to sabotage Omega's mission. She wanted another chance; they had inadvertently given it to her.

Here and there a first-magnitude star managed to struggle through the man-made pollution, making its presence felt. Kobalt knew that stars were looking down on her, judging her with their cold, cruel light. That feeling of being found wanting had arisen in her since she was just a child, when she would run out of the house after doing something wrong, something that would surely garner her a stern and outsized punishment. Slowly, her eyes closed, for some reason feeling comforted by Ermi's waterlogged head on the seat beside her.

The child Bobbi threw herself down on the lawn and stared up at the stars, absorbing their relentless light and their objective judgment of what that light illuminated in her, allowing the celestial judgment to become part of her. Gradually, that judgment would undergo a mysterious process, be transformed by her subconscious as if into a burr lodged under her skin, there to be a constant reminder that she was different from her sister, utterly and irretrievably detached from her mother and father. She was opposed to them in every way imaginable, and, years later, after their deaths, it was a constant struggle for her not to feel that way about Evan, who knew nothing, and hopefully never would.

That's why she liked it when her sister came outside, looking for her. And when she lay down beside her, took her hand in hers, she had no doubt about Evan's love for her. She knew the time would come when the adults would be gone, and Evan would take care of her. Call it a premonition, call it whatever you wanted. The fact that there were secrets she kept to herself, secrets she knew and Evan didn't, was a way of feeling better about having to rely on her older sister.

"Kobalt."

She heard Zherov's voice as if from far away. Closer to, she became aware of the wind through the masts of the boats in the marina, the lapping of water against hulls, a sharp cry from a seagull disturbed from sleep.

She opened her eyes but did not look at him; her gaze was still fixed on a point only she could see. "Listen to me, Anton," she said in an almost dreamy voice, a voice she had used many times before in other difficult settings. "There once was a cat and a rat. This was a long time ago, in a world not so different than ours. The cat has the rat cornered. The cat isn't particularly big, the rat isn't at all small. Anyway, the rat is trapped, knows it, and starts to plead for its life. This rat has a particularly convincing manner about it, a sincerity most rats lack. The cat is impressed, as any cat would be.

"'I bet you don't even like rat meat,' the rat says. 'You look like a discerning sort of fellow, someone I could even admire. You know rat meat is sinewy and gristly, no fit meal for someone such as yourself. I bet mouse is more your cup of tea. Nice plump mouse is a dish fit for someone as astute as yourself. Am I right?' 'It just so happens you are,' the cat replies, impressed, despite itself. 'And you're hungry,' says the rat. 'Am I right?' 'It just so happens you are,' comes the reply. 'Well, then, we can strike a bargain. You let me go, you promise not to harm me or my family, and I'll lead you to a nest of mice fat as houses, biggest you've ever seen.'

"The cat agrees. Why wouldn't it? Sounds like a great deal. So the cat backs up, lets the rat go. And what does the rat do? It speeds off around the corner, leaving the cat sitting on its haunches. But the cat is cunning, too. It puts its nose to the floor and follows the rat back to its own nest in time to see the rat's hindquarters about to disappear into a hole it has gnawed in the baseboard.

"The cat pounces, digs it claws into the rat's back, drags it out, and bites off its head. Then the cat shoves its forepaw into the nest, drags out the rat's family and, one by one, bites off their heads."

"What am I, a five-year-old who scares easily?" Zherov spread his hands, still careful not to get too close to Ermi's head. "Why are you telling me this story?"

Kobalt's gaze swung toward him at last. "It's not a story, really. It's a parable. There's a point to it, a moral."

"And what would that be?"

"Your sympathies are naturally with the cat. Cats are nice, right? They're clean, they make you laugh at their antics, they're empathetic to humans. Rats are, well, they're rats; they're dirty, they eat garbage, they spread disease. They're rodents, for God's sake."

"So?"

Kobalt snapped her fingers several times. "Are you being deliberately dense, Anton? When you come down to it, the cat and the rat—they're both the same. They lie, they betray others and themselves. And they're vicious as hell."

Zherov sat still for some time. The seagull's cry came again, this time joined by others. It was the hour before dawn, when the light in the sky was as uncertain as the future.

"Dima," he said at length.

"Yes, Dima. Our boss. In your mind, he was the cat. But reading Ermi's ledger, seeing how he profited from betraying his own people, you now know he's the rat. The cat and the rat are one and the same."

"In other words, no one's on your side." He inclined his head toward her. "Except you, of course."

"Oh, Anton, me least of all." For once her smile was genuinely benign. "But you knew this about me going in. And I know it about you. That's our advantage. That gives us an edge. Neither of us are pretending we're the cat."

"Rats till the end of the night."

"And beyond. Perhaps."

Zherov considered this for some time. He glanced down at poor Ermi's head. "Rat," he said.

"No, Anton. It's true he gave us up. But he also gave us a priceless gift." She slid out the leather-bound ledger, the damning evidence against Dima Nikolaevich Tokmakov. "We have the electronic keys to his bank account in Cyprus. With that hoard we can fashion a new life, in our own image, not Dima's, not the SVR's, not the FSB's."

Zherov got up. "I need a drink."

They returned below, rummaged through Ermi's stash of liquor, which was more extensive than the one hidden bottle in his office.

"Vodka!" Zherov proclaimed, holding high the bottle he'd fetched from the small freezer. "Beluga! Say this for Ermi, he had excellent taste in liquor."

Kobalt got down a pair of glasses and Zherov poured the vodka. They looked at each other for a long time before they clinked glasses and threw the icy liquor down their throats. Zherov immediately refilled the glasses and the contents were downed in seconds.

"Now." He kicked the door to the head closed so Ermi's headless corpse was out of sight, if not out of mind. "I've been puzzling over something. If Omega killed Ermi, they're also responsible for the ex-con at the knife shop."

She frowned. "The trouble with that theory is unlike the SVR, Omega would never hire anyone—Russian ex-cons included—to do their dirty work."

He spread his hands. "So, what? The SVR and Omega were both here in Istanbul at the same time, centered on you?"

"Omega I can understand; they want revenge." She shook her head. "But the SVR? That doesn't track."

She poured them both a third round. This time, though, she took up her glass and sipped the vodka, savoring its unique flavor. It was made in Mariinsk, where the Trans-Siberian Railway crossed the Kiya River, and the artisanal water was superb.

"To be honest, I don't get it either." He regarded her levelly. "Listen, about what I said before about you screwing up your Omega remit in Odessa—"

"Forget it."

He nodded and drank up.

When they had finished, she rose. "It's almost dawn. Time to get out of here. You unplug us and cast off the lines. I'll get the boat ready to move out."

"You know how to drive this thing?" Zherov asked.

She looked at him archly. "And you don't?"

***

When they were far enough from the marina to have reached deep water, she cut the engines to idle. Zherov had found a large tarp in which they wrapped Ermi's corpse. Together, they hauled it topside. She added the head and the boat's anchor, while Zherov added his tie and jacket, both of which were smeared with blood, then they secured the package with two of the nylon lines, one around the ankles, the other around the shoulders.

After they rolled it over the side, heard the heavy splash, and watched Ermi vanish into the deep, they sat and finished off the vodka, taking turns drinking directly from the bottle. The sky had turned pink, the light edging ever so slowly from blue to gold. Wind gusts were weak and fitful. Not a good day for sailing.

They had not exchanged a word for some time, fully absorbed in their tasks. At length, Zherov set the empty bottle aside. "Will you tell me more about your time with Omega?"

"It took more than six weeks of living in Odessa as Alina Kravets," she heard herself saying. "Naked, without any backup whatsoever, without even a Moscow-based exfiltration plan should I run into trouble."

"And you did run into trouble."

Kobalt nodded. "Eventually. But not the kind you think. I was only a *sluzhashchiy*—an acolyte. I wasn't privy to their inner circle. Someone must have ratted me out. They came for me in the hour of the wolf—just before dawn. Strictly training book protocol. They felt they needed three of them, but they were wrong. I killed them one after another, and then I got the hell out of Odessa."

It seemed to Kobalt that Zherov was seeing her in a new light, but that might simply have been the rising of the sun.

"What did you mean when you said the trouble you ran into was not what I think?"

"Mm. Well, as I told you Omega's foundation is deeply religious."

"Calling you an acolyte was a dead giveaway. In any event, with extremists that's hardly new."

"This one is. Their liturgy is in Church Slavonic, which is almost identical to Russian. During one of the interminable services I slipped out."

Out at sea, boats could be seen, at first just smudges in her vision against the rising sun, but gradually revealing details, as if she were watching an artist layering in color onto her canvas. The water had turned from black to cobalt, lighter where the morning touched it.

"I was sent to infiltrate, discover their mission, and to sabotage it. They were open about the mission—to cleanse the world of evil, what they considered evil, anyway—but I still had no idea how they planned on accomplishing it. I needed to penetrate their inner sanctum—papers, files, email or text conversations.

"All the files were housed in a central building—a place I wasn't allowed to enter. I had formulated a plan to get in unseen, during a service, but I never made it. A limousine came through the gates, rolling slowly, almost majestically, I thought, through the compound. I could only stay where I was and watch. It stopped beside the entrance to the central building. Two huge men in shiny black suits emerged—bodyguards, I had no doubt. When their surveillance of the area was complete, another figure stepped out. A woman."

Ermi's boat had been drifting all this time. Now that there was water traffic, Kobalt rose and went to the cockpit, drew the engine out of neutral, and set a course parallel to the shore.

"This woman, who was she?" Zherov had come up beside her.

"Unknown." Kobalt was staring straight ahead. "But my guess is she was the leader. She was certainly treated that way, not only by her bodyguards but by the people who appeared out of the central building to greet her."

"Did you see her face? Would you recognize her?"

"I tried, but by that time the service was over. There were too many people in the compound. She was tall and slim. She didn't walk like a woman."

Zherov frowned. "What? She walked like a man?"

Kobalt shook her head. "Not that either, exactly. To be honest, I can't put my finger on it."

She guided the boat onward.

"Where are we headed?"

"We need to scuttle this boat."

Zherov grunted. "And how will we do that and get back to shore without being seen?"

"Do you know how to swim, Anton?"

"Of course."

"Then all will be well."

He shook his head for a moment. It seemed that she utterly perplexed him. Every time he turned around, she did or said something that surprised—or even shocked—him.

"One important thing I did discover before I left Omega is that Odessa wasn't their home base."

"Where is it then?" Zherov asked.

She gave him a penetrating look. "We're going to go back to Odessa to find out."

17

WASHINGTON, DC

Evan is dreaming again of her sister. This time she is with Bobbi in Copenhagen. She is nineteen, Bobbi two years younger. They are holding hands. Bobbi's face is alight with wonder and excitement. They had been in Sumatra, but had cut the beach lounging short because Bobbi had suddenly insisted they spend more time in the Danish capital, among all the tall, handsome blond men.

So. Copenhagen. One minute the sky is sunny and clear, the next gray and low. Ominous rumbling abounds from all sides, as if the oncoming storm is descending upon the city from every direction at once. Even before the wind begins to pick up, lifting up coat flaps, upending the most careful hairdos, swirling newspapers in tiny gyres, Evan knows they should be seeking shelter. But the streets are full, clogged with more and more people. Moreover, she does not know which way to turn. As a consequence of her fear and indecision, she is rooted to the spot. A swirl of people, coming out of nowhere, denser than the rest, shoulder by, and Bobbi's hand is wrenched out of hers. Almost at once, Bobbi is swallowed up in the chattering throng.

Evan tries to call out, but she has no voice. She screams Bobbi's name but it's as if her vocal cords are paralyzed. She tries to run after her sister, but she cannot find her way, and cannot recall in which direction Bobbi was headed when she vanished amidst the dense knot of strangers. Then, as the clouds open up and rain begins to pelt her, she finds that she cannot even remember her sister's face.

Cold sweat bathed her. Gloved hands clamped around Pine's throat, her eyes refocused. They had heard him enter the building, heard his raised voice coming closer and closer.

"You're cornered now. I have you up a tree. The only escape route is through the front door. Believe me, I won't hesitate to shoot out your kneecaps. My orders are to bring you in alive. No one said anything about what shape you need to be in, as long as you're conscious."

"Who are you working for?" Evan shouted just before she and Ben scuttled from one room to another.

"I'll share that bit with you," Pine called back, "after I've shattered your knees." His voice echoed through the empty building.

"Will's dead," Ben called. "And soon you will be too."

This time, they stayed put. They let him come at them, then, according to plan.

Evan took him down just after he jumped Ben, sending Ben tumbling against the far wall. She heard the throttled gurgle of Pine's breathing, she was aware of his arms beating against the floor helplessly as he tried to drag oxygen into his starving lungs. She concentrated on Pine's face—his bulging eyes, his ruined nose, blackened, stump-like, the rictus of his grimace, the trembling of his lips, lifting away from his bloodstained teeth.

Then she felt strong hands on her shoulders, trying to lift her away. She resisted. A voice in her ear, but the words meant nothing to her. She was in another time, another place. The hands lifted from her shoulders, grasped her wrists, trying to pull her hands from Pine's throat. She resisted. Her thumbs dug deeper into his windpipe. A moment more and she would crack open his cricoid, the ring of cartilage that protected his trachea. That would be the finish of him.

"Evan. Evan!" It was Ben's voice buzzing in her ear. "Let him go. Evan, take a deep breath and let him go."

"Why?" Her voice was thick, curdled, seeming foreign even to herself.

Ben said, "We need what he has to tell us." His voice was urgent but calm. That was her Ben.

She nodded numbly and let go.

Pine was striped with the pale lavender illumination from a construction fixture lying on the floor that Ben had found and plugged in. Luckily, the construction company hadn't had the electricity turned off.

"Now you'll tell us everything," Ben said from over her shoulder.

Pine did not acknowledge Ben's existence. His eyes were fixed on Evan as he took a long shuddering breath. Then he smiled. And gnashed his teeth, his smile morphing into a smirk.

The acrid smell of bitter almonds came to her. Her head jerked away.

"Ben!"

But Pine's lips were already turning blue. A baby blue foam bubbled up through his smirk.

Ben pulled her away. "Cyanide," she said thickly.

"In a false tooth."

"Old as time." She teetered back on her haunches. Her muscles ached, her head hurt like the flaming spires of hell. Her mind vomited up the image of Onders's gun to the back of her head, his words dripping like poison from his lips. Her entire body began to shake.

Ben slid down, his back against a bare wooden stud. "Jesus wept, Evan." He reached out and put his arm around her, and this time she didn't brush it away, but curled into him until the shakes subsided.

She looked around at the severely abused room in this falling-apart building. As if seeing it for the first time. She sat up straight. "Are we alone?"

"Nobody alive here but us, the rats, and the roaches."

Evan rose, holding on to a girder. She stared down into Pine's face. The blood from Pine's nose, smashed by her hammer blow, was a black stain, overrun by the last dribble of foam. The cyanotic lips looked livid purple. She bent, looking more closely. Four parallel scratches on the left side of his neck were dark with dried blood.

Ben crab-walked over to the corpse, systematically plundered his pockets, finding only pocket litter—the usual detritus of restaurant receipts and the like meant to help authenticate his legend. He ran his fingertips down all the seams of Pine's clothes, looking for anything that might have been sewn in. The last seam he checked was on the collar of Pine's jacket. "Something here." Using his knife, he carefully slit open the seam, slipped out a small, 2x3 photo of a woman from the waist up.

He held it up for Evan so see. "Recognize her?"

Evan took out the photo taken outside Cologne, put the two side by side. "It's Ana," she said. "The same woman who was with Onders two years ago."

"Ideas?"

"Her hair's shorter here. They were both her lovers?"

"Huh."

"Anyway, Pine called him Will, the photo is 'To W,' so I'm thinking William Onders really was his name."

"That would be a break," Ben confirmed.

He rose, took her elbow, and together they left Pine there.

It was an open question what would get to him first—the rats or the roaches.

"When I had my hands around his throat, I was thinking of Onders, his gun on me, his words in my ear. I was terrified and elated all at once." She gave him a searching look. "Does that make sense?"

"Perfect sense." Ben cleared his throat. "Look, you've just gone through more traumatic events than most people—even in our business—experience in their lives. So cut yourself some slack."

"I can't." Evan put her head in her hands. "Not when Wendy and Michael are missing."

They sat across from one another at a booth in the roadside bar and diner within walking distance of the Lethe motel, where they had holed up the night before. They had chosen the booth that had the best view out the plate glass windows at the parking lot and the traffic on the interstate behind.

Evan gulped down mineral water; she wasn't yet ready for alcohol. Ben was turning the glass holding his bourbon and ginger beer around and around between his hands. Watching the light play off the tops of the ice cubes.

She stared at her glass, frowning. "There's something else. Something buried."

Ben said nothing, looking at her expectantly. He was not about to push her.

She drained her glass. Ben did the same with his, never taking his eyes off her. "After Bobbi turned sixteen," she began, "I told her that as a present I'd take her anywhere she wanted to go. We spent some time planning, and inexplicably—well, it was inexplicable at the time and for years afterward—she chose Copenhagen. I'd chosen Sumatra, and we did go there afterward. She was seventeen by the time we made the trip."

Ben refilled her glass from the bottle of mineral water, called for another drink for himself. "Drink more," he said, and she did.

"It seemed odd at the time. So bland a choice. I mean, this was our first trip outside the States," Evan went on. "But then we had such a great time there, Bobbi—my morose, teenage sister—was so happy, happier there than in Sumatra, although I know she enjoyed that too . . . the thought never occurred to me. Until I got to Sumatra and saw that dossier."

"What thought. What do you think happened in Copenhagen?"

They both sat back and kept quiet as the waitress set down Ben's bourbon and ginger, their plates of spaghetti and meatballs, a shaker of Parmesan cheese and a basket of cut Italian bread, sprinkled with a handful of foiled pats of batter.

"Anything else?" But the waitress was already turning away, Ben's empty cocktail glass on her tray, and in any case, they needed to get back to their conversation.

"Bobbi got recruited, that's what happened there. The FSB got to her somehow, someway."

Ben twirled spaghetti around the tines of his fork. "The meet must have been prearranged, Evan. You must know that."

"Of course." She bit her lip. "Whoever it was I'd like to do to him what I did to fucking Pine."

"The question is how far back does the contact go?"

"It had to have been before she was sixteen, clearly. She had to have been in touch with the FSB before we went to Sumatra and Denmark because she begged me to spend more time in Copenhagen than we had at first planned. But my sense is that she was first recruited early on."

"Why would you think that?" Ben asked. "She'd be just a kid. Why would she be susceptible—"

"Something triggered her, something profound," Evan replied. "I don't know what, but it's the only logical explanation." Her eyes shifted. "See, the thing is I don't think she needed to be convinced. I think she wanted to be recruited."

Ben's eyebrows lifted. "What? Like she was waiting for it?"

Evan nodded, which only made the pain in her head flare up so badly she had to put her head in her hands.

"Bad?"

"Like an insane clown posse is riding through my brain, firing at every nerve ending in sight." She finished off the bottle of mineral water, then called for a beer. She was ready for a real drink. Then she attacked the food with all the gusto of an avid orca.

Though it was already past 3 A.M., the place had actually filled up, or at least the bar had. Apart from the two of them, no one was eating. Men in rumpled suits come from parties, whores' arms, other bars, stood shoulder to shoulder with working men—truckers, all-night maintenance crews, getting smashed on their triple-overtime. It was mob-deep at the bar with more trailing in. The place was a nexus, a kind of oasis in the midst of the post-industrial desert of the interstate. The decibel level kept rising. Somewhere Miley Cyrus's voice was blaring "Nothing Breaks Like a Heart" from the neon-lit speakers of a digital jukebox.

"Miley's right." Evan tore a bit of bread in half, buttered it savagely. "The world hurts you deeply and leaves a scar."

"Bobbi?"

She wiped tomato sauce off her mouth but said nothing.

"I know you feel guilty that you weren't in DC to protect her."

That isn't it, she thought. *That isn't it at all. It was Bobbi who hurt me deeply, not the world. It was Bobbi who left the scar, just like I left a scar in her.* But she didn't say any of this to Ben; she never would. Not even on the point of death.

He took a large swallow of his drink. "Let's get this train back on track."

Evan nodded. "I was Onders's assignment. I was meant to be tortured—by who I don't know. But I'll bet it was Onders who was going to shove the death gag in my mouth when they killed me."

"Oh, God."

"And you were Pine's, according to the death gag we found in his hotel room."

"And the one in Paul Fisher's mouth?"

She considered a moment, then shook her head. "I don't know. Onders and Pine were sent to deal with me and you. And Onders was on my flight ... but Pine was already here when the kids were abducted and Paul murdered. So maybe Pine was involved with that, or there was another team sent out for the kids and Paul."

"Two teams then perhaps—but one group."

Evan nodded. "My contact tells me that Onders and Pine were part of a group that calls itself Omega. They're the group that Bobbi was assigned to infiltrate."

Ben's face clouded over. "Why did you keep this from me?"

"There hasn't been time, Ben. And I'm telling you now."

"Do you not trust me?" His expression was even darker now. "Is that it? And, again, where is this intel coming from?"

"I told you—I can't say. For my contact's own protection." He was still tense, still had his antagonistic face on. "Come on, Ben. Don't be a dick. You know I'm doing the right thing—adhering to strict security protocols."

He looked away from her, but his shoulders came down from around his ears.

"Okay. I'm sorry. Let's just stick to the situation we're in now. What we do know. Omega has taken your niece and nephew, murdered their father, and the group has—had—at least two members resident here in America." He spread his hands. "What else?"

"There's the Germany connection in those photos and the

cigarettes," she said. "And I'm willing to bet that's where both Onders and Pine were trained."

That refocused his attention. His gaze snapped back to her. "In Germany. Of course. The photo from outside Cologne. But that photo of Ana and Onders is two years old."

"Which is when the training could have taken place." She tapped her forefinger on the tabletop. "We need to find Ana. Both Onders and Pine carried her photo. She's the key."

"Hold that thought," Ben said. "Our FBI shadows have finally found us."

Evan turned. Tennyson and Leyland had entered the diner. Tennyson hitched up his pants as he looked around. Then he spied them and headed in their direction. Like the Red Sea, the boisterous crowd parted for them.

Tennyson, eyes narrowed menacingly, loomed over them. "Get up." He snapped his fingers. "Get up now. We're arresting you for tampering with a federal crime scene and violating national security."

PART THREE

PART THREE

18

ISTANBUL, TURKEY

"Children."

"Anton, when you say that word it sounds like 'Martians.'" Kobalt shot him an icy look. "Wendy and Michael. Those are my children's names."

Zherov shifted from one foot to another. "How old were these children when you decided to leave them?"

"Three and a half years younger than they are now."

He made a sound that might have been disgust or irritation, as if to say, *Women. They can't be trusted.* "But you left them without a backward glance. You were exfiltrated out of Washington, DC, out of America. Out of your life. Which, if the reports aren't *dezinformatsiya*, you despised."

She turned the wheel over hard to starboard. "I despised my life. I despised my husband."

"And your children?"

"I felt nothing. I feel nothing. And now I'm dead to them. That's the way it was always going to be."

"You left them with a man who you despised."

"They have my sister," Kobalt said.

"Don't you despise Evan, as well?"

"Perhaps. But I also trust her."

"How odd."

Kobalt took a deep breath, exhaled slowly, allowing her anger at him to move freely out of her. "Tell me, Anton, have you any siblings?"

"I'm an only child."

"Then you wouldn't know." It would take more than one breath to get all her anger out. "So. Have you any children?"

He gave a peculiar little laugh, not unlike a hiccup. "I haven't been married."

She cut the boat's speed to one quarter. The day was already growing warm, the humidity thickening. Soon it would cover the city like a blanket. "I didn't ask whether you were married."

He turned away from her. "I want to be back on dry land."

"Don't we all." She cut the engines.

Belowdecks, she opened the fore hatch, sat down at the edge, and kicked hard at the hose attached to the sea cock. The hose and the seal attaching it to the sea cock was a weak point in all boats. As water started to fill the boat below the waterline, she rose, went back up on deck where Zherov stood waiting for her.

"I've started the scuttling process," she said. "Get ready to swim."

They moved to the port railing. She tied her jacket around her waist.

"You didn't answer my question, Anton."

He jumped and she went just after. In the water, she directed him. They swam for perhaps a hundred yards, into an area where the water abruptly turned aquamarine. Shortly thereafter, they reached the sandbar Ermi had pointed out to her during their cruise together.

"Brave teens sometimes swim out here to get away from

their parents," she told him as they took a breather on the wet sand, "and to fuck their brains out."

"I've never done it on a sandbar," Zherov said.

"And you won't today either." She wrung water out of her jacket. "But keep obfuscating, by all means."

He sat beside her, opened his sopping shirt wider, then wrapped his arms around his drawn-up legs. "So," he began, then stopped completely as if the clockwork mechanism inside him had suddenly run down. He shook his head, wiped down his hair. "So. There is someone. A daughter."

Kobalt wasn't surprised, given his previous reactions. "How old is she?"

"Not sure. Nine or ten, I think."

"What's her name?"

"I don't know."

She turned to him. "You don't know the name of your own daughter?"

"I've never even seen her. My former mistress forbade it."

"She *forbade* it?"

"She's a high-ranking apparatchik inside the Kremlin." His voice had taken on an unfamiliar tone, darker, more sinewy, as if all his bravado had been short-circuited. "And to be honest it didn't bother me. I hated her then, hated her for leaving, for getting pregnant. I felt she had no right." His hand cut through the air like a knife. "Then, too, I was wrapped up in my work. I was wholly focused on killing enemies of the State on foreign soil and coming back alive. I didn't care. I forgot."

She knew there was more. "Then."

"Yes, then." He looked miserable, and, all at once, he seemed more than a killing machine honed by Dima and his Zaslon instructors.

"And now?"

"Now? I'm a decade older. The thirties are not like the

twenties, not at all." He pursed his lips. "Now I feel as if I've lost something and I don't even know what it is."

They sat like that, engulfed in a strange sort of silence freighted with their pasts.

Kobalt had turned her face up to the sun, closed her eyes, and thought about being reunited with her children. How strange even that idea was to her. To want to see them, talk with them, be with them.

At length, she opened her eyes. "Have you ever read *Peter Pan*? Or seen the films?"

"What? No."

"Peter Pan was one of London's Lost Boys who never grew up. Instead, he found his way to Neverland. He returns to London and takes three children, Wendy, Michael, and John, with him back to Neverland."

She laced her fingers together, broke them apart, laced them back together again. "Here is what I'm offering you, Anton. We work together. We find Wendy and Michael, my lost children, and once they're safe I will find a way to bring you and your daughter together."

He gave a little laugh that contained a nervousness that sparked like electricity. "If only you could bring her to Neverland. I have made inquiries of late. Her mother does not treat her well. Perhaps the child reminds her of me."

She regarded him in all seriousness. "We'll deal with that then."

He studied her face for some moments, perhaps needing to assure himself that in this she was being sincere. Then he grasped the hand she held out.

Kobalt rose, stepped to the water's edge. "I don't know about you, but I need a good breakfast and a stiff Bloody Mary."

Then she dove in, and, with powerful strokes, headed toward shore. Zherov followed soon thereafter.

Behind them, the boat was just a memory.

19

WASHINGTON, DC

"I hope you know what you're doing," Ben said to her, under his breath.

"You'll be the first to know if I don't." The noise level in the bar covered their asides. Then she turned to the agents as if she hadn't heard Tennyson's declaration of war. "What a surprise, gentlemen." She gestured. "Have a seat. Take a load off. Your knees must be killing you after all the tailing you've done today. Am I right?"

Tennyson's face pinked up.

Ben's expression was unreadable. "Like the lady said, Tennyson, take a pew."

"I think we'll stand. We don't want to spoil your dinner."

"Too late," Evan said without the slightest inflection.

Leyland took a step toward her, brushing past his boss. Bending forward he said, "Show's over." He put his hand on the butt of his holstered sidearm. "Get up. Now."

She looked up at him, batted her eyes. "Take a chill pill, Daddy-O."

Leyland goggled at her. Tennyson's mouth was a grim line.

"She's just winding him up," Ben said equably.

Leyland turned to his boss, but shrugging, Tennyson said, "This is good experience for you, Jason."

Evan dug the transmitter Leyland had placed under their car from her pocket and threw it on the table.

"I really do think you want to sit down, Tennyson." Ben gestured. "You're going to want to hear what Evan has to say."

The agent stared at the transmitter as if it were a scorpion ready to strike. "I don't—"

"I have more presents for you," Evan said.

Ben nodded. "And then you're probably going to want a drink."

Tennyson looked at Ben, glared at Evan, then looked around the jumping bar, possibly hoping for the cavalry to come riding to his rescue. Then he said, "Fuck," and sat down.

Leyland's nose wrinkled as if in response to a foul odor, but he kept quiet. Maybe he was learning. He stood, like a sentinel, observing the scene as it unfolded.

The juke had segued into the Rolling Stones' "Gimme Shelter," Jagger's voice hauntingly augmented by that of Merry Clayton.

Tennyson sighed, ran the heel of his hand across his sweating forehead.

"I think he needs that drink stat," Evan said.

Ben raised a hand, ordered a bourbon neat when the waitress responded to his hail.

"Make that a double," Tennyson mumbled. "It's been a long day."

When the drink came, he downed it in one, set the glass back on the table. "Okay, let's have it." His eyes watered and his cheeks were taking on a rosy glow.

Ben sat back. This was Evan's show and he wanted to enjoy it.

"The first thing I checked after I ID'd Paul Fisher's body was for material under his fingernails."

"Defensive wounds. Forensics is on it." Tennyson nodded. He looked bone weary, as if he'd aged a year in a day. "Tell me something I don't know."

"You don't know the identity of Paul's killer." Evan placed the baggie that had housed the passport, license, money, and death gag on the table. In it now was the stubbed-out cigarette butt they had found on the bathroom sink. This is what she had gone back into the bathroom to retrieve before she and Ben had fled through the hotel room's window.

Tennyson glanced at the baggie, then gave Evan a gimlet-eyed stare meant to stop an oncoming lineman in his tracks. "Yeah. So?"

"Your forensics team will run DNA on this butt and find that it matches the material found deep under Paul Fisher's fingernails." For once, Tennyson had nothing to say. His mouth hung half-open. "On the fourth floor of an abandoned building across the street from the Majestic Hotel"—she added the address—"you'll find the body of the man who buried Paul alive. He's got a line of scratches on the left side of his neck where Paul got to him before he was thrown into the pit."

"I'll be fucking banjaxed." Leyland squinted at Evan.

His boss said, "Please don't tell me you know who this bastard is, too."

She handed him Pine's driver's license.

"An American," he growled.

"Or something else entirely," Ben said.

Leyland frowned. "Meaning?"

"There's a German connection." She slid over the pack of cigarettes Ben had found in Pine's hotel room.

"Pine might be American," Ben said. "Or he might not."

"Either way," Evan added, "the tobacco is fresh. It's clear he's been in Germany recently. So . . . our bailiwick."

Tennyson stowed away the driver's license, along with the cigarettes, the baggie, and the now disabled transmitter.

His head swung slowly from side to side. "You fuckers."

Evan lifted a forkful of spaghetti. "You're welcome."

He looked at her for some time, rapped his knuckles twice on the table before setting his card down in front of her.

"The full resources of the FBI are bent on finding your niece and nephew. I will find them. That's a promise."

She nodded.

That was as close as he could come to recognizing her as a professional.

20

NIGHT FLIGHT

"You don't really believe Wendy and Michael are still in the States."

"I don't," Evan said. "But it doesn't hurt to have Tennyson believe that they are, because if I'm wrong..." She let the sentence sink of its own weight.

They were seated in the first-class section of the Lufthansa flight to Frankfurt. From there it would be a short hop to Cologne. Ben had paid for the tickets. When she had said, only half-jokingly, that if they went on like this he'd blow through his severance in no time, he had just shrugged and told her not to worry about it.

They had boarded the plane last, as they always did. Strict protocol, checking out all the passengers before they stepped aboard. She heard him on the phone with Zoe while they waited, even though he'd stepped away. She turned her back to him to give him privacy, looked out over the tarmac, watched a plane, lights blinking, come in for a landing.

Then she heard Ben's voice behind her. "Someone wants to

speak with you." He was holding out his cell. He was smiling. She took the phone.

"Hey, Poppet."

"Hi, Deckard."

Pirates of the Caribbean and *Blade Runner*. Their two favorite films, which they watched whenever they were together. They used to argue about whether Rick Deckard was a Replicant, even placed a bet on it, until they saw *Blade Runner 2049*, which settled the issue. Evan still owed Zoe a dinner out, having lost the bet.

"Everything going okay?" Evan said.

"Everything is everything," Zoe said. Translation: I'm fine. "I miss you guys."

She turned to glance at Ben. "We miss you too, Poppet."

"Evan . . ."

She gripped Ben's mobile more tightly. Something serious was coming. "What is it, honey?"

"I just heard about Wendy and Michael being missing. I'm guessing that—"

"No guessing," Evan said. "Promise fiddle." Translation: pinky swear. "Okay?"

"Sure. I get it."

"There's the girl."

"Will I see you soon?"

"Soon as we get home."

Zoe was smart enough and used to their comings and goings not to ask when.

Ben was tapping his watch.

"Gotta scoot."

"Deckard, take care of him."

"Always, Poppet. Always."

★ ★ ★

"You're not wrong," Ben said, continuing their conversation as they finished their dinner. "There was no ransom contact made."

"Nor will there be," Evan affirmed. "What Tennyson doesn't get is that this abduction is beyond the scope of normal guidelines. It doesn't fit into the picture he's already assembling. There was no point in telling him because he wouldn't understand."

She paused as the flight attendant took their dinner trays and told them the dessert cart was on its way.

"So what *do* you think the abduction is all about?"

"What gives me pause is Paul's murder. It wasn't a spur-of-the-moment idea to get him out of the way. It was as carefully planned and orchestrated as the abduction."

"By Omega." Ben turned to her. "So much for my theory about Wells orchestrating the abduction."

Evan closed her eyes for a moment, aware that her heart rate had become elevated. She struggled to keep the terror of Wendy and Michael's unknown fate in a far corner of her mind. In the face of the unknown she tended to imagine the worst. If she allowed that to flood her, the powers of reasoning and planning she relied on would be muddied, beyond useless. She did not open her eyes until she had regained full control of her emotions.

"That never made sense to me," she said. "Paul was doing a lot of Wells's dirty work through Wells's Super PAC. He certainly wouldn't want him murdered. So we might rule out Wells being part of Omega."

He frowned. "You don't look certain."

"I wish I was."

Ben put his head back against the seat rest. "I so would like to sleep." He closed his eyes.

Evan rose, went forward to the toilet, locked herself in. She stood in front of the mirror. Her attention was drawn to the single orchid stuck in a slender glass vase attached to the wall.

"You poor thing," she whispered, "stuck in here with no sunlight or any way to escape."

Sudden tears overran her eyes, slid down her cheeks, leaving tracks shining in the artificial light.

Oh, Wendy, oh, Michael, she thought. *Where are you?* She watched her reflection weeping and wondered who that was. *I will find you. Wherever they have taken you, wherever you are, I will find you.*

Ben hadn't turned his seat into a bed, nor were his eyes closed. The privacy screen was still down between their shells. He glanced at her as she slid back into her seat, saw the red rims around her eyes.

He looked straight ahead at his screen, where *Wendezeit—1989, A Spy Story* was silently running, but he didn't seem to be paying attention.

Evan wiped at her face, more a gesture of anger than pulling herself together. "I'm sorry I lost it with Pine."

"He wasn't going to give us squat," Ben said gently. "I think we both suspected that from the get-go."

"Still." She took a breath. "We could have tried."

"What's the point, Evan?" He turned to her. "Unless you're getting a masochistic kick blaming yourself."

She looked him in the eye. "I *am* blaming myself, but not so much for that."

He waited, patient now. The dessert cart arrived, and she asked, "Any Butter Brickle ice cream?"

And Ben understood now. Still, he would wait for her to tell him in her own time, in her own way.

"I'm afraid not," the flight attendant said. "But we do have butter pecan."

"Yes," Evan said, brightening somewhat. "Hot fudge sundae with two scoops, and extra fudge."

"Make that two," Ben said.

"I didn't know you were a butter pecan fan," Evan said.

"I'd prefer Butter Brickle," he replied. "But this will do."

She gave him a questioning look, then a brief nod of acknowledgment.

When dessert had arrived and they were alone again, she dropped two pain pills into her mouth, took a couple bites of her sundae before she put her spoon down. "So I've been thinking . . . I've spent a lot of whatever downtime I've had with Zoe."

"Don't think she's not grateful. She thinks of you as her aunt. What you've done for her is just what a girl who's lost her mother needs."

"It's what Wendy and Michael need, too. I've spent as much time with them as my job allows, but I'm away so much . . ." She shook her head. "And now that they're gone I'm racked with guilt."

"Evan, you spent a great deal of time with them," Ben said. "How often did you bring Zoe over to play with them?"

"But still I feel like something was missing."

"Ideas?"

She stared down at the small crater she'd made in the rapidly melting sundae. "What I suspect . . . because . . . because of my . . . complicated relationship with Bobbi, I didn't get as close to them as I could or should have."

"That's nonsense and you know it. First, there was their father, who didn't like you, to put it mildly. Second, all you need to do is recall how their faces lit up every time they saw you."

She bit her lip. "Maybe I was being selfish." Perhaps she wasn't listening.

He reached out, placed a hand over hers. "Evan, you're the least selfish person I know. You had only so much off time— the nature of your work wouldn't allow a moment more. You gave your love to Zoe and to Michael and to Wendy, I'm sure in equal measure, and they're all the better for it."

"But if they're lost. If they're somehow . . . gone forever." She choked. "I'd never be able to forgive myself."

"That's not how this chapter of our lives is going to end."

Her eyes held steady on his, enlarged by her incipient tears. "You can't know that."

"We'll make it so." His hand squeezed hers. "Together."

After, with the lights low, their seats made into beds, heads on pillows, covered with duvets, Evan slept, and in sleeping, dreamed. She dreams of being in the stream near their house. Bobbi is with her. Bobbi is laughing at her, repeating over and over, *I have the power, not you.* Never you, but in the manner of dreams, she doesn't understand what that means. Anxiety builds in her to unbearable heights.

That's when Bobbi reaches out, places both hands on the crown of Evan's head—*You want power? Here's power*—and pushes her down under the water. When Evan struggles, Bobbi wraps her legs over her sister's shoulders, and keeps her down.

Down . . .

Down . . .

Down.

21

DAY PART

The Russian-built aircraft, one of a small fleet that was the pride and joy of the SVR, sat grounded due to mechanical trouble. Kobalt and Zherov had already boarded the plane, changed into fresh clothes, and were preparing for takeoff when the captain informed them of the problem and suggested they would be more comfortable waiting in the diplomats' lounge in the private section of the Istanbul airport. He was right, because since this was Turkey and the jet was Russian built, what had been promised in an hour or two might well wind up taking twenty.

They were now in the process of demolishing yet another bottle of ice-cold vodka, sitting side by side at the semicircular bar, on plush stool-like chairs with low backs. At some point, the bartender placed before them an array of *mezze*, which they picked at now and again.

"The question must be asked," Kobalt said, "Who was the Russian criminal, the tattooed ex-con, working for?"

The lounge was modern and over-air-conditioned, an open rectangular space with a few scattered sitting areas. Blown-up photos of the city hung on the walls were interspersed with framed posters for Turkish Airlines. Spare but comfortable, impersonal indirect lighting. By contrast, sunlight threw itself against the plate glass windows, creating splashes of butter-yellow lozenges along the carpeted floor. Apart from the two of them and the bartender, no one was in the lounge. Outside, on the tarmac, they could see their plane. It was impossible to tell whether the mechs who had been swarming under and over it for hours even knew what they were doing.

Kobalt rotated her glass a quarter turn and drank from it. "There are a number of entities who would use a man like him—a murderer inside prison and here in the real world."

Zherov's expression was pensive, even perhaps concerned. "I was just thinking—for the past six months or so SVR has been using ex-cons to do their wet work. It's a neat trick, since if anything goes sideways there's no blowback. SVR's hands are clean."

"SVR's hands are never clean."

"Well, but you know what I mean."

She frowned deeply. "I've been entertaining the same idea."

"Well, if you ask me, it's the right one," Zherov said. "It seems clear that Ermi was a lawyer of no little repute. He was discreet, and also dirty as sin, as we ourselves have seen. He may have been the clearinghouse for any number of SVR or FSB upper echelons."

"You're saying he sold me out for a client who was paying him more than I did."

Zherov nodded. "What seems most likely is that someone inside SVR or the FSB got wind of this mission of yours." He watched her. "They don't like personal initiatives. You must know that. I know Dima does."

"But the intel about my children came straight from our own HUMINT division," she countered.

He shrugged. "A leak? In any case, someone in SVR has

decided you're not trustworthy. Maybe he thinks you're a double." He peered at her. "You're not, are you?"

She snorted. "Don't be absurd. My heart is Russian." She gestured. "It's curious, though."

"What is?"

"That this SVR attack on me comes right after Omega abducts my children."

"If you're distracted by what's happened to them you're singularly vulnerable," he pointed out.

She squeezed the bridge of her nose between her thumb and forefinger. "You've been in this game longer than I have. Maybe you could tap a few contacts and find out who has voiced distrust in me."

He reflected for a moment. "I can try," he said. "And now that I think of it, the pool of suspects can't be too big. My understanding was this remit was between you and Dima."

"Apparently not." Her eyes narrowed. "There's HUMINT, whoever there received and passed on the intel to me. And then there's you, of course."

His incipient laugh died on his lips. "You can't possibly suspect me. I'm Dima's man, he sent me. And I was the one who engaged with that psycho in the knife shop."

She smiled. "Now I suspect everyone, even Dima, though God alone knows why he'd want to kill his golden goose."

"He wouldn't. You're his pride and joy." He smirked. "Even though you won't let him into your pants."

"Right." She made a sarcastic sound. "But not to worry overly, Anton, you're at the bottom of the admittedly short list."

Zherov blew air out through his lips. "You really are some piece of work." He took a sip, shook his head. "I wish I'd gotten the Russian to talk. I'd love to know who inside SVR hired him."

"It would have been a waste of time," she said. "There's only one thing a man like that does, and it's definitely not talk." She finished off her vodka, poured herself more. She was aware that she was drinking more than Zherov, but then again, she suspected she could hold her liquor better than he could. "He was a specialist; he was only interested in killing." She smacked her lips. "A psycho like him gets his jollies from watching people die."

"Jollies?"

"Killing is his heroin."

Zherov nodded. Here was something he could understand down to its roots.

She studied him for a moment. "It felt good, didn't it?"

He frowned. "What?"

"Killing him."

"I tried not to."

"You didn't try hard enough," she said. "Clearly." Her gaze kept steady on his face. "So. It felt good. It was freeing. Society wasn't in the equation; it had ceased to exist. It was you and him. Until it was only you."

Zherov narrowed his eyes. Then, abruptly, he laughed. "Has it been an hour already? I owe you a hundred dollars."

"Psychoanalysis is more like four hundred an hour these days." Her lips turned up at the corners. "But, of course, that comes with a prescription for something that will put you right out of your misery."

"As if you never felt freed by killing someone."

"I've never killed anyone." She didn't know why she lied; maybe it was a compulsion, maybe it was just plain bloody-mindedness.

"I don't believe you."

She shrugged.

He leaned in, his gaze intense. "You know why I don't believe you? Because you're intimate with the psychology. The mechanism inside us that makes us do what we do. And yes,

I mean *us*. In this, if not in anything else, we're the same, you and me."

Kobalt took a time-out to calm her breathing, to return her rage to the little wooden box she had fashioned for it when she was younger. She had spent the better part of a year on that project.

She sat back to further calm herself. Also, to distance herself from him. He was the strangest of bedfellows, but she needed him as a buffer. "They swept you up out of the gutter, didn't they, Anton?"

"Actually, they resurrected me out of prison."

"How old were you?"

"Twenty," he replied. "Almost."

"And why were you incarcerated?"

"That time?" He took up a bit of hummus on his fork, swallowed it down. "I knifed a man in a bar."

"You were involved in a fight."

"Not at all. The prick said he knew my kind. He said I was nothing, that I'd always be nothing. He laughed at me, shamed me. I watched him die with a smile on my face."

Something deep inside Kobalt felt chilled. "So you felt nothing."

He took up some more hummus. "What d'you mean? I felt elated, vindicated. Finally. He got what was coming to him. He asked for it." Zherov tossed his head. "Up to that point everyone treated me like a piece of shit they cleaned off the soles of their shoes. Never again. Now people were afraid of me. Now I had status." He ate the rest of the hummus. "Even the cops who took me in were impressed. They must have told someone high up. I was only inside a week before they came and got me."

"The FSB."

"Initially. But I was too much for them; after three weeks, they sent me down to SVR, where I trained. I came under the jurisdiction of Dima. He plucked me out and gave me my first remit. When I came back, he brought me into Zaslon."

He took a drink of vodka. "You look shocked, Karin." He was careful to use her current legend here though only the bartender was around.

She shook her head. "Shocked, no. Aggrieved." She emptied the bottle, called for another. "Aggrieved that you were the one Dima assigned as my nursemaid."

"It worked out in the end." He poured from the new bottle. "Didn't it?"

"So far, anyway." She looked away, squinted into the bright sunshine spinning off the fuselage of their wounded bird.

"What's with you? Every time I think we've come to some kind of accord, you pull the rug from under me."

"Now you know how I've felt ever since I came over."

"Meaning?"

"Meaning Russians. They think just because they're men they're entitled to fuck me."

He shrugged. "That's the way it works here."

"Not with me."

He made a face. "I wish I understood you better."

"Don't expect any help from me."

"I won't," he said sourly. "Now."

She needed a break. Rising off her stool, she crossed to the window, studying the incomprehensible activity surrounding their plane and learning nothing. But at least the vise around her chest had loosened, her breathing flowing freely again.

Zherov waited some time for her to come back, nibbling and drinking. When she evinced no sign of moving, he came to her, standing too close for comfort. She was about to step away when he said, "Why are you being like this when you've asked for my help?"

She picked up a date dipped in honey and coconut from a small bowl on a nearby table, held it out to him.

His neck turned ruddy. "Thanks, but I don't need a payment."

"I thought you were making it clear you did." She popped the date into her mouth, chewed reflectively. "Either you try to help us both out—because, Anton, it's clear that you're in as much danger as I am—or you don't. It's entirely up to you."

She cocked her head. "Do you remember how contemptuous of me you were when you first walked on the plane?"

"That was then, this is now." His hands were busy doing nothing. He knew he'd made a series of mistakes with her but had no idea how or what he needed to do to rectify the balance of power. "Besides, I was pissed at Dima for sending me to be your nursemaid."

"No more than I was."

The mood developed the thickness, the darkness that comes just before an electrical storm. They regarded each other for long minutes, then he pulled out his mobile phone, stepped away and made a couple of calls out of her hearing.

"Okay, done," he said when he returned. "I may hear something, I may not."

The sunlight was fading. Still, she felt it even through the glass. "If I thought you had a heart, Anton, I'd feel sorry for you."

He shook his head, pulled at his earlobe. "Evan Ryder. The American *shpion*. She's your sister, yes?"

She stared at him.

"Is she anything like you?"

"She's too much like me."

Zherov shifted his weight from one foot to the other. "Then we could use someone like her."

At length, Kobalt shook her head. "I know Evan. Not even on the point of death."

He grinned. "I imagine that, too, could be arranged."

Outside, darkness had descended.

22

AFTER HOURS

At the violet hour—that is, just after sunset—the Moscow Aquarium was all but deserted. Here and there the night crew went about their appointed tasks silently and efficiently. A contingent swept up the debris that children and adults alike left, cleaned out corners, mopped the floors until they gleamed like gold in the low lights. Others with doctorate degrees, trailed dutifully by their note-taking assistants, glided between the tanks on steel catwalks that overlooked the open tops. Now and then, one or another would stop, kneel down, check on certain charges, dictate to their companions. The susurrus added to the soft background sounds that could only be heard at this time, when the crowds had filed out, the gates closed.

But the aquarium never slept; at least its denizens never slept.

In the dusky evening, a man bundled in a heavy overcoat, its lambs-wool collar turned up and a wide-brimmed fedora jammed onto his large head, was escorted through the discreet employees' side entrance by two grim-faced SVR agents. They left him inside the door, from where he was ushered into the aquarium proper by a marine biologist with whom he'd gone to school in St. Petersburg, a man who inexplicably—at least to the bundled figure—chose science over the FSB, science over money, a dacha in the Moscow hills, and mistresses plentiful and sparkling as Christmas ornaments.

The man in the heavy overcoat held a small satchel in one hand. He spoke to his friend as he had when they were at school, confiding secrets to each other, sharing a trust that needed no words to explain. The man in the heavy overcoat was Director General Baev, head of the SVR, the marine biologist by his side was Dr. Morayev. The amusing appropriateness of his name was never lost on him. In fact, he used to joke with Baev that his family name was why he chose marine science over the FSB. All his friends called him Morayev, even Baev, whom Morayev in turn addressed as Slava.

Director General Baev was a compact man, burly, with an intimidating manner, armor against his personal insecurities. His features were lopsided, one eye slightly higher than the other, and on his nearly lipless mouth, which lifted on one corner, was what appeared to be a perpetual smirk or snarl, depending on his mood. He had thick, slicked-back hair the color of a mink's pelt, and an unfashionable full beard. The backs of his hands were forested with coarse black hair.

In contrast, Morayev was small and slightly round-shouldered from his studies through a microscope. He was a bachelor, and often spent weekends at Baev's dacha when the sparkly Christmas ornaments were in attendance. He enjoyed a good time as much as the next man.

Morayev accompanied Baev only as far as the enormous shark tank, where another man was already waiting, hands crossed over his bathing suit, the only article of clothing he wore. Morayev stopped dead in his tracks a very healthy distance from this man, as he always did. He was terrified of him even though Baev often made sport of his phobia. Great whites or tiger sharks didn't bother the marine biologist one whit, but just the sight of Minister Darko Vladimirovich Kusnetsov, director of the FSB, gave him heart palpitations. Kusnetsov was a curious amalgam of the venal and the righteous. Like most men in high government positions he was open to money grabs, payoffs, and sending his ill-gotten gains to safety offshore. On the other hand, he would not countenance in himself or anyone under him trafficking in drugs or human exploitation. Those who dared vanished without a trace.

"I will leave you now, Slava," Morayev murmured and, without waiting for a reply from his friend, turned on his heel and, as far as he was able, beat a hasty retreat.

The two officials—the director of SVR and the head of its parent organization, the FSB, the Federal Security Service—met above the center of the shark tank, shook hands, then embraced as Russian comrades. Over the years, they had formed an uneasy truce. Minister Kusnetsov would never call it a friendship; Baev was his inferior in rank, and Baev himself was not foolish enough to think it so. And yet on some level neither would admit to, there was an unspoken bond between them. One of the reasons was that they were in agreement on their rules of corruption. The other was right here below them.

Baev opened his bag, took out his bathing suit and two towels, stripped down, and climbed into the suit. They then both drew masks and freediving carbon fiber fin blades from the bottom of their bags. One after the other, the men lowered themselves into the tank. They were both champion swimmers and expert free divers. This activity they had years ago devised for themselves required them to swim with sharks without gear or protection.

After super-filling their lungs without churning their legs, they sank down. Flexing their legs, they moved in the same rhythm with the sharks. There was the usual assortment of non-threatening animals: reef sharks, lemon sharks, lemon-tip sharks, and the couch potatoes of the breed, nurse sharks. The fact was sharks were by nature shy; a far cry from the one depicted in *Jaws*.

Baev, however, was particularly drawn to bull sharks because they were the most aggressive, and adaptable: they could swim in both salt and fresh water.

For his part, Kusnetsov preferred the tiger sharks. He loved their lean lines, feral eyes, and predatory stare. Over the years, he'd stared down several of these fellows. He'd never been hurt; neither of them had.

The danger and ineffable beauty were only part of the benefits the two men found in the depths of the shark tank. There was also the silence—so absolute they swore they heard their hearts beating, the blood circulating through their veins and arteries. Nowhere else in their busy lives could they find the profound peace they basked in here.

Baev found the eight-foot bull shark he'd dubbed Ongendus, the first king of Denmark, or possibly the great beast found him, for Baev was certain that by this time Ongendus recognized him. They swam side by side, Baev so close to that primitive heart, wanting to touch it and all it signified, without knowing how. This was as close, he thought, as he would ever get to the mystery and wonder of life itself.

Twice they surfaced to refresh their lungs. Once a curious lemon-tip followed them almost to the surface, hanging with them as they breathed, then lost interest as they dropped down again into the green depths. And when at last they both tired, Baev found himself, as always, reluctant to leave Ongendus's side.

Afterward, they sat on the catwalk toweling off. Baev brought out a thermos of iced vodka from which the men took turns drinking.

Later, clothed and energized from their swim and the vodka, they repaired to an office within the aquarium they always used.

Baev plunked himself down on a small sofa while Kusnetsov sat in a swivel chair behind the desk. He was long, slender, and sleek, like his beloved tiger sharks. His bald pate held a fringe of salt-and-pepper hair that on anyone else would have looked monkish. Not on the minister, though. His eyes were glittery, black, and insatiable. Like his tiger sharks you never knew what he was thinking or what he would do next, though Baev had a long history of making correct guesses.

"So." Kusnetsov clasped his hands behind his head, his favorite position for off-the-record conversations. He wore a dark suit, white shirt, and red tie. Each item of clothing fit him perfectly. "Has Dima bedded her yet?" There was no need to clarify who the "her" referred to. Often, it seemed to Baev that all their conversations about Dima started with the same question. But, in fact, he was beginning to believe that they were about Kobalt herself.

"She has resisted every advance, even the most subtle." Baev considered a moment, then dared to say, "I find that commendable."

The minister appeared to brush aside his words of praise. "And yet he continues to bend the rules for her," he mused. "This makes their relationship . . . questionable. Any woman who can get whatever she wants from Dima without fucking his brains out is to be watched closely. We both know how dangerous Dima is under his preening surface."

"Well, that's his MO, isn't it? Time and again, he offers you the chance to think he's ineffectual as an enemy."

"The question is whether he chose wisely with Kobalt."

"She's a stone-cold killing machine," Baev reminded him. "Anouk, Leda, the American Lila Butler. The Swede Elias Larsson, the Chechen Alu Islamov—she terminated them all with perfect efficiency and no sign of remorse." He took a breath. "Kobalt is a weapon, but she's a weapon Dima wants for himself."

Kusnetsov grunted. "As proof of your thesis, it is my understanding that Dima leant Kobalt one of our planes so she could fetch her children back from whomever took them."

Baev nodded. "That would be a logical assumption, but the fact is she's going after Omega again, the group she was sent to infiltrate six months ago."

"And the children?"

"They think she's dead, quite naturally. It seems she wants to stay dead to them too."

For a long time after that, the minister remained silent. He stared down at his fingertips as he tapped them together. At length, he looked up. "It seems my assessment of Kobalt may be somewhat off base. Two question marks have been erased. But . . ."

Here it comes, Baev thought.

"There's the third, namely the fact that her remit for Omega ended in failure."

Baev was careful to keep his surprise off his face. "If you read the minutes of her debriefing on that remit, you'll see that she provided us with crucial intel. Omega is a fanatic God-based cult. They're indoctrinating Russians citizens, turning them against the Federation."

"Unacceptable, absolutely. But what she failed to do was bring back *actionable* intel. Who is Omega's leader, what is Omega's ultimate goal? How far along are they toward achieving it? And where, precisely, is their main headquarters? The compound in Odessa was merely a satellite."

"That is why I haven't reprimanded Dima for sending her off," Baev said. "She's been given a second chance at completing her Omega remit."

"As far as I am concerned, the jury's still out. Kobalt has still to prove her worth to me." Kusnetsov's strong hand swept through the air between them. He cleared his throat, forearms on the desk, his torso leaning slightly toward Baev, indicating he was now prepared to discuss the core of their conversation. "My chief concern is Evan Ryder. She is Kobalt's sister."

"They hate each other."

Kusnetsov lowered his head, a bull about to charge. "Nevertheless, Ryder is a possible temptation for Kobalt, a conduit to the West. These possible loopholes in Kobalt being iron-bound to us I will not tolerate." He glowered. "I have expressed this very concern a number of times, Slava, and yet—" His hands opened like shovels as if, Baev thought, about to scoop out Baev's grave. A ball of ice instantly formed in Baev's lower belly. "And yet Ryder remains alive and well." Kusnetsov's nostrils flared as if he had sensed a foul odor. "Where does your Ryder remit stand? Do you even know where she is?"

"Indeed, I do." Baev ventured a breath without choking on his anxiety. "We have finally located her. The abduction of Kobalt's children gave us the opportunity we needed. HUMINT indicated that she, not Kobalt, is trying to track down the children. I have dispatched a pair of 'farm hands' to terminate her."

"Farm hands?" The minister glowered. "What are you talking about?"

Baev cleared his throat. "'Farm hands' are *blatnoy*"—criminals—"newly released from *fenya*." Prison. "All of them are handpicked. They ran murder-for-hire operations on the inside. All they live for is murder; they do it better than anyone else."

"Including Ryder."

Baev nodded. "Including Ryder."

Kusnetsov lifted a palm from the table, lowered it silently, deliberately, which, as Baev well knew, held more weight than if he had slammed it down. The minister was at his most dangerous when calm. "All right. But listen well, Slava, I want this over and done with. No fuckups, no dangling threads. Terminate Evan Ryder, quickly and neatly."

Baev rose to his feet like any good soldier having been given his marching orders, answered formally, "I understand completely, Minister Kusnetsov."

Baev should have gone straight home, but he didn't feel like it. He had an itch he couldn't scratch. Home was the last place he wanted to be. Dismissing his driver and bodyguard, he slid behind the wheel of the armored Navigator. He was better off driving when he needed to work out an issue, especially one that had been on the periphery of his consciousness for some time.

As he drove along the embankment to the Moskva, he deliberately turned his mind away from the problems vexing him. Moonlight in Moscow. How that took him back to his youth, when he would stroll along the riverbank with his current girlfriend, while the silver light on the black river worked its romantic magic. But that was a long time ago. Tonight, it seemed further away than usual. When had he lost his taste for romance? Was it the same time he fell out of love with his wife? Perhaps he had never loved her. Perhaps the carapace of cynicism created by working within the clandestine services had already made him immune to love—to normal, humdrum human concerns altogether.

He shivered, feeling more alone than he had in some time. He could always go to a club, get smashed on vodka and wind up with some young woman, as vapid as she was gorgeous. He had numbers in his cell, women who'd gladly take his money for a night of debauchery. But neither of those things appealed to him. With a start, he realized they hadn't in a while. His job had consumed him completely, and now he resided in the belly of the beast: powerful, wealthy beyond his wildest dreams, and absolutely, totally alone.

Taking a police exit, he drove down the ramp to the water's

edge, and parked. He felt trapped, and he almost stumbled in his haste to get out of the Navigator. Pulling his overcoat more tightly around him, he walked a distance along the service road. Across the river lights glimmered, their reflections dancing over the water. He stared out at the Moskva, but his gaze was turned inward.

"*Her remit for Omega ended in failure*," Kusnetsov had said, speaking of Kobalt. That was the received wisdom by the handful of people who had read the report of her debriefing. Everyone simply assumed she had failed, that she had slipped up, given herself away somehow. But Baev wasn't so sure. Agents like Kobalt were in their own way fanatics; their attention to detail was almost superhuman. So if she hadn't slipped up, then what? The only other possibility was that she was betrayed. Which meant someone inside SVR, possibly even Zaslon, wanted her dead. Who and why?

Drawing out his cell, he made a number of calls, asking the questions that needed answering. Once—but only once—he was forced to raise his voice.

Back in the SUV, he turned on the ignition, waited for the heater to warm his extremities. He paused a moment, then made one more call.

He drove deeper into the night, away from his lavish apartment, his wife, his teenage children, who were hardly there anyway. He did not think about any of them, allowed a mental scrim to slide down over their images, relegating their existence to the shadowed recesses of his mind.

Twenty minutes later, in the thin traffic, he pulled up onto the concrete apron of a modern townhouse, one of a long, snaking line, a three-story, four-bedroom residence three blocks off the Novorizhskoe Highway. It was quiet here, outside the Ring Road, and high barrier walls effectively muffled the traffic noise from the highway.

He was just about to step out when his mobile buzzed. He

listened for perhaps thirty seconds, said, "Understood," and rang off.

The front door opened and there stood Kata in high heels, thigh-high stockings, and nothing else. She grinned when she saw him.

She welcomed him inside with a kiss on the side of his neck that quickly turned into a little nip. "I'm pleased you decided to extend your stay."

23

KÖLN, GERMANY

"Once upon a time, this was my kind of city," Evan said. "In the medieval age many of the guilds were run by women."

"An open city," Ben replied as they took a taxi into town from the airport. "But that's history. Now, today, and from now on it's Moscow Rules." Which meant they were in enemy territory, they should assume nothing, blend in as much as possible, and take coincidence as opposition action.

Clouds chased each other across the sky, like children playing tag. The sun winked in and out, sending inconstant shadows skittering across streets and sidewalks. Ben had told the taxi driver to drop them off across the street from the thorny twin steeples of the gothic Church Cathedral of St. Peter, home to the archbishop and the archdiocese of Cologne. Evan was looking at it—the third tallest church in the world, its first stones were laid in 1248, but what with the extreme turbulence of history, it was not completed until centuries later, in 1880—when her mobile vibrated. An encrypted text had arrived in the sandboxed section. She opened it and began to read.

"Evan," Ben said, "we're here."

"Have the driver keep going," she replied without lifting her head from the screen.

Leaning forward, Ben told the driver to keep going. The driver shrugged and drove them on.

The text was from Lyudmila. Via her sandboxed mobile, Evan had texted her their current names, Carla and Len Johnstone—legends they had used before—their flight number and arrival time in Cologne as soon as Ben had made the reservations. Lyudmila had responded with a name, an address, a time, and detailed instructions for the meet. Glancing at her watch, Evan saw they had about three hours to spare.

"We'd like sausages, kraut, and beer," she told the driver. "Take us to the best place on Ebertplaz."

The driver nodded, turned at the next corner. Twenty minutes later, they were walking through the glass doors of Liebchen, an old-school beer hall with wooden tables and floors shellacked black from decades of shoe and boot soles, a testament to its popularity. It was overheated and vaporous with steam from huge cauldrons of potato and cabbage soups.

When they seated themselves at a table halfway back, a slim waitress set out silverware and glasses, handed them menus, and went off with their beer orders.

"Bratwurst or weisswurst?" Ben asked.

"Brats, definitely." Evan put her menu aside. "Sauerkraut and potatoes."

The beers came, and they ordered. The waitress took their menus and departed.

Evan shook out a single painkiller and washed it down with a gulp of beer. She winced. "*Nein.*" Pushed the beer over to sit side by side with Ben's. Catching the eye of the waitress, she ordered a large bottle of mineral water. Drank down an entire glass when it came.

Over their food, Ben said, "Does your mysterious contact know you're here with someone?"

Evan was cutting into her brat while trying not to let the juice spray her. "No."

"Good. Let's keep it that way."

She needed to concentrate on the two gold Omegas, Paul's horrific end, and the children, the death gag with Ben's name on it, and how they all fit together. In order to do that, she knew she had to block out her history with her sister. In the present circumstances this she could do without too much difficulty, but there was another issue that needed to be brought out into the open now.

"Ben," she began, "if we're to continue working in the field together we have to talk about that night here in Germany."

He put down his fork. "Maybe better to discuss the aftermath."

"I know. We were both complicit in keeping the truth from Lila."

"My wife was a good person. She didn't deserve to be lied to."

"And if you had confessed? What would have been gained, Ben? She would have hated you, demonized me, and your marriage would have imploded. Is that what you would have wanted for Zoe? For any of us?"

"No, of course not. But . . ." The end of his thought dangled in the air like a loose thread on the hem of a coat.

"But what? We spoke about it at the time, remember?"

"Yes. Long into the night."

"Face it, Ben. The only reason to tell Lila was to assuage your guilt." She took a breath. "Unfortunately, the truth doesn't always earn you forgiveness."

He nodded. His face was sallow and drawn. "I can't help missing her."

"No, you can't."

He lifted his head up. "And I can't help feeling . . ."

Abruptly, he pushed his plate away, rose, and went toward the rear where Evan assumed the toilets were. She wondered what he'd been about to say, and what had stopped him from voicing it. She wondered whether his hesitation had something to do with Isobel Lowe. She wondered about their history— how long was it, how had they met, what did they mean to each other? She had seen for herself how strikingly beautiful Isobel was, how compelling her personality was. It was not at all inconceivable that Ben was in love with her. In fact, now that she thought about it, the two of them made a likely couple. Not a happy-making thought. Not at all.

Movement in the periphery of her vision made her lift her head. Ben was coming back. He had more color in his face and his hair was damp. He must have thrown cold water at himself.

As he slipped back into his seat, he said, "I was about to thank you for what you did back there in Anacostia."

"One good deed begets another. You pulled me out of the flaming wreck I'd made of my Charger."

Ben shook his head. "I don't know. Pine gave me more grief than I had expected."

"Do you need a refresher at the Farm?" The Farm was the closely guarded campus deep in the hills of Virginia where recruits were schooled in the dark arts of tradecraft, Moscow Rules, and, for some, wet work.

"Ah, no." He shook his head. "This is the only way to hone my instincts."

"Of course." Evan smiled. "Those instincts never die, Ben, they're just buried under an avalanche of paperwork."

He returned her smile. "The natural result, I suppose, of having been half man, half desk for years." He chewed on a brat, swallowed it down with a swig of beer. "Imagine my striving for that, thinking running my own shop would be the pinnacle of my career"—he spread his hands—"when I realize now how much I've missed the adrenaline rush of the field."

She waited patiently, sensing there was something more he wanted to say.

He cleared his throat. "What I want to say is that we have a special bond, an intimacy that, I think, gave us permission to have sex that night. But it's only now I realize that the intimacy we share is bound by violence. We have killed people together and in each other's presence. And I find it so odd, so inexplicable because this is something no one else can share; it's ours alone."

She nodded. "For better or for worse."

"Hm. It's probably both, don't you think?"

"I do, as a matter of fact. But we've chosen this life, Ben. We found it, it didn't find us." She placed the two gold Omegas on the table. "Shall we continue?"

"Of course."

"All right." She set the two photos down beside the sigils. "Clearly, Onders and Pine were members of this group"—she tapped the Omegas—"whatever it is."

"But is Ana?" Ben turned the photos around to look at them more closely. "At the very least, she's the link between the two men. But there must be more to it than that."

Evan put the Omegas away. "Isn't that why we're here?"

24

ODESSA, UKRAINE

They came into Odessa in filthy weather. It was that curious time of day between afternoon and evening when nothing looked quite right. Nevertheless, after the hair-raising descent through the worst turbulence Kobalt could recall, it was a relief to be on the ground.

The plane ride from Istanbul had been short; time only for a catnap. Zherov stayed awake, however, staring at Kobalt while she slept, as if he could read her better this way than when she was awake and aware of him.

They took an Uber to Ekaterininskaya Square. It left them off at the entrance to Le Pechêur, The Fisherman, the best hotel in the city, where successful importer-exporters would be expected to stay. She looked at the façade, which was built in the classic Parisian style, and thought that these days no matter what city you were in, you were in the same place you started from. *I could be anywhere,* she thought. *Except for the fact I hate it here.*

Inside, just like at Versailles, enormous chandeliers depended from the high vaulted ceiling, throwing crystals of light across everything: the marble floor, the plush sofas and chairs in perfect sitting arrangements, even the liveried personnel *click-clacking* across the floor. It was not yet high season, so it was easy for Kobalt to have her choice of two-bedroom suites. She asked for a suite that had a view of the Black Sea. They were given key cards and shown the way to the elevator bank by a young liveried man.

The suite was spacious and luxurious, with large bay windows that overlooked the street down to the sea a block away. The water was rough, the color of gunmetal, as if the secrets at the bottom had been churned up. She set down her small weekender and her briefcase.

They took dinner in the bar, an opulent rectangle of perpetual twilight, the lamps in wall sconces turned low. She ordered bourbon and, after a moment's hesitation, Zherov followed suit. They drank through the appetizers and the main courses. She didn't order dessert, but Zherov ate a large square of cherry cake. Afterward, they strolled down to the water. The weather had cleared. They could see lights moving on the now-calm water, tankers and freighters lumbering through the dark.

"What exactly do you expect to find here?" Zherov was leaning, forearms on the top iron railing below which waves lurched and sucked against the seawall. To their right, the beach stretched away, and above it the aqua-colored pools of the major resorts glimmered in the mercury-vapor security lights like a string of blue jewels.

"Omega." Kobalt was staring out across the Black Sea, as if she could look all the way across to Istanbul on the southernmost shore. "I'm going to find out who that woman in the limo was. I'm going to find out if she's the head of Omega, and then I'm going to find out where the headquarters is. These answers will come to me, either through hell or high water. I will get them no matter how many people inside the Omega compound have to die."

The Zherov who had first stepped onto the FSB jet outside Moscow would have been skeptical, would have given her a contemptuous, almost amused, look. But the Zherov who stood beside her tonight, listening to the wash of the water, the screaming of the last gulls heading in for the night, was only impressed.

"You have a plan." He meant it as a question but somehow it didn't come out that way.

"I always have a plan." She said this without any trace of self-aggrandizement. She possessed not one iota of braggadocio, and this impressed him more even than her quiet self-confidence.

She turned her back on the shoreline. "We both need to sleep. We move out at 4 A.M."

Back in the suite, they retired to their respective bedrooms. Zherov kicked off his shoes, unbuttoned his shirt, slid off his trousers, hung his clothes neatly in the closet. They had both changed on the flight over, but he needed a shower. Padding into the bathroom, he turned on the taps while he cleaned his teeth with the toothbrush and paste from the hotel's amenity kit.

After showering, he wrapped himself in the oversize terry cloth robe hanging on the back of the bathroom door. Checking his mobile phone he saw that he had one call-back message. He punched in the number and had a short conversation with his contact on the other end of the line. Mostly, he listened to what the man had to say, then began a shouting match that escalated until Zherov rang off in fury.

He was so angry that, without getting dressed, he padded across the room and passed through the door connecting his bedroom to the living area without giving his state of undress a second thought. She was sitting on the sofa, drinking vodka from a glass, a half-filled bottle of Beluga Gold Line on the glass-topped cocktail table in front of her. The TV was on, but the sound was muted. Not that it mattered since the TV was showing *Metropolis*, Fritz Lang's Expressionist masterpiece. She didn't seem to be paying any attention to the images flickering across the screen, though; she was lost in thought. She was still dressed in the stylish business suit she had changed into on the plane. It was navy shantung silk, a short jacket with standup collar and a pencil skirt. She had pushed her feet out of the black pumps with three-inch heels, sensible but still flattering to her figure.

He stood there watching her, feeling slightly unnerved. But then he always felt unnerved around her—it was only a matter of degree depending on the situation and how acid her tongue.

When she didn't acknowledge his presence in any way, he thought about clearing his throat, but realized that would make him feel like a schoolboy again. He had hated school, had fought with fellow classmates more than he studied, was disciplined almost daily.

Shaking off shadows from the past, he crossed to the sideboard, got himself a glass.

He poured the vodka as he sat down beside her. He took a sip, then said, "When is news not news?"

"When?" She did not look at him or seem in any way surprised he was there. Possibly, she had registered him in the periphery of her vision.

He ran his hand through his still-damp hair. "When there's nothing to tell."

Now, at last, she came out of her semi-trance and looked at him.

"My contacts are all too terrified to go deep enough to find out who's put this deep-cover termination order out on you."

"So . . . someone high up."

"Okay, but you're the department's shiny new toy. No one would—"

"But someone clearly has. It's a bear-eat-bear world we're in. I stepped into it with my eyes wide open and I will continue on with it. But there are lines I will not cross, like fucking Dima, no matter what the consequences."

"And that's something I admire in you, Bobbi."

It was the first time he had called her by her real name— her American name. The gesture touched her. She found the stirring of her emotion utterly surprising.

She regarded him silently for some time. "Anton, we're on the cusp of something more dangerous than I had imagined when I set out. Someone with a great deal of power wants me gone."

He laughed. "You're not trying to frighten me off, are you?"

When she made no reply, he said, going for the simple truth as he saw it, "Often, and now would be one of those times, I feel as if we're communicating from different planets through the vacuum of outer space."

She upended the bottle, refilled both their glasses. "You've made it clear that you don't trust me."

"That was then," Zherov said. "This is now."

After some thought, she nodded. "All right then. I suppose I should come clean. I'm giving you my trust. Understand, this is a very difficult thing for me to do. It always has been, ever since—" She waved away what she might have been about to say, erasing the slate. "The abduction of my children keeps filling my headspace. I don't want it to, but there it is, bright as noontime. In return, I must have your trust. In just a few hours we'll be infiltrating the Omega compound. It could well be that we're walking into a life-or-death situation. If we can't trust each other completely one or both of us are liable to wind up dead."

His eyes engaged hers as they had not before. "I told you about the daughter I've never seen." His tone was earnest. "I want to see her. I want to be a part of her life, so I understand the filling of your headspace as you aptly put it. When I spoke to you about my daughter, you listened. You said you would help me see her. It's important to me you understand that I will be eternally grateful for anything you do on my behalf."

"So." Her hands lay in her lap. "We trust each other?"

He sat back, eyes half-closed. At this hour and without sleep he was actually feeling the liquor racing through his system. "At school I was always getting into trouble—fighting, I loved to fight, especially boys bigger than I was. It was a genuine pleasure to knock the shit out of them. Of course I got disciplined every day, not that I minded so much. It was the head of school calling my father that was the problem." He took another swallow of vodka. "After the third call, my father got fed up. He began what became his nightly routine of physically punishing me—belt, chains, what have you. But always my mother would steal into my room after my father had begun his nightly snore fest. She'd feed me a wedge of cake, the bottom half of which was made up almost entirely of cherries soaked in kirsch. Later, when she deemed me old enough—sixteen or seventeen, in my memory—she substituted a shot of ice-cold vodka."

He finished off the vodka in his glass. "I still bear the scars across my back." She poured him more. "I've never told anyone that. The women I've slept with never once asked. Never. Who knows, maybe they were scared. Anyway . . ." He turned to her. "In a few hours I will be trusting you with my life. Again. So, yes, Bobbi, we trust each other."

The meeting of their glasses echoed through the suite.

25

KÖLN, GERMANY

The Köln Kino was a large birthday cake of a building with thick layers of curlicue cement frosting running across its frontage. The marquee above the entrance danced with colored lights day or night, giving it the aspect of a carnival arch.

The lobby was dim, swathed in fabric the color of oxblood and wooden panels stained a rich mahogany. The carpeting was lush, though worn in the center by the multitudes entering and exiting the theater.

At this time in the afternoon there were only a handful of people scattered around the orchestra and no one at all in the balcony or side loges. The side walls were draped in a curtain-like fabric, the seats were upholstered in the same oxblood color as the lobby.

They came in on the middle of a *Die Hard* festival. Bruce Willis was battering someone while exuding his characteristic smirk. There was a lot of noise. Also blood. An explosion or two couldn't be far behind.

"Who are you supposed to meet?" Ben said over the sound effects.

"His name's Otto Vimpel." Evan scanned the sparse audience. "I'm to sit in the sixth row from the rear, first seat off the far right-side aisle that runs along the side wall."

"Are you absolutely certain you can trust your contact?"

"For the hundredth time . . ."

He responded to the annoyance in her voice. "Go on then." But he longed to know something—anything—about the mysterious contact who had shown her the dossier on her sister. "I'll hang back here in the shadows." He surmised the contact was Russian, FSB or SVR, high-ranking; that made the most sense because they had met outside Russia. But why would Evan trust that kind of Russian? "That way I'll be able to keep an eye on you without being seen."

He watched her walk all the way to the right and down the narrow aisle. As she slid into her appointed seat he scanned each member of the audience again. By their silhouettes, his trained eye marked their gender and approximate age. He counted six middle-aged men, each one sitting alone, two women in their twenties or early thirties, sitting together. A couple of an indeterminate age were seated closest to Evan. The farthest away were a trio of old men, perched like crows on a fence. And that was it. None of these patrons set off any alarm bells.

Arms crossed over his chest, Ben leaned against the rear wall, his gaze quartering the immediate vicinity around Evan every thirty seconds. His mind was filled with Evan; he couldn't help it. Like a fully wound clock, he could not stop. He thought of their hours spent in the fuggy atmosphere of the beer hall. He thought of her face, of the way her lips moved when she spoke, how her eyes could hold him in a vise-like grip. He experienced again the painful thrust of her seething anger. He wanted more than anything for them to find the children, to bring them home safe and sound. For him, finding Ana was merely the next step in rescuing Wendy and Michael. And yet, in the end, like a serpent eating its tail, he inevitably returned to the moment when his iron control, weakened by what he and Evan had been through in the last several days since she had returned from Sumatra, almost betrayed him. When he nearly told her how he felt about her. He had been so appalled that he'd had to excuse himself, take himself somewhere—anywhere—away from the magnetism she exerted on him—her moon to his earth, rising the tides within him as she came closer.

He stiffened, his arms unfolding as a stocky man entered the theater. The man stood for a moment while his eyes adjusted to the darkness on the periphery of the film's glare. Then he stepped to his left, went halfway down, and found a seat.

Ben's muscles relaxed.

On the screen, a skyscraper at night, the top floors lit up. Sirens screaming as if in pain.

A woman entered the theater—blond, buxom, late twenties, early thirties, large eyes, high cheekbones, pointed chin, too much makeup. In a skintight dress beneath an unbuttoned jacket and four-inch heels. He marked her as an escort. She stood very still; only her eyes moved, glittering like opals in the changing light of the projection. She found Ben last or seemed to at least; he had the tingling sense that she had marked him the moment she stepped into the theater.

Ben watched her approach out of the corner of his eye. Her hips swayed provocatively as she passed right by him without even giving him the briefest of looks. He watched her as she went down the right-hand aisle, seated herself in the first seat in the fifth row from the back—directly behind Evan.

Ben stood up straight, even took a step in their direction. Evan had been told her meet was with Otto Vimpel. Had she gotten the name wrong? Was this woman simply a moviegoer who happened to choose the seat right behind Evan? Or was this, indeed, Otto Vimpel?

The woman dressed as an escort flicked open a lighter, put the flame to the end of a cigarette. She blew smoke upward, then bent forward. Was she talking to Evan? It was impossible to tell over the rush of sound from the speakers. A close-up showed a timer ticking down the seconds until detonation.

In the periphery of his vision, Ben noted movement, and he turned his head fractionally to the left in order to bring it into view. The couple looked like they were changing seats, scuttling along, bent low so as not to block anyone's view. They were in the same row as Evan. They had been sitting off to the left. It looked as if they were going to center themselves to the screen, but they kept on coming, past the center section, moving faster now as they approached the area where Evan sat listening to the woman dressed as an escort, who might or might not be Otto Vimpel.

Ben silently cursed Evan's Russian contact as he leapt over the seatback in the last row on a course to intercept the scurrying couple. Then, reaching over Evan's seatback, the woman grabbed Evan, pulled her violently down.

Evan first became aware of the presence behind her as a scent of heather and lime. But apart from her hands she did not move. These she readied, curling them on the tops of her thighs. The key was to keep her upper body relaxed while her inner energy—*ki* Japanese termed it—gathered in her lower belly. If there was to be hand-to-hand or even if she felt a wire rising over her head from behind, she was prepared. She felt no fear, only anticipation. She tried to clear her mind of that, too. No thought. Action.

A metallic click raised the downy hairs on her forearm until the sharp odor of tobacco smoke reassured her. Moments later, the heat of a female in close proximity, as if a missile were aimed at the back of her neck.

Then she felt the breeze on her right ear. The breeze said, "You know me."

It was the beginning of the parole Lyudmila had sent her, the recognition call and response. "We met at Magda's Christmas party," she responded in turn.

"No. It was New Year's," came the husky reply, ending the parole.

Evan turned her head. The woman who was supposed to be Otto Vimpel spoke German with a French accent. She was slim, quite beautiful, with dark, wide-apart eyes and a wide, sensual mouth. She looked to be several years younger than Evan.

"I was expecting Otto."

"I am Ottavia," she said. "My friends call me Otto. Now listen, there's not much time. This woman you seek—"

It was at the precise moment that both Evan and Otto became aware of the scuttling movement to their left. The flash of steel as the knives came out, slender, wicked-looking blades leveled at Evan.

"*Merde!*" Otto husked. "*Pisse! Les con!*" Reaching over Evan's seatback, she grabbed the collar of Evan's coat, dragged her up and then pushed her down to the floor. Then lying flat on the floor of her own row, she stretched out her arm and, with a flick of the lighter, set the flame to the hem of the curtain hanging in front of the side wall.

Ben smelled the smoke first. Then the first flame flickered off to his right, more flames quickly rising, like a field being set on fire by a fleeing army. He was now close enough that the couple became aware of him as he leapt seatbacks like a hurdler. A full charge of adrenaline spurted into his system. He felt only elation at being in the field, being his old fighting self, realizing that he could shake off the last of the man-desk rust.

He was only a row away when the female of the couple

broke off to engage him, while her partner carried on toward Evan. She was smart. She caught him in mid-leap, landing a punch to the point of his chin that rocked him back, entangling him in the seats. Climbing, she came at him with her knife blade bared, ready to spit him like a pig.

The fire Otto had started burst into full flower, flames running up the heavy folds, feeding on the highly flammable fabric. From her position on the floor, all Evan saw was a shadowed figure arcing toward her with the knife extended and murder in his eye.

Otto was trying to drag her into the aisle when the knife slashed down, ripped open the back of her coat. Evan slipped from Otto's grasp. The shadowed figure flipped her over onto her back and lunged at her.

Ben let her get close—frighteningly close—before he drove his knuckles into her throat. The woman reared back, and her wig fell off. It wasn't a woman at all, but a man whose Adam's apple he had bruised. The man started choking, but Ben made the mistake of going for his knife. As he wrapped his fingers around the man's wrist, he saw the blur of a second knife, felt a flash of pain, and then the warm trickle of blood.

Evan had gathered herself. With smoke swirling, leaves of ash flying, and the handful of patrons running for the exit, she slammed the heel of her boot into the man's face. He took the blow, dropped his knife, and grabbed hold of her foot by the heel and ankle, twisting hard. Evan bit her lip as a streak of pain shot up her leg, through her knee, into her hip. His blue eyes bored into her as he prepared to break her leg.

* * *

Ben saw the blue ink tattoos first—the manacle around the wrist, the horrific skull with a demon's bared teeth on the back of his hand—then the dizzying stink of the man's body odor, as if he'd slept in the same clothes for a week. And he thought, *Left triceps, no big deal*, and ignored the pain and the blood. Then he thought, *Jesus, Russian prison.* His scalp began to itch, his heart to pound, and he took a right hook to the jaw—shaken but undeterred, he fought back, using kites, the edges of his hands weapons that would inflect tremendous damage if they found their mark. Trouble was, each of his blows were taken on Manacle's sturdy forearms. It wasn't only the demon's skull that was grinning at him—it was Manacle himself, his long tobacco-stained teeth bared from his pulled-back lips.

Evan breathed as shallowly as possible. Her eyes had begun to tear as the heat from the fire dried them out. Her cheeks felt like they were already on fire. Above her, Otto appeared. Lunging her torso over Evan's supine body, she flicked her cigarette butt into Blue Eyes's face. His hands came up reflexively, releasing Evan's ankle, needing to brush tobacco ash out of his eyes. These precious few seconds were enough for Evan to free herself. She gave him another shot in the throat before Otto finally got a solid grip on her, levered her away.

Pulling Evan into the aisle seemed at first a foolish move, as a whoosh of flames loomed up in front of them. But the flames were a hindrance to Blue Eyes as well. He was only steps behind them when Evan leapt straight up, grabbing handfuls of curtain that had not yet caught fire. Using her whole weight, she pulled it down between them and Blue Eyes. The wall of fire flared up in his path as the new material caught and burst into flame.

No time to look back. They raced to the front of the theater, vaulted up onto the stage, past the edge of the screen, and into the gloom of whatever lay beyond.

So chaotic were the last several minutes that it wasn't until they were halfway up the iron maintenance stairs that she remembered.

Ben! I can't leave him there!

They were almost at the head of the stairs when she turned back.

"What are you doing?" Otto cried. She grabbed Evan's arm. "You can't go back down there! It's death!"

With a violent motion, Evan freed herself, took a step back down. "I've got to find—"

She stopped, paralyzed, as Blue Eyes, clothing blackened by his brush with the falling curtain, rushed up the stairs, a PB semi-automatic pistol with integrated silencer aimed at her heart.

Manacle had Ben in a choke hold. Ben's back was to him. He had one arm across Ben's throat, the other at the back of his head. One swift motion would lay his throat open, blood gushing, consciousness failing. Death. Time seemed to dilate, each second felt like a minute. Ben saw the fire burning along the theater's right-side wall. He saw Evan and the woman who should have been Otto Vimpel scrambling into the aisle, saw the man attacking them stumble after them, saw Evan pull down the curtain, the man entangled as they ran off. Saw him reappear, bat flames from his clothes, smother the fire in order to free himself, then light off after them.

Ben absorbed all this input in the time it takes a heart to complete its double-beat. Then he set about his work. Grasping Manacle's forearm with both hands, he made room for his chin to come forward. At the same time, he stepped back, a maneuver Manacle wasn't expecting. It threw him momentarily off-balance, and in that instant, Ben levered his body forward into a crouch. Manacle came up over the top of him, and his back slammed down onto the hard edge of a seatback. He groaned and rolled over. But if Ben had expected the aikido move to put him down permanently, he was mistaken.

Manacle rose, arched his back with a frightening crack like a tree limb breaking off under a blanket of wet snow. He drew a pistol. Later, Ben would recall that it was a PB semi-automatic pistol with integrated silencer, but for the moment he was solely concentrated on staying alive long enough to finish off this fight.

The 9mm bullet *spanged* off the iron so close to Evan she felt the staircase shudder and cry out. Or that might have been Otto, who was just ahead of her.

"Let's go," she pleaded. And this time Evan listened. Much as she wanted to there was no way she could get through Blue Eyes alive. As she watched Otto clack up onto a catwalk that accessed the loge, she ducked away just as she heard the *phutt!* of another bullet, and then the ringing of the treads behind her as Blue Eyes came on. He was coming fast.

There was a move to disarm a gunman at close quarters that had been taught at the Farm for decades. Ben knew it as muscle memory, but his years in the field had taught him that it didn't work in all circumstances. This was one of them.

The problem was the wrist of the hand holding the gun. The instructors at the Farm taught their acolytes to bend the wrist with a hard blow. Too often that didn't work; the wrist of a trained assassin was like iron; you could hammer it all day and not get it to bend. The alternative technique, which is what Ben used now, was this:

He slammed his hand against the inside of the wrist to move the pistol aside and at the same time grabbed the slide of the gun itself, turning it hard to the left, thus making it possible to wrench it from Manacle's grip. The maneuver was tricky; timing was essential, but so was speed. If you couldn't do it fast enough you were dead. This was not a moment for thought; it was a moment for action.

When Ben had the gun in his hand, he smacked the butt into Manacle's temple. When that didn't stop this human tank, when, with a maniac's bulging eyes, Manacle head-butted him, Ben managed to remain conscious, stay on his feet, and shake the exploding suns out of his vision. He turned the gun around and shot Manacle point-blank between the eyes.

26

ODESSA, UKRAINE

Back in Moscow, when she had seen Anton Zherov climb aboard the plane Dima had arranged for her, Kobalt had to tamp down on the anger she felt at being given a babysitter. He was Dima's man, which annoyed her even more. It was at that moment that she had begun to consider and to plan. If Zherov was to accompany her, it would be so much better if he was her man. Was he susceptible to corruption? Almost everyone was—she only had to take her husband, Paul, as an example. He'd been corrupted by the money funneled to him through Wells's Super PAC. Running it had made him a millionaire many times over. His corruption was just the most intimate of the series of corruptions she was privy to living inside Washington's Beltway. Was there anyone left in DC who wasn't corrupt? The system disgusted her. Worse, Paul's slavish worshiping at the altar of wealth repelled her. He wore made-to-measure suits, shirts and, incredibly, to her, shoes. He had bought a Ferrari, a Rolls, was looking for the right boat for his ever-rising status. He had begun talking of selling the house, moving to a larger one in a tonier area. When she thought of

Paul there was only rage, a stone in her heart at the sacrifice she had made for Russia. As for her children, since coming over she had convinced herself that they didn't exist, or if they did sneak into her thoughts or dreams every once in a while, they were hazed and indistinct, as if she were looking at someone else's kids.

It was not such a difficult thing to do. Her heart had been turned to ash by the knowledge that the couple who had called themselves her and Evan's mother and father were no such thing. They, too, had been corrupted—with money, money they needed desperately when their tin mine collapsed and lawsuits came flying out of the rubble like vampire bats. All the lawsuits magically vanished, the mine was rebuilt, stronger and with the most modern equipment, just for taking on the burden of raising two children.

And what of our real mother and father? This was a question that tore at her insides. They were Russian by birth; they were sleeper agents. *They left us in America while they returned to the Motherland. They abandoned us, threw us away. They didn't want us. Maybe, like me, they were only doing their duty to the Motherland.* She should have hated them too, this nameless couple who had birthed them only to hand them over to true Americans. But the opposite had happened. The moment she had read the letter hidden away at the bottom of her father's closet, when she was not yet ten years old, she felt free—no, not exactly free, but herself. Her real self. For the first time. She felt the thick heavy Russian blood running through her veins, and yet she felt light, as if a great weight had been lifted off her. Before, she'd look at herself in a full-length mirror and wonder why her posture was so bad, why her back was hunched, her shoulders up around her ears, as if expecting a blow from some invisible person. From that moment on, she was able to stand up straight.

And then, starting when she was eleven, the texts began—

unsigned—short but cogent, and she knew they were from a Russian source—or maybe sources, she couldn't tell. She hoped they were from a variety of sources because then she would have a family—a real family—for already she had pulled away from her sister, seeing nothing of a compatible nature in her. The culmination of these contacts came when she was four months from her seventeenth birthday: a face-to-face rendezvous, at last! In Copenhagen. Evan had already planned the trip to Sumatra. She was forced to beg her older sister to tack on several days in the capital of Denmark. She hated doing that, but she had kept her mind on the outcome, on the in-the-flesh meeting. She was so excited she could hardly stand it. Of course, Evan misinterpreted her enthusiasm as being for Sumatra, which suited her just fine.

Brushing away the past like so many strands of a spiderweb, she turned her mind to more recent events. To Zherov. To making sure he was her man. Money, power, ideology, sex, or if you will, blackmail—these were the traditional coins used to turn an enemy agent.

There had to be a better way to recruit someone, she thought, than using blackmail, intimidation, or money. Blackmail bought you fear, fear caused hesitation in your recruit; hesitation in the field is what got someone killed. Intimidation bought you resentment, which made your recruit vulnerable to being turned. And money—well, money bought you nothing at all. There was always an opposition agent willing to pay your recruit more.

Nevertheless, blackmail, intimidation, and money were the currencies Dima used to bind his field agents to him. Dima was old-school. That didn't mean he wasn't dangerous; the opposite, in fact, was true. What it did mean, however, was that he had vulnerabilities one could take advantage of, if you were both bold and clever. Kobalt had devised a better method, a way to bind Zherov's loyalty to her until death did them part.

These were Kobalt's thoughts as she and Zherov made their way toward the Omega compound at 4:20 in the morning.

The compound inhabited an area of the city more run-down than most and far away from the ritzy—or what passed for ritzy in Odessa—strip bordering the Black Sea. This was to be expected. In July and August that seafront strip would be buzzing with Muscovites and tourists from as far as away as Tallinn. But now it had minimal traffic, which meant that the area where the compound crouched like a cur in a cardboard box had virtually no traffic at all. This necessitated that Kobalt and Zherov arrive on foot, furtively and silently as foxes. They followed the geometric pattern the blue shadows threw along the narrow sidewalks.

Before leaving their suite, Kobalt had unlocked her briefcase and chosen the weapons she wanted, stowing them away in the numerous pockets of her suit jacket. By this time, it was clear to Zherov that she had her wardrobe custom made to her exacting specifications. It amused him to imagine the SVR support and document directorate having a field day working on such iconoclastic clothing.

The compound itself was walled off and distanced from its neighbors on all sides by a perimeter layer of unused and dilapidated warehouses, bought up at rock-bottom prices by Omega. No one else had any use for them.

Access to the compound was through the warehouse on the eastern front. A door of a size to admit one person at a time was inset into a much larger door, this one big enough to accommodate a tractor-trailer or a couple of buses side by side. The lock on the smaller door wasn't strong enough to give Kobalt much of a pause. Inside, they found the cavernous space completely empty. Dark streaks of dried oil stained the unsealed concrete floor. At the far end, a narrow staircase led up to a small office with windows to overlook the main floor. A light shone through one of the windows.

She signaled to Zherov, but he had already snapped the Scorpion's stock in place and had it at the ready. Pistol out, he moved across the floor. Halfway across, Zherov, according to plan, hung back to cover her while she light-footed it the rest of the way, ascended the staircase, and opened the door to the office. She waited a full thirty seconds before she ventured inside.

A desk, an old wooden chair, three steel-cased filing cabinets with their drawers open and empty were all that the office held. No sign of a human or even of human habitation. She signaled an all clear to Zherov as she stepped out and came back down to the warehouse floor.

"There's something I don't understand," Zherov whispered. "Along with the report of your debriefing I also read your recommendation of sending a Zaslon team in to terminate the residents. But it never was acted upon."

Kobalt grunted. "Dima dismissed the recommendation. He told me that the current environment, with talk of a Russian takeover of Ukraine, made a raid on Ukrainian soil out of the question."

They moved on, slowly and silently.

Where is everyone? Zherov mouthed.

She shrugged, but her furrowed brow conveyed more than words could have.

She led him to the exit along the right-hand wall, and via a wooden loading dock they entered the compound proper. Again, there was not a soul in sight.

"Okay," he said in a more normal voice, "this can't be right."

"And yet it is." At a fast jog, she led him across the open space and into the compound's main building—the place she had not been allowed to enter when she was here the first time. From what they could immediately see of the two large main spaces, this building, like the warehouse, had also been cleared out, stripped of every last vestige of Omega, including logs, records, dossiers—anything at all pertaining to the group.

"They're gone," he said, stating the obvious. He turned around to see Kobalt squatting beside a number of dark smears not unlike the old oil stains they'd found in the warehouse. She had switched on her flashlight app, was running the beam this way and that over them.

Zherov joined her on his haunches. "Found something?"

"This isn't oil, old or otherwise," she said. "It's blood."

"They didn't go quietly?"

"Or there was a purge, brought on perhaps by a schism within Omega."

He looked around. "If that's the case, where are the bodies?"

She stood up and he with her. "They could have taken them with them."

"Dissidents?" Zherov shrugged. "I wouldn't bother."

Kobalt nodded. "Neither would I."

Because she had never been inside the main building, she had no idea of its interior layout. They began to explore. Beyond the two larger main spaces was a warren of rooms, clearly used for sleeping, meetings, or storage. They were all empty. At the end of a hallway was a door down to what appeared to be a basement. The two of them gave each other a significant glance, then started down. The steps were concrete, crumbling at the edges. As Kobalt's flash played over them, the dark stains became more pronounced.

It became colder and colder—the damp was deep, seeping into their bones through their clothes. It was a long way down to the basement floor. They did not, however, need to descend all the way. Three-quarters of the way down, the beam of light picked out dazzling reflections that at first blinded them. They moved much more cautiously down the steps until they could see a pane of thick glass from floor to ceiling, stretching to either wall. It was sealed at every edge. Behind the glass they saw corpses, over a dozen of them, sprawled grotesquely, as if, standing just where they were now, the perpetrators had somehow killed the people without giving them a second thought.

"Most of them have been shot," Zherov said, "but not all of them."

He was right, and now a dreadful chill invaded Kobalt's body. As Zherov began to move downward, she grabbed his arm.

"Don't," she said. "Don't take a step nearer."

"What?" He turned to stare at her. "Why not? We've got to find out how they were killed."

"Look closer, Anton. They're on medical tables. Their reproductive organs have been removed. In other cases—there, one or two—strange-looking organs have been sutured in.

"When I was here before, the services invariably focused on the Book of Genesis, and most specifically on the figure of Noah, and God's pact with him. It seems more than likely that Omega's ultimate mission is to create a new world—the Paradise on earth God promised him after the flood." She tilted her head toward the wall of glass. "If that's the case, we can intuit from this that they mean to do it in much the same way as the Nazi doctors tried."

"They're insane. I mean certifiable," Zherov said. "That's the reality we're facing."

They retreated back up the stairs. When they reached the hallway, they smelled food cooking. A door to the left of the one they had just emerged from opened onto a short corridor.

Kobalt pointed toward it. "I guess the kitchens, and probably beyond that the mess hall."

Zherov nodded, moved ahead of her, Scorpion at the ready.

They found her in front of a wood-fired stove, stirring a pot set on one of the rings. Kobalt came up to Zherov, pushed the Scorpion down to his side.

"Marta?"

The woman turned as Kobalt came into view. "Alina Kravets. But I doubt that's your real name." A smile, swiftly fading. "After what I heard about you, I never thought I'd see you again." When she caught sight of Zherov, she laughed. "Is this your backup? Doesn't matter, you're too late." She shook her head. "Omega is gone. It's a new, far more militant cadre than anything you knew when you were here."

"Why are you still here?"

There were dark circles under Marta's eyes and in them a haunted look. "Where should I go?" She shook her head, and Kobalt could see the dark bruises on her neck. "I have nowhere else." She turned back to her stirring.

"How did you stay alive?"

She stretched up her neck, exposing the full extent of the bruising. "I killed one of them. Then I hid in the woodpile, curled up, quiet as a fetus. No one found me. She had important work to perform, which she did. Then they left. I could hear the roar of the trucks from where I was hiding. I waited a long time after that, to make sure they were all gone and not coming back." She made a face of extreme distaste. "I made the mistake of looking at the remains after they left."

She shuddered. "The stuff of nightmares."

Zherov had backed up. He was standing in the doorway to the short corridor, Scorpion cradled in the crook of his left arm, a loyal sentinel.

The kitchen table was no more than a cutting board held at waist height by four rough-hewn wooden legs. They sat on rickety wooden stools that seemed at any moment ready to come apart. Marta poured them tea she had brewed. It was Russian Caravan, stale, black, and bitter as sin. Taking his cue from Kobalt's expression, Zherov did not leave his post to fetch his glass.

"You said 'she,' Marta. That she had important work to do.

Do you mean the woman who came with her entourage the day I fled? Can you tell me anything about her?"

Marta's hands closed around her glass. "Did you see her? Did you see Ana?"

"Just a glimpse," Kobalt said. *Ana*, she thought.

"Strange woman." Marta took a sip of the tea without wincing. "All she did was pass by me at a moderate distance, but the impression she made on me is stamped into my memory, especially because she was no more than twenty-seven, maybe twenty-eight, breathtakingly young to have such ultimate power." She paused a moment, as if arranging her thoughts, then went on. "She brought some people with her—scientists or butchers—depending on your point of view. They stayed ten days. You saw for yourselves the obscene horror they left behind."

Kobalt waited for the other woman to go on. She considered taking another sip of the hot, caustic tea, then thought better of it. After a moment, she urged Marta to continue. "Marta. How was this woman, this Ana, strange?"

Marta gave a grunt. "Easier to say how wasn't she strange. She was tall, I remember that vividly. And she spoke with a deep voice—almost a man's voice. And it had a commanding tone, a kind of—I don't know—a bewitching note. It was enticing, captivating. And I'll tell you that the upper echelon that coalesced around her that day were certainly captives— *her* captives. I got the distinct impression they would do what she wanted when she wanted them to do it."

Kobalt vividly recalled Ana's gait—not a woman's walk nor a man's stride. It was something else altogether, something she had never seen before. "She sounds formidable."

Kobalt pushed her glass away. "Marta, do you know where Omega went?"

She shook her head. "But somewhere far away. Maybe Romania somewhere in the Carpathians? I seem to recall something to that effect. But my mind is a little muzzy."

Kobalt leaned forward, careful not to upset the table. "Do you know where in the Carpathians?"

Marta shook her head. "If I did know, Ana would have hunted me down. I wouldn't be alive now."

27

KÖLN, GERMANY

Evan wasted no more time watching Otto scrambling up the iron stairs and onto a narrow iron catwalk that led to another one higher up. The woman had taken off her shoes, the better to run. Evan now held one of them in her hand. She waited, muscles tense, trying to clear her mind of everything except what she had to do. She had had only seconds to think about it, but the simple fact was clear: she wasn't going to leave Ben. It was unthinkable. She'd never be able to live with herself again. She thought about Ben now, but every time she did so, her mind went back to the night they had spent making love while the German rain beat down against the roof of the building in which they had holed up. She remembered every single detail: her animal cries, his hands sweeping along her skin, his mouth on hers, her mouth on him, her legs drawing up, gripping his hips. And then, afterward, the dripping of the faucet in the kitchen, the squeak of a mouse, the tiny insect sounds outside as the rain subsided. The utter peace of lying in his arms. The rest of the world had fallen away. It might have existed outside their bolt-hole, but at that moment she wasn't even sure of that. They might have slept, or not. Try as she might she could never remember. Then dawn had slid in through the rotted blinds, and with it a new smell . . .

The rank smell of Blue Eyes struck Evan like a wall. She was hidden at the top of the stairs. She was ready. He reached the top of the staircase, all his senses alert. It was the PB she saw first, the ugly snout of the silencer, a weasel scenting its prey. Now! She swung around, oriented herself to him, and drove the stiletto heel of Otto's shoe through his left eye, through the jelly of the vitreous humor. He took a reflexive step back, and she saw that he had taken off his half-burned clothes. Bare to the waist, she could see the Russian prison tattoos. With bared teeth and rage fueling her, she jammed the heel in farther, past the ocular orbit. How deep it went, she never did discover. With a violent shove, she sent him plummeting down the stairs.

It was only when his head smacked into the bottom like a sack of wet cement that she saw Ben standing there, peering up at her.

There was a large and unsightly hole in the back of Manacle's head, like a pink and red mushroom flowering out, leaving its mass over three seats. Ben stepped over the mess, ran down the right-side aisle, leapt over the charcoaled curtain, wisps of smoke still rising from it as if it were a gigantic cake just pulled from the oven. He sprinted to the front of the theater, following the path Evan had taken. His mind was solely on her. Yet his trained eyes noted there was not another soul in sight. What other patrons had been in attendance had fled. He knew it wouldn't be long before the authorities drew up in front of the theater. They had to be gone before that happened, and leaving through the front entrance was out of the question.

He saw the tattoos on the man with the high heel through his eye before he looked up to see Evan standing at the top.

Eight-pointed stars on each shoulder, signifying he was a commander, a knife going through the top of his torso, signifying he had been an assassin for hire in prison. He had continued his profession upon release.

Vaulting over the murderer, he rushed up the stairs. They embraced, but it was an awkward gesture, as if both of them were pulling away at the same time they came together. Awkward and brief. Once safely at arm's length, they studied each other, checking for injuries, not the least of which was the egg-shaped swelling on his forehead from Manacle's head-butt. Ben won that one, if winning was the right term.

As she led him up to the second catwalk, through a metal door and into a narrow maintenance passageway, through another metal door that led out to the loge where, she hoped, Otto was waiting, Ben said, "Both our attackers were Russians, ex-cons for hire. Does that ring a bell?"

Evan searched through the memory files in her mind but could come up with nothing. When she shook her head, he said, "I'd like to remind you that your contact, who set up this meet with Otto Vimpel . . ."

"Her name's Ottavia."

"Okay, but back to your original contact: Russian, FSB or SVR. Am I correct?"

"Ex-SVR," Evan admitted. And because she knew where this was going, "Also ex-Politburo."

"Lovely." Ben rolled his eyes. "And you don't think your contact set us up?"

She was about to answer when from below came a hellish commotion.

"The authorities have arrived," Ben said. "We've got to get out of here. Where's Ottavia?"

Evan pointed. "This way." They passed through the loge and climbed the inner staircase up to the balcony. Voices echoed, shouts were raised as the bloody burned mayhem in the orchestra was discovered. The police would have no idea what happened or why, but it wouldn't take them long to find the armed Russian with the prison tattoos and the stiletto heel through his eye and come up the staircase hunting for the perpetrators.

They found Otto up in the last row. She had her remaining shoe in her hand, heel outward. A look of profound relief flooded her face when she saw Evan.

"You put my other shoe to good use," she said in her French-accented German.

Evan nodded. "They're both dead."

"Both Russian ex-cons," Ben said. "Murderers."

Otto lifted her chin. "And who is this specimen?"

"My partner. Ben."

Otto's expression turned wary, her eyes dark and haunted. "I was told the meet would be with just you." She turned to go.

"Wait," Evan said. "The authorities have entered the theater. We need an escape route."

Otto turned back. "What happened to the other one?" She was looking at Evan, but when Ben raised the silenced PB, her eyes opened wide.

"I shot him in the head," Ben said matter-of-factly.

"Dead?" Otto asked.

"As a poisoned rat."

That made her smile. She tossed her head. "Okay. Follow me."

This theater was clearly part of her bailiwick. She led them up past the projection booth, out onto the roof. Evening had descended with the usual Germanic heaviness, as if it were orchestrated by Wagner. They could hear the sirens clearly now, see the revolving blue-and-white lights from the police cars, the ambulances, and the fire trucks. The clatter drowned out the chatter from the crowd that had amassed across the street, the closest the cops would allow them to the crime scene.

The building itself was quite large, and Otto led them to the rear, where the low parapet overlooked the roof of a smaller building. The walls abutted, so there was no space in between the buildings. They clambered over the parapet, dropped down onto the lower rooftop, and found a protected spot to hunker down. Otto stepped away for a moment to throw her remaining shoe down an airshaft, before returning to them.

"The Russian I shot had a manacle tat around his right wrist, signifying a prison sentence of more than five years," Ben began. "He had a demon's skull on the back of his hand, signifying defiance against Russian law. My guess is he managed to escape and took his commander with him."

"The question," Otto said, "is who were they working for?"

Ben gave Evan a hard look. "Not your contact, huh?"

"Lyudmila?" Otto gave a curt laugh. "Don't be absurd."

And then it all clicked in Ben's mind: Evan's contact was ex-SVR, ex-Politburo, and her given name was Lyudmila. He had to work hard to keep his jaw from dropping open. "Lyudmila Shokova? Evan, your contact is Lyudmila Alexeyevna Shokova?"

Even in the semidarkness of the rooftop, he could see Evan's cheeks coloring in the blinking lights of restaurant signs and other brightly lit marquees.

"Wasn't Shokova purged from the Politburo a year, year and a half ago?"

Evan nodded.

"So why isn't she dead? Defenestrated, killed by hit-and-run, poisoned at their favorite restaurant, or arrested on some bogus charges. That's what happens to the purged in Russia."

"She fled," Evan said.

"She's exceptionally clever," Otto added, like an exclamation mark.

Ben shook his head. "She was also FSB. Aren't they trying to find her?"

"They're certain she's dead. Died in a flaming wreck after speeding around a hairpin turn in the Moscow hills." Otto was studying her nails. "I helped arrange that moving tableau." She picked her head up. "It was very convincing, down to the smallest detail."

Ben turned to Evan. "Did you know all this?"

She shrugged.

Ben's gaze swept over both of them. "Why was she purged?"

"She's a woman," Evan said.

Otto spread her long-fingered hands. "It's Russia. Who can understand anything?"

Neither of those was the answer he was looking for, but it seemed it was all the answer he was going to get. He shifted uncomfortably. His head hurt where Manacle had butted him. Now he knew something of what Evan felt. The commotion on the street had not abated. He glanced over to the roof of the theater. "Are we safe up here?"

Otto nodded. "Perfectly. The police won't come up to the theater's roof. The detectives are a lazy bunch and once they see the tats there'll be no reason for them to follow up, unless they want to bring the matter to the Federal Foreign Office. But again that involves paperwork so . . ." She shrugged her shapely shoulders.

Evan scrolled through her mobile until she found the photos of Wendy and Michael. "Have you seen either of these children? They're my niece and nephew. They were abducted from their home in DC three days ago. Their father was murdered."

"I haven't," Otto said. "But I've seen the photos. Lyudmila sent them to me. She distributed them to everyone in her network. She's trying hard to find them."

Evan glanced at Ben, but he seemed to be scarcely paying attention. She kicked him with the heel of her boot. He glared at her, folded his arms across his chest.

Best to ignore him, she thought, as she brought out the two photos to show Otto, turning on her flashlight app. "Do you know this woman? Her name is Ana."

"Without a family name . . . But hold on now . . ." Otto frowned, took the photo of Ana and Onders in the countryside somewhere outside of Köln, looked at it more closely. "I know this place. Yes, this photo was taken in the Bergisch Gladbach countryside. It's only about an hour's drive northeast."

"That photo is dated about two years ago," Evan said. "The other is undated."

"Hmm." Otto tapped the image of the hazy building in the background. "That's the Schneller Psychiatric Clinic. I myself have never been inside. It's rather famous for its experimental treatments on psychiatric patients. I've heard they are often quite successful." She looked up at them. "Perhaps the woman in the photo was a patient there—or if you're in luck she still is."

Ben massaged his temples. "That's where we need to go next."

"Ask for Dr. Reveshvili, he runs the clinic," Otto said. "He ought to be able to locate this Ana you're looking for. Either she's still at the clinic or she's been sent home."

"How well do you know him?"

"Just by reputation, which is excellent."

Over Ben's covert objection, Evan held out one of the disk-like black cases in her palm, opened it to show Otto the gold Omega. "This mean anything to you?"

Otto shook her head. "It's the Greek letter omega, but I'm guessing you already know that."

Evan raised her eyebrows. "So, nothing else?"

"Sorry, no." She looked at them quizzically. "Look, night is falling, it's getting dark and I'm getting cold. And I suspect we could all use some fuel." She pointed. "There's a fire escape at the back of this building. I know a snug place to get some food and put our heads together regarding tomorrow's foray out to the clinic."

When they didn't move, she looked at Ben. "You don't like me."

"I don't trust you."

"Lyudmila sent me to help you."

"I for sure don't trust Lyudmila Shokova."

"Guilt by association from an American," she said, rising. "As a German born in Alsace that's no surprise." Her mouth gave a little quirk. "A German with a Russian friend, that's irony for you, right?" She turned up the collar of her jacket. "As I said, I'm in need of some good Russian vodka and a comforting Alsatian dinner to fill my stomach." She indicated the far side of the roof. "You can either accompany me or go your own way."

She started off and, rising, Evan followed. "Do as you wish, Ben. Just don't take your time deciding."

28

MICHAEL

I wake up into darkness. Or maybe I'm not awake at all. There is no sound: no trilling of the songbirds that nest in our backyard, no buzzing of spring flies, no sound of wind in the willows—if we even have willows, which now that I think about it, we actually don't. But even though I'm already nine years old, my favorite book is still *Wind in the Willows*. I've lain in bed at night so many times rereading chapter after chapter, and then, finally switching the light off when my father—Paul, he says in his sternest voice—yells at me to go to bed, I don't sleep right away, I stay awake in the dark and imagine myself in the riverbank world of Moley, Badger, Toad, and Rat—who, I discovered in Wikipedia, is really a European water vole, which so far as I am concerned, is a whole lot better than a rat. I don't much like rats, or moths, or, worst of all, hairy millipedes, which give me nightmares. But I do like badgers—I like them very much.

In this darkness of nothing-at-all, I call out to Wendy. She hears me because a moment later her hand finds mine and holds it tightly.

"Wendy, where are we?" I whisper because the darkness of nothing-at-all seems made for whispers.

"Somewhere," she whispers back.

"Not home?"

"No, Mikey. Not home."

Stupidly, I begin to cry.

"Oh, don't do that, Mikey." She squeezes my hand. "It will turn out right."

It was Aunt Evan who first called me Mikey, and now Wendy knows it. I don't mind. Especially now. I'm surprised, but I'm not angry that she shares my secret with Aunt Evan. I like hearing my sister call me "Mikey." I love Wendy, and I stop crying because she has also said "It will turn out right," which is the song by someone called De-Phazz that she listens to at night. When I hear it coming from her room, it always calms me. But I do wish Aunt Evan was here. I feel safe with her.

I love Aunt Evan. She always spends time with me, which is more than I can say for Paul. He pays no attention to me whatsoever. He's too busy, he says. But I don't understand what that means. And Mama . . . for a time I was just so angry at her for leaving us with Paul, who isn't really a father at all. But then one day Aunt Evan caught me crying and when I told her how I felt she said that was normal, that she had been angry too, and I didn't feel so alone. Then she said something that I hold on to. She said that Mama's leaving wasn't her fault, it was no one's fault, and anyway, what good would it do holding on to the anger. She's right, I know she is, but there's something missing, a hole inside me I don't know how to fix. *Time*, Aunt Evan said, *holes take time to fill in*. The first time Wendy and I looked at snapshots of Mama, I said, "She doesn't look like I remember. Does she look like you remember?" and I thought Wendy was going to say something, but she didn't. She sat silent as the owl that visits our backyard now and again just after twilight disappears. I tried to look at where she was staring but I couldn't see anything, and I was too scared to ask her what caught her attention.

It seems to me sometimes that the owl is waiting for me to come out of the house. Then its head swivels and it stares at me as if bringing wisdom from far away, as owls do. The kids my age that I know would name the owl Hedwig, after Harry Potter's snowy owl, but not me. In the first place, my owl isn't a snowy owl, something anyone who has studied owls like I have would know in about a second. In the second place, I think Hedwig is a stupid, stupid name. I have named my owl Omega, which might sound like a weird name for an owl, except there is this wonderful owl named Omega in Winnie-the-Pooh's Hundred Acre Wood, a story Aunt Evan reads to me every time she comes and that she even got Wendy to read to me, when her head's not buried in her Peter Pan books.

Aunt Evan once told me that there's a space inside her where nothing lives, a space where Mama used to be. She said, *I know you can't understand that, Mikey*, but I did. I understood it completely, but I've never known how to tell her, I get all tongue-tied when I try, it's like trying to tell her I understood what breathing is. I don't have the words, but I'm sure she can see what I'm feeling in my eyes. I have the same space inside me where nothing is, a space reserved for Mama that was never filled. And the reason I'm sure Aunt Evan knows is because she tells me all about her own time with Mama, how they grew up together, played tricks on each other, how they argued and made up. *Just like you and Wendy*, she says, but her eyes are clouded, and she seems to me troubled, though I can't make out why. But I've learned many things about Mama from Aunt Evan, which makes me love her even more. Sometimes I think of Aunt Evan moving into the empty space inside me so it's filled, and she will put an end to the ache I feel all the time. I love best the stories of how mischievous Mama was, how she was drawn to forbidden things, like her father's liquor or her mother's cigarettes. Hearing about Mama being bad makes me shiver like the scary movies Wendy likes so much. I would never dare taste liquor or puff on a cigarette, but I'm secretly thrilled that Mama once did.

Once. Mama is gone now. Mama is dead. I still don't understand death. But then I can't quite grasp life, either. Or time. When Wendy says something about next year, I have no idea what she means. I know about next week, which often makes me groan aloud because it takes ages and ages to come about.

I wish Mama would come back, but Wendy tells me there is no coming back from being dead. *Why not?* I ask her. Dad comes back from all his trips. All of them. Wendy says, *It's not the same, Mikey*, but she can't explain why.

But Aunt Evan does. She tells me there is one place—and one place only—you can't come back from, not even next week. When I ask her why, she tells me: *because if you're in that place, it means your time here in this place is over. And when your time here is over, you must cross over a bridge—the bridge to forever—to that other place. The bridge is one-way only; once you cross over you don't come back.*

"I still don't understand," I say to her. If I said this to Wendy, she would make me feel stupid, but not Aunt Evan. She never makes me feel stupid, she never talks down to me like Wendy sometimes does because she still thinks of me as a child, even though I'm only two years younger than she is.

Aunt Evan is ever so clever, and she tells me, "Remember when I took you and Wendy downtown, and I showed you there was no J Street?" When I nod, she smiles. "Okay, then, but somewhere there is a J Street, we just can't see it."

"Is J Street across the bridge?" I ask her. "The bridge to forever?"

She laughs and claps her hands. "How clever you are!" I'm

bursting inside, I want to be clever like Aunt Evan. "That's just where your mama is. She has crossed."

"She's walking on J Street," I say, trying to imagine it, and failing. "I hope she likes it."

Aunt Evan tousles my hair. "I'm sure she does, Mikey. I'm sure she likes it a lot."

Now, in the darkness of nothing-at-all, I turn to my sister and whisper, "Are we on J Street?"

"What?"

"Maybe we'll see Mama."

At that moment, a door opens. Blinding white light destroys the darkness of nothing-at-all, and a voice hurts my ears.

Wendy says, "That's not Mama's voice."

We have not crossed over the bridge. We are not on J Street.

29

ODESSA, UKRAINE

The opalescent dawn contrasted harmoniously with the dull gray of the buildings. As usual, their hotel stood out—a peacock in a land of pigeons. As soon as they stepped inside, the night manager, about to go off duty, handed Kobalt a slip of folded paper, bid her good morning and stepped outside, disappearing into the tender light. She opened the paper, read the handwritten note. Her head snapped up. She ordered Zherov to take the weaponry back up to their suite.

"Where will you be?"

She gestured to the bar. "I need to do this alone."

He hesitated a moment.

"It's okay," she reassured him. "I'll be fine."

He nodded, then walked away.

She waited until he stepped into the elevator and the doors closed before she made her way to the bar. Only in Odessa would a hotel bar be open at the crack of dawn. Possibly it never closed.

For a long moment, she stood on the threshold, taking the temperature of the room. It was nearly deserted, just the bartender, a disconsolate businessman in a disgracefully rumpled suit, taking vodka shots one after the other without so much as a pause to take a breath, and the woman at a semicircular banquette off to the right. She was seated so that she had a full view of the entrance, so she must have seen Kobalt, and yet she made no sign of recognition. Her ice-blue eyes passed over Kobalt's face as if she were a part of the bar's décor. Her blond hair was pulled back from her sharp-featured face. Her nose was too long, her mouth too wide, her chin too prominent, and yet when taken all together, through some mysterious alchemical means, she was gorgeous in a manner most women only dreamed about as they leafed through *Vogue* or *Vanity Fair*.

Since ignoring people seemed the order of the morning, Kobalt crossed to the bar. The businessman smelled of metal and canned air and sweat, the way you do after a twenty-four-hour flight. The bartender, a barrel-chested man who might have been police or military in his former life, studied every inch of her from the top of her head to the toes of her boots, after which he greeted her in a surprisingly soft voice.

She looked over the bartop. "What are you mixing there?"

He had a shaved head and a face like an extremely intelligent bear. "I'm trying out a new type of Negroni." A toss of his head indicated the businessman. He winked. "For all the sophisticates."

"Too early for a Negroni."

"Why, yes, it is." He put a filled shot glass on the bar along with an ice-cold bottle of Mamont Siberian vodka. The bottle was shaped like the curved tusk of a Yukagir mammoth. He indicated with his chin. "Courtesy of Madame."

Kobalt sat at the bar, two stools away from the wrecked businessman, but soon moved farther away. The bartender tasted the Negroni, found it wanting, and threw it out. He drifted closer to her just as she threw the shot he'd poured for her down her throat.

"Don't you want to see Madame?"

Kobalt looked him in the eye. He had an honest face, odd for an ex-whatever he'd been. Maybe that was his new hobby. "I'm working up the nerve."

He gave her a knowing smile.

She cocked her head. "You know her?"

"I work for her. Have for a long time."

"Even when you were in law enforcement?"

He laughed softly. "There is no law enforcement here." He winked. "She and I go way back." He kept polishing the bartop. He was about to turn away when he added, "If you know her at all you know she doesn't like to be kept waiting."

"Which is why I'm here talking with you."

"Ah, a strategy." He gave her a sardonic look. "Good luck with that." He moved away to gather up the shot glasses in front of the drunk businessman.

Time passed with the slowness of a clock running down. Kobalt could feel her heart beating through the sludge-like unreality of the moment. Her heart had risen into her throat, threatening to make her gag.

She realized she'd finished her third vodka. When she could no longer prolong the inevitable, she took her glass and the bottle by its long neck and crossed the room, slid into the banquette close enough to feel the other woman's heat. Her signature scent of lime, cinnamon, and musk was exotic and at the same time familiar.

She filled both their glasses, using every ounce of concentration to keep her hand steady.

"For a dead person you're looking mighty fine." It was disconcerting to Kobalt to hear how rough and yet reedy her voice had become.

"I suppose that's one way to say hello." Lyudmila Alexeyevna Shokova took her time in responding.

"Another way would be, What the hell are you doing showing your face in public?"

The bartender arrived with a tray which held two coffees, a creamer, a container of sugar cubes, a pitcher of whole milk, two white china bowls, two spoons, and two individual boxes of Kellogg's Special K cereal. Without saying a word the bartender set everything on the table and then returned to his place behind the bar, where he unfolded a newspaper and began to read.

"Special K." Lyudmila tore open the top of one of the boxes. "My favorite breakfast." She spilled the cereal into one of the bowls. She pointed to the other box. "And you?"

"I prefer to drink my breakfast." Kobalt's stomach was in knots.

"Spoken like a true Russian." Lyudmila ripped open the second box, spilled that, too, into her bowl. She added milk, took a spoonful into her mouth, chewed, and swallowed.

"To answer your question, I'm not out in public. Zoltan is in charge of this room." The slight incline of her head indicated the bartender. "I'm safe here." She took another spoonful of Special K. "Safer than you, anyway."

Kobalt's brows knit together. "What the hell does that mean?"

The drunk businessman chose that moment to topple off his stool, puddle on the burgundy-and-teal carpet. Zoltan continued reading his newspaper. When the businessman began to snore, Zoltan made a call, possibly because he didn't want the noise to disturb Madame. Moments later, a pair of burly men sporting the colors of the hotel entered the bar, picked the businessman up, and dragged him away.

Lyudmila took a sip of her coffee, set the cup down. She'd added no milk or sugar. "People are after your ass, Kobalt. Exceedingly serious people."

"And you know this how? You've been out of the FSB loop for over a year."

Lyudmila laughed her low, sultry laugh. "Zoltan told me."

Kobalt was through with feeling her heart in her throat. "No wonder." She'd rather have a knife in her side. "I have no doubt you've been fucking Zoltan, just like you've fucked every male superior on your way up the FSB ladder—all the way to the Politburo."

Lyudmila's expression was proof she hadn't taken offense, at least on the outside. "In Russia, this is the only way to get anyone to pay attention to you. That is why you see only beautiful women in positions of power. I pity the ugly female; all she gets are scraps from the table—and a lowly table it is, at that." Her lips twitched ever so slightly. "Of course, you being American would find this state of affairs deeply upsetting."

"I'm not American. I'm Russian." She found herself smiling with her jaw clamped firmly shut. "You said I drink like a Russian."

"Or perhaps an American in Russian clothing."

Kobalt was instantly on her guard. "What the hell does that mean?"

Lyudmila chose to dismiss her comment. "It's only a matter of time for you, Kobalt. If you want to remain a vital part of Dima's directorate, you'll have to bed him."

"You're not the first person to tell me that."

Lyudmila took another sip of coffee. "It's not a pleasant experience, believe me. He is a man of, shall we say, unsavory tastes when it comes to his sexual proclivities. Consider yourself warned."

"I've already taken steps to counter that."

This appeared to surprise Lyudmila. "Is that so." She put her elbows on the table. "I would so like to hear about it."

Sure, Kobalt thought. *Any minute now.*

She felt dislocated in time, another surge of the unreality she experienced at the bar. The present dissolved into the past . . .

Three and a half years ago, she lands in Moscow at a military airfield ringed by high fences topped with coils of razor wire, after spending one disorienting day in Istanbul, mostly in a second-floor FSB safe house inside the Grand Bazaar, with one brief accompanied foray to a local café for a Turkish coffee. In the safe house, her ears are filled with the shouts, cries, and imprecations of vendors, which slowly resolve into a wall of sound which lulls her into a shallow, anxious sleep.

It is late at night when she arrives in Moscow, the promised land—somewhere between eleven and midnight. The taciturn handler who guided her through immigration in Istanbul and stayed with her all day, guides her along the tarmac to a gleaming Mercedes G-class SUV, but he does not get in with her. She is alone with an even more taciturn driver. She expects to be taken to another FSB safe house. She pictures a dacha, perhaps in the Moscow hills, painted red and black, snow piled on the pitched roof, surrounded by pines drowned in snow.

Instead she is taken into Moscow Center, to Lubyanka Square in the Meshchansky District. The enormous neo-baroque building looms up in front of her, home to the FSB and, below, to the infamous Lubyanka prison. Legend has it that the prison is like the Roach Motel—suspects go in, but they don't come out. But of course they did, a handful, anyway; an old joke names Lubyanka as the tallest building in Moscow, since Siberia can be seen from its basement.

To her dismay, it is to the basement she is taken. It is so dark and silent down there she soon feels as if she is drowned. She is led into a room built of concrete. Apart from a metal table bolted to the bare concrete floor, two chairs, one on either side of it, and a shaded light hanging from the ceiling, there is nothing in the windowless room. A large drain is in the center, where the floor dips down. The concrete has dark and ominous stains around the drain. The room stinks of metal, blood, and fusel oil, overlaid with the lingering miasma of terror.

It is in this ghastly place where she first meets Lyudmila Alexeyevna Shokova. Apparently, it is Dima's judgment that a female interrogator would be less intimidating than a male one. Or maybe utilizing Lyudmila this way was a cruel joke, since, as it turns out, she cannot imagine a male interrogator being anywhere near as intimidating as Lyudmila.

She sits at the far side of the table, reading a well-used hardback copy of Ivan Turgenev's *Fathers and Sons*.

The door closes behind Bobbi and she sits in the opposing chair. The metal is cold and hard, and she shivers slightly. She waits for Lyudmila to look up from her reading. At some point, she wonders if she will wait forever, so she says, "I've had a long flight from America here. I'm tired and filthy and I'd like to go to my hotel room."

After a moment, Lyudmila's head comes up and she fixes Bobbi with her ice-blue eyes. Bobbi sees that even in this atrocious light this woman can effortlessly command a room. She is regal-looking. Bobbi can imagine her as a tsarina, facing down men who would block her ascent to power.

"'Nothing is worse and more hurtful than a happiness that comes too late,'" she says in her deep enthralling contralto. "This is Turgenev's opinion anyway." She closes the book, slides it halfway between them, rests her folded arms on the table. "I would so like to hear if this is what has happened to you, Bobbi. Has your happiness come too late?"

"I don't know," Bobbi says truthfully. "I'm here, aren't I?"

"That is to be determined." Lyudmila's eyes narrow. "I imagine you're wondering why Dima isn't running this debriefing. He wasn't allowed. When it comes to you, he can't be relied upon to be objective." Her hands are very still on the table, like small animals waiting for their chance to strike. "There are those among us who think you're too good to be true: living inside the Beltway, married to a man who runs a conservative Super PAC. What could be more ideal?"

"And yet you decided to exfiltrate me."

"What, we are thinking, if you are a double? What if the Americans got onto you and turned you? After all, they have your husband, your children."

"They don't do that sort of thing in America."

Lyudmila ignores her snide remark. "What a coup for them, don't you agree?"

Since the answer is obvious Bobbi decides no answer is necessary. The one thing necessary here, her gut tells her, is to keep her gaze locked with her interrogator's. If she looks away, she suspects she may be here in the Lubyanka basement for longer than she wants.

"But on the other hand," Lyudmila is saying, "we have your husband under constant surveillance."

"Useless," she says. "I hate him. His idea of sexual fun was to hit me in places that would never show."

"Is that so?" Lyudmila cocks her head as if this is news to her. "Why then didn't you leave him?"

"You know very well why. I couldn't leave him because he was part of my cover. Divorce would have brought too much attention to me. I was explicitly told to keep as low a profile as possible."

"Yes, you were. And you did. Admirably." Lyudmila's voice is perfectly neutral. "We needed to make sure where your loyalty lies. Ordering you to leave your family behind was the first step. This is the second."

Her lips purse. "But your children."

Bobbi leans forward. "Listen to me very carefully. I decided before they were born that I was fated to leave them behind."

"Do you hate them?"

"They think I am dead. They are dead to me."

"Yes, undying loyalty, Bobbi. This is what we ask of you. And in return we give you everything you want, and everything you need to carry out the assignments we expect you to complete."

"Whatever is expected of me I swear I will carry out to the best of my abilities."

For several endless moments Lyudmila sits perfectly still, her face a mask. At length, she nods, seemingly satisfied. "Come now." She rises and, as if by magic, the door to the interrogation room opens. "Time to rest. A dacha in the Moscow hills has been arranged." She raises a finger. "But never forget that you are on probation. Everything you say, every move you make will be scrutinized. Is this understood?"

The plush Belle Epoque interior of Le Pechêur swam back into focus. Zoltan was behind the bar, still reading his paper, but as she glanced at him, he looked up, engaged her eyes, and smiled. Lyudmila had finished her double portion of Special K. The scent of lime, cinnamon, and musk was dizzying, but it was preferable to that of metal, blood, fusel oil, and terror.

And yet fear was slowly but surely sucking the oxygen out of the room. Lyudmila was here in Odessa, at this hotel, on this day, at this ungodly hour—surely not a coincidence. *Which means she's keeping track of my movements*, Kobalt thought. *I'm once again in her sights. For the love of God why?*

Think carefully now. Put one foot in front of the other slowly and thoughtfully.

Kobalt's eyes glittered in the lamplight, but her hands below the table were trembling. Curling them into fists gave her the illusion of protection, at least. "'If we wait for the moment when everything, absolutely everything is ready, we shall never begin.'"

"Turgenev." When Lyudmila Alexeyevna Shokova smiled

the entire room lit up. "You remembered. What a clever little vixen you are!"

"That answers your question about the steps I've taken to counter Dima."

She considered Kobalt with her gaze. "Then you have begun."

"I have."

"With Zherov."

"I have ensured his undying loyalty."

"How did you manage that?" Lyudmila used the disconcerting tactic of turning a simple dialog into an interrogation.

"I offered him my trust."

Lyudmila opened her eyes wide and laughed, a bell ringing in the clear dawn light of a mountainside. "You have learned. And learned well."

Kobalt acknowledged the compliment with the faintest of nods. She needed to get her shoulders lowered from around her ears. She worked on this now.

"Who's put the termination order out on me, Lyudmila?"

Instead of answering, in true Lyudmila style, she asked another question. "Did you ever find out who ratted you out to Omega?"

She shook her head. It took her a minute. "Do you think it's the same person?"

Lyudmila shrugged. "It's a thought."

"And a good one. Zherov called in some favors, but everyone was too frightened to dig deeply enough to find out who wants me dead."

The termination order was what had forced Lyudmila out of seclusion in order to help safeguard Kobalt, whose career trajectory was a vital part of her overall plan.

"One thing is for sure, Kobalt. Dima was a first stepping-stone for you. He is riddled with delusions of grandeur. I imagine he will try to make a move on Baev, but that dick will squash him like a bug under his boot sole. No, the further you distance yourself from Dima the better."

"Then I have no one but Zherov."

Lyudmila pushed her milky bowl away. "So. Like me."

Kobalt was unsure of her meaning, but she knew she had to come at it obliquely. "I never did understand what happened with your career."

Lyudmila called for more coffee and another drink for Kobalt. "Joseph had a coat of many colors that was coveted by his brethren. I have many secrets, all of which are coveted by my former brethren. Some of them were getting too close to discovering what they were. You and I were exfiltrated in precisely the same way. To the world at large, we're dead."

Zoltan appeared out of the kitchen, a tray held high. He took a step, opened his mouth to say something. A soft *phutt!* sounded from behind him, and he stumbled, the tray and its contents flying in all directions. Then he fell flat on his face. Two bullet holes blackened the middle of his upper back, like the flags of the victorious enemy.

30

KÖLN, GERMANY

"You drink like a Russian."

Evan poured herself another vodka, raised it to Otto, who was standing at the stovetop, cooking them some food. "*Za nashu druzjbu!*"

Otto took a moment out from stirring the contents of a pan to raise her glass in response. "Yes, to our friendship."

This was the third toast to Otto Evan had made. The first was "*Za zdarovje!*" *To your health*, the second, "*Za vstrechu!*" *To our meeting*.

For his part, Ben had not participated in any of the toasts. He was leaning against the frame of the open doorway into Otto's small but well-stocked kitchen. This was a woman who liked food.

Otto had called an Uber to take them to her apartment across town.

"Aren't your feet cold?" Ben had asked Otto on the way over. Evan sensed the nasty edge to his voice and wondered if Otto picked up on it. She hoped not.

And possibly she didn't because she smiled at Ben as she

wriggled her bare toes. "With my childhood this is nothing, believe me."

Evan suspected Ben wanted to snap, *I don't believe anything you say*. But happily he kept his mouth shut. She wondered at his immediate antipathy to Otto, even though she had helped them out of a difficult situation and had been in as much danger as they had. She wondered at his absolute antipathy to Lyudmila, even though Otto had told them she had her entire network looking for Wendy and Michael. But then again Lyudmila was Russian, ex-FSB, ex-Politburo, and it seemed to make no difference to him that she had been purged from both those posts. That she had become a pariah within Russia made no impression on him. Perhaps he felt her precipitous fall from grace was *dezinformatsiya* that Evan had fallen for. Clearly, the fact that Evan was using her as a source enraged him. She wondered whether she'd ever be able to square that with him, or when this hunt for her niece and nephew was finished, they'd take separate paths. Right now, that was an outcome she preferred not to contemplate.

In the warmth and cozy comfort of Otto's apartment, they had showered while Otto threw their clothes into the wash. In between shots of vodka, Evan was sewing up the back of the beautiful coat Isobel Lowe had generously given her where Blue Eyes's knife had ripped it. Otto had offered to give her one of her own coats, but Evan, already in love with this one, declined, thanked her, and asked instead for needle and thread. The slash was a straight line, no problem, even for Evan who was no seamstress.

"Whatever you've prepared is making my mouth water," Evan said as Otto brought the heavy pan to the table. Using a metal spatula, she delivered a third of the contents onto each of the three plates she had set out.

"Choucroute garni," she said with a grin. "Sauerkraut and fresh Strasbourg sausage. A true Alsatian plate."

Evan put her coat aside as Otto sat down. Ben stayed where he was, observing the two women as if he were across the street, watching them through binoculars.

Evan took up her fork and knife. "Come on, Ben. You must be as hungry as I am."

Otto gave him a sardonic look, reached over, stabbed a piece of sausage off his plate. "It's not poisoned, I promise." She popped the meat into her mouth, chewed delightedly. "See?" She gestured. "It's been a long, exhausting day. Please enjoy yourself while you can. We'll eat. We'll sleep." She wiped her mouth. "You'll want to be well rested. The clinic won't be a walk in the park, believe me."

Ben came away from the wall at last, sat down at the table. "Don't you think you've had enough to drink?"

Evan glanced at him. "Unless you're sweating vodka you can't talk to these Russians."

"What Russians? Otto here is German."

The look she gave him was like a razor scraping over his skin.

"Right." Picking up his cutlery, he began to eat his choucroute garni.

"Benjamin," Otto began, "just so you don't think I'm an Orc or a Nazgûl—" She grinned. "I'm a Tolkien scholar, seriously." She took a mouthful of sauerkraut. "I was born into poverty—abject poverty. Being Germans in Alsace, the French took everything from my family. They shot my grandfather and left my grandmother for dead. My father died five years ago, my mother no longer recognizes her children. My older brother is an officer in the military, my younger sister is a therapist in Berlin. She oversees our mother's care. I'm unmarried and have no children."

"You left out one thing," Ben said flatly. "You work for an ex-FSB officer."

"Ben." Evan paused, fork partway to her mouth. "We are in

Otto's home. She has let us clean ourselves up, laundered our clothing, and fed us."

But Otto appeared unfazed by his stark rudeness. "Lyudmila and I are friends first and foremost. She's an extraordinary woman. She saved my life when no one else would. I owe her everything."

Ben, filling his mouth with Strasbourg sausage, said nothing while he chewed. "So," he said finally, before forking another bite of sauerkraut and sausage, "what can you tell us about Reveshvili, other than what we can find out through Google or any other search engine?"

Otto poured herself more vodka. "While you were both getting cleaned up, I did a bit of research, down and dirty," she said. "It seems he works from eleven in the morning until midnight or 1 A.M., but it's virtually impossible to get in to see him once he's in the clinic." She put down her knife and fork. "However, every working day, he takes his breakfast at Gästehaus Wald, a small family-run inn at the edge of the Gierather Wald. That's the same forest visible in one corner of the photo you showed me. It's only a few minutes' drive from the clinic." Her expression became thoughtful, and after a moment she added, "He is a fanatic about the benefits of a good breakfast. And he's fascinated by the subject of twins. A few points around which you might engage him."

"Okay, so you want Evan to talk with him." Ben did not look happy about this. "But she needs protection."

Otto shook her head. "I very much doubt she'll have anything to fear from Herr *Doktor*, so allow Evan the space to talk with him." She turned her attention to Evan. "Anyway, many people believe him to be a genius. Whether or not that's so, you'll judge for yourself. But one thing is clear, the patients' success rate at the clinic has been nothing short of stellar."

* * *

"You really can be a shit," Evan said, as they drove out of Cologne the next morning in a rental car, Evan behind the wheel.

Ben stared out the window. "Part of my job description."

"You know," she said, steering around a lumbering truck, "it occurs to me that you were fine as long as you were taking care of me, but now that Otto's put me in the driver's seat literally and figuratively you've grown an attitude."

She moved into the left lane of the highway, accelerating. "And it's an attitude I don't much care for."

For the next thirty minutes or so they traveled without a word being exchanged. Evan moved over to the right and, following the directions Otto had given her, took the next exit.

"Evan, why did you go to Sumatra, of all places?"

Ben's voice echoed in the car's interior like a clarion call to war.

As soon as she was clear of the off-ramp, she pulled over to the side of the road, put on her hazard blinking lights, and turned to him. "I went to Sumatra because that's where Lyudmila was. She called me to her, and I went."

"Why?" His voice was hoarse, thinned out, vibrating like a wire. "Why would you do that?"

How could I be so wrong? she asked herself. *His hatred of Lyudmila and everything she touches has nothing to do with her being Russian, with her being ex-FSB, ex-Politburo. It strikes much closer to home.*

But just to be sure, she said, "After taking down Nemesis in Bavaria I was burned out. I needed a rest. In Sumatra, there was nothing around us but the sun, the water, and the macaques." And though he tried to hide it, she saw. "You're jealous of her. Oh. You are, you are."

He reacted predictably. "You're nuts."

"She's a friend," she said softly.

"She's a Russian. And not just any Russian. She was with SVR. She was a member of the Politburo, for God's sake."

"That was then," Evan said. "She's quits with all that now."

"Oh, Evan, come on. You're never quits with our world. Once a spy, always a spy."

"Listen, as far as anyone knows—and this includes the Russians—Lyudmila's dead. I'm one of just a handful of people outside her private network who she trusted to tell that she was still alive. And she told me the truth about my sister. And now she's helping to find Wendy and Michael. I trust her, Ben. You need to trust my instincts."

They sat like that for some time, the engine humming beneath them, cars passing on the road to their left, the world indifferent to their deep-seated dilemma.

"So," Ben said. "What do we do now?"

"Aren't you curious whether I'm jealous of Isobel Lowe?"

"Why should you be?"

"Hm. Let me think." Her tone was sarcastic. "Well. For one thing you hid your relationship from me."

"Operational security. She was instrumental in making my shop a reality and getting Aristides to be my boss. It was imperative that no one else know of her involvement."

"Need to know, in other words."

He nodded. "Precisely."

"I'm not asking you to, but under the circumstances, you have to put your bias about Lyudmila aside. Please."

"I don't *have* to do anything."

He had nothing, but he needed something in order to save a bit of face. She knew that, too.

"Okay. Then I *am* asking you, Ben. Please let this thing between us go, at least for the time being. It's already starting to fuck up our working relationship. We're under Moscow Rules. We can't afford this. We have to be on the same page all the way down the line. Sooner rather than later we'll forfeit our lives if we don't."

The silence between them was coming to seem like an ocean neither of them had the equipment to cross.

Ben ran his hand across his eyes. "Sorry, Evan. I have been acting like a shit. I know it. Being terminated, having the whole shop blown up, the transition back to field work has been far tougher than I expected."

"I understand. We're under no one's auspices, we have no backup. We're out here in a kill zone completely naked." She leaned toward him, her heart softening, because, as usual when it came to the emotional side of things, she was a couple of steps ahead of him. "But that's not all, is it?"

He took his hand away from his eyes, turned to watch her watching him. "I saw the whole thing happen—the car T-bone the light post, the awful wreck I didn't think anyone could survive. In that instant, I felt more helpless than I've ever felt in my life.

"When I went to pull you out of your car, I thought you were dead. My blood ran cold—it's a literary cliché, but damn that's exactly how I felt. And when I discovered you were alive and not seriously injured something broke open inside me." Hands spread. "And now . . . now that it's out of its shell I don't know what to do with it." He took a breath, let it out in a rush. "Particularly because I have no idea how you feel about me."

Evan felt the pain in her head, which had never fully gone away, becoming acute once again, and she winced. "I don't know what you want me to say, Ben."

"I don't *want* you to say anything. But what's the truth?"

"There is no truth here, not one that I can get my mind around right now."

"So you don't know—"

"Why push it, Ben?" She had to intervene; she was feeling overwhelmed. "Let it alone."

"Now is not the time, is that it?"

"Jesus, you know it's not."

He nodded. "Okay," he said. "Okay."

31

ODESSA, UKRAINE

They came in very quickly. Zoltan was down, gone—a shock tactic that hit home. The two men entering the bar were big and heavily armed. One had a tattoo of a multi-pointed star on his forehead, the other, shorter, square of both body and face, sported a jagged scar that drew down the outside of his left eye and left a fissure that split his cheek in two unequal parts.

They seemed to ignore Lyudmila—they obviously did not recognize her—fixating on Kobalt.

Scar grinned. "There you are."

Star nodded. "Take her down."

Scar leveled his machine pistol at Kobalt, but before he could pull the trigger, she hurled the bottle of vodka at him. He recoiled as the glass shattered against the weapon, splashing the liquor over his face. Star's weapon came up, but before he could do anything with it his head exploded in a volley of sound, fury, blood, and bits of bone. Scar whirled only to get a three-round face full of bullets from Zherov's Scorpion. At that very moment, Lyudmila bolted out of the banquette. She had a gun drawn, a Ruger SR40c. It held sixteen rounds of

.40 S&W, arguably the most powerful small handgun on the planet.

Kobalt was right behind her as she disappeared through the doorway into the kitchen. She stepped over the threshold; Zoltan lay unmoving, all breath gone. She heard the four shots, one right after another, and stumbling into the kitchen, came upon Lyudmila standing in classic two-handed shooter's stance. A man, larger even than Scar and Star, lay spread-eagled across the grill, his shirt and jacket smoldering. The volume of blood pouring from the man's wounds was more than sufficient to smother the burners, and the stench of gas was already infiltrating the kitchen. The terrified staff was huddled in a far corner, trembling and whimpering.

Ripping past Lyudmila, Kobalt turned off all the unlit burners to stop the gas flow. As she did so, she saw the patch sewn into the inside of his jacket: *Поліція-Politsiya*. *Ukrainian Police*.

An instant later, Zherov came bounding through the kitchen door, threw Kobalt's tricked-out jacket to her, and the three of them headed toward the rear exit without a word being said among them. Time for introductions and explanations when they were well clear of what had become a kill zone.

"I'm sorry about Zoltan," Kobalt said.

Lyudmila nodded, but said nothing.

Kobalt knew her time in Odessa was at an end; there was nothing more to glean here. But with Lyudmila as their unexpected companion, she and Zherov could not return to the FSB jet. She knew without having to ask that he wanted to ditch her. She knew Lyudmila made him nervous. Zherov was out of his depth, stranded in what was for him terra incognita. She hoped he was a fast learner, otherwise he'd be the one who was ditched.

She had no choice but to follow Lyudmila as they exited the hotel. Lyudmila was far more conversant with the byways of Odessa than she was. As they hurried away, she thanked Zherov, but that was the extent of their conversation.

Just north of the vast container shipping complex that was the heart of Odessa's port lay a docking complex large enough for navy vessels and pleasure boats, though the latter were few and far between. Soon they were ensconced below deck on a sixty-five-foot yacht docked no more than a stone's throw from where the Krivak III–class frigate in the Ukrainian naval fleet was tied up alongside a brace of Island-class patrol boats.

From below, they could hear the rubberized footsteps of Lyudmila's crew as they moved back and forth topside on their mysterious rounds, like nurses in a hospital. It seemed they were preparing to get under way.

Zherov had already taken a giant slug of vodka and Lyudmila was pouring him another. They sat around a polished teak table with a thick central post bolted to the deck. The cabin, more spacious than seemed possible, was lined with teak and another wood Kobalt couldn't identify. On the table was a nautical map of Odessa to the north and Constanta in Romania to the southwest. Kobalt had no idea what Lyudmila was up to and was about to ask her just that, when Lyudmila herself spoke up and answered at least one of her questions.

"Be assured we are safe from the police here," Lyudmila said. "This yacht is an asset of a legitimate software company I own through a maze of shell corporations. The ship's registry is in Panama."

Kobalt nodded.

"It's time I tell you why I risked coming out of hiding."

"You think now that every concern you had about me is true."

"What I know, Kobalt, is that you have done everything

they have asked of you. But in the process you have become something else—a killing machine."

"I'm just following in your bloody footsteps."

Lyudmila pinned her with a gorgon's look that caused her bones to ache, just as if she had fallen a long way before reaching the stony earth.

"Unlike you, Kobalt, I feel remorse for every life I've taken. The dead return at night with their gaping wounds, their accusatory stares."

Kobalt did not know where she was, what was expected of her, only that she was being judged, and judged harshly. So of course she said the worst thing possible. "Then I feel sorry for you."

"I am human," Lyudmila said after a thoroughly uncomfortable pause during which Kobalt felt as if fire ants were crawling over her body. "What are you?"

Kobalt knew she had to reverse course before the hole she had fallen into became too deep to climb out of. She cleared her throat.

"What?" Lyudmila leaned in, the space between them turned gelid. "What was that?"

"I'm sorry." Kobalt shook her head because she was. She was sure that Lyudmila had broken her cover to punish her. "I misspoke. . . . Stupid of me."

Lyudmila lifted a hand. "However, what you have done at their behest is no longer my concern. I am not one of them now."

So Lyudmila really was quits with them, Kobalt thought. What, then, did she want? She did not seem to be someone to retire to Tahiti or Sumba to live out the rest of her life in eternal sunshine, sea breezes, gentle surf, and unutterable boredom. She was like a shark: if she wasn't moving forward it was because she was dead. Kobalt wanted to be like that so badly she could taste it.

"On the other hand I am bound to ask you a question before moving forward. About your children."

Kobalt knew that this was her final test, that if she failed she would never be like Lyudmila, would never have her wisdom and connections no matter how much of Ermi's money she had sequestered. She took a deep cleansing breath let it out. Time to trust, time to tell this person whom she admired so much, the truth. "In the almost four years since I was exfiltrated I have never thought of them. Certainly, I haven't missed them. What were they to me, anyway? They might have been birthed and raised by someone else altogether. I never had a maternal instinct; it's alien to me. They're alien to me."

Lyudmila made no move, nor did her stony expression change. "Really. And yet it is because of them that you're here."

"No." She shook her head. "I'm here because I have a job to do, and I'm going to destroy Omega, even if it kills me."

32

BERGISCH GLADBACH, GERMANY

Evan and Ben crested a rise and were greeted by the Gierather Wald—the dense blue-green forest, at the near edge of which sat Gästehaus Wald, the half-timbered inn where, according to Otto, the director and lead researcher at Schneller Psychiatric Clinic, Dr. Konstantin Reveshvili, took his breakfast.

If he looked like anyone, Evan thought upon entering the inn, it was a dark-haired Max von Sydow—long face, pale eyes, saturnine mouth, thinning hair combed straight back off his wide forehead.

She stood in the entryway, as if unsure whether to come in or not, but in reality, making meticulous mental note of her surroundings. The ground floor was actually two rooms—the one on the right a restaurant, the one on the left, two steps down, was the inn's public space with comfy-looking sofas and upholstered chairs set in small groupings, along with side tables laden with newspapers and magazines and shaded reading lamps.

The ceiling was low, the heavy wooden beams and floor blackened by woodsmoke and burned ash of cigarettes, cigars, and pipes. A massive fireplace in the far wall of the restaurant was merrily blazing. It was much cooler here at the edge of the forest than it had been in the city. In fact, the trees seemed to dominate the inn, as if they, too, were its patrons. The blue-green gloom of Gierather Wald seemed to have permanently leeched into the rooms. Branches were used to hold light fixtures in the restaurant area, the tables and chair frames appeared to be hand-hewn, using local wood. The chair cushions were a handmade forest pattern. Heavenly smells swirled out of the kitchen: woodsmoke mingling with the scents of melted butter, fried potatoes, grilled meat, and caramelized sugar.

Evan seemed, for the moment, rooted to the spot. Her conversation with Ben had rattled her deeply. So many emotions chased themselves through her mind, and she couldn't catch any one of them. Everything seemed to be slipping through her fingers. Part of her raged, *How could he?* Another part quailed, terrified of possibilities that she had dared not contemplate. Still another part was hell-bent on keeping her life just the way it was.

The innkeeper, a heavyset man with cheeks like glowing coals, came bustling up to her, interrupting her inner agony. After a moment's blankness, she realized he was asking whether she was looking for breakfast or a room to rent or both. She had to pull herself together. This was no frame of mind in which to begin an interview with someone who could bring her closer to Wendy and Michael.

When she told the innkeeper that she was meeting Dr. Reveshvili, he bowed his head, nodding, as if she were royalty. He discreetly pointed out the good doctor and ushered her over himself.

"*Reveshvili takes his breakfast alone—always,*" Otto had told her before they had left her apartment. "He will not be happy to be interrupted. You will need a method to sink the hook deep into his palate so he cannot escape you."

Reveshvili was seated by himself at a prime window table. He was staring out past the gravel driveway to the forest beyond, where the treetops bent as if to his will. He wore a rather old-fashioned, charcoal-gray pinstripe three-piece suit that fit him so perfectly it must have been made to measure. An unfashionably wide cream tie completed the picture. She imagined him wearing polished thick-soled brogues.

"Herr *Doktor*," the innkeeper said when they arrived, "your friend is here."

Reveshvili was slow turning away from the forest view. When he did, he looked from the innkeeper to Evan. "What friend?"

Evan put the flat of her hand to her chest. "Carla Johnstone." Then she held it out to him. "We made this appointment last week via telephone. Don't you remember, Herr *Doktor*?"

"I do not. And I certainly do not book appointments during my breakfast hour." But as she leaned subtly forward, he took her proffered hand and studied her face intently, with a curious, slight frown.

"My apologies, Herr *Doktor*," Evan said in a reverential tone, "it was certainly not my intention of disturbing you during the most important ritual of the day."

This brought him up short. "Do you think so, really?"

She bobbed her head. "Absolutely."

He cocked his head slightly, as a scientist might at the unforeseen outcome of an important experiment. "So you share my theory on the importance of a sound breakfast."

"Herr *Doktor*, that is why you agreed to allow me to join you this morning."

He continued to study her a moment or two more. Despite herself, Evan felt sweat break out under her arms.

"Armand."

"Yes, Herr *Doktor*."

The innkeeper had not moved. In the event this young lady turned out to be an interloper he was fully prepared to lead her away from his best patron's table.

"Please bring a setting for Fraulein Johnstone. This beautiful young lady will be joining me for breakfast."

"At once, Herr *Doktor*." Armand scurried away.

Evan had only just seated herself in the chair opposite Reveshvili when Armand rushed back with a place setting. He filled her glass from the bottled water already on the table and asked her what he might prepare for her.

"Fraulein Johnstone will have what I am having, Armand."

So that's the kind of man he is, Evan thought. She was hardly surprised, but nevertheless pleased to have confirmation.

"Very good, Herr *Doktor*. Right away."

A waitress replaced him, pouring coffee for Evan and topping off Reveshvili's cup.

"Now," Reveshvili said, switching to perfect English, "how may I help?"

"My sister and I—"

"You have a sister." His head had come up. His nose seemed to twitch as if he were a hunting dog out in the forest across the road.

"My twin sister, Bobbi." Evan painted a smile on her face. She hadn't meant to use Bobbi's real name, it had just slipped out.

"Ah."

Reveshvili was about to continue when their plates arrived. Evan had eaten nothing at Otto's before they set off, so that she could authentically assure Reveshvili that the two of them were simpatico on the devout pleasures of a sound breakfast. She would have to pace herself, but she was prepared to impress him in devouring the feast set out on the massive plates before them: fresh multigrain rolls, slices of black pumpernickel, butter, five kinds of cold salami, sausage and Black Forest ham, four different cheeses, marmalade, homemade preserves, and more strong hot coffee.

She started eating, slowly but with evident great pleasure, keeping one eye on the Herr *Doktor*.

"So," he said, after washing down several mouthfuls of breakfast with a swig of black coffee, "tell me why you have come to see me."

"My sister and I—"

"Your *twin* sister."

"Yes." Otto was right, Reveshvili was for some reason interested in twins. "Bobbi and I have a good friend. We met her in Köln while on holiday maybe five or so years ago. We kept up a correspondence for a while, then all of a sudden, her texts stopped, her mobile number went out of service. We've been worried about her ever since."

Two parallel lines formed above the bridge of Reveshvili's patrician nose. "You have my sympathies, dear lady. Nevertheless, I cannot fathom why you have come to me."

Here we go, Evan thought. *It's showtime.*

She pulled out the photo of Ana and William Onders, keeping the second photo in reserve. Placing it on the table between them. "That's Ana," she said. "And that, in the background is, I believe, the Schneller Psychiatric Clinic." Before Reveshvili could say a word, she turned the photo over and showed him the inscription: To W, from Ana I love you-countryside Koln: a breath of fresh air.

"You see," she added, "it's dated the twenty-seventh of June, only two years ago." Turning the photo over again, she tapped the hazed building. "That has to be your clinic, Herr *Doktor*. There can be no doubt about it."

"Hm." Reveshvili took up the photo, the better to study it. "And do you know this man?"

Evan was so focused on gleaning information about Ana that she was momentarily stumped by the question, but quickly realized that anything she might learn about Onders could be useful as well. "That 'W' is for Will—William Onders, I believe."

Reveshvili made no reply.

"Herr *Doktor*, do you know this woman, Ana?"

The lines above his nose deepened. "I do. But I am wondering what she is doing here with this William Onders."

"I was hoping you could shed some light." Once again, beads of sweat made their appearance under her arms.

"I'm afraid not." Reveshvili set the photo down as carefully as if it were an heirloom of great value. "This man"—he tapped the photo with his long spidery index finger—"I have never seen him before." He looked up at her. "You're interested in him as well as in Ana?"

"Sadly, he's dead," Evan said, carefully studying his face.

"I see." Most of the time when people say "I see" it's a placeholder, something perfectly neutral to say to fill a conversational silence. But Evan had learned that every once in a while, it had real meaning. Reveshvili appeared to be lost in thought.

At length, he came out of his reverie. "And where, might I ask, is your twin sister now? Is she here with you, close at hand?"

Reveshvili possessed that unique talent of the best interrogators of changing the subject without a hint of warning. "She, also, is dead, I'm afraid," she told him.

He set down his knife and fork, and for a long moment, he said nothing. "What a great pity," he said at last.

His face had turned to stone. His gaze seemed far away. She found it odd that he hadn't offered her his condolences. She cleared her throat, and the sound brought him back.

He looked at her as if she had just sat down. "I have a particular interest in twins. My studies, you see. I am interested in how their thought patterns run parallel at times and then, at others, work at cross-purposes. Quite strange—and, it goes without saying, fascinating."

She needed him to get back on track. She smiled and said softly, "Herr *Doktor*, what if anything can you tell me about Ana?"

"What? Oh, Ana. Yes." He shrugged. "She was a clinician here. At barely twenty-one, by far the youngest we've ever had at the clinic. She was a genius, really."

"But she's no longer at the clinic?"

"Ah, no. She left some time ago." He tapped his lower lip. "Three years, perhaps four."

"Why did she leave?"

"Our clinic was not the place for her. Her main interest was in psychopharmacology. That's not the main thrust of my therapies. Frankly, I distrust drugs, except in the most extreme cases, such as bipolar disorder. There, lithium has been a godsend."

"What exactly was Ana working on while she was with you?"

Reveshvili waved a hand. "Oh, you know, experiments—far more outré, frankly, than I was comfortable with."

She was about to ask for more details, when he said, "But look here. You're injured."

Evan touched the healing wound on the left side of her head. "It's nothing."

Reveshvili clucked his tongue. "Even from here I can see it's not 'nothing,' Fraulein."

"Of course, Herr *Doktor*."

"I am impressed, Fraulein." He smiled. "You understand the essentials of German formality."

They were way off-topic—her topic. But she was interested now to learn where he was leading the conversation.

"You must allow me to take a look at your wound. I would very much like to make certain it's healing properly. Did you go to the hospital originally?"

"I . . . didn't think it was necessary."

"There's no question. You will come back to the clinic with me after breakfast and I will clean and rebandage it."

"It's really not necessary."

"Nonsense. You are coming with me and that is the end of it."

She had one more physical card to play. Drawing out the second photo that had belonged to the man she and Ben knew only as Jon Pine, she placed it in front of Reveshvili. "Here is a photo of Ana, but in close-up. It was found in the possession of a man called Jon Pine. Does that name ring a bell?"

Reveshvili took up the photo, held it in front of his face as if he were nearsighted. Something seemed to go through him, a tremor of intent not acted upon. What had stopped him? Evan wondered.

He continued to stare fixedly at the photo. "I do not know Herr Pine," he said, after a time.

Evan made certain not to show her disappointment. "So about Ana . . ."

"Yes?"

She realized that she couldn't ask him Ana's last name; they were supposed to be friends. *Improvise*, she told herself. "We knew her as Ana Logan. But after she disappeared, we could find no trace of anyone with that name who looked like our Ana."

"Really?" Reveshvili pursed his lips. "How curious! She presented herself to us, with her impeccable curriculum vitae, as Fraulein *Doktor* Ana Helm."

33

HIGH NOON

It is noon when Wendy and Michael are led outside. The sun blazes down, making them squint, bringing tears to their eyes, as if there wasn't already sufficient cause for weeping. But, if truth be known, following the seemingly interminable days and nights of their incarceration they are all cried out, even Michael, who grasps his sister's hand with a desperation granted only to children.

Curiously, no one has accompanied them past the door, and when they are able to look back through clear eyes, they see not a prison at all, but a castle so beautiful it seems to have appeared straight out of a fairy tale.

"Wendy! Michael!"

As one, they turn from the castle toward the voice calling their names to behold a very tall, very beautiful young woman, who might easily pass for a princess were it not for her short hair and her large, piercing eyes. They are bewildered how someone so beautiful, so unknown to them knows their names. And then they see her smile. It is a wide smile, a generous smile, and one which, were they a decade older, they might have recognized as a very, very wicked smile, indeed.

She is crouching down in the walled courtyard beyond the door of the castle, at the edge of a cobbled circle surrounded by a ring of tamped-down dirt. The walls, crawling with ivy, are high and look thick, as well.

She holds out her arms. "Come here, my darlings." She wears a suede jacket the color of whiskey over a man's lightweight wool shirt. Below are riding breeches with inner thigh pads and high, polished boots with, Wendy knows from her insatiable reading, thin soles, meant for riding a horse, not tramping through fields on expeditions.

Wendy feels Michael's small hand sweaty in hers as she leads him hesitantly toward the beautiful woman. Sunlight spins off her hair, and now she rests her elbows on her powerful-looking thighs. In fact, now that they are closer everything about her looks powerful, excepting her long, swanlike neck.

"How are you two?" she says in her singsong voice, as if they just arrived at the castle.

"Where are we?" Wendy asks. "Why have you brought us here?"

For his part, Michael says simply, "What's your name?"

"Ana," sings the beautiful woman.

There is something about her eyes. Perhaps their enormity causes them to be mesmeric. Or maybe it is the intelligence behind them.

"My name is Ana." That smile again, creeping across her face like liquid mercury. "You have nothing to fear from me. You have been secluded for your own protection. America is changing. You were no longer safe there, although it's my opinion you really never were."

"But America is our home," Wendy says.

"America is where you were born and raised for a short

period. But it wasn't safe. Not for your mother and not for you."

Wendy frowns. "Whatever do you mean?" She likes saying "whatever" instead of "what," just like the heroines in the novels she reads.

Ana's face darkens for a moment, a trapdoor suddenly visible. But it's only for the blink of an eye, and possibly it was never there at all. "Your father was not a nice man. He cheated and stole from people."

"Did not!" Michael shouts.

"He amassed a fortune in other people's money."

Michael jumps up and down, his face empurpled. "Did not! Did not!"

"Worse, even, he hit your mother, over and over again."

Tears spurting. "Did not, did, not, did not!"

"Hush, Mikey." His sister squeezes his hand all the more tightly. Flashes in her mind of her father shouting, of a dish or a glass crashing to the kitchen floor, of a slap like a wet bag against concrete that made her jump and then shake. And once a deeper sound, thicker, heavier, and a strangled cry from mom. They thought she was asleep. They thought grown-up things could be kept from their children. But evil had crept in the door and lodged itself inside the house, crawling out at night when the lights downstairs were low, when upstairs there was no light on at all, and fear hung from the ceiling like a rafter full of bats.

All these hideous memories flash through Wendy's mind as she stares at Ana. "I knew," she says in a whisper.

"I think you both knew."

Wendy hugs Michael to her, his shoulders shaking, a thin wail escaping his mouth. Ana's face is a mask of sorrow. Tears tremble in the corners of her eyes.

"Now you are safe, protected from all things harmful and

evil." She opens her arms again, and this time Wendy, dragging Michael with her, steps inside that shelter.

"I have brought you into God's own house," Ana sings, her voice atremble. "I've brought you all this long way to meet your family."

PART FOUR

34

MOSCOW, RUSSIA

Dima Tokmakov's office was a dismal affair, suitable for his job as director of Zaslon. It inhabited a corner of the seventh floor of the Lubyanka building. That its window overlooked not much at all bothered Dima not at all. When it came to the subject of nature or artwork, he was a full-on philistine.

Apart from his massive desk, his chair, and two others on the opposite side, there was precious little to indicate that the space was currently inhabited. On his desk were two laptops, side by side and linked electronically. On the right corner was a framed photograph of Nadya, a candid snap—a selfie. Dima always got a little thrill when he looked at it, knowing she took it while she was naked and wet, just out of the shower. Not that a viewer could tell, since it was a close-up of her face.

He was thinking of the unique sound Nadya made when she orgasmed, a laugh that sent shivers through him when, like a grimalkin in the forest of the night, Ilya Ivanovich Gurin appeared in the open doorway. How he always managed to get past Feliks was another mystery Dima had yet to solve. When queried, Feliks swore he never saw Gurin, but Dima worried that his adjutant had been suborned.

In any case, Gurin was here now. He said not a word; there was no need. The expression on his face was message enough: Baev, the director of SVR, awaits.

Dima rose with a deep sense of foreboding. He knew, of course, that his banker in Istanbul was dead—killed in a particularly gruesome manner. The implications of Ermi Çelik's murder were as yet unclear to him. He had checked his Cyprus bank statements. They were, thank Saint Matrona, wholly intact. But if the murderer somehow got their hands on Çelik's ledger, he was sunk. These were the thoughts that occupied his mind as he followed Gurin down the stairs all seven flights to Baev's first-floor office. Baev, a fitness freak who swam at an indoor pool in lieu of breakfast and played four-wall handball every evening in lieu of dinner, never took the elevator, which meant Gurin never did either.

When Dima entered, he was standing at the window behind his desk, staring out at the saints alone knew what. His hands were clamped at the small of his back. As Dima stepped into the carpeted office, Gurin closed the door behind him.

The space was the polar opposite of Dima's. The walls were crowded with photos—photos of the director general with every member of the Politburo, either in a group or singly, but pride of place was reserved for Baev with the Sovereign, the leader of Mother Russia, the most powerful man within the Federation. If these photos were meant to intimidate the visitor, they succeeded admirably.

Dima stood for some time waiting for Baev to turn around. When he didn't, Dima cleared his throat, said, "You wished to see me, Director General?"

At the sound of his voice, Baev turned. "Did I?" He appeared to be actually considering this, which unnerved the already-on-edge Dima.

Abruptly, Baev snapped out of it, "Ah, yes. Dima, do you know why my office is on the first floor?"

Dima did not answer; an answer was neither required nor expected.

"Below here is the prison," Baev continued. "Sometimes I can feel its vibration—the vibrations of pain, of suffering, of men breaking, men on the point of dying, men begging for their lives." He unfolded his hands from the small of his back, pointed a finger in the air. "When one chooses a life of crime, of dissidence, of betraying the State, there are consequences of the most serious nature. Do you not agree, Dima Nikolaevich?"

"I do, Director General."

"Do you find those vibrations as gratifying as I do, Dima Nikolaevich?"

Baev grinned, a particularly terrifying sight. He gestured, coughing or laughing, it was impossible to tell which. "Come, come, sit. Be comfortable."

Having done just about everything in the first few minutes to ensure Dima's discomfort, this last was a sublimely ironic statement. Not lost on Dima, the charade made Dima hate Baev all the more. Baev was unspeakably difficult to work for, let alone work with. Dima never knew what he was thinking, never knew what his decisions would be on issues big or small. He had, to put it another way, not even the vaguest inkling of Baev's process or method. He always came to a meeting in the dark and left it without the light of knowledge he needed.

Baev had left the window and fastidiously seated himself behind his desk. As he was sitting down, Dima saw a dossier open on the desk. It was a black-jacketed folder, and though he couldn't see it, Dima knew that it had a red stripe across the upper corner. It was the dossier on Directorate 52123, better known to him—and surely to Baev as well—as the Kobalt dossier.

He stared at the open folder as Baev tapped it with the

perfectly manicured nail of his forefinger. In a low, calm voice, he said: "This dossier is close to both our hearts, Dima Nikolaevich, would you not agree?"

Dima nodded. "I would, Director General." No one knew Baev's given or patronymic names or, more accurately, no one inside the Lubyanka would use them either in front of the director or behind his back. That was an unwritten rule of the FSB as stringently adhered to as insistently refuting the existence of Zaslon.

"It's also been not only a priority of yours, but one that has been locked away from the world both inside the Lubyanka and outside. Is this not so?"

"It is, Director General."

"And you have made every effort to keep it that way, is this not also so?"

"Of course, Director General."

Baev's fist came down on the desk so hard the dossier rose into the air for a brief shaky flight. "Then how the fuck has it been lifted?"

"Lifted?" Confusion made Dima sound like an idiot.

"There's been an infiltration of the SVR server, Dima Nikolaevich!" Baev thundered. "A *black* infiltration."

The modifier *black* sent a chill through Dima's bones. Red meant an infiltration from within the FSB. Black meant the infiltration came from *outside* the Lubyanka.

He stood up, bent over, placing his own fists on Baev's desk. "Have we been able to trace the infiltration back via an ISP address?"

"Don't be naïve. So far we've been led around in an electronic circle." Baev shook his head. "All we do know is that this is a private enterprise, definitely no hallmarks of it being state-run. And in any case, none of the usual suspects . . ." he counted off on his fingers ". . . China, North Korea, Israel, Iran. Forget GCHQ, the British don't have the expertise. None of them have any knowledge of Kobalt, let alone interest."

By this time, Dima's armpits were shamefully wet. Beads of sweat rolled down his spine. And yet his mouth was as dry as the Gobi Desert. He straightened up and coughed into his fist before he found his voice. "Which means—"

Baev tapped the Kobalt dossier, this time with a knuckle. "Which means that whoever poached the dossier has penetrated Kobalt's identity. Find out who that is and terminate them at once."

"Eminently, Director General."

Ilya Ivanovich Gurin watched Dima's hasty retreat out of the corner of his eye. Then with a smirk he rose from behind his narrow desk and entered his boss's office, where Baev was talking low and indistinctly on a mobile phone. He held a hand up and Gurin remained in place by the closed door. Shortly thereafter, Baev's call ended. He put away the mobile and beckoned Gurin over.

"You put the fear of God into Dima, sir," he said as he came to attention before Baev's desk.

Baev sat down but did not give his adjutant leave to do so. "For the love of Stalin, Ilya Ivanovich, get your head out of my butt."

Gurin, who had endured much worse during his tenure with Baev, said nothing, steeled himself to brush aside whatever he was feeling. There was an office pool as to how long he'd last as Baev's adjutant. It had taken the last man just three weeks to be fired, and the one before that a little over a month. Gurin had been at it four months already and had pissed off fully nine-tenths of the pool's participants whose guesses had long expired. There was a sense of pride in this, but also of shame for the verbal abuse he was required to put up with. Every hour of every day that mountain of abuse grew higher, blotting out the horizon that might have been Gurin's future had he stayed in FSB narcotics, instead of excitedly transferring into SVR where it felt as if he was required to navigate the confusing intrigues at the court of a Byzantine emperor.

Baev sat back, folded his hands across his stomach, which had not the slightest bulge to it. He watched his adjutant like a hawk circling its prey.

"A grave disappointment."

Gurin leaned forward slightly. "Kobalt?"

"Dima." Baev bit his lower lip, always a bad sign. "Kobalt isn't a disappointment because nothing was expected of her. She's Dima's little 'experiment.' The SVR—indeed, the entirety of our clandestine services—is not the venue for experiments."

"I agree entirely, sir."

He snorted. "You know, your nose is starting to feel nice and comfortable up my ass." He lifted a forefinger. "But mind I don't fart. You won't survive."

Gurin's cheeks flamed, despite his best efforts.

"Two down," Baev said now. "Two of your recruits—dead."

Gurin noted sourly his boss's use of "your" instead of "the." Of course, this was his fault; whose else could it be, certainly not the great Baev.

"Evan Ryder has proved more . . . formidable than—"

Baev smiled thinly. "Gurin, Gurin, Gurin, did you not read the dossier on her. It's quite comprehensive. Thick as a brick. Ryder has been a knife in our belly for years." He gestured. "You only have to review the notes on the operation outside St. Petersburg to realize how deadly she is. And as difficult to catch as a will-o'-the-wisp."

He splayed his fingers on the desktop just as Kusnetsov had done in their last meeting after the shark swim. "My fear, dear Gurin, is that her sister—the defector—will prove just as deadly. Perhaps even to us." He ran the top of his tongue around his lips. "What's your opinion?"

"Mine?" Gurin looked taken aback.

"I'm grooming you for bigger things, Gurin, assuming, that is, you can finish the job on Ryder."

"I will not fail you, sir."

"Good, good, that's what I want to hear." He frowned. "But now, what about Kobalt? She screwed up the Omega remit."

"That was a big one to screw up," Gurin said with a nod. "But was it a *deliberate* screwup? That's the question."

Baev appeared to consider this for some moments, though the hesitation was strictly for Gurin's benefit. "Never underestimate the Americans." He was leading Gurin on, so that he would be certain what happened next was the right course of action. "Their current administration is in disarray—and of course we both see our hand in that—but the career *shpiony* work, spinning their own webs of deceit."

"Sir, if I may, I suspect that Kobalt is the most ambitious operation they have thrown at us in quite some time. But how can we trust her? Evan Ryder and Kobalt are sisters. Blood runs deep, sir."

Baev nodded as if he had made up his mind. "Intriguing theory, Gurin, in that event, Kobalt was never what Dima Nikolaevich purported her to be: an asset. She's a black widow that has invaded our web. The very fact that our central server was breached and the Kobalt dossier accessed proves my point. The Americans are checking up, making sure their mole hasn't been tumbled."

He gave his adjutant a rare smile along with his usual penetrating stare. "So, what do you think? Should we dispatch an SVR field agent to terminate Kobalt?"

"I think that is the wisest course of action," Gurin said, stepping into the trap Baev had laid for him. "And, in my opinion, the sooner the better."

The trap snapped closed, as Gurin's tone of voice, the hardening of his eyes, his choice of words all clearly confirmed to Baev his adjutant's preening ambition and his hostility toward Kobalt. His eagerness to get rid of her turned Baev's stomach.

The director held his smile, and Gurin's eyes with his own, for an unnaturally long time without responding to Gurin's confidently stated opinion; he took inordinate pleasure in watching this greedy underling squirm in discomfort. Finally, he dropped his gaze to the desktop and said, "Yes, yes, Gurin, but one thing at a time. As Minister Kusnetsov reminded me at our last meeting, our target has been, and is now, Evan Ryder. Using convicted killers from the zone as assassins is a recent innovation I myself sanctioned. It's brilliant—no connection back to the State. And in this case, necessary. It seemed to me too dangerous to use SVR personnel for this termination.

"*But . . .*" His head came up and his torso surged forward, chest against the edge of the desk. "Two dead. You sent two of these ex-cons, these so-called 'farm hands,' to Cologne and what happened, eh. Eh?" He pointed a blunt finger. "That's on you, Ilya Ivanovich. You chose the men; they failed. Just remember it's the singer not the song."

Gurin made the mistake of giving his boss a bewildered look.

"My *idea* is sound, it's been a success time and again," Baev said in an irritated tone of voice. "It's your handpicked executioners who failed." He put his hands flat on the desk. "Now I choose, Ilya Ivanovich, hear me? You will go to the club where you found the first two assassins. You will wait at the bar for a freelancer named Kata."

Gurin blinked. "That club is always packed, sir. How will I find this Kata?"

"Just stay put." Baev's smile was as wide as the Cheshire cat's. "Kata will find you."

35

BLACK SEA COAST, UKRAINE

"Omega murdered your husband and abducted your children," Lyudmila said. "Have you given any thought as to why Omega would do these things?"

"To get back at me for infiltrating their compound here in Odessa."

"Killing your husband, that I can understand. But what has abducting your children gained them?"

"Maybe it's you, Bobbi," Zherov offered.

They both looked at him.

"Isn't it possible that Omega," he said, expounding on his theory, "wants to draw you to them."

"Into a trap," Lyudmila added.

Kobalt's eyes were alight. "That's precisely what Omega is doing. But they've made a mistake that will prove fatal." She looked tellingly at Lyudmila. "Omega expects me to hunt my children down. They're counting on my maternal instincts taking over, making me careless. Making me vulnerable. The very opposite is true. I will find their headquarters—"

"It's somewhere in the Carpathian Mountains," Zherov interjected rashly.

Kobalt shot him a look that would have stopped a charging rhinoceros in its tracks. It certainly shut him up. But Lyudmila was too quick.

"If the compound was deserted, how did you find this out?"

Kobalt did not, at this stage, want to share the fact of Marta's existence or what she had told them. She still didn't trust Lyudmila's motives; she was the most enigmatic person Kobalt had ever encountered. Everything about her was obscure, unknowable. She thought quickly. "It's a best guess. We found scorched fragments of Romanian liturgical literature. There are a number of remote monasteries, churches, and castles once owned by religious leaders in remote sections of the Carpathians."

Lyudmila nodded, drew out her cell, and stepping away, made a call. When she returned, she said, "We'll soon find out whether this lead is good or a dead end."

"I have confidence in it," Zherov said. Kobalt wanted to punch him. He had no idea the deep water they were in with Lyudmila. Like the shark she was she'd chew him up and spit out the inedible parts as soon as look at him.

Wanting desperately to change the subject, Kobalt said, "You were going to tell me why you came out of hiding."

"Not now," Lyudmila said.

She rose abruptly and, without another word, went back up on deck. Keeping well away from her crew, she leaned against the port railing, shook out a cigarette and lit up. She was not much of a smoker, in fact she could take smoking or leave it, but the small movements, the precise ritual, calmed her mind, allowing it to work unencumbered.

She now had more complete information than either Evan or Kobalt had separately. But it remained unclear to her why, if Omega had indeed abducted Kobalt's children to gain revenge or leverage on her, they had involved Evan? This was not a question she could put to either sister, as neither was aware of the other. A major difficulty was that, unlike Nemesis, she knew so little about Omega. At every step, her people had come up against a stone wall. A couple of them had been killed trying to dig into the organization. But if Kobalt and Zherov were telling the truth, then she was closer to the nerve center of Omega than she'd ever been.

She had just learned a basic tenet of field work, an area for which she had had no training and had never been cut out for, mainly because she was simply too beautiful, her face too memorable to allow her to get lost in any flow of people, no matter how large. Hers was a supremely ordered mind. Someone ignorant of her inner workings might have mistaken her mind for that of a bureaucrat. She was far too clever and calculating. She could—and sometimes did—eat bureaucrats for breakfast, one of the aspects that made her too dangerous for the Politburo. She was simply advancing too quickly, especially for a female.

The problem she was currently grappling with was this: plans are by definition fixed, whereas field work was mutable. What she had learned today was basic to field work but was absent from her own training in the FSB. When in the field, you not only had to have a plan B, but also plans C, D, E, and F, in order to ensure success.

Everything was going according to her clever and calculated plan until Kobalt's children were abducted, throwing a gigantic spanner in the works. It was as if a moment ago she was hurtling full speed down the highway she had carefully chosen, and now she had been forced to a halt by a tractor-trailer jackknifed across the road.

She took the smoke deep into her lungs, let it out in a slow stream. She looked across to the Ukrainian frigate. Its decks appeared nearly deserted, but she wasn't fooled. The Ukrainian Navy was always on alert.

When she engineered her own extraction from Russia, she had been freed of so many burdens they were impossible to count. For some time before that, she had prepared herself to continue her clandestine work, which was why she had gathered her own private network around her.

If what Kobalt had told her regarding her children was true, then her plan was back on track—or would be shortly. In Lyudmila's opinion nothing good ever came from children— they threw you off course, muddled your mind—made you, in effect, crazy—useless for espionage on any level, especially for field work. During the grueling vetting process three and a half years ago she had gone to great pains to query Kobalt time and again about her attachment to the children she left behind. Time and again, Kobalt had assured her she had no attachment to them whatsoever.

At that moment, she felt a presence behind her. Kobalt. She did not turn from her contemplation of the Ukrainian ship. She was unsurprised.

She said nothing; she could wait Kobalt out.

Kobalt cleared her throat, and Lyudmila knew she was nervous. Kobalt was not alone in that—apart from Evan, most everyone was nervous around her. She possessed that kind of heat lightning. Furthermore, she knew how to deploy it.

"We're getting under way soon?"

Lyudmila contrived not to hear her. "Where is Zherov?"

"Asleep. We've had hardly any rest in thirty-six hours."

"And yet here you are." Her voice was tart and clipped.

"I, uh . . . I wanted to talk with you."

"And here I am."

There was a tense silence between them that she knew Kobalt was struggling to understand. *I should write a book*, she thought, *detailing all the ways to keep people off-balance. I'd call it* The Little Bitch Book *and put it under lock and key so no one but Evan would learn my secrets.*

Kobalt cleared her throat again. "Did you know that we were attacked in Istanbul?"

"I know everything that happened to you and Zherov in Istanbul."

Not everything, Kobalt thought. *You don't know that I now have control over the millions of dollars Dima has been stealing and stashing away in a bank in Cyprus. You don't know that, seeing he had already checked the account, I've drained it, using Dima's ID and password. I transferred the money into a dummy account I had set up before my exfiltration just in case I ran into trouble in Russia. From there I bought Bitcoins. Two minutes after it cleared I sold the Bitcoins. I took a 2 percent loss, but that was more than acceptable, and now the money, absolutely untraceable, resides in my own account in a prominent Lichtenstein bank. You don't know that I've ruined Dima.* She said none of this to Lyudmila, of course; she still did not trust her. But there was another reason. Ever since she had stolen into her father's closet, read the truth, Russian-through-and-through, she had been addicted to secrets. Hoarding secrets made her feel safe, as if they were stones in the walls of the castle she was building around herself. Secrets made her strong; if she gathered enough around her, she would be invincible.

Instead, she said, "You must suspect who sent the ex-convict Russian assassin after us."

"You'd think so."

"So you don't?"

Her gaze passed over Kobalt, making her shiver. "I know that for the past six months or so SVR has been employing ex-con mercenaries to carry out their wet work. Very neat, very clean. No blowback to the State."

"I have come to the same conclusion. With none of Zherov's contacts willing to talk, he and I are thinking maybe Director General Baev is behind the move. I've made myself extremely valuable to Zaslon and to the SVR. Maybe Baev didn't expect that. Maybe he doesn't want that shine on Dima."

Below them the engines started up. The lines had been secured, and they began to move, the slip they were in slowly sliding away. Soon enough they had picked up speed as they paralleled the coast, heading southwest. Despite all her protection, Lyudmila felt a distinct relief at leaving the warship behind.

Having waited in silence while the yacht departed, Kobalt now turned to Lyudmila, one elbow on the railing. "Now might be the time to tell me why you stuck your head up into the waking world. Down below, you said, 'Not now.' But I think what you meant was, 'Not now, not here.'"

Lyudmila shook out another cigarette. When she offered it to Kobalt the younger woman shrugged and shook her head. Placing the cigarette between her lips she lit it. For some time, they stood in an uneasy silence, Lyudmila smoking, Kobalt gripping the rail with pale knuckles.

The yacht headed steadily southwest, the shoreline slipping by in a haze of beaches, candy-striped umbrellas, whitewashed one- and two-story resorts, sunbathing figures, and hollering children splashing in the surf.

At length, with smoke drifting out of her half-open mouth, Lyudmila said, "You may be right. There is the war between Baev and Dima."

"A war?"

"Between Baev and his directorate heads there is always a cold war being waged beneath the surface. It's the same between FSB and the GRU. It's merely a matter of how nasty these wars get. The fact is Dima and Baev hate each other's guts. That doesn't happen so often, not within SVR, anyway." She took another draw deep into her lungs. "You know, don't you, that holding on to power is far more difficult than gaining it. Of this Baev is acutely aware. Retaining his power means, sooner or later, he must destroy the influence of those below him before they become a real threat."

She ran a hand distractedly through her hair. "This was my sin. Can you believe it? Because I am a woman only. I knew how to play the game. When SVR became too small for me, I moved up into the Politburo. I did what Baev does, what any politician worth her salt does, I began to obliterate my competition." For a moment, she stared at the glowing end of her cigarette. "Had I been a man, I would have been hailed. Instead, as my power and influence grew, I frightened those above me. They formed a cabal and ousted me. In Russia, a man's power and influence will always win out over that of a woman's, no matter how smart, how clever she may be."

A gull swept down, crying, then cut sharply in toward shore, where wicker and plastic picnic baskets were being unloaded onto blankets and gaily striped beach balls lofted into the sunlit afternoon.

Behind Lyudmila's eyes her mind lit up like rocket flares. "But I mean to change that."

"How?"

Lyudmila dragged smoke into her lungs, let it out through her nostrils. "All in good time, Kobalt. Now I will tell you why I came out of hiding. I've discovered the whereabouts of your parents—your birth parents."

Kobalt's heart seemed to skip a beat and then another and another. She lost the ability to breathe. It was a good thing she was gripping the railing, otherwise she would have stumbled and fallen to her knees.

Lyudmila's eyes bored into her. "I am of the belief that you want to know about them. Is this correct?"

"Yes." Kobalt nearly choked on the word.

"It is also my belief that you would like me to take you to them." Another drag on her cigarette. "Is this correct?"

"It is," Kobalt said, in a strangled voice.

Lyudmila placed a hand on Kobalt's shoulder. "Then it is done." For the first time, her smile contained genuine warmth. "It is for this—for you—that I have revealed myself."

Kobalt, still in shock, did not know what to say, so she said nothing. Concentrated simply on breathing.

Lyudmila was finished with her cigarette. The shoreline sliding past them was now deserted beach; all signs of civilization had vanished.

36

BERGISCH GLADBACH, GERMANY

At some point when she was lost in her increasingly taxing conversation, Ben had entered the inn. He was sitting at a table, drinking coffee and pretending to read a local paper he had picked up from the wooden rack beside the front door. She dearly wished there was some way she could tell him that Ana was a clinical psychologist who had been working at the clinic under Dr. Reveshvili.

"Herr *Doktor*," she said now. "Do you know where Ana Helm is now?"

Reveshvili patted his lips fastidiously, set the linen napkin back on his lap. "The truth is, I don't know. She left here under something of a cloud."

"Can you tell me what happened?"

He pushed his plate away, took a deliberate sip of coffee, set the cup back down precisely in the center of the saucer. "We had a disagreement over her commandeering more and more of the laboratories. Other clinicians were complaining that their own work was suffering as a result. At first, Ana put me off, saying she just required a bit more time to verify her work.

She said she was very close." He grimaced. "The disagreement escalated from there. As time went on, she contrived to evade me, until one night I returned to the clinic to find her feverishly working in three lab spaces at once. I realized then that her experimentation had become unacceptable, dangerous."

Evan forced herself not to lean forward, or in any other manner give away her heightened interest. "What was she working on, Herr *Doktor*?"

He raised his hand, and Armand was at his elbow, refilling his coffee cup. "Do you wish anything else, Fraulein?"

"Thank you, no." She returned his smile, then turned it toward Armand. "Everything was delicious."

"You are too kind, Fraulein." He did everything but click his heels. Then he was off to see to another table.

She turned her attention back to Reveshvili. "The experiments, Herr *Doktor*. Ana Helm's experiments."

"Yes, of course." He rubbed his chin. "Ana was experimenting with organophosphorus compounds. More specifically those that deal with the human neurotransmitter acetylcholine."

"Toward what end?" Evan asked.

Reveshvili shook his head. "This was the crux of our falling out, and my subsequent order for her to leave." He called for the check, signed it. Clearly, he had a house account. He left a generous amount as a gratuity, unusual for a European. Bills always included a tip, modest by American standards.

"Ana claimed that she was creating a chemical that would rebuild neurotransmitters in the brain, in order to help victims of stroke, seizures, calamitous accidents, that sort of thing."

"And you didn't believe her."

"I did not. She was clearly lying to me, hiding the truth."

"Have you any idea what her true aim was?"

"Unfortunately, no. Her work was exceedingly complex; she left no sera, no notes behind. She worked alone, so there were no assistants to query."

He cleared his throat. "Now, if you will be so kind as to accompany me. I will drive you to the clinic so I can take a look at that head wound of yours."

Reveshvili's car was a vintage MG convertible the precise color of the forest that rose not a hundred yards from where it crouched on the far edge of the gravel. The doctor opened the passenger's side door for her, and she got in. Standing, he was quite a bit thinner than she had imagined. Taller too, several inches over six feet, she estimated. His shoes, though, were just as she imagined. As he rounded the grille to get behind the wheel, she saw Ben hurrying out of the inn, looking at her with a furrowed brow. There was no way to contact him, as Reveshvili was already beside her. He turned the key in the ignition, the MG rumbled to life, and he pulled out of the parking area with more speed than she thought necessary.

Almost immediately, it was clear that the doctor loved driving, loved his car even more. The engine hummed happily along, by which she knew he—or, more likely, an ace mechanic—kept the vehicle in perfect running order.

The drive up to the clinic was level and straight, almost to the end, when the road curved to the left, sweeping around a steep grade, then heading right toward the side of the clinic where, it seemed, there was a private lot for the use of the staff.

They entered via an unprepossessing door and were immediately in a corridor. He preceded her inside. As she was at the threshold, she glanced back over her shoulder, saw Ben silently getting out of his car. His eyes were riveted on her. She gave him a quick smile, then passed into the interior of the clinic, following Reveshvili's narrow back. Without turning her head, she noted the CCTV mini camera aimed at the doorway, as well as someone who might at first be mistaken for a doctor or an orderly but by the width of his shoulders and the set of his stance she knew to be a guard. In the brief glance she caught of him she couldn't tell whether or not he was armed.

She followed a number of turns, memorizing each one. Behind her the clinic stretched away, seeming like a labyrinth. The corridor gave out onto a suite of offices. Apart from a faintly medicinal odor, she could have been in the core of any business on earth. As they entered into his office suite, into the anteroom to his surgery, his pace abruptly quickened. With a rapid motion he turned over a framed photo, locked it away in a drawer of his magnificent Biedermeier desk.

"Come, come, Fraulein," he said brusquely with his forefinger crooked. "This way." He had become the doctor and she the patient. His territory.

To Evan's trained eye the anteroom might have been that of a Prussian general—which is to say a gentleman as well as a battlefield commander. Everything had its place, everything within the office was just so. Not a pen, not a sheet of paper, not even a paper clip was out of place. And yet, despite its precise formality it was neither austere nor inhuman. It was clearly a lived-in space. CCTV mini camera in here as well, and she supposed the entire clinic was thus protected from intruders and wandering patients.

Though it was as orderly as Reveshvili's office, the surgery was as cold as a stainless-steel ice chest. To their left was placed a reclining leather sofa, common to any therapist's office, and, some six feet away, a high-backed chair upholstered in a well-worn tweed, thick as an English winter mackintosh. To their right rose a doctor's examining table, covered in a sheet of disposable paper. It was on this Reveshvili indicated she should lie, while he washed his hands at a sink against the wall. No guard here so while his back was turned, she crossed through the doorway in the rear wall, peered down a corridor that led farther into the clinic's interior. She saw two more guards chatting away. At that moment, she saw a light go on in the right-hand wall of the corridor, over an elevator. The illuminated B moved to 1, the door opened and as someone stepped out, she ducked back into Reveshvili's exam room. As he dried his hands, she hoisted herself onto the table.

She was still assessing what she had noted: the turns in the outer corridor, the CCTV cameras, the guards, and the elevator, as he brought over a hooded lamp, a magnifier on a gooseneck stand, and a rolling metal tabouret, in which, presumably, he kept his instruments.

"Please be good enough to lie down, Fraulein," he said in a matter-of-fact tone. "I need to examine the wound."

He sat on a stool, snapped on a pair of latex gloves and, stooping over her, brought first the light, then the magnifier to bear on the left side of her head.

"What happened here?" He could as easily been talking to himself as asking her.

Nevertheless, she felt compelled to provide an answer. "The hazards of being in a foreign country and not knowing one's way around, Herr *Doktor*."

To this, he made a sound: a good old-fashioned harrumph. Evan almost laughed. She didn't know anyone harrumphed in this day and age. But, then, in some ways, Reveshvili seemed to belong to another time, a bygone age when men were ruled by honor.

He spent an inordinately long time examining not only the wound but her entire face, a slight frown on his countenance that might have indicated a kind of puzzlement.

"Is everything all right?" she asked. "Is the wound infected?"

"Please remain still, Fraulein," Reveshvili said sternly. "I am injecting you with a subcutaneous anesthetic. You will feel no discomfort whatsoever beyond this tiny pinch." He worked in silence for the next ten minutes while she stared at the ceiling and tried to unravel the mystery of Fraulein *Doktor* Ana Helm—if that was, indeed, her real name. Who was she? What was her connection to William Onders, the man who had tried to kidnap her? Was she involved in some way, or was that photo of the two of them a remembrance of a fleeting romance? And why was Pine, Onders's partner in crime, also carrying a photo of Ana? Only one thing was clear at the moment: Reveshvili wasn't going to provide the answers. At least not willingly.

37

SCHNELLER PSYCHIATRIC CLINIC,
BERGISCH GLADBACH

"You seem uncommonly tense, Fraulein," Reveshvili said when he had finished, and they were seated in his office. He cocked his head again, just slightly. "I haven't overstepped myself, have I?"

"Not at all." She and Reveshvili had glasses of freshly brewed coffee he had poured from an insulated carafe on a polished wood sideboard. The coffee was strong and delicious. They held their glasses by their handles.

"Mm." He took a sip. "But I imagine trying to find a friend who has disappeared can cause tension, yes?"

She nodded. "It can."

He sat back, lifted his head as if looking at the ceiling. "I look at you, Fraulein, and I think of myself at your age. But, you know, the older I get the harder it is to picture myself." His head came down and his eyes fastened on her. "I can see the setting—school, ballfields, winter skiing trips to the mountains, summer excursions to a small house by a lake. A very still lake. Still and very, very deep." He shook his head. "But there is no me in those memories, or if there is, I'm so blurred I cannot make myself out."

Evan was intrigued despite herself. Once again, his demeanor had done a ninety-degree turn. "What about home? Surely you can see your younger self at home."

He continued to stare at her with the same intensity as when she was lying on the table in his surgery. "Home?" he said at length. "I have no memories of home at all." His voice had taken on a kind of singsong quality, inviting her to sink into it. "And to that, dear Fraulein, I wonder whether I had a home at all."

"But you must have. Everyone has a home." Did her own voice sound slurry, or was she imagining it?

"You know, it is a strange and perplexing fact that I was and remain afraid of that lake. It was so large, so dark, so deep that no swimmer could touch bottom." A peculiar calm swept over her—a certain warmth. "And do you know, as I remember it, the water was always black, as if something in it—a mineral possibly—repelled the sunlight. What was down there, I wondered in my youth. Monsters. My own monsters, perhaps." His voice had changed again. Like the sirens of *The Odyssey* it had become a beguiling song. "And even though I still feel the fear, that *gottverdammt* lake is what I remember with crystal clarity."

He took a longer drink of his coffee as if this memory still had the power to unnerve him. At length, he got around to answering her question: "I was a ward of the State. I was raised by the State. Whatever other memories I might have once had of that time have been obliterated."

"I'm sorry, Herr *Doktor*." Somewhat to her surprise, she found that she was.

He did not acknowledge her sentiment. "My patients often tell me that you cannot miss what you never had. But home, parents . . . In this I think they can be very wrong, yes?"

"It's possible, I suppose." Evan felt disoriented, as if she had been dropped into the black pool inside the caverns of her youth or that black lake of Reveshvili's childhood. She fought to regain her sense of equilibrium, but it seemed to be a losing battle. In fact, she didn't seem to want to regain it. She felt as if she were lying on her back, looking at the summer sky through the dappled shade of a huge apple tree. Back and forth the dappling went, swung by a breeze. Back and forth.

"I told you before that you appeared to be inordinately tense. But I sense that you are also distraught."

"My sister—my late sister's—children have been abducted. I'm trying to find them."

"Ah. I think now you tell me the truth. And you think Ana is somehow involved?"

"I don't know. But the man she was with in that photo surely was. Since he's dead, I have to find Ana and ask her."

"Mm. Possibly I can help with that."

"How? Tell me how."

"Nurture or nature—"

"How does that—"

"Indulge me if you will. Nurture or nature, which plays a greater role in the formative years of a child? This question is endlessly debated, most fiercely, without a shadow of a doubt, in the psychiatric community. It has been my experience that when we examine the early life of a single child, we inevitably find that nature is triumphant. The single child must rely on him or herself more and thus his or her traits are forced to the fore more quickly, more forcefully. Whereas, with siblings the opposite is true. Because siblings rely on each other in their formative years, nurture is the primary guiding force."

A gentle rustling. "Are you with me so far?"

"Mm." She laughed softly. His voice had become aqueous—the lake itself or the underground pool—they seemed to have merged. The apple tree was gone. In its place, shadows passed across the jagged rock ceiling like clouds. Her eyes were closed as she sank into the dark icy water.

"So. Then what do we learn when we are confronted with twin sisters—or brothers, hm? Curiously, I have discovered that these two siblings—it must be two for this to hold true—are opposites. In other words, for one nurture takes the upper hand, for the other, it is nature."

She found herself tumbling backward in time to when she and Bobbi were young.

"I find myself wondering, dear Fraulein, whether this is the case with you and your sister. I am very much interested in your response. Perhaps you will be kind enough to enlighten me."

"I was born on the last day of the year in the Black Hills of South Dakota. My sister, Bobbi, came two years later, almost to the day. Our parents owned a large horse ranch, along with tin and copper mines. Drive an hour or two west and you'd be in Wyoming. I loved to explore the nearby hidden cave system."

"What about Bobbi?"

"Bobbi liked the caves, or said she did . . ." The shadows skittered away from her every time she looked for them on the inside of her closed eyelids ". . . up to a point."

"Up to what point?" Reveshvili asked in his soft singsong voice.

"I don't . . . remember . . ."

"Of course you remember," Reveshvili urged gently. "Every memory of your life is stored inside your brain. It is merely a question of opening the right door."

"This door . . . I think this door is locked."

"Mm, and who locked it, dear Fraulein?"

Evan became confused. "Who?"

"Carla." Reveshvili leaned forward. "That is your given name, yes?"

A pause. "Yes . . . No . . ."

"What shall I call you now," Reveshvili said, "as it appears Carla is not your real name?"

"Ev . . . Evan."

"Ah." He allowed a short silence to fall, as if at the end of the first act. "So, Evan, who locked that particular door?"

"I did."

"Then you must have the key."

"I don't . . . What if I don't want to open it?"

"I think," Reveshvili said, "that it is already unlocked."

The black water purled all around her.

"I think you have unlocked it," Reveshvili said. "You have unlocked it right here, right now."

He was right, she knew he was right. The veil between the world inside her and the world outside seemed to have vanished. She swam through the door. "I did it." Her voice was hoarse, throttled.

"You did what?" Reveshvili asked.

"I left her in one of the caves . . . Bobbi."

"When was this?"

"I was . . . almost thirteen, I think. So Bobbi was ten, almost eleven."

Evan took a breath, let it out with a soft hiss. "It was growing dark outside and she wanted to get back, be home. I didn't. She kept badgering me. We fought. She broke down crying and it was too much. I left her there."

"You left Bobbi in the cave for how long?"

"Overnight."

"Did she ever tell your parents?"

"No."

"Did you talk with her about it subsequently?"

"I couldn't."

"And she wouldn't." Reveshvili made a low humming sound between his half-open lips. "Why is that, do you think?"

"I don't know." Another deep breath, ragged this time. "But

nothing was ever the same between us after that, not on the inside anyway. On the outside, we needed each other, especially after our parents were killed."

Reveshvili leaned even closer. "Evan, can you say why you left Bobbi in the cave?"

"I already . . . She got on my nerves."

"Overnight."

Evan drew another breath, even more ragged this time. "Yes. Overnight."

"You fought in the caves."

"Yes."

"What did you fight about, Evan?"

The shadows were moving ever faster; vertigo took hold of Evan, its sharp nails digging into her flesh.

Two vertical lines appeared above the bridge of her nose. "Bobbi had a secret."

"A secret."

"Yes. She knew something I didn't. Something important. I knew it was important because she told me she found it among our father's papers when she was skulking around the house being bored."

"Why do you think she wouldn't tell you."

"She could be a bitch when she wanted to be."

"And?"

"I tried to find it, but I couldn't. And she would never tell me."

"I believe you know that is not what I meant."

Evan hesitated for some time. Finally, she said so softly, Reveshvili had to lean over to hear her, "She felt helpless in the caves. She wanted . . . she needed some control."

"But you wouldn't let her have it."

"I was so angry."

Reveshvili sat back, hands in his lap. He watched her carefully, carefully marked the emotions scudding across Evan's face.

"Evan," he said at last, "I believe very strongly that you have the answer to Bobbi's secret. It is inside you. It is a secret you both share."

"I don't know . . . I don't . . . Where should I look?"

"Memories—memories of you when you were very young, four, possibly three."

Silence. Then, "Toys, games, seeing Bobbi as a baby. One day, just like that, as if she was delivered by a stork."

"Perhaps she was. What else?"

"N . . . Nothing. But . . ."

"But what?"

"I used to have a dream. It repeated, it . . ."

"Can you say what it was about?"

"Shadows, shadows moving on the wall, across the floor, fast as a bat's wings."

For long minutes Reveshvili was lost in thought. "You know, Evan, dreams and memories, they are not so very different." He smiled. "Every once in a while there is no difference at all."

"But they told me . . . my parents told me it was a dream. To just forget . . ."

His smiled faded. "Tell me please, Evan, how many fingers do you have on one hand?"

In her current state, the question didn't seem odd. "Five."

"Five, yes. There is your key, Evan: the number five."

"I don't . . . I don't understand."

"In time you will," Reveshvili said. "Have faith."

She was asleep now. Fast asleep. She had reached the end of her tether; she couldn't go on. Rising, Reveshvili understood this. He scooped her up, laid her gently down on the sofa. He placed a pillow under her head. For long minutes he studied her. It was a deep meditation, as if he were committing every last inch of her to memory.

He covered her with a light blanket, turned off the lights, and silently as a shadow retreated back to his desk, where he unlocked a drawer, drew out one of two dossiers, opened it to the correct page and, taking up his beloved Montblanc fountain pen, began to write. Every so often he would glance up, his eyes resting on Evan. It was impossible to know what thoughts were now filling him up.

38

MOSCOW, RUSSIA

It was after 1 a.m. of a star-spangled morning when Gurin invoked his FSB ID to get past PP&J's velvet curtain. PP&J, on Tverskaya Street, not far from Red Square, was a nightclub, strip joint, restaurant and, of importance to Gurin, a private club. Each section was gifted with a different décor. The bar was typically gaudy—a polished copper-top stainless-steel affair presided over by four female bartenders, all of whom were in constant motion serving drinks to the young, rich, wild black-clad revelers crowded three deep. The restaurant was a poshly seated affair, with tables far enough away from each other so discreet conversations would be no problem. Here, minor government officials and their mistresses rubbed elbows with middle-management criminals and their plasticized models moonlighting as escorts. The pole-dancing was off to the left. Nicknamed Siberia, it was for goggle-eyed businessmen, intent on dropping as much money as they could before they got laid.

The private club was an animal of a genus altogether different. The lizard-world was confined to the first floor; up here on the second floor was where the charismatic megafauna roamed, grazed, and plotted destruction and wealth.

The club was accessed by a deliberately narrow staircase at the top of which stood a pair of ex-wrestlers, probably sprung out of prison expressly for the purpose of keeping the riffraff out, no matter how many bills they waved in their faces. The pale Norwegian wood paneling started on the way up, interspersed with small shaded wall lamps.

The club itself was split into three separate areas: the lounge, with its low leather chairs draped with sheepskins and the ubiquitous quartet of Andy Warhol's lithos of Marilyn Monroe, each in a different colorway. In the middle was a bar, smaller than the one down below, and not in the least bit glitzy—all of that had been left to the riffraff and non-members. The third area was the inner sanctum, where the club elite—high-level mobsters and their main contacts in the legitimate world—smoked cigars, drank iced vodka, toyed with their arm candy, and eventually, after the girls were temporarily exiled to the lounge, got down to the serious business of cyber-extortion, blackmail, money laundering, and worldwide cryptocurrency scams.

The lights were lower here, the music Frank Sinatra and Dean Martin instead of Venom and Alcest, black-metal bands whose hellhound music was prone to give Gurin an ocular migraine.

Even Gurin's normal FSB card, identifying him as an adjutant, would have no sway up here, but he was carrying a different card, one that made him out to be a full colonel, which bought him an immediate entrée.

Gurin saw the group of men who, for a usurious fee, had recommended the professional murderers to him, the two men who had failed to kill Evan Ryder and were now no longer among the living. He needed to go several steps beyond these people, who had once seemed so formidable.

He cut right, sat at the bar, and ordered three shots of vodka, downing them one after the other without a pause. When the bartender asked if he wanted a refill, Gurin waved him off. He had chosen a swivel seat that had a clear view of the door to the inner sanctum, three steps up from the other areas. The guard looked like an automaton, his flat Slavic face devoid of any expression, let alone emotion. No one was admitted, no one even made the attempt, and after twenty minutes of this Gurin was considering what his plan B might be when the door opened and a woman stepped out. Gurin caught a brief glimpse of the interior, which was so befogged with cigar smoke the occupants were reduced to two-dimensional shadows.

The woman came down the three stairs as if she were a queen descending from her throne. Unlike many of the showgirls here and downstairs, she was elegantly clad in a little black dress that sheathed her curves perfectly. A gold choker was around her throat, a ring sporting a square-cut emerald as big as a baby's knuckle on her right index finger. Diamond studs pierced her earlobes.

She was a veritable ice queen—pale skin, pale blond hair, pale gray eyes. She wore nude lipstick. When she walked over to the bar her hips swayed provocatively. *Click-clack* went her high heels against the granite floor. *Click-clack*.

She was striking without Gurin understanding quite why. In other circumstances—when she woke up in the morning, for instance—she might have even been plain looking. But right now in this milieu, dressed as she was, she was anything but.

She sat next to Gurin without looking at him. She was an inhabitant of another world. To her, Gurin scarcely existed.

She ordered a vodka martini, dirty, with a raft of three olives. She knew what she wanted, and the bartender knew it. He knew her as well, for he said, "Immediately, Ms. Hemakova." And she received it immediately, precisely as she asked for it. She took her first sip, put the glass down, and lit up a cigarette.

Sinatra was singing "In the Wee Small Hours of the Morning." Without looking at him and at the same time exhaling a plume of smoke, she said, "I've often wondered whether this song is optimistic or pessimistic."

At first, he wondered whether Ms. Hemakova was actually talking to him because he couldn't for the life of him imagine why she should. Then she turned to him slowly and deliberately and he knew that for some reason beyond his comprehension she had been speaking to him.

He cleared his throat, realizing he felt a bit giddy. "Well, it certainly is melancholy."

"So much of Sinatra's repertory is, don't you think?" She gave him the once-over, assessing him with the same sharp knowledgeable gaze an assay officer might turn on a lump of shiny ore to ascertain whether it was iron pyrite or gold.

"I do," he said at length. "But as for this specific song I come down firmly on the optimistic side. I think he will see her again, finally tell her he loves her, before she falls into his arms."

"So you're neither an optimist nor a pessimist," she said. "You're a romantic."

"Aren't all Russians?"

She shrugged her beautiful shoulders. "That's what Lermontov would have you believe, anyway." Mikhail Lermontov was a poet and novelist of the mid-seventeenth century, Russia's leading Romanticist. She laughed, a low lovely purr. "As a girl I used to have a crush on Pechorin, Lermontov's greatest creation."

All at once, she held out a hand, slim and long fingered. "Kata."

He looked at her as if she had just landed from Venus. This was the assassin Baev had sent him to meet? The idea fairly took his breath away.

A Mona Lisa smile transfigured her face.

He took her hand and was immediately astonished by the

flash of heat that went through him. This was followed by his surprise at how tough and calloused the palm was. "Yuri." He gave her the false name on his ID.

"So." She took another puff, shot the smoke out of the corner of her mouth away from him. "Yuri, are you not a Russian Romantic?"

He smiled sheepishly. "I'm afraid I am normally too much of a pessimist."

"Mm. That must be on account of your work."

"You know what my work is?"

"FSB. Word gets around. As to the specifics, I am content to remain in the dark."

He smiled. He liked this woman, which was unusual for him. Now he needed to gather himself to say what he needed to say. "Kata, I am looking for someone."

"And you believe that I can help you."

"That is my hope, yes."

"Hope. This is not the precinct of a pessimist."

He laughed into her smile. "So. Perhaps you have unearthed a bit of the optimist in me."

"You know, Yuri, we have been talking for perhaps ten minutes and not once have you made an off-color remark or made a move on me."

"Are you pleased or disappointed?"

That purring laugh again. "I like you, Yuri. I really do."

"Thank you, and I return the compliment."

They stared at each other while Dean Martin sang "My Rifle, My Pony and Me."

"This song," she said with a wry twitch to her lips, "I would think the Sovereign has this playing every night after dinner." Her lips formed a moue. "Or shouldn't I say that in front of an FSB officer?"

Gurin smiled. "I would think, Kata, that you're the kind of person who can get away with saying anything she wants."

Again, he felt the intensity of her gaze as she reassessed him. "You said you wanted to find someone," she said, stubbing out the butt of her cigarette. "I will help you."

He looked at her more closely, trying and failing to judge Baev's choice. "Kata, are you someone who will kill without either remorse or regret?"

"Precisely so." She drained her glass

"Full disclosure. This target is a stone-cold killer. She has no remorse. She will not hesitate to kill you."

A slow smile spread across Kata's face. "Just my type of target."

"Kobalt is indeed."

Gurin knew that Baev mistook him for a spineless toady who would never buck an order, and Gurin had made good use of that misconception recently. He had already tried to kill Kobalt twice, the first time by clandestinely betraying her identity to Omega, the second by hiring a "farm hand" to go after her in Istanbul; good thing he didn't have to pay that fee.

Baev never knew, he was quite certain, so it wouldn't occur to Baev now that Gurin might give Kata a remit other than the one he was sent here with—to have Kata kill Evan Ryder. But Gurin had no intention of setting this supreme assassin after Ryder when he could manipulate her into terminating Kobalt, who he knew, with the confidence of the short-sighted, was a threat to the State and to his own lofty ambitions. He was already imagining the kudos he would reap when his initiative in ridding Russia of an American mole would be revealed to his superiors.

"Kobalt is one of your own, so I'm given to believe." Kata shook out another cigarette and lit up. "That's quite a problem you have there, Yuri."

He nodded. "I'm painfully aware of that."

She started laughing.

He frowned. "What's so funny?"

"No, no. Not you. But the situation itself is, you must admit. Here you are an officer in the FSB asking me for help in terminating one of your own." Her eyes crinkled. "The irony tickles me pink."

He did not share in her hilarity. "For a number of reasons, the killing cannot be traced back to . . . the FSB." In his quaking heart he meant "to me," but knew Kata would interpret this to mean "to Baev," since as far as she knew, and would ever know, the remit he was here to give her came straight from the good Director General Baev himself. He suspected she had made sure the FSB, and Baev, had been carefully distanced from any number of previous assignments Baev had given this terrifying woman.

"Mm," she said, sobering up. She pulled out the olives from her glass. Her teeth crushed through them, one by one. "Poor, poor Yuri." Her hand cupped his face. Then she laughed again and said, "Have no worries, Kata can keep a secret." He felt her warmth, but only for a moment, before her hand was back on the bartop. She stubbed out her cigarette. "Let us now repair to a place that affords us privacy."

"As you wish." He nodded. "Lead on."

He followed her toward the private room, but at the last moment she veered to their right, taking him down a short corridor. *Click-clack. Click-clack.* The walls were covered in flocked fabric, the sconces gold rimmed. At the end, she opened a door and they stepped into a smallish room, square, windowless, that looked to be an office, at other hours of the day. Perhaps at this time of the night it might also serve as a venue for a private lap dance or two. A narrow desk, a swivel task chair, and a pair of club chairs were the furnishings. On the wall was a framed poster of Muhammed Ali in a boxing ring, standing over Sonny Liston, exhorting him to get the fuck up off the mat. Indirect light rimmed the room where the walls met the ceiling.

She closed the door behind him and said, "There now. This is an atmosphere more conducive to the finalization of our contract."

"How much do you want?" He was eager to consummate the deal—his deal, not Baev's, he thought smugly.

"Let's not get ahead of ourselves, Yuri." She stepped closer to him, watched his nostrils flare. When he told her he liked her perfume, she laughed her husky laugh. "Oh, Yuri, I never wear perfume."

She turned away to light up another cigarette, then turned back to him and took another step closer. "Now Yuri, back to business."

"Yes. I asked about your price."

Kata's eyes twinkled. "All right, let's start there. I think . . . let me see, oh, I don't know, one million should get it done."

"Rubles?"

"Don't be absurd." She tapped ash from her cigarette into a square dish, took a small drag so the lit end glowed brightly again. Blew the smoke into the air. "American dollars. Always."

For the sake of saving face, he considered this for a beat or two. "That can be arranged."

"Then you'll provide me with all salient details."

He handed over his mobile, open to where he'd already loaded the parts of the Kobalt dossier he wanted her to see, the information she would need to get to Kobalt. She sighed out another cloud of smoke as she read the intel. When she was finished memorizing, she looked up. "Since you've made it quite clear that the target will prove difficult, I shall require 70 percent up front."

"The usual payout is fifty before, the balance afterward, but in this case I'm willing to go to sixty up front."

She smiled into his eyes. "I don't bargain. My terms are non-negotiable."

He nodded. He was in too deep now to back out. All his

chips were on the table and she'd seen his hole card. He took back his mobile, and she gave him the name of her offshore bank and the account number. His fingers moved over the keyboard, then he handed her the phone again. "Done," he said. The money Baev had earmarked for Ryder's termination, now put to much better use.

She checked her account, saw the $700,000 had been electronically deposited.

She nodded. "But, Yuri, darling, you haven't heard all of my terms." She slipped his phone into one of his jacket pockets.

"What? But—"

That was when she leaned forward, pushed the glowing end of her cigarette into his left eye.

Gurin screamed. His body tried to jump back, but she had a firm hold on him, and she was strong. Her hand clamped him like a vise.

"My eye! My eye!"

"Yes, Yuri. Or should I call you Ilya Ivanovich? No, we don't know each other well enough. So. Gurin, if you ever want to see out of your left eye again, you'll tell me precisely how dangerous the target is. Very, I think, otherwise you would not have come to me."

"Please!" He nearly screamed. "Yes, yes, she's very dangerous. She evaded a trap in Odessa, and in Istanbul she killed one of our farm hands—" He paused, panting. "You know what a farm hand is."

She wriggled the cigarette slightly and Gurin would have slid to the floor if she hadn't been propping him up. "One of us is a moron, Ilya, and it isn't me." When he whimpered, she laughed. "You were right to seek me out. Clearly, brute strength and blunt force will not work on your target. This is your lucky night, Gurin. What you need, my friend, is someone with guile and the expertise to deploy . . . how shall we say . . . unorthodox methodology." Kata's eyes seemed to have glazed over. She was talking more to herself than to him. "She dodged death twice. Oh, killing her is going to be such fun." Silently, she thanked Baev for sending her this assignment, and of course the easier one she was about to finish. He really did know how to make her happy.

Gurin's face was blue-white, like a snowbank. His muscles were in spasm. She was expending more and more energy just keeping him upright.

He was weeping out of his good eye. "Please," he whined. "Please take it away."

"Sure thing." She shrugged. And reversed her ring, dragged the emerald in a scimitar line across his throat, stepping smartly away before the first gout of blood could sully her outfit. Without even a backward glance, she walked away. *Click-clack. Click-clack.*

39

BERGISCH GLADBACH, GERMANY

"Ana Helm."

Evan nodded. "Fraulein *Doktor* Ana Helm. According to Dr. Reveshvili."

Ben gave her a critical look. "You don't believe him?"

"I don't know what to believe, to be honest." She paused, looking around the lounge area of their inn to once again make sure they were alone. Security had become something of a tic with her since leaving the clinic. "For sure he's been lying to me about some things."

Ben's eyes narrowed. "But not everything?"

"No. That's my sense, anyway." She pressed her fingers into her eyes, rotating them slowly.

"Are you okay?"

"That's about the hundredth time you've asked me that, Ben."

"Well, a, you were in there far longer than I expected, and, b, you came out looking a bit spaced out."

"I'm just tired, that's all."

Ben grunted. "Being tired isn't your thing, Evan. What the hell happened in there?"

"I already told you. Reveshvili took care of my wound, and then we talked about his interest in twins, nature versus nurture, those kinds of things."

"And what else?"

She frowned. "I don't recall, exactly. More of the same, I guess."

Ben gave her a concerned look. "And about Ana? You think he lied about her name."

"At the very least he didn't tell me everything he knows about her."

"So how do we find out the truth?"

"Guards who didn't look like guards and a state-of-the-art CCTV system."

"No alarm?" Ben asked.

"If there was one," Evan said, "I didn't see it. And believe me I was looking."

They were crouched behind the manicured hedge that bordered the side of the staff parking lot farthest away from the clinic. At night, the hulking structure seemed to take on an altogether different aspect, larger, somehow muscular, as if it were a crouched animal waiting to lash out at its prey. Lights were on all over the building, which was only to be expected at a place like this when emergencies among the patients were apt to erupt at any time, day or night.

Evan led them around to the rear of the building, but there was no way to gain entrance. Continuing on, she saw that the land dropped away on the far side, and her pulse rate quickened. If there was an outside entrance to the basement, it would be there.

Coming around the corner, she raised a hand, and they froze in the deep shadows of the eaves. Ahead of them, a pair of men in clinic whites stood in the halo of a security light, smoking and chewing the fat. Every once in a while, they'd check their mobiles. They looked bored out of their minds.

Evan's heart was pounding. She shook her head, trying to clear it of the fuzziness that had been her close companion since she exited the clinic. She recalled a lake, black as this starless, moonless night. She recalled monsters deep beneath the surface. She recalled the cave system she explored in her youth. She recalled Bobbi's face, white as milk in the beam of her flashlight, her mouth opened wide. She recalled Bobbi tripping her as they ran down to the stream's edge. She recalled Bobbi laughing at her. She recalled Bobbi sobbing in bed when she was certain Evan was asleep. And she recalled the next morning when Bobbi had to explain why she had put her fist through the wall beside the place she slept.

Her vision cleared for a moment and she looked at her hand. Five fingers, she counted them off. Five. What did Reveshvili mean? The dream shadows moving across the wall, the floor.

"Evan." Ben whispered in her ear. "Evan, they're gone."

She refocused her attention. Through the vanishing cobwebs of the past, she saw he was right. The guards had moved on, leaving only the butts of their cigarettes ground in the grass beneath their boot heels.

"Did you see where they went?" she asked.

"Down. There's the entrance to the basement."

They crept forward, silent as the unstirring pines off to their left. They paused just outside the circle of light, saw it illuminated a wide, well-worn staircase. At the bottom of the short flight was a metal door set into the building's stonework.

Ben ran his fingertips around the edges. "No wire. No sign of an alarm."

She looked at the keys on the electronic locking panel. Standing to one side, she shone the light from her mobile on it from an oblique angle. The keys last used by the two men shone with the oil on their fingertips. She tried the combinations. The door opened on the fifth try.

They slipped inside. The basement was dimly lighted. It was clearly used mainly as storage. Boxes, crates, oxygen tanks all had their sections, all were stacked or lined up neatly. To their right a walk-in refrigerated unit such as would be seen in a butcher's shop, to their left the elevator and, beside it, a flight of ascending stairs. There was no one around, not that she expected there would be at this time of night.

Stepping over to the refrigerated unit, Evan pulled the lever, opened the door. She didn't know what to expect but she was hoping she wouldn't find anything grisly, such as body parts, jars of eyeballs swimming in fluid, the sort of evidence that was the stuff of pulp fiction. There was nothing like that, but rather glass cases lining both side walls, in which were arrayed sera in racks, clearly marked and numbered.

"Anything?" Ben asked when she had stepped out. He'd been keeping a lookout.

She shook her head as she closed the door. "Nothing of interest." She turned. "But then it's Reveshvili's office that interests me."

He indicated with his head. "We're best off taking the stairs."

They were moving toward the steps, when the elevator opened and Jon Pine stepped out.

Ben drew his pistol. "You're dead," he said incredulously.

Jon Pine raised his hands, but he was laughing good-naturedly. "Please be good enough to stand down, Herr Butler."

Ben's eyes narrowed. "You know my name."

"Consider what an absurd statement that is." Jon Pine was clad in a neatly tailored three-piece suit in pin-striped lightweight wool, a snow-white shirt, and a pale-blue tie. His feet were clad in tasseled loafers, shining brightly even in the low light.

"Ben, put the gun away," Evan said. She took a step forward. "You look exactly like Jon Pine. If you're not him, you must be his twin."

The man inclined his head. "Indeed, Fraulein Ryder. My name is Leonard Pine, and I am Jon's twin brother." His smile was genial, with not even a hint of guile. "I am the clinic's night manager."

Evan took another step forward. "You know both our names."

Pine's smile never faltered. "Dr. Reveshvili has many resources at his disposal."

She frowned. "Then why did he keep up the masquerade?"

"Ah, Fraulein Ryder, it was your masquerade. It interested Dr. Reveshvili." He lifted a hand. "Now if you will step into the elevator . . ."

Though Ben had stood down, he'd never returned the pistol to its holster in his armpit. It was aimed at the floor, but it was still an active threat. "Now why would we do that, Herr Pine."

Leonard Pine held the elevator door open. "Because you are both expected." He stood aside for them to enter.

A proper English tea, complete with ginger scones, clotted cream, tiny assorted cakes in a triple-decker metal stand, and, of course, a pot of Earl Grey, judging by the scent of bergamot wafting upward from the spout.

This midnight repast was set up in Reveshvili's office, although the Herr *Doktor* was nowhere in evidence. Evan asked where he was. "Resting," Leonard Pine said laconically.

Ben, having had the good sense to finally holster his weapon, said, "None of this makes any sense."

"Now," said Leonard Pine.

"Now what?" Ben said.

"It doesn't make sense now, at this moment." Was that completely benign smile ever going to leave Leonard Pine's face? "But it will."

The English tea service had been set up in the center of a small café table that might have been imported from Les Deux Magots in Paris or Berlin's original Café Einstein. A pair of black-and-white wicker chairs were on either side.

Leonard Pine gestured to Evan. "If you would be so kind."

As both she and Ben moved toward the chairs, Pine said, "Just Fraulein Ryder, if you please."

Ben turned, bewildered. "What about me?"

Leonard Pine stood, back straight, hands clasped at the small of his back. "You will accompany me, Herr Butler."

"And leave Evan here on her own." He shook his head. "Never happen, my friend."

"Ben, please." Evan took the chair indicated by Pine.

"Allow me to reassure you, Herr Butler, Fraulein Ryder is perfectly safe," Pine said in his stiff-necked manner. "There is no danger to her here. Her safety is vouchsafed by the Herr *Doktor* himself."

Still, Ben did not move until Evan gave him a look with which he was all too familiar. Only then did he step to Pine's side.

"Is everything to your satisfaction, Fraulein?" the night manager asked.

"You've got to be kidding," Ben muttered, but over him Evan said, "Yes, thank you, Herr Pine."

"It is entirely my pleasure, Fraulein."

She looked pointedly at the empty chair. "The tea is getting cold."

"I think not, Fraulein."

Ben took a more direct tack. "Someone else is expected."

"Indeed, Herr Butler."

"Would it by any chance be Reveshvili?"

The briefest flicker of displeasure at Ben's lack of manners passed across Leonard Pine's face before the professional smile returned. "The Herr *Doktor* is resting."

"As you said." Evan's smile was thin, inelastic. "But not indisposed, I trust?"

"He is quite well, Fraulein," Pine assured her. "Thank you for inquiring."

She was beginning to feel like Alice during her first few minutes at the Mad Hatter's tea party. She needed to shake things up. "Herr Pine, I regret to inform you that your brother Jon is dead."

"That does not surprise me," Pine said without one iota of change to his masklike expression.

"He attacked us—Herr Butler and me. We were forced to defend ourselves."

"Again," Pine said, with maddening sangfroid.

Evan looked at him searchingly. "This fact doesn't surprise, let alone disturb, you?"

"In no way, Fraulein. Knowing my brother as I did, his demise was only a matter of time."

"But we killed him."

"So I gather." His head briefly inclined to just the correct angle. "You are to be congratulated."

Ben stared at him, his mouth half-open.

"And now, Fraulein, Herr Butler and I will take our leave." With that pronouncement Pine turned on his well-shod heel. Ben accompanied him out, leaving Evan for the moment alone with the elaborate and inviting tea service.

Evan watched them out of Reveshvili's office. As she rose and stepped to his desk, she thought about the instant déjà vu she had felt upon first seeing Leonard Pine as he stood in the open doorway of the elevator. What a head rush! Dressed as he was, and with his impeccable manner, he was like looking at Jon Pine in a distorted funhouse mirror.

At Reveshvili's desk, she immediately went to the drawer in which he had locked away the photo he hadn't wanted her to see. The drawer was still locked, but it was with one of those small, flimsy mechanisms typical of desks. It took her less than ten seconds to jimmy it open, and there lay the 8x10 frame facedown.

With a quick glance at the open doorway to ascertain she was still alone, she lifted out the frame and turned it faceup. She stared at the photo for either seconds or hours, her buzzing mind had lost all sense of time and space. Without realizing it, she found herself seated in Reveshvili's chair. Despite her best efforts, her heart kept skipping beats. She could scarcely believe what she was seeing.

The photo showed a family of four, standing in dappled sunshine. The parents were on either side of their children—two prepubescent girls of extraordinary beauty. Already at this young age they both possessed the kind of faces the camera loved, faces that drew you in mesmerically. In this sense, she was already seeing preternatural adults. She looked from one face to the other and could not tell them apart. Identical twins, and there could be no doubt whatsoever. Both had the face of Fraulein *Doktor* Ana Helm.

Evan put a hand to her head, thinking of the two photos they had found. The one with William Onders was surely Ana, but the one they had found as part of Jon Pine's possessions could very well be of the twin. Turning on the desk's task light, she took out the photos, placed them just below the framed photo. She looked from one to the other—the two faces she and Ben had assumed were the same woman. But now she looked closer, she could see a tiny scar running through the left eyebrow of the woman in Pine's photo. Ana's twin. She took a couple of deep breaths while she put her photos away because the 8x10 held other revelations for her.

Of the parents standing on either side of their two girls, one was recognizable as Herr *Doktor* Reveshvili—younger, his face not as lined, but just as stern, dignified, the expression defined by gravitas even, as here, at rest. So Ana was Reveshvili's daughter. No wonder he was so cagey when talking about her. Neither had he said a word about the twin when Evan had shown him Jon Pine's photo of her, but she clearly recalled the expression on his face, the ever so brief hesitation before he spoke. Now, both took on an importance she could not have dreamed of earlier. This family portrait changed everything.

And now, at last, her attention was drawn to the fourth figure—Reveshvili's wife, the mother of Ana and her twin. She was tall—as tall as Reveshvili, which was saying something. Slim and fit, she had dark, wavy hair down to her shoulders, wide-apart eyes, and a generous mouth. She reminded Evan of someone, but she couldn't think of who it might be. A movie star in Hollywood's heyday? Hedy Lamarr, maybe? In any event, she could see where Ana and her sister got their looks. In all, this was one striking family, something out of fable or legend. And yet they were real.

At that moment, she heard a noise. Her head snapped up, her eyes locked on the figure standing in the doorway—slim and fit, wavy hair down to her shoulders, but no longer dark: a startling silver, lent an almost feral glow from the office's warm lamplight.

She was looking at Reveshvili's wife, mother of Ana and her twin sister.

40

SCHNELLER PSYCHIATRIC CLINIC, BERGISCH GLADBACH

"I see you found what you were looking for."

"Frau Reveshvili." Evan, standing the portrait of the family up on the desk where it had been when she had first walked into the office earlier in the day, rose and came around the desk toward the laden café table. "Finally, we meet."

The Herr *Doktor*'s wife did not move from the open doorway. Rather, she leaned against the frame. She was enrobed in a silk dressing gown embroidered with cranes in the Japanese style. Her feet were bare. She was riveted on Evan's face as if her eyes were magnetized.

"Please feel free to ransack my husband's personal papers."

She said this with such a lack of emotion, it was like receiving a text. On curiously stiff legs Evan made it to the table, stood with her hands gripping the back of one of the chairs. "The table has been laid," she said. "Won't you join me?"

Ana's mother said not a word in response. Instead, she drew out a pack of cigarettes, plucked one out, placed it between her lips. It was at that moment that Evan realized she wasn't wearing a speck of makeup, not even a scrim of foundation. From the pocket of her gown, she produced a gold lighter, flicked it open. But her hand trembled so badly, she had difficulty bringing the flame to the end of the cigarette.

Without a second thought, Evan crossed the space between them, took the woman's hand in her own, moved the flame so she could draw smoke into her lungs. This she did, but to Evan's surprise she let go of the lighter so that it fell into Evan's hand. Surprise turned into astonishment to see Reveshvili's wife silently weeping as she smoked.

Alarmed, Evan said, "Frau Reveshvili."

"My name is Frau *Doktor* Rebecca Reveshvili."

She never took her eyes off Evan. She never stopped crying, tears overflowing her eyes, running down her cheeks, plip-plopping in the space between them. The cigarette, forgotten, hung awkwardly from her fingers.

"I don't—" Evan felt a constriction, like a tightened metal band, around her heart. "I don't understand."

"Of course not." Rebecca's voice was unsteady. "Why would you?"

Again her hand dug in her pocket, and this time she handed something to Evan: a snapshot.

Evan was looking at much younger versions of Reveshvili—Konstantin—and Rebecca. They cut a dashing couple, but there was something in both their eyes—the same emotions: sorrow, resignation, and something more, something darker, deeper: a discordant eddy of incompatible sensibilities. The faint heartbeat of impending judgment, of a future clouded by their own questionable actions. How she could discern all of this from the photo she would not, even in retrospect, fully understand. For the moment, though, she was taken over by these observations as if they had been made part of herself.

The charismatic pair were bookended by two children—both girls. Not twins, though. One girl looked to be about five or six, the other a toddler—maybe two, three? But what struck her dumb was the background. It was as familiar to her as the lines in her palm, as her own reflection gazing back at her from a long-ago mirror. Reveshvili and his wife were standing in front of the Black Hills of South Dakota, in front of the very house where Evan and Bobbi grew up.

"You were five years old then." Rebecca's emotion-clotted voice came to her as if from a distant past.

Five. The number of fingers on her hand. The number of years she was alive.

Evan's knees turned to jelly, her heart felt ripped asunder, and she collapsed onto the floor, into Rebecca's tears.

41

COAST OF ROMANIA

The sea slapped against the side of the boat, the black water rising and falling in the rhythm of a living thing. The sea was, in fact, an organism alive with a multitude of life, some stranger than others. *Just like people*, Kobalt thought. She lay in her berth, but even the gentle rocking motion failed to lull her to sleep. There was too much to think about, too many forks in the road that, when she began had seemed so straight and uncluttered.

She heard the lines slap against metal, felt the boat rock more forcefully as the wind began to pick up. No matter: she had a cast-iron stomach. She raised her head, saw a figure in the doorway. She sat up as the figure entered, turned on a lamp.

Lyudmila. She was wearing a rubberized waterproof jacket. Silently, she held out a second one. Kobalt slid out of her bunk, slipped on her boots, and took the jacket. Taking a cue from Lyudmila, she did all this silently. Then she followed, as the other woman turned on her heel and went out.

Seen from the deck, to Kobalt's eyes the coast was dark and brooding, nothing more than a pencil sketch against a blasted charcoal sky, as if she was looking at the remnants of an enormous celestial burn. Turbulent clouds thickened on the horizon, coming their way. She saw no lights out on the water and was reassured.

When she gave Lyudmila a querying look, the Russian pointed over the port side. Craning her neck, she could make out a small launch with an outboard motor. One of the crew was in the stern, swinging the outboard out of the water. As the women climbed down a rope ladder that had been unfurled over the side, the crew member took up a pair of oars. *No noise tonight,* she thought.

The moment they clambered in, the two tie lines holding the launch to the yacht were loosed. They sat, facing each other, while the crewman began to row with powerful strokes through the rising chop toward the shore.

The two women looked at each other. Not a word was spoken. Kobalt had given up trying to winkle out Lyudmila's mood, let alone her thought processes, by her facial expressions. It was like trying to read tea leaves or the thrown bones of foxes.

Kobalt glanced back over her shoulder at the receding yacht, where others lay sleeping, oblivious to whatever Lyudmila had planned. Looking over the Russian's shoulder at the oncoming shore, she could now make out the beachfront glimmering in the ghostly glow of the port of Constanta, just to the south.

Because the outboard was raised, the launch was able to slide all the way up the shingle until the bow was grounded in sand. The women stepped out, and into Romania. It was a cool and desolate shore, rocky and somehow foreboding. Kobalt, thinking of Viola in Shakespeare's *Twelfth Night*, who was shipwrecked on a foreign shore, moved swiftly up the sand, boots sinking in bit by bit, up toward the jagged rocks, and beyond, the wall of the corniche. The hiss and suck of the water, the instability of the wet sand, grainy as couscous. The wind scouring the shingle. A shiver of apprehension chased through her.

As they crested the rise upon which the corniche was built, they could see off to their left the baroque cupolas of the grand casino rising from a promontory reaching out into the water, ugly as a boil on a fat man's behind.

There was a dark-colored Opel Erebus sedan waiting for them, its engine running. It was only then that the full extent of Lyudmila's meticulous planning came fully home to Kobalt.

"What is this all about?" she asked Lyudmila after they slid into the backseat and the sedan started off, heading south, toward Constanta.

"We're going to see your parents," Lyudmila said. "That's what this is all about." She turned to Kobalt. "This is why I came to meet you in Odessa, to take you here, where they are."

Kobalt's pulse should have quickened, her heart skipping a beat, her stomach contracting. Something. "Here in Romania? In Copenhagen I was told they were Russian agents."

"True enough." Lyudmila nodded. "Their parents were Romanian. They emigrated to Russia when they were in their teens. By all accounts, your parents were precocious in every way."

That should have been Kobalt's first clue, but she was too busy wondering whether she actually wanted to meet her birth parents.

"At the tender age of seventeen, they were taken in by the FSB, specially trained. As a couple, they were sent to the United States as part of a long-range program to create agents-in-place from, shall we say, the ground up."

"Russians in American clothing."

"Exactly." Lyudmila frowned. "The program was an experiment. As such, it failed. The majority of the children growing up in America became addicted to the American capitalist way of life. They rejected recruitment outright when approached."

"Except for me."

Lyudmila nodded. "Except for you."

"When? The letter wasn't dated."

"They left when you were three."

As the Opel slid through the empty nighttime streets, Kobalt lapsed into a deep silence. Ever since she had found the goodbye letter from her birth parents to the American couple who, for ten years, had been the only parents she knew, she had felt that she was walking on eggshells around them, and especially Evan, lest she somehow give away the vital information she had stolen. She felt split in two: an outer layer concealing the new one birthed inside her. She couldn't help feeling a distance between her and the Americans, seeing them in a different light. The mooring ropes that connect a child to her parents had been severed for Bobbi, and she felt herself drifting away toward a breach that had appeared in her world. And on the other side of that breach stood the woman in whose womb she had grown, absorbing the hushed Russian conversations the woman would have had with her husband—Kobalt's father—as they echoed through the amniotic fluid in which she floated.

From the outset, she knew that Evan wouldn't share her feelings, that Evan was bonded to their American parents with a weld that could not be broken. Evan was nothing if not fiercely loyal. She should have felt loyal to Kobalt as well, but she didn't. For some reason she didn't. She would never drift toward the breach in the world that had so drawn Kobalt the moment she had read the letter, felt that it had been written to her, not to the Americans. From that stunned time on she had thought of the people who reared her as "the Americans." Now she had crossed over that breach, entered an entirely new world, a place she belonged. And of course she wanted to see her real parents, there was no doubt in her mind. None at all.

She turned to Lyudmila. "Have you seen them? Have you spoken to them? Do they know I'm coming?"

Lyudmila smiled and seemed to nod. But there was something lurking in the corners of that smile Kobalt recognized only in retrospect. That should have been her second clue. But she was too excited now. She had worked herself up, thinking of all the things she would say to them and, above all, what she would say first. "*Mama, Papa, hello!*" "*Mama, Papa, I never thought this day would come!*" "*Mama, Papa, I'm so happy . . .*"

And then the Opel drew up to the gates of *Cimitirul Anadalchioi*—the Anadalchioi Cemetery.

The graves of Galina and Maxim Chernyshevsky occupied one-half of a square plot shared with the Cherniceanus, clearly Maxim's parents before their names were Russianized by the FSB. A waist-high iron fence that had seen better days marked off the plot, with a little gate that squealed like a stuck pig when Kobalt opened it. Out of respect, Lyudmila stood several paces behind her, hands clasped in front of her, quiet and still.

At this ungodly hour no one else was in the cemetery. Even the crows were asleep. The wind sweeping in off the sea whistled tunelessly through the aisles between the gravestones and polished granite monuments. Not a flower was in sight, not even a dead one. *Those six feet under wouldn't mind,* Kobalt thought as she stood in front of her birth parents' graves. Flowers, like funerals, were for the living, the gateway for grief, for respect, for remembrance. She had none of those gifts to present to Galina and Maxim. How could she? She had never known them. She'd been handed off to the Americans without her consent, which was an absurd thought. How could a three-year-old give her consent to anything?

And yet, she felt resentment; had she been consulted she surely would have opted to go with them back to Russia. Why would she want to be left behind, like yesterday's papers? Who would want that? But she already had her answer to that: Evan, clearly. Evan, who was on the other side of the breach in the world and would forever remain so.

She felt wetness on her face. Not tears, no. Rain—or, more accurately—a chill drizzle. She buttoned the top snap of her slicker, felt her hair begin to mat down. She thought she ought to say something, a greeting—*privet kak dela segodnya*, Hello, *how are you doing today?*—a farewell. An acknowledgment. Nothing came to mind. A prayer, maybe, a eulogy for the dead. Nope, not those either. She felt dry, hollowed out. The place where her Russian parents had been was a well without water—the water to nourish her. It had run dry when they had left her in America, returning across the breach. She could bow her head—at least she could do that, but not for long, she was too restless. She did not like being in Romania. The energy was all wrong, something tearing at her skin, a sleet of biting insects.

At length, she stepped back, seemed pushed, as if some kind of force pressured her chest.

"Are you all right?" Lyudmila asked.

She nodded. She was having trouble breathing. Shallow breaths were no good, and yet these were piling up inside her like waves beating against the shore.

"I thought you deserved to know."

A surge of anger flushed through Kobalt. "This intimacy. You and me here with my parents, you the agent of this—what would you call it?—not a reunion, surely!"

Lyudmila did not react as she had expected to the verbal slap in the face. Instead, she said in a perfectly level voice, "I don't think 'reunion' is the wrong word."

Kobalt's eyes flashed as she threw Lyudmila a murderous look. Turning on her heel, she strode quickly away, down the avenue of the dead. Feeling dead herself. All this time she had thought she had crossed the breach, when she now realized she had fallen into it. She was nowhere, a rolling stone, pushed back and forth inside the abyss.

"You're wrong," she spat as Lyudmila came up beside her. "There's nothing here for me, not even a single, solitary memory."

"You think I shouldn't have brought you here."

She rounded on the Russian. "I think you're manipulating me. I think this was a stunt to bring me into your fold, to make me beholden to you." Her eyes blazed; they felt hot and swollen, as if something had rubbed them raw. "Wrong a second time. Dead wrong."

They had exited the cemetery now and were heading back toward the waiting Opel. They had plunged into those hours before dawn when night loses its hold, when it reluctantly begins to retreat into the west. The wind had all but disappeared, leaving the drizzle behind like a footprint soon lost to light.

"It was a mistake to bring you here," Lyudmila said, "to think it would give you some solace."

Those words rooted Kobalt to the spot. Her anger lifted color into the points of her cheeks. Not an apology, never an apology from this one. "Why are we here? Really."

"Really?" Lyudmila huffed, as if reluctant to go on. "Years ago, I brought a nephew of mine to England, to live with another family. To protect him. And protect him I did, until I couldn't anymore. He was murdered several months ago. He was especially dear to me. I supervised his repatriation to Russia, his burial. I think of him often, and when I do, I picture the place I chose for him to rest in peace. I find solace in the image, in picturing myself there. I speak to him, sometimes. It helps. Well, it helps me." She ducked her head. "That's why I thought . . ." Her voice was lost in the rain. "But, of course, everyone is different." They were standing by the Opel, but neither made a move to get in. It was as if they had forgotten about the vehicle altogether.

"But you knew him, Lyudmila, your nephew. You watched him grow up. While my parents left me on someone else's doorstep while they . . ."

"They did what they were meant to do," Lyudmila said softly, soft as the drizzle. "What their duty to Russia dictated. Do you imagine it was easy for them—especially your mother—to birth two little girls only to give them up before they even knew you? I have no doubt it was the most difficult thing she did in her life—the most heartbreaking thing any woman would have to do."

"You're wrong, Lyudmila, for the third time. What I did— giving birth to two children I was ordered to have, two children I never wanted, was the most difficult thing I've ever had to do."

Lyudmila seemed struck dumb. Her eyes were the only clue as to the wildness Kobalt's confession caused inside her. Kobalt sensed she didn't understand. She wondered whether she possessed the fortitude to explain it. This nighttime sojourn into Romania had exhausted her.

Kobalt closed her eyes. "Have you ever had an itch you couldn't scratch—or, worse, a pain? Those things kicking at my stomach from the inside, eating away at me, taking a part of me with them when I squeezed them out between my legs. And then the endless howling, the shit and piss, the neediness, the relentless mouths at my breasts, gnawing away at my nipples until they were raw. They were anchors, weighing me down, warping my life out of shape. I did all this for the State, another layer of varnish shining my cover, my false identity, a candy coating like an M&M. But I didn't love them. I didn't even like them."

She took a breath. "Shocked? Am I shocking you? You don't know what to think of me now, do you? A monster, you think, right? But I'll tell you something I never told you at my intake interview, something I never would have told you even if you'd pressed a red-hot knife blade to my flesh: those times after the children were born, before I was exfiltrated, I had never felt so helpless in my life. I was a prisoner and they were my jailers. Paul's depredations were nothing compared to what the children did to me. When Paul struck me it was over in a heartbeat and then life went on. But the darkness my children brought into my life was every second I drew breath—no respite, no surcease. None."

She stopped, for the moment out of breath. She could feel her blood beating fiercely in her temples, like a gun to her head: *boum, boum, boum*! For a moment, the shame of what she had admitted threatened to overwhelm her, thinking, *What if my mother was like me? What if she didn't love us, what if she didn't even like us? What if her time with us was a nightmare? What if she couldn't wait to give us away? What if she was like the couple who raised me, who I called Mother and Father, who lied, who denied me my birthright?* She shuddered inside, her breath hot in her throat. *I hate them. I hate them all.* But then she pulled herself together for the final volley. *But, really,* she thought, *parents were the least of it.*

"You want to know fear, Lyudmila? Well, my children taught me fear."

The sky was gray, storm clouds being shredded high aloft, though down here among the mortals it was as still as a held breath. The thick clouds had bundled the heavy, suffocating air with them. Kobalt could smell the sea, its freshness, its mineral tang; she could taste its limitless expanse, its freedom.

"I need a drink," Lyudmila said thickly.

"Vodka," was all Kobalt could manage.

A gull, large, graceful, gray-and-white, determined in its militancy, swooped low over them, a fresh fish clamped in its pale beak.

42

SCHNELLER PSYCHIATRIC CLINIC, BERGISCH GLADBACH

"There is your key, Evan: the number five."

"I don't . . . I don't understand."

"In time you will," Reveshvili said. *"Have faith."*

She had faith; she had to have faith. And yet . . .

"No, no, no. It can't be." Evan on her knees, staring from the photo taken in the Black Hills of South Dakota to Frau *Doktor* Rebecca Reveshvili's tearstained face. As she took in the photo, at herself at five years old, Bobbi at three, she thought of the dream shadows, moving across the walls, the floor. Not a dream then? Were they memories?

Rebecca placed her hand on the crown of Evan's head. A benediction or a welcome home? Both, perhaps. But try as she might, Evan could not get her head around what seemed to be happening. It was too much, too fast. So many revelations unfurling in her mind, one on top of the other, until an unsupportable weight fell upon her shoulders, and her head bowed.

No, no, no, she chanted to herself. *You can't be my mother.*

I know my mother, I know my father. They raised us. Isn't that proof enough? But it wasn't proof of anything; deep down, she knew that. Raising a child was not the same as birthing her. Not at all. But, but, but . . .

"I cried when it came time to go home, back to Russia." Rebecca's fingers ran through Evan's hair, slowly, gently. "That surprised me. I thought I had steeled myself because my path was set from the moment Kostya and I set foot in America. This was our mission. Our duty, which we had accepted willingly. We knew. We thought we knew."

"There is your key, Evan: the number five."

She was five in this photo, five when Rebecca and Konstantin Reveshvili had left America to return to Russia, the place of their birth, having done what the Motherland had asked of them. And there was something else, something just as telling: she could see herself in Rebecca, not simply in her body type, the shape of her face, some of her features, maybe, but in smaller things—the way she used her hands, the set of her shoulders, her freckled forearms. Like Evan, like Evan, all of them. Only in retrospect, with this knowledge front and center did she wonder why she never noticed that neither she nor Bobbi looked anything like their mother and father—the couple who raised them. Why would a child even consider such a thing? You took it for granted that the woman who took care of you, who you called Mom was your mother. The man who set you on his knee, played ball with you, read to you at night before bed, who you called Dad was your father. And they *were* Mom and Dad—but now, only in a sense. Here was the woman who had borne her for nine months, who had pushed her out of her womb, whose blood she shared. Here was the man who had colluded in her birth, whose blood she also shared.

And then, all at once, it hit her head-on like a Mack truck: she wasn't American; she was Russian. Bobbi wasn't American; she was Russian. This was the truth that Bobbi had known about their parents, their real parents, the secret she wouldn't share that night in the caves of South Dakota. This was why Bobbi became a spy for Russia.

Rebecca's soft voice filled Evan's senses. "From the moment I first held you—beautiful pink baby, close to my chest, feeling your heartbeat against mine, your tiny fingers curl around my forefinger—all the defenses I had built against loving you crumbled to dust. That dust tried to choke me, bring me back to where I had begun, but that place was gone, dead and buried. I was no longer the woman I had been passing through immigration in New York, to begin this mission in America.

"You . . . you changed everything for me. Giving you up ripped out a part of my heart. Now it beats more softly, more erratically. There have been times I thought it would stop altogether. Ask your father; he will tell you. Or perhaps he won't. Kostya is more secretive than I ever was. He holds his secrets close, hoards them like a Tolkien dragon its gold. But, make no mistake, he loves you fully as much as I do."

Evan could not stop the tears rolling down her cheeks. Reaching up, she took her mother's hand in hers, rose to face her. She placed a hand on her mother's cheek, wet also with tears.

"Tell me this isn't a dream."

Rebecca smiled wanly. "This isn't a dream, Evan."

They embraced. Her mother felt as frail as a bird. Her heartbeat came clearly to Evan, fast and fluttery.

Alarmed, she stepped back. For the first time, she took in what Rebecca was wearing—the nightgown, her bare feet. She frowned. "Are you all right? Why are you dressed like that?"

That wan smile, tinged now with sorrow. "I live here. I have for some years now."

"Live here?" Evan shook her head. "You mean . . . ?"

"Yes. I'm an inmate."

"But why?"

"Oh, Evan, what shall I say? Such a simple question, such a complicated answer—an answer, unfortunately, without end."

Evan half turned, aware now that Reveshvili—Kostya— had come into the office. He had brought a third wicker chair, which he placed alongside the others at the small table.

"Perhaps we should all sit down." His smile was pained when he looked at both Evan and his wife. "Such grand food should not go to waste."

Evan walked arm in arm with her mother to the table, seating her first, before she sat. Kostya was the last to be seated. He poured them Earl Grey out of the teapot. It was still hot.

He sipped his tea, then set the cup down precisely in the center of its saucer. "Your mother has a hole in her heart. It causes her weakness in times of stress."

Absurdly, Evan thought of Rebecca saying that giving her up had taken a piece of her heart. But, of course, that couldn't be right. "How . . . how bad?" she stumbled.

"It's not only the physical," Kostya went on. "Your mother's problems are emotional."

"Oh, Kostya, why beat around the bush? Evan's our daughter, she deserves to know." Rebecca turned to Evan. "I'm bipolar. I'm under constant medication to . . . well, to keep me on more or less an even keel."

"Sometimes the meds work," Kostya added. "Sometimes they don't."

Rebecca smiled wanly. "I'm here for my own safety."

Any appetite Evan might have originally had at the sight of the sumptuous tea service had flown to a high branch of a tree whose top she couldn't see. She began to weep again.

"Oh, no, Evan." Her mother reached across the table. "No, please don't. I'm fine here. Your father takes excellent care of me."

"I warned you, Becca."

But Evan spoke over him. "But you're not free."

"Who among us is free, Evan?" Her mother squeezed her hand. "Are you? If you think so, you're fooling yourself. Think of your obligations."

Evan opened her mouth to refute her, but she knew her mother was right. She was on a specific path—she had an obligation to find and rescue Wendy and Michael, she had an obligation to find Omega and, as with Nemesis before it, shut it down. She wasn't free, not at all.

She squeezed her mother's hand in return. "Will . . . will you be okay?"

"I have my . . . difficult moments. I get overwhelmed by dark thoughts, fears, night terrors"—she laughed without humor—"like you had when you were two. But, yes, overall I'm as okay as I'll ever be." The smile she gave Kostya glowed with love. "As I said, your father takes good care of me."

"May I ask you—?"

"Anything, Evan. We're through keeping secrets, isn't that right, Kostya."

Dr. Reveshvili nodded reluctantly.

Evan's heart was pounding as she tried to keep her emotions in check. "Are you . . ." Her mouth dried up, necessitating her to start again. *Deep breath, let it out all the way.* "Are you two still FSB?"

"We were never FSB," Rebecca said.

"Your mother is correct." Kostya smiled. "We were only ever freelancers, cutouts. From the moment we left Russia we ceased to have a case officer. Our monthly stipend came from an entirely benign entity in Germany."

"No case officer." Evan shook her head. "I've never heard of such a thing."

"Nor will you ever again. That element was part of the experiment. It didn't work, which was why the program was shut down quickly and completely."

"All right, you were freelancers," Evan said, "but you still had knowledge of the program, so . . ."

Kostya's smile broadened. "Great minds think alike, Evan. It happened that I came into possession of a piece of material— never mind how—the Sovereign would dearly love to get his hands on. It is something that, were it to get out, would cause him great humiliation. It is not here with me, and naturally it is not in Russia. It is in a secure location where no one but I can get to it."

"What about you, Mama?" She used the Russian word.

Rebecca reacted with a brief, grateful smile. "I know nothing of this material, nor its hiding place," Rebecca said. "Kostya was adamant about that."

Reveshvili's mouth formed a firm line. "I won't have FSB thugs trying to get to me through her."

"You see how he is, Evan," Rebecca said.

"We never expected to see you again." Reveshvili's voice was raspy with emotion.

"But I found you." Evan, dizzied from one startling revelation after another, felt as if she had been set adrift on a storm-tossed sea, with no sight of land anywhere. "And you recognized me, even after all these years."

"Not immediately, but as we spoke, I began to see Becca in you—then, in a rush, more and more, and I knew it had to be you. And then I started thinking about how to tell you who I was—and about Becca, of course—and, being a medical man I decided to take a certain course."

"You drugged me."

"Very lightly and very safely, I assure you," he said. "Just enough for your subconscious to be accessible, to create a pathway for me to try and lead you back to your early childhood, the truth about your origins."

"And what you told me about yourself—the black lake, your lack of family."

"The haunted black lake is all too real, I'm afraid, as is the cabin beside it." Kostya kept turning his cup around and around on its saucer. "In fact, everything I told you . . . the entire session was based on truth. If I had lied, you would have known—your subconscious would have picked it up." He shook his head. "I withheld certain knowledge—about Ana and her twin—but I judged you weren't ready to hear about them back at the inn."

He was right again; she hadn't been ready then—not by a long shot. This was an immensely difficult situation, fraught with wrong turns that could have blown up in both their faces. "You handled everything well," she said sincerely. And in the end, he had allowed her mother to tell her what she needed to know. "Very well."

"I appreciate that." Kostya looked and sounded like he meant it.

Evan chewed all this over for some time, then, "I need to ask you another question."

Kostya spread his hands.

"About Bobbi . . ."

"Ah, Robin."

"Robin?" Evan's brows knit together. And she thought, *I don't even know my own sister's real name.* "We only called her Bobbi."

"Her American nickname," Kostya said, clearly showing his distaste.

"She was unlike you," Rebecca said. "She was a blue baby, premature. She came out of me cold as ice. I thought she was dead. I wept over her, until the nurse took her away from me."

"Robin was in an incubator for the first ten days of her life," Kostya informed her in his even, professional voice. He might have been speaking of a patient, someone else's child. She was also acutely aware that he had not come close to her, had not acknowledged she knew he was her father. What was wrong with him?

"The differences didn't end when she was brought back to me. She was an unholy terror," Rebecca said.

"It doesn't change what she was." Kostya took a pastry, delivered it to his wife's plate. "Here, eat something, Becca. You're looking pale."

"It's not from lack of food." She closed her eyes. "Talking about Robin always does this to me." Her voice held a tremor. She gathered herself and when she spoke again her voice was steady. "Terror or not, I could not have loved her more. I doted on her, spent more time with her than I did with you."

"Robin fed off that," Kostya said, refilling his cup.

"She needed me more," Rebecca retorted. She didn't appear angry; she was giving Evan her side.

Reveshvili turned to Evan. "And how did you get along with her, Evan?"

She wished he would call her daughter, or dear. *Something* other than her name, as if she were an acquaintance of her mother's asked to tea. *But then, why should he*? she thought. He scarcely knew her.

"Not well," Evan said softly. "We never really meshed, never got each other. And then she defected to the FSB."

Silence at the table, in the office, in the connecting corridors.

"Anyway the good news is she has two children, Wendy, eleven, and Michael, nine, both of whom I love." That Bobbi had become a Russian agent did not seem to surprise them, but they seemed not to know of the children, nor about Bobbi's death. She almost told them but then considered that there were enough earthshaking changes in all their lives for the moment. She made a mental note to warn Ben to keep Bobbi's murder to himself.

"Our grandchildren," Rebecca said, in the reverential tone reserved for the progeny of their offspring. "Kostya, we have grandchildren. Evan, tell us. What are they like?"

For the next ten minutes, Evan spoke about Wendy and Michael, winding up telling them about the kids' love of Snickers bars and Butter Brickle ice cream.

Rebecca was laughing and crying at the same time, and Evan knew she had made the right decision to hold off on telling them of Bobbi's death.

"They had a difficult upbringing," Evan said now. Her mind was still buzzing. "At some point, it became clear to me that Bobbi—Robin—never wanted children. She didn't know how to be a mother and had no patience to learn. We had many fights over that, I'm ashamed to say."

"Don't be." Rebecca squeezed her hand briefly.

"And their father?" Kostya continued, always the analytical scientist.

"Indifferent at best. At his worst he was downright cold." She spread her hands. "To tell you the truth I don't know why my sister ever got pregnant."

Reveshvili and Rebecca exchanged a glance. "It was mandated, I'm sure," Reveshvili said. "Another layer for her cover."

"So she had been contacted by then."

"Very early on, so we were given to understand."

Evan felt a blanket of depression settling on her shoulders. "I am not like her, you know," she said after a time.

"We do," her mother said, rubbing the back of her hand reassuringly. "Of course we do."

"Really?" She turned to Reveshvili. "Then why do you still speak to me as if I'm a patient or a client?"

Kostya seemed momentarily taken aback, but the abashed look vanished as quickly as it appeared. "We didn't . . . that is, I did not want to presume."

"Presume?"

"On your memories of your other parents—the couple who raised you as their own."

Rebecca nodded. "It was a tragedy what happened to them."

"A distinctly American tragedy," Kostya added.

"Mary and Joe Ryder were nice people," her mother said. "Sympathetic and empathetic. We would never have left you girls with them if they had been anything but so very kind."

"Mary had been trying to conceive for two years when we were directed to them," her father continued. "They were overjoyed, didn't ask questions."

Rebecca smiled. "They fell in love with both of you on first sight."

Evan took her time digesting this. Her eyes filled, but the tears refused to spill over. Perhaps she was all cried out, possibly she was simply in shock. "I saw . . ." She cleared her throat, began again, "I saw the photo of your other daughters," she said after another silent interval.

Kostya's cup was almost to his lips when he stopped, set it down. "The twins," he said.

Evan nodded. "Ana and . . ."

"Ana and Luzida."

"Is Ana's last name really Helm?" Evan asked.

Reveshvili sighed. "Yes. Ana changed her name to Helm when they—"

"Broke away," Rebecca said bitterly. "When they renounced us."

"Ana did work here, as I said." Kostya's shoulders were hunched as tension rode through his large frame. "I threw her out nearly three years ago."

"Not soon enough!" Rebecca cried.

Reveshvili gave her a look before turning back to Evan. "What she was working on—in secret—was not in the clinic's best interest."

"She was experimenting on his indigent patients," Rebecca cried. "Three of them died. She killed them! Our own daughter!"

"With drugs," Evan said to Reveshvili, "right?"

"With drugs?" Rebecca said. "No, not at all."

"Then what . . . ?"

Kostya took up a knife, sliced off a pat of butter, ran it over the top of a scone. Rebecca said nothing more. When Evan glanced over, she saw that her mother was staring at Reveshvili. It was only when her gaze returned to her father that Rebecca continued.

"They ruined me, those two."

"Now, Becca."

Her eyes were blazing. "Well, it's true. You know it is. It's because of them I'm in here."

"That's not—"

"But it is, Kostya. I told Evan no more secrets and I mean it."

He stared at his scone, sighed, and set it down. "All right, Becca. As you wish."

"You should wish it, too," Rebecca said quietly but firmly.

Evan paused for a moment to allow emotions to settle, then she said, "What was Ana really working on?"

Reveshvili's face twisted. "She was experimenting specifically on the patients' reproductive organs."

Evan could see the horror in her mother's eyes.

Kostya nodded. "What she was doing was . . . yes, horrific. At first I couldn't believe it."

"But I could," Rebecca said. "She's become a demon."

Now Evan was as horrified as her mother. "Did you contact the authorities?" she asked.

"Of course not." Kostya gave her a sharp look. "Bringing outsiders in would have started a wholesale investigation. The authorities would have shut us down. Where would my patients go? They all have serious conditions that can only be treated here, under my supervision." He shook his head. "She left us in an entirely untenable position."

"The bitch," Rebecca spat out with considerable venom. "I

curse the day I gave birth to those two. There must have been something rotten in my womb."

"Becca, stop it," Kostya said in an anguished tone. "I beg you."

She subsided, head bowed, hands in her lap.

Evan looked from her mother to her father. "But . . . what is she planning . . . ?"

"I have no idea," Kostya said.

"Maybe it has something to do with the fact that she and her sister cannot reproduce. Maybe she's trying to find a way—"

"Becca, that's insane," Kostya said with a tremor of fear in his voice. "You're talking Eduard Wirths—Auschwitz abominations."

"Kostya, you must face the fact that Ana is a psychopath," Rebecca spat out. "She and her sister. They hate the world and everyone in it."

"It's true Ana has a messiah complex," Kostya said. "They both do. But especially Ana."

"Ever since she was a child," Rebecca continued, "in her twisted mind she was obsessed with the biblical flood, God's promise to Noah that humankind would start anew." Her voice filled with anguish now. "Messiah! She is no messiah, she is a destroyer, babbling about the end of the world, the Omega of humankind she'd say, obsessing over her foolish symbols!"

Evan froze. She could practically feel and hear gears turning and grinding in her brain. "Symbols? Omega?!" A sudden terror gripped her. "Oh my God, Mama . . . I don't know how to say this to you . . . Bobbi's children—your grandchildren, they were abducted several days ago. I am sure now it was Ana who took them. That's why I'm here, I'm trying to find them. Up to now I assumed it was revenge for Bobbi infiltrating an organization called Omega, but in light of what you've just told me it's clear that Ana *is* Omega, and a much uglier reason for her taking the children rears its head."

Rebecca's eyes opened wide. "What?" She nearly screamed. "What are you saying? You can't mean she might be using them as subjects?" She gasped. "No, it can't be."

Kostya wiped his forehead with the back of his hand. "From what we saw of her work here, Becca, she had no success on adults."

Rebecca closed her eyes. "Please refrain from defining this in strictly scientific terms."

He spread his hands. "But the scientific method is the only way to get to the underlying cause of what is happening."

Evan nodded. "I'm sorry, Mama, but he's right." Her voice was none too steady.

Rebecca flinched, let loose with a tiny whimper. "God help us all! This is a nightmare."

Evan took a breath. She and Ben needed to get going. She rose, went to her mother, put her arms around her shoulders. "This will be taken care of, Mama. I promise you."

Rebecca looked up at her, eyes clouded with tears. "Death," she whispered hoarsely. "Death is all I see."

Evan kissed the top of her head. "It's all right."

"I won't lose you, Evan. Not after you've come back to us. I won't allow—"

"Becca." Kostya's voice was soft, gentling. "Nothing is going to—"

"Ana will kill Evan if she gets the chance!" Rebecca's eyes blazed through her tears. "You know that, Kostya."

"There is much more at stake," Evan said. "I have to stop her."

Rebecca was sobbing, her thin shoulders shaking.

Unconsciously, Evan ran her fingers through the hair on the crown of her mother's head, just as her mother had done to her moments before. "If I don't, who will?"

Reveshvili nodded. "She's right. Becca. You know her training as well as I do."

Evan's head snapped up. "How do you know about my training?"

"We've been following your progress and—"

"Oh, Kostya, can't you ever stop lying to her?"

"Wait a minute," Evan said to Reveshvili, "you knew who I was all along?"

"You're my daughter," he said simply.

Kostya then spoke to his wife. "I made a promise, Becca."

"But I didn't." Her mother turned to her. "It was Lyudmila Alexeyevna who informed us about Robin being successfully recruited. And she has kept us informed about you as well."

Lyudmila! she thought. *She's the reason I'm here now. Lyudmila must have shown them pictures of me as an adult, no? Did he know who I was all along?* But perhaps not, because it occurred to her that Lyudmila hadn't told them about Wendy and Michael, and had kept them in the dark about Bobbi's death.

"You and Lyudmila Alexeyevna are friends," Rebecca said. It wasn't a question.

Evan nodded. "But it seems even friends have secrets from each other." Still, Evan trusted Lyudmila, trusted that whatever secrets surrounded her orchestration of this meeting were being kept for Evan's benefit. And for that of the Reveshvilis.

Rebecca eyed her. "Do you not have secrets from her?"

Of course I do, Evan thought.

"We are very proud of you, of what you have accomplished. Of the fear you have struck into the heart of the FSB," Rebecca said with a fierce pride.

"Indeed we are, *moya doch'*." *My daughter.*

Something in Evan's core melted. *At last*, she thought. *At last!* And she said, "Tell me, *Otets*." *Father*. "Tell me everything I need to know."

43

ROMANIA/BERGISCH GLADBACH

"Experiments."

"Yes."

"On her own people."

"People who no longer believed in their leader's methodology." Kobalt's lips pursed. "Zherov and I saw the hideous results in the Omega compound."

Lyudmila nodded. She and Kobalt were standing on the deck of her yacht, along with Zherov. The seas had calmed, the day was clear, the sky directly above cobalt blue, but it would be bleached white by noontime. It was already hot.

"Which means we've got to find and neutralize Omega quickly." This from Zherov, who was looking better since getting eight hours of sleep. He knew nothing of the two women's trip to the cemetery; there was no need.

They were interrupted by the buzzing of Lyudmila's mobile. She excused herself, stepping away toward the bow. The call was sandboxed. Her pulse accelerated. She heard Evan's voice on the other end of the encrypted line.

"I met my parents—my birth parents," Evan said.

"How?"

"You know how," Evan said. "You sent me to them."

Lyudmila nodded. "Well, at last you were better prepared to meet them."

"I owe you, bitch."

Lyudmila gave a low laugh. "I'll bank it."

"You know what Ana is up to?"

"Yes. She's been experimenting on humans," Lyudmila said, preparing to lie to Evan again, for her own good. "I went to Omega's compound in Odessa. There were people she shot, but others looked as if they had been victims of medical experiments."

"That's what she was doing at the clinic. And my parents are terrified of what she might be doing now. But, Lyudmila . . . some good news . . . they discovered where Omega's headquarters is."

Lyudmila's eyes opened wide. "At last!"

Evan told her. "Meet there?"

"Back to you with an ETA. You have transport?"

"My father is arranging it."

"It must feel odd saying that, no?"

Too loaded a question for her to answer now. "I'll send you my ETA when I know." Evan cut the connection.

Well, Lyudmila thought, pocketing her mobile, *perhaps sometimes, against all odds, the plans of mice and women do have a chance to turn out the way they were meant to.*

Kobalt and Zherov were waiting for her.

"Kobalt," she said, "call your pilot. Tell him to get over to Constanta Mihail Kogalniceanu Airport as quickly as he can."

Kobalt's eyes lit up like the inside of a circus tent. "You found Omega's location?" she asked even while she was punching in the direct code. She spoke briefly, verified a flight plan being filed, and severed the connection. "Forty minutes to an hour," she said.

"We'd better get going, then." Lyudmila was already at the port side. She started her climb down to the waiting launch, and one by one they all followed.

Ben drained his glass of tea. "Can you not tell me what's going on?"

"Alas, events occur without us," Leonard Pine said in his proper tone.

They were sitting in the clinic's kitchens, which were vast, clad in stainless steel and, at this time of the morning, all but deserted. Several lonely figures in smocks were at work on the other side prepping breakfast. The atmosphere was clean and bright.

Ben decided to switch topics. "Tell me about your brother."

"Mm. Jon and I were like oil and water, we always were." Pine's eyes had a faraway look as he peered into the past. "Where I thought white, he thought black. We fell right in line with Herr *Doktor* Reveshvili's theories on twins. Jon was born bad. I, on the other hand, absorbed my parents' ethical and moral values." He paused for a moment to wet his lips. "Personally, I believe Jon's life could have been salvaged, but then he met Ana here at the clinic. He fell head over heels under her spell. She dazzled him, ravished him. He did whatever she said. He said he'd follow her anywhere, and he did. She had that effect on many people." Pine blinked, his eyes refocusing on Ben. "And now he's dead." He sighed. "The sad truth is I miss him."

"Why sad?" Ben said. "He was your twin brother."

Pine waved an elegant hand. "Oh, we were never like that, thinking each other's thoughts, finishing each other's sentences. Jon's mind was a complete mystery to me. I found Ana terrifying rather than mesmerizing, and I would never be tempted to join her end-of-the-world cult, what did she call it, her Omega group."

Ben's jaw nearly fell open as the pieces of the puzzle fell together. Ana was Omega. "What can you tell me about this Omega?"

Pine shrugged. "I can tell you about Ana." He refilled Ben's glass, then his own. "She is certifiable."

Ben cocked his head. "In what way?"

Pine made a small sound. "In what way is she not? In my opinion she's a narcissist, a megalomaniac in the grip of a vicious psychosis. She is convinced the world needs to be scourged, that humankind needs to die in order to be born again."

"Under her leadership."

Pine pursed his lips, as close as he ever got to showing distaste. "And all Caucasians, the superior race, in her twisted opinion. According to Omega doctrine, which is, of course, Ana's doctrine, the mixing of races, of colors, has caused a rift in mankind's evolution, a branching down a wrong path. It must be stopped in its tracks because it is already on the brink of going too far."

"Nazism taken to its illogical extreme."

"Precisely so." Pine's hands swept over the top of the stainless-steel counter at which they were seated. "Another thing. Ana's also bipolar, which is why her grip on Jon was so unshakable."

"He was also bipolar?"

Pine nodded. "She took him off the medication protocol prescribed by the Herr *Doktor*. She told him he didn't need it and he believed her."

"He wanted to believe her."

"Precisely. She took him with her when the Herr *Doktor* kicked her out."

"It seems to me that she should have been a patient here."

"Oh, we all thought so." Pine shrugged. "But there was no holding her back. To be brutally honest, she could become quite violent. She would have hurt someone—or worse—without a shred of remorse. The Herr *Doktor* could not take that chance. Ana is their daughter, you see." He shook his head. "She hates her mother with a venom that is frankly terrifying."

Ben frowned. "Why does Ana hate her mother so?"

Pine shrugged. "Perhaps because her mother is the only person who can see right down to the core of her. Ana fears her mother as much as she despises her."

"It seems to me you're describing a creature, not a human being."

"That is one way of putting it." Pine leaned forward, his voice lowering. "Listen, Herr Butler—"

"Call me Ben, please."

Pine produced his professional winning smile. "It's my training." He drew his glass of tea closer to him but did not drink from it. "I feel compelled to tell you something I have not shared even with the Reveshvilis."

"Keeping secrets from your employers. Is that also your training?" Ben said this last in a semi-bantering tone, in order not to cause offense.

"Ah, no. Absolutely no. But when I confide in you, you will understand." He bit his lip as if, at the last minute, he was having second thoughts. Then, with a rush, he plunged ahead. "Ana knows about your companion, Fraulein Ryder, and her sister."

Ben's brows drew together. "Meaning?"

"Ana was the one who engineered the abduction of the sister's two children."

A chill ran down Ben's spine. "We suspected as much. It was the only possibility we found that made sense. A long-held grudge, revenge for Bobbi's mission against Omega."

"Yes," Pine said gently. "That is possible. But more likely it's that they are family. She is without issue."

"What?"

"She's barren. I don't doubt she will find a way to use the children. I believe she will indoctrinate them into Omega's extremist religion. If she has her way—if she is not stopped—she will ensure they become Omega's future standard-bearers."

Ben sat perfectly still. His heart thundered so hard in his chest he could scarcely breathe. "What . . ." his voice cracked, forcing him to start over. "What did you mean, family? How on earth could Bobbi's children be family to Ana?"

Before Leonard Pine could answer, three people stepped into the kitchen: Evan, Reveshvili, and a woman—a wan beauty, willowy and alluring, who Ben had never seen before. He stood to meet them, as did Pine.

"Ben Butler," Evan said in a formal manner Ben felt odd in the extreme, "I'd like to introduce you to my parents: Herr *Doktor* Konstantin Reveshvili and Frau *Doktor* Rebecca Reveshvili."

44

CONSTANTA, ROMANIA

Less than a quarter mile from the airport squatted a nondescript building that might have been the regional headquarters of a since defunct import-export business. That's what it looked like from the outside. Once inside, however, it became clear that nothing could be further from the truth, for this was a former black site, used by the CIA a decade ago for the interrogation of terrorists known and suspected.

Even ten years later, the interior held on to the smells of blood, brain matter, sweat, pain, fear, and human waste, which, like cigarette smoke in a pub, had seeped into the porous bare concrete walls, giving the place a gaggingly thick atmosphere like few other places on earth.

Apart from the stench, the first thing that drew their attention when they switched on their LED flashlights was the four industrial-size water spigots protruding obscenely from the walls. Then the three enormous drains sunk into the floor. The concrete surrounding those drains served as indelible evidence of the strenuous work performed by the previous occupiers. The stains were dark, wide, and deep as lakes. In a far corner, a pyramid of the huge glass bottles used to fill industrial water dispensers rose, mottled with myriad spiderwebs.

They had arrived in the area early. Lyudmila had rightfully decided they should not wait at the airport, where their presence could be questioned or reported. They wished to remain unheralded and unsighted in Romania.

While Zherov checked out the space in detail, Lyudmila had her final talk with Kobalt—final in the sense that after this they would both be changed. Or they would be dead.

"Kobalt, I won't lie to you. I have been given the location of Omega's headquarters."

"That last call you got."

Lyudmila nodded.

"Then we're all set to go as soon as my plane lands? How far are we going? Will it require refueling?"

"You and Zherov are returning to Moscow."

"What?" Hands on hips, feet at shoulder width, an altogether aggressive stance. "You've got to be joking."

"You have urgent business in the capital."

"More urgent than taking down Omega? I don't think so."

"I'm going to take care of Omega." She had no intention of telling her that she would be meeting Evan there, just as she had no intention of telling her that her real parents were alive and living in Germany. "You had your chance with them, and your failure, no matter the reason, has gotten you in hot water with those inside the FSB who control your fate."

"Dima."

"And his boss, Director General Stanislav Budimirovich Baev." She reached out, gripped Kobalt's shoulder. "Hear me, Bobbi, if you're ever to have the career at FSB we both want, you—"

"'We'?" Kobalt echoed. "How does my career involve you?"

"You're alone, Bobbi—totally alone. None of your superiors

can be trusted an inch. Do you really believe you can find your own way when I could not?"

Kobalt looked away, at Zherov peeking into corners, looking for what she could not say.

"I've learned from my mistakes. But in the conventional sense it's too late: I'm persona non grata in Moscow. I'm an exile. And yet I have all this knowledge. Ironic, don't you think? But this is knowledge vital to you. It can guide you past the pitfalls, the internecine warfare that riddles FSB and all its offshoots."

Kobalt rubbed her temples. "Why should I trust you?"

Lyudmila shrugged. "Don't, for all I care. But know this: we both want the same thing."

"And what is that?" Kobalt's tone was blatantly skeptical. "This better be good."

"We both want to be in the game, while remaining free— our own people." She peered at Kobalt. "Is that not what you want, Bobbi, or have I read you wrong from the moment I first met you?"

Kobalt took a long time in answering. She seemed to be gathering herself around a center she was not yet altogether sure of. At length, she cleared her throat. "No, Lyudmila. You're not wrong."

"Then fly back to Moscow and clean up the mess you made."

"The mess *I* made? Someone ratted me out. The same person who coerced Ermi into giving me up in Istanbul."

"And you must find that person and air them out," Lyudmila said. "The sooner the better. Whoever it is, is a danger to you. Being undermined from inside is a long walk off a short pier."

"I want to finish what I started with Omega. Dima gave me the remit—"

"And how did that end?" Lyudmila shook her head. "Think with your mind, not your emotions, Bobbi."

"But I had already formulated a new plan. Dima was about to accompany me to an interview with Baev to present it when I got the news about the abduction."

"Lucky for you. That interview would not have gone well. Baev would have raked you over the coals." Lyudmila shook her head. "No, you need to tend to business back in Moscow right now."

"If you know all this, what do you need me for?"

Lyudmila smiled, showing sharp teeth. "What comes to me now is second- and thirdhand. With you on the inside and rising up the hierarchy everything will change for both of us. You get the career you deserve, and I get straight intel. In addition, you will be protected."

Kobalt turned away, but there was nothing to see in this place, the bones of an abattoir financed and overseen by the darkest of American forces.

"Take the plane," Lyudmila said. "Return to Moscow, use the leverage you've unearthed."

"And how d'you propose I do that?"

"Assert yourself, Bobbi."

"I have the means to destroy Dima, a list of payouts for giving up the missions outside St. Petersburg, Berlin, Kiev, and Aleppo that blew up in SVR's collective face."

"But it isn't enough to destroy Dima. You have the power to damage Baev, as well. Dima was his hire, and even though they are at war, this war is par for the course inside FSB."

"Then . . . ?"

"You must take your information to the one man who distrusts you more than anyone else: the director of FSB, Minister Darko Vladimirovich Kusnetsov."

Kobalt started as if hit with a cattle prod. "That's insane. A suicide mission. You're insane."

"Kusnetsov is, above all else, a pragmatist. This pragmatism is what has allowed him to stand above the fray, watching those below him eat each other. He is a man acutely aware of just how treacherous the balance of power inside FSB can be."

"What if I think your plan is nuts? What if I think you're using me to gain your own ends? What if I shake the Omega location out of you?"

"No need. I'll give it to you," Lyudmila said deadpan. "If that's what you want. But Omega will be expecting you. You'll encounter your children. In all likelihood they'll find out who you really are. And back in Moscow your own personal antagonist mole will continue to undermine you.

"Look, I know you have doubts. You think I'm lying to you. But the irrefutable fact is what you've uncovered on Dima is seismic. In Kusnetsov's hands, it will shift the balance of power all the way down the line. And the truth is if you agree we'll be using each other. We'll know that up front."

Kobalt considered. This was the same argument she used to recruit Zherov. She meant it and perhaps so did Lyudmila. One thing was true—she needed to tamp down on her seething emotions. She had allowed her failure—for whatever reason—at the Omega compound to get under her skin. It was clouding her judgment, Lyudmila was right about that. What if she was right about everything? As she continued to ponder the imponderable, she ticked off her own list: she had Dima's fortune banked, she had recruited Zherov, but, yes, other than these positives she was alone, again as Lyudmila pointed out. What use was money without an infrastructure, without her knowing the ropes? She could say no here and be on her own, but with all the new information was that really a wise idea?

Ermi's money set her free. But even walking away had its pitfalls, for surely her Russian masters would come after her, hunt her down, kill her. Alternatively, she could operate on her own. But doing what? Hiring herself out to the highest bidder? She already knew who some of those bidders would be: warlords, arms dealers, international drug traffickers, authoritarian heads of state—human scum she had no intention of working for.

Belatedly, she realized that she had been so wrapped up in this second chance at breaking up Omega, she had not thought her future through. Ermi's money had changed everything, as huge amounts of money will. It gave her freedom, but it also could become a prison, an overseer to which she became enslaved. But if, for the time being, she ignored her cache . . . she could envision the way forward Lyudmila was offering. So . . . what was it to be?

At last, she nodded. "All right. I'm in."

"Good. You have two Moscow remits," Lyudmila said. "The first is to get in to see Kusnetsov. The second is to ferret out your mole and terminate him."

"I don't know a thing about Kusnetsov," Kobalt confessed. "How do I handle him?"

Lyudmila grinned, her teeth shone in Zherov's flashlight beam as he returned from his recon. "Once you're with him, this is what I suggest."

45

FLESH/METAL/BONE

Two persistent rumors running through FSB lore centered around its head, Minister Darko Vladimirovich Kusnetsov. The first was that he never slept; the second was that he slept in a coffin. Like most rumors there was a kernel of truth to both. Kusnetsov slept on average two hours a night. He also had an aversion to direct sunlight. He was never seen in daylight without his signature wide-brimmed hat, black as a raven's wings.

Director General Stanislav Budimirovich Baev had cause to think on these things as he made the two-mile journey from his home to Permskaya Ulitsa, on the northeast outskirts of Moscow. No light penetrated the car's blacked-out windows, keeping him shadowed as he was driven through the city and out past the Ring Road. Usually, he disliked getting up at 5 A.M., but today was different, for he'd slept hardly a wink. Besides, this was the best time of the day and week to meet with Kusnetsov; his news couldn't wait for their next shark tank dive tomorrow night.

But inevitably, possibly lamentably, his mind turned to Kata in whose townhouse he had been staying the past couple of nights. Long after they would cease their bouts of sex the taste of her flesh would linger on his tongue, like a bite of the best chocolate slowly revealing its constituents, its secrets, as it melted. That complex taste kept him from normal sleep, in a kind of suspended state, not quite awake, but floating on a sea of her hot flesh. He closed his eyes, and her taste came to him, risen from his memory. It was dangerous to think of her naked body now, to become aroused when he needed all his attention focused on the imminent meeting, but her fragrance was too alluring to resist. But last night, he lay in her bed, inhaling her scent like attar, and listened to the silence of the house, for the first time alone in her townhouse. Odd. The place seemed dead without her electric presence.

His reverie broke apart as his driver turned the car in to the entrance to the Poryan Meat Processing plant, a cluster of neat blue-and-cream-tiled buildings. Concrete and asphalt dominated, dotted here and there with small patches of grass and a rather sad-looking line of plane trees scarcely out of their infancy. The sodium lights were still on, illuminating the car park and the antiseptic fronts of the buildings. The sky radiated the sickly yellow of the nighttime city, like an old man's rotted teeth, blotting out all stars.

Inside the spotless stainless-steel interior the night manager, still on duty this early in the morning, greeted Baev formally and, sweeping one arm out, ushered him into the cavernous building. They passed beef carcasses hanging on hooks, enormous vats where meat and its byproducts were ground, until the whine of rotary saws and the heavy, wet *thwacks* of cleavers striking raw beef presaged their approach to the butchering station.

The glassed-in cubicles were aligned side by side. Each featured a pair of waist-high benches, a rotary saw, an array of knives, cleavers, and the like, along with a pewter slop sink. Kusnetsov, clad in a thick neoprene butcher's apron, occupied one such booth. The night manager stopped, pointed wordlessly, and left Baev to navigate the butcher's row on his own.

Kusnetsov's apron was splashed with blood, but not nearly as much as Baev would have expected. Uncharacteristically for him, his hair held beads of sweat, his forearms were bare and glistening with his efforts with a mighty cleaver, which he wielded with frightening aplomb. His grandfather had been a butcher in a small town outside of St. Petersburg. And legend had it that he taught Kusnetsov all there was to know about butchering. Of course, as legends will, this one became entangled in the absurd—mainly the notion that Kusnetsov plied his beloved sideline on humans—traitors, criminals, even oligarchs who dared to defy him. Looking at him now, however, Baev could believe the legend.

Even before he came abreast of the cubicle in which Kusnetsov labored, he began to swagger. The bearer of glad tidings, he had good reason to feel buoyed up.

"Minister Kusnetsov," he said loudly and in his heartiest tone, but before he could go any farther, Kusnetsov waved him backward.

"Stand clear, Slava. You want your suit to remain spotless." So saying, he applied a powerful blow with his cleaver, slicing through red muscle, pale sinew, and bone pink with blood.

Peering down at the portion he had cleanly separated from the mass, he nodded, satisfied. Tossing the mass aside, he drew another large slab of meat to him. "You know, Slava, the rumor about me." He slammed the cleaver down through muscle and bone. "It's not just animals I butcher."

Baev shuddered. "I have heard them of course, Minister, but I—"

"They're true, Slava." *Slam* went the cleaver. "Absolutely true. Look here, who's to say this is a side of beef, eh?" *Slam* went the cleaver. Baev felt his gorge rise. "This could very well be the side of . . . Well, anything, really."

This fairly took Baev's breath away. "You mean Anatoly Vasiliev?" Anatoly Vasiliev Ivanovich was a senior officer of FSB Border Service. Baev had worked with him a number of times when their remits in counterintelligence overlapped. Baev had found him to be an unremarkable man, easy to work with.

"The same." *Thwack* went the cleaver. "We discovered he's been selling secrets to the enemy, using his position to cross the border to make the exchange: intel for cash." *Thwack*. "I will not countenance traitors." *Thwack*. He held up the lozenge-shaped piece so Baev could see the split bone. "Fatty. Still it might make a base for a decent stew."

Baev put a hand over his mouth. He'd heard that human flesh was inordinately fatty.

Heaving the sigh of a job well done, Kusnetsov dropped the meat and turned. "Bad news for Anatoly Ivanovich, and his boss. A complete purge of the directorate has been carried out."

Alarmingly, Baev noticed he hadn't let go of the cleaver, which now hung at his side.

"There are no traitors in your service, are there, Slava." Again, not a question.

"Certainly not, Minister!"

Kusnetsov smiled, at last putting aside the cleaver. He washed his hands at the sink. Stepping forward, Baev handed him a clean towel off a pile.

As he dried his hands, Kusnetsov evinced a more relaxed mien. "It is good to see you this morning, Slava." He tossed the towel into a trash bin. "You bring good news, I expect."

"Indeed." Baev did not want to look at the red-and-white striated meat behind Kusnetsov, but the stench of the raw meat, blood, and offal dizzied him. It was all he could do not to heave up the meager breakfast he had hurriedly consumed standing in Kata's kitchen. Now, swallowing bile, he put as genuine a smile on his face as he could muster.

"I have discovered the source of the security breach that allowed the Kobalt dossier to be hijacked."

"And you have closed this breach." It was not a question.

"Oh, yes. And the source already has been terminated."

"Good." Kusnetsov's brows came together. "Was the source internal or external?" Ominously, his voice dropped half an octave, or so it seemed to Baev.

"Internal, Minister." Despite his better judgment, his eyes flicked to the bloody cleaver and back to Kusnetsov's face. "A single individual," he continued, his bravado fading. "An adjutant, as it happens." He wasn't about to tell his boss that it was his own assistant.

Kusnetsov's eyebrows rose. "Is that so?"

Baev ducked his head, but only slightly. "A lapse in judgment. It won't happen again, I assure you."

"See that it does not, Slava, or there will be hell to pay."

Baev absorbed this body blow as best he could. *Better a body blow,* he thought, *than a cleaver to his rib cage.* Once again, he shuddered inwardly.

"Now, as to Ryder."

"I'm on it," Baev said.

Kusnetsov turned on him. "No, Slava, you most certainly are not. I have read the report from Cologne. Both the farm hands you sent scraped off the floor of a certain theater there. I've had to dispatch one of my lieutenants to mollify the local constabulary."

Baev felt the tickle as a line of sweat ran down the back of his neck. "They were the wrong men to send, I admit. I have changed tacks."

"Again."

"If at first you don't succeed, Minister." He waited for a response. Receiving none, he plowed relentlessly on. "I believe I now have the answer. I've decided to use a more . . . unorthodox . . . route to ensure Ryder's termination."

Kusnetsov's eyes seemed to bore into Baev's skull. "You know, Slava, for some time now I've been contemplating a shake-up within the FSB. This business with Anatoly Vasiliev has accelerated my thinking."

A jagged icicle slid between Baev's ribs. The threat to him was implicit and immediate. His elevated pulse trip-hammered in his ears. He desperately wanted to ask a question, but instinct, long honed on FSB politics, kept him silent. He dared not look away from Kusnetsov now, even for an instant.

"Yes," Kusnetsov nodded, as if to himself, "the time for change is imminent."

He smiled at his subordinate. Baev read all kinds of consequences in that smile. Was it friendly, icy, sardonic, contemptuous? In this mentally hyper-kinetic moment, he could not read Kusnetsov at all.

Then his boss took up the cleaver, dismissing Baev, returning to swing it again, down through muscle, sinew, and bone. Another bloody piece separated from the whole.

46

WENDY/MICHAEL

"God is alive! His fiery hand is the burning sword!"

Mikey and I are sitting on a carpet spread on the stone floor of the citadel's chapel. Mikey is listening to Ana with rapt attention, as if she's a sorceress. And why not? There's this ginormous burning sword behind her, I don't know how many feet long, standing upright on a carved stone base black as a moonless night. Whatever it's made of is black, too. The flames run up its length. The flames never stop. The sword never burns. Maybe the length of an adult's height behind the sword is a plain cross, gray, sharp-edged, big as the sword itself. Looks like what they make pavement out of.

"It is eternal," Ana is saying, as if she really is this sorceress out of any number of fantasy novels whose worlds I've been plunged into, "for it is God's handmade manifest in our world."

Mikey remains wide-eyed, astonished, completely spellbound. As for me, I don't know. Call me a skeptic—I think that's the right word; I'll have to google it when we get out of here. *If* we get out of here. But, no, I don't want to think that; I'll start to cry and Mikey will get scared. I have to make sure he isn't scared, so I have to hold tight on to my own fear and push it way down.

The thing is Ana told us she's Mom's sister. Come on, what are the odds? But then, I looked at her really close, and, *bam!* I saw that she actually does have Mom's eyes. And chin. And I thought, *What if she is Mom's sister. Our aunt, like Aunt Evan.* But no one ever said they had another sister, and I don't know about Mom, I was probably too young, but for sure Aunt Evan would have told me—at least me. I'm a big enough girl now, aren't I?

Anyway, if Ana really is Mom's sister why did she tell us not to call her Aunt Ana? "You must call me Mother Ana," she said. But she's not our mother. On the other hand, from what I can gather, she's running a kind of religious order, and I did read somewhere that the head of female religious orders is called Mother Superior. But then she insists we're all family: she and Mikey and me. Family. There's a word I've never heard when applied to Mikey and me. Mom surely never said it, and as for Paul . . .

"God has plans for us, my darling children. Just as He had plans for humankind when he spoke to Noah. This is what God said, his voice like thunder in Noah's mind: 'Now the earth is corrupt in My sight and is full of violence. I see how corrupt the earth had become, for all the people on earth have corrupted their ways.' And God said to Noah, 'I am going to put an end to all people, for the earth is filled with violence because of them. I am surely going to destroy both them and the earth. So make yourself an ark.'"

Ana's eyes swing to us—to Mikey and then to me, and I feel pinned in place, just as if she actually is some kind of siren with a golden tongue. "And God kept his covenant with Noah. On the seventeenth day of the second month—all the springs of the great deep burst forth, and the floodgates of the heavens were opened. And rain fell, covering the earth for forty days and forty nights, until all the lands were under heaven's water. All except the crest of Mount Ararat, where Noah and his family made their way, and started humankind again."

Her eyes, it seems to me, have turned dark—dark as the stand the flaming sword is set on. But they're also as fiery as that arrow. How to explain that. I can't. And now I've got a funny feeling in the pit of my stomach that makes me want to take Mikey and run—run as far away as we can. But I know we can't. Mother Ana or one of her people will stop us, and that makes the funny feeling in my stomach spread.

And Mother Ana is speaking. "And God said to Noah when the ark has landed on the top of Mount Ararat, and Noah and all his family are safe, and the water starts to recede, 'Thus I establish My covenant with you: Never again shall all flesh be cut off by the waters of the flood; never again shall there be a flood to destroy the earth.'

"These were God's very words to Noah, His chosen one, my darling children. But the descendants of Noah have broken their covenant with God. Once again, humankind is full of sin, of violence, of corruption that has entered every soul on earth, eating away at them all from the inside. You and Michael will help me forge the Paradise God promised Noah after he landed on Ararat."

To tell you the truth, sitting here next to Wendy, I think Mother Ana is pretty cool. I mean, she said she was Mama's sister. I asked Wendy about that when we were alone and she said she can see parts of Mama's face in Mother Ana, so maybe she really is our aunt. Oh, but I'm not allowed to call her that. Anyway, I guess part of Mother Ana's coolness is that everyone else here listens to her and does what she says. I'd like to be like that someday and, guess what, Mother Ana says I will be. How cool is that? I have to keep that promise—she calls it a covenant, like she says God has with her—close to me, so I won't be too scared. I mean, I am scared, but Wendy isn't so I guess things are okay. I'm still confused about where we are and why we're here, though. Wendy doesn't seem to know, either. Another thing I can't think about because I'll get scared all over again, and I hate, hate, hate feeling scared.

Now Mother Ana is going on with her story about God and Noah and the ark and the flood. I'm glad Noah is safe on that mountain with the funny name, Ararat. I wonder where it is. Maybe I'll ask Wendy to google it when we get out of here, but by that time I'll probably forget.

So again I tune in fully to what Mother Ana is saying. ". . . Once again, humankind is full of sin, of violence, of corruption that has entered every soul on earth, eating away at them all from the inside."

She's looking at me now, and even though we're family, that look makes something inside me squirmy, like I've eaten a handful of worms. Yuk! Gross!

So there's that sin, and violence, and corruption thing again, and it makes me wonder whether she's talking about the video games I play. Anyway, she's saying, "Here in the present, God has spoken to me, His voice like thunder in my mind. He has said, 'Once again the earth is corrupt in My sight and is full of violence, sin, and corruption, for all the people on earth have corrupted their ways.' And God has said to me, 'I have put in your hands the means to start anew, to recreate humans as they were meant to be in the time of Noah. For this you will need children, children of your womb or your sister's womb. You will be My architect and they will be the catalysts to people Paradise on earth.'"

But what about Aunt Evan? I think. *I want her to be saved. She's like Mama, only there.* I open my mouth, almost say it out loud, but something—I don't know what—stops me, and I clamp my mouth shut. I don't understand. Is any of this real or am I in a dream? All I want is to wake up, but I've pinched myself so many times I have bruises all along my arms.

I look up. Ana's arms are stretched out at the height of her shoulders, her fingers cupped, as if to wrap me and Wendy like Christmas presents. "And so, my darling children, I have brought you here to be safe within my ark, which is protected by God Himself, so that here with me, with your family, we can start anew."

And now she moves, and I see behind her, behind the fiery arrow, is a symbol, its golden skin glittering in the firelight, making it seem as if it's writhing, as if it's alive. It's a kind of round horseshoe with two feet, and after a minute or two I see what it is. I take Mikey's hand in mind and grip it tight as I can, because now I am scared—real and truly scared, and it takes everything I have not to burst out crying . . .

"Tomorrow is the seventeenth day of the month," Ana's voice rising like the sun at dawn. "The seventeenth day of the second month as reckoned by the calendar used by God in the time of Moses. In our time, modern-day time, it is the fifth month: May. Tomorrow is when the second flood—which is not a flood, but a method given to me by God himself—will be unleashed. Tomorrow is when all mankind, except the precious few, handpicked by God, will be wiped from the face of the earth."

. . . because I know Greek letters; they're part of an online game I play. You pick a team symbolized by a Greek letter, but you're not allowed to pick the last Greek letter. It is Omega, the end of all things. Omega is death.

47

BETWEEN HEAVEN AND EARTH

"Here, you are loved," Rebecca said just before Evan boarded the big helicopter squatting on its circular pad out behind the clinic. *"Here you will always be loved."* While Ben spoke with Leonard Pine, the clinic's night manager, Rebecca embraced Evan, tenderly, fiercely, and Evan drew in her scent. She smelled of the great forest beyond the clinic, clean and fresh and piney, as if she spent hours wandering between the resiny trees.

Kostya Reveshvili stood very close, his voice low but penetrating through the *whup-whup-whup* of the rotors. *"Now, listen,* moya doch'. *Your sister Ana is a master at psychological warfare. Beware her every mood, her every word."*

"I will, *Otets.*"

He smiled. Kostya was so close his lips were almost touching Evan's ear. And, as time was growing short, he kissed her on both cheeks. *"Come back to us,* moya doch'. *"*

Now, as they lifted off and tilted away from the two figures below, Evan sat, noise-canceling headphones on, arms wrapped around herself. Ben wanted to talk with her, at least ask her how she was doing, but he knew there was so much information for her to unpack that he was better off thinking his own thoughts. Besides, the roar of the helicopter rotors made conversation virtually impossible.

Below them, the countryside gave way as they passed over the seemingly endless forest, into grasslands, farming country, dotted with tractors and stone houses from which thin trails of smoke drifted skyward. Above them, the clouds rolled and tumbled, climbing to airless heights.

She and Ben were in the clinic's silver-and-blue Airbus H155 headed southeast. The helicopter was fast; they were flying at over 200 mph. Still, it would take roughly six hours—including a stop to refuel at an airfield outside the Austrian city of Graz—to reach their final destination deep in Romania's Carpathian Mountains.

"Dracula territory," Ben had said as they took off, his words all but lost in the chatter of the rotors.

Evan put her head in her hands. Knowing that her parents, her real parents, were alive, that they loved her, had never rejected her, but were merely accomplishing the last part of their remit seemed a larger concept than her mind could contain, like discovering the existence of the fourth dimension. They inhabited the same world as she did, as Bobbi had, therefore she understood them, understood everything they had done as no other child could. The question of forgiveness never entered the picture, which made acceptance, if not exactly easy, then surely less difficult. Still, there was a seismic shift in her world, proof positive of an unknown element—a crucial one—so long withheld from her. With that thought came another wave of hatred for her sister. Bobbi had known, known for years and years, and yet held on to that knowledge for what—spite? resentment? insecurity? malice? All four, possibly. Ah, but what did it matter? Bobbi was dead.

And yet it did matter. It mattered very much. Even while part of her clung to the rage, another, more mature part, knew that she needed to let the anger go, flow through her, and away, to vanish into the past.

She felt ripped in half. She was not who she had been before Konstantin and Rebecca had revealed themselves. She had never been aware of a breach in her world, a before and an after, so she had crossed it without even knowing it was there. But now, looking back over her shoulder, she could see it, dark and wide and permanent. She could never go back, never be the person she had been yesterday morning when she had walked into the forest inn and seen Konstantin Reveshvili eating breakfast. She did not know who this new Evan Ryder was. She had been born Evan Reveshvili—she was still a Reveshvili. Russian blood coursed through her veins, as it had coursed through Bobbi's. Was that truly the reason she defected? Or was it another example of her spite, resentment, insecurity, malice? Knowing her sister, it was probably malice aforethought.

Her teeth rattled, her spine tingled, the vibrations from the aircraft rising up through the soles of her boots, firing each and every nerve ending. An insupportable weight had fallen on her shoulders, the weight of another universe, of another life unlived. The knowledge of her birth parents, the joyful experience of meeting them, vied with her remembered love of the couple who raised her, who she had always called Mom and Dad, who never corrected her because they couldn't, because, perhaps, they didn't want to, pressed down on her with crushing force. She felt squeezed in a vise, heart hammering, breathless. She had to keep repeating, *This is not a dream* over and over in her head while pinching the flesh of her forearm in order not to lose her shit. Her head felt like it was splitting apart—nothing existed, not Ben, not the pilots, not the helicopter, not heaven above or the earth below. There was nothing in her universe except Kostya, Rebecca, Mary, Joe, and herself, each revolving around the others, a mini–solar system, real and symbols of the earthquake that had her in its grip.

Then she took her face out of her hands. She looked out, saw the clouds, the sky, the speed at which they were flying, and her mind was filled with Peter Pan. In her mind's eye, she saw Peter, and beside him Wendy and Michael, their arms spread wide, the wind riffling their hair. She could see the perfect ovals of their faces, their eyes shining, flying toward her, excited smiles wreathing their faces. She felt them in her arms, rocking her back on her heels. She felt her love for them warming her, settling her. They had no mother, no father. But they had her. And now they had grandparents. Such a wrenching turn of events.

And, all at once, she knew she had to pull herself together. Out of the darkness, into the light. Wendy and Michael were ahead of her, hidden in the Carpathian Mountains, having been abducted by her sister Ana. Ana, the psychopath, the solipsist. The self-proclaimed messiah.

And, leaning forward, she shouted at the pilots via her mic, "I'm betting you can take this baby up a notch, fellas! Am I wrong?"

She wasn't wrong. They touched down in Graz in record time. While the pilots climbed out to supervise the refueling, Evan stood outside the radius of the rotors. The afternoon sun was growing old and tired as it slipped toward the west. A chill was in the air. The wind sent up tiny eddies, but there was no hint of inclement weather.

She faced the wind, trying to rid herself of the feeling of unreality that had overwhelmed her the moment she understood who the Reveshvilis actually were. But now, in the open air, standing alone on the small airfield's tarmac, her eyes burning, tears at last overflowing, running down her cheeks, shivering in the wind, she surrendered to the surges of emotions buffeting her.

She felt Ben's approach. She stopped herself from cringing away, from keeping herself—what was happening to her—a raw wound, as if she had been shot—at a firm remove from any other human being.

"Evan—"

She turned her face away. It must be puffy and swollen. "Not now, Ben."

"Evan, I'd like to say I'm sorry—"

"Don't say anything, okay?"

Beyond the copter's behemoth fuselage there was nothing much to see. A cluster of nondescript low buildings, an ugly radio tower, not a soul to be seen, apart from the tech helping with the refueling. It was like standing at the edge of a windswept desert or looking out at the post-apocalyptic world.

"But I'm not sorry."

Ben had clearly made up his mind, he just wasn't going to give up. "Frankly, I don't care whether you're sorry or not." She had other things on her mind; Ben was last on the list or on another list altogether.

"Evan, it's imperative we talk now."

"Oh, Ben, we're at the end phase of our remit. We've got to find Wendy and Michael and get on with it. They're all I care about. They're all either of us should care about."

"I can't help caring about you."

"Which is why you're not cut out for field work anymore. Ben, I've said this before. You've spent too many years being a handler, sitting behind a desk, working out remits."

But she saw that it was he whose face looked puffy and swollen, even though his cheeks had hollowed out. The whites of his eyes were threaded with red; the eyes themselves looked haunted. For the first time since meeting her parents her thoughts turned outward beyond herself.

Ben looked away for the moment, then back at her. "You're right, of course. I don't belong out here." He straightened his back. "But I'm here now, and there's something I need to tell you."

She nodded. "Go ahead."

"Leonard Pine took me aside just before we boarded. It may seem trivial compared to what's ahead of us, but not to Leonard Pine. He has a wayward sister, young and wild. Sadly, he learned that she followed Jon and joined Omega as a fierce fighter. Her name is Helene, but she now goes by Hel, the Norse goddess of death, which, I believe, tells us all we need to know about her. Nevertheless, she is beloved by Leonard, and now she's his only living sibling. He asked us to spare her. If we could bring her back to him, he would be most grateful." Ben looked pale and drawn. "He said we'll know her by the necklace with a gold cross he gave her."

"Noted." She searched Ben's face. "Anything else?"

Ben shook his head.

She squeezed his shoulder. "For what it's worth I'm not sorry you're here with me."

He gripped her arm briefly, before turning away, a smile nowhere in evidence.

48

MOSCOW, RUSSIA

The low sky over Moscow pressed down like an iron on a shirt. A late afternoon on the sixteenth of May, the military airfield was quiet, almost sleepy. The air was utterly still, not a breath of wind anywhere. Thick clouds were the color of mercury. Though it would be at least five hours until sunset, a peculiar twilight had settled over the city. The air was difficult to breathe, as if much of the oxygen had been sucked up into the glowering sky.

The SVR vehicle was waiting for them on the edge of the tarmac. The driver who, Kobalt noted in passing, was a female, held the door open, nodding to them deferentially as they climbed in.

As they drove off, Zherov gave the driver his home address.

"Too many days in the same clothes," he said as he settled back in the seat. "I need a long hot shower, a half-bottle of vodka, then a new outfit."

Kobalt checked her watch. "Fine. I'll need you by five though. I'll text you the address."

Then she turned her attention to the driver. The rearview

mirror showed a thin strip of skin around gray eyes as pale, almost, as water. She was a blonde with skin almost as pale as her eyes. *Clearly a desk jockey,* Kobalt thought.

"Driver, what's your name?"

"Kata Romanovna, Colonel."

Kobalt was not used to being addressed by her rank. "Okay, Kata Romanovna, please find out where Minister Darko Vladimirovich Kusnetsov will be in one hour and take me there."

"At once, Colonel," the driver confirmed.

Kobalt saw Kata reach for her mobile and press a button. The tinted bulletproof glass privacy screen slid up, cutting them off from the front of the SUV.

Zherov was already frowning. "I don't like this idea of going to see Minister Kusnetsov."

"You don't like it because you weren't in on the decision."

"Okay, you and Lyudmila worked something out between you. You won't tell me what that is, and, yes, that pisses me off. But I tell you, I still don't trust her. No matter what you say or what she tells you, we don't know her real motivations."

"I think I do, Anton."

He grunted, crossing his arms over his chest. "Even if you do—which is a big 'if'—it's still an extremely dangerous course to take."

Kobalt stared out the window as raindrops began to slide down the glass. A hundred tiny eyes staring at her. "Maybe, but at this point it's the only course."

Zherov shifted uncomfortably in his seat. "To tell you the truth, I don't like the idea of us coming back to Moscow at all. I mean, why take the chance? We have Ermi Çelik's money, away from here we had our freedom."

Kobalt turned back to him. "That freedom is illusory, Anton. Do you really want to be like Lyudmila, always on the run, not knowing when a Zaslon hit team might be around the next corner?" She shook her head. "That life's not for me."

He stared at her wordlessly. He wasn't about to contradict her, but he was still fuming inside as they crossed the Ring Road.

"Don't be angry, Anton. There's too much hard work— dangerous work—for us ahead." She smiled. "Right up your street."

He stared up at the roof of the SUV, then back at her. "Why the hell did she take you off the boat in the middle of the night?"

Kobalt let a moment's silence pass. Then, "This woman who you so don't trust took me to meet my parents."

"What?" Zherov was openmouthed. "Your parents were American. They died when you were a kid."

"As it happens, no. The American couple adopted me and my sister." She nodded at his astonished expression. "That's right, both of us—Evan and I—are Russian. Galina and Maxim Chernyshevsky. They're dead, Anton, buried in the family plot in a cemetery outside Constanta. Our lineage goes back to Romania. That's why she took the yacht there. It was important that I have closure on a secret I knew since I was very little. Until that moment, I had no idea who my birth parents were."

"I . . ." He choked. Whatever he was going to say seemed stuck inside him.

"Turns out I'm one of you. Shocking, isn't it? That's what you were going to say."

He looked stunned. "Or something like it, anyway. I mean, *'tchyo za ga'lima?*" *What the fuck?*

She laughed at his complete consternation.

"Give me a minute, or three. Please." He was struggling with this new reality. "I don't . . . I couldn't have imagined such a thing."

"This was a gift Lyudmila gave me. A precious gift. You understand?"

He nodded, lost in thought for some time. "Perhaps I've misjudged her."

"The only way forward is to accept what is in front of you."

"In any case . . ." He sighed deeply, closed his eyes. "I'll tell you what I want out of this . . . a reward for this life. A big one."

"And you'll have it. Now you know you will."

He nodded. "You know what? I'm thinking of a wide, crescent beach on a tiny Thai or Indonesian island, lying back in a hammock, listening to the surf and the palm fronds clatter in the onshore breeze."

"When we retire," she said with a certain amount of cynicism.

"Sure, sure," he answered, choosing to ignore her tone.

"Anton."

He opened his eyes.

"The next few hours will be as delicate as they are crucial. I need to know I can count on you."

A laugh and a nod. "Always, boss. I told you that."

Reaching out, she squeezed his shoulder. "Good man."

"A guy can dream, can't he?"

Kobalt thought about this. "Sometimes," she said, "dreaming is all that makes life livable."

Moments later, having bypassed the teeming traffic using the clear lane reserved for government eminences and foreign dignitaries, they reached Zherov's apartment building. The driver pulled over to the curb and stopped. She slid out, opened the curbside rear door for him.

"See you at five," Zherov said. "Whatever you have up your sleeve, good luck."

Kobalt nodded absently, her mind already on the options for penetrating Minister Kusnetsov's day-to-day defenses without raising an alarm. It all depended on where he would be twenty minutes from now, and whether that place would be advantageous to her. Her preference was to get to him while he was out of the office. Less interference and levels of security to go through, not to mention less officious personnel to get past. This close to the finish line she was impatient for action.

Out of the corner of her eye, she saw Zherov trotting up the steps to the building's front door.

Out of the corner of her eye, she saw Kata draw a pistol, take a shooter's stance, and fire a bullet into Zherov's back.

49

CARPATHIAN MOUNTAINS, ROMANIA

Lyudmila was waiting for them as the copter landed in the center of an open field. She and Evan had been in almost constant touch since Lyudmila arrived here, in what in Roman times had once been the Kingdom of Dacia, before it was conquered and became a province of the far-flung Empire. Dacia had a storied history, being conquered by the Huns long after the Empire fell, then the Lombards, and, finally, in 791, by Charlemagne's army. That was when the Slavic people arrived. Later, much of Dacia became known as Transylvania, the high, toothed mountains forbidding, the legends even more so.

The sky was a pellucid blue directly above them, even though shadows thrown across the open space were growing long spider legs. The air was crisp and clean. Even at this time of year snow glimmered on the higher peaks like trapped moonlight.

The moment she saw Evan exiting, Lyudmila waved her over. Evan scuttled forward under the slowing rotors, standing up straight well outside their radius. Ben followed but was smart enough to busy himself with shouldering the two khaki duffels containing the equipment, selected by Evan and her father and loaded into the helicopter.

"Thank you," Evan said when she came up to her. "Thank you for finding my birth parents and for leading me step-by-step to them."

Lyudmila smiled, placed her palm against Evan's cheek. *Now the circle is closed*, she thought. *They, each of them, have the closure they needed. And both of them are shielded from the full truth. Kobalt thinks her birth parents are dead. Evan thinks her sister is dead. Now their worlds will never collide. They will never face the dreadful reality of rending each other limb from limb to avenge deep-seated betrayals.*

Evan brought her up to date on what she and Ben had learned from her parents and from Leonard Pine.

Lyudmila nodded. "I know what Leonard knows," she said. "He's one of mine. As for the rest, it's both illuminating and terrifying. Your sister Ana is completely out of control. She must be stopped. There's no alternative. What she has planned for your niece and nephew is unspeakable. It must not happen."

"There's something else," Evan said. "I think we're on a deadline and it's tonight at midnight."

They both looked at her as if she had grown another head.

Lyudmila came out of shock first. "Explain, please."

"From what my parents told me, Ana is obsessed with Noah and the Flood, which started on the seventeenth of the month. Today is the sixteenth."

"We're going to head out before nightfall." Lyudmila squinted up at the lowering sky. The wind had picked up, thick with moisture. "Heavy weather coming our way. That will lower visibility, at least."

Ben dropped the duffels and, kneeling, zipped one open. "How far are we from the Omega citadel?"

Lyudmila produced a Samsung Note from her backpack, fired it up. The GPS took a moment to sync with the appropriate satellite signal, then, "Here we are." She pointed to a spot on the topographical interface she overlaid on the Google Earth map. Her fingertip moved roughly northeast. "And here is the citadel."

She swiped right, revealing a close-up photo of the castle. It stretched itself skyward within a heavily forested glen. In the background, mountain peaks crowded out the sky. There was a central tower crowned by a kind of brightly lit open-air hall. The rock on which the castle had been built climbed halfway up this tower, making the citadel seem as if it had risen from inside the earth itself. To the right was a circular turret with a long, sloping conical roof not unlike a cartoon dunce cap. On the left, a smaller conical roof was anchored by another brown-brick turret. Lyudmila glanced at Evan before swiping right again, bringing up a rear view of the citadel.

"You can't see it for the trees," Evan's forefinger stabbed out, "but according to my father, right here close to the stone wall a small stream runs more or less across the castle's back. At the base of the rock wall, there's an outlet for a storm drain."

Ben glanced up from the photo to Evan. "Are you proposing we gain access to the citadel by crawling through what must be centuries of muck?"

"You and Lyudmila," Evan said. "A diversion is required."

"With all this brush around we could start a fire," Ben suggested.

Evan shook her head. "Not with the kids inside."

Lyudmila swiped the screen, stowed away the Note in her backpack. "Anyway, Evan has a better idea."

"While you and Lyudmila get in through the channel in back," Evan said to Ben, "I'll be going in the front door."

Ben huffed. "You'll be doing what now?"

"Listen, Ana is expecting Bobbi. I have suspected all along that's one reason she took Wendy and Michael."

"Which means she doesn't know Bobbi's dead," Lyudmila said.

"Right." Evan nodded. "Just as Rebecca and Konstantin don't know that Bobbi, their Robin, is dead." She exchanged a meaningful glance with Lyudmila, her eyes expressing an understanding and gratitude that needed no words. Lyudmila inclined her head ever so slightly.

Evan continued. "We know why she wants them, we know in all likelihood she'll start experimenting on them at one minute after midnight."

"So . . ." Lyudmila prompted.

"I'm going to give her precisely what she expects, what she wants: my sister Bobbi, her sister Robin," Evan replied.

"Excuse me," Ben broke in, "but we don't know why she wants Robin."

"And we won't know until she and I are together." Evan's eyes were alight with the prospect of the confrontation. "The point is, Ben, my appearance should allow you two enough time to infiltrate the citadel and get the kids out."

"I think you're nuts," Ben said. "And that's a professional opinion."

"Do you have a better idea?"

"Yeah, we all get mucked up, grab the kids, and get the hell out of there."

"Too risky. In a firefight, Wendy and Michael are vulnerable."

"All of us together makes no sense," Lyudmila said. "If we run into trouble, it's—"

"No, no. Hell no." Ben waved away her words, but his eyes were on Evan. "I know what this is all about. It's personal, Evan. You want the chance to confront your sister, to be the one who takes her down."

A strained silence ensued. Just the wind in the treetops, a birdsong, the whirring of insects. They could almost hear the last of the sunlight as it slanted across their grim faces.

"Family," Lyudmila said softly, breaking the tension. "You can't fight it, Ben. It's a losing battle."

"I don't believe that," he said, a little too quickly.

"Think of Zoe," Evan said. "Think how you would feel if someone abducted her. Ben, Wendy and Michael are my family. I'm not going to—"

"What if she shoots you dead," Ben interrupted her. "The moment she sees you."

Evan shook her head. "She won't do that."

"Why the hell not?"

"Family," Lyudmila repeated. "Ana will be curious. She'll need to talk with a sister she's never met, a sister from a lifestyle totally alien to her. Ana won't harm her."

"At first." Ben's eyes narrowed. "Can you even guarantee that?"

"Nothing in life is guaranteed," Evan said. "Especially with the lives we lead."

"So . . ." Lyudmila said.

"We go." Evan and Lyudmila started out.

"Wait," Ben said. "What happens after we get Wendy and Michael?"

Evan turned back to him as Lyudmila tapped her backpack. "We blow that fucker into kingdom come."

50

FIRING LINE

As Zherov pitched onto his face, the car's door locks clicked down and stayed down. Kobalt scrambled over the backseat, blocking out the shock, her own survival at the forefront. Whipping around, she threw herself against the glass partition, to no avail. All the glass was bulletproof. What good would her hitting it do? Still, human nature. Thrashing, she watched the driver slide behind the wheel, put the SUV in gear, and zoom out into traffic. In New York, that maneuver would have presaged a blare of horns and shouted invective. Here, in Moscow, there was nary a sound. No citizen would dare raise a protest against an official government vehicle, no matter how dangerously it was being driven.

She was weaponless, having left them all on the plane. There was no way she was going to be received by the head of the FSB while she was weaponized. But she did have her mobile. Without thinking, she was about to punch in Zherov's speed-dial number, then, finger hovering over the keyboard, realized, with a gut contraction, that Zherov was bleeding out on the front steps of his apartment building. She tried to call emergency services instead, but she had no signal. With a string of juicy expletives, she thought about Dima. She was in an SVR vehicle whose driver knew precisely when her plane was landing. Another inside job, like her betrayal at the Omega compound in Odessa? At the knife shop in Istanbul? It seemed the most logical explanation. She shook her head. It astonished her how things could get so shitty, so quickly.

She tried to communicate with the driver—the chance of her real name being Kata Romanovna was next to nil. The intra-vehicular communication system was working perfectly well, but the driver remained mute as a Trappist nun. Nevertheless, Kobalt kept at it.

"Where are we going?" she demanded, and then in an even more commanding tone, "Where are you taking me, Kata?"

"There is a time and place for everything."

Finally a response. "Where is it, then, our destination?"

The driver smirked at her in the rearview mirror. It was at that moment Kobalt noticed the ring with its enormous square-cut emerald. She took another look at the driver with the incongruous ring that must have cost a fortune, assuming the emerald was real and not paste. The mystery deepened. Not only did she not know who this woman was, she now could not imagine who she was working for.

At length, Kobalt sat back, turned her mind to other, more practical matters.

They reversed direction, headed northeast, crossed the Moskva River via the Bolshoy Bridge. It had a longer name, but no one used it. They headed along the northern embankment road, still on a northeast course. They had long since left the upper- and middle-class residential neighborhoods, and were in one of the poorer, industrialized sections of the city. Soon enough, they were passing hulking warehouses and electrical plants that were so long outdated, beyond repair or rehabilitation, that they had been abandoned by all but the most destitute pilgrims from far away, those who had lost even a vestige of hope of finding employment. Here and there, enclaves of the homeless could be spotted, their drugged-out denizens sprawled, insensate.

Presently, the canal ended, and they rolled sedately through Andronyevskaya Square. The space was entirely deserted; not a soul was visible. Rising up and facing each other were a pair of enormous structures, probably apartment buildings, judging by the number of windows pockmarking their filthy yellowish façades. The glass in every window was blown, as if from titanic blasts from inside at some time in the past. The buildings had a haunted aspect, as even from the outside it was clear no one was bedding down inside them. Not an area any tourist would be taken to. Although street crime was exceptionally low in Moscow, poverty wasn't.

The SUV pulled in to the curb near the building on the western side of the square.

"Last stop," Kata said without a trace of irony. She killed the engine, then stepped out. Moving to the rear passenger's door, she unlocked it, swung the heavy door open. What Kata was wearing beneath her black ankle-length duster was impossible to say.

"Out," she ordered curtly.

Kobalt expected to see a pistol pointed at her, but, curiously, there was none.

"Tell me who you are."

In a blur of motion, Kata whipped out an electric cattle prod and, leaning in, jabbed it hard against the left side of Kobalt's chest. Kobalt spasmed backward as if she had been shot. She lay on the backseat, seeing flashing lights amid the darkness at the edges of her vision. Her heart seemed to be skipping beats, then throbbing like a runaway train.

The next moment, she felt herself being hauled out of the

SUV. Immediately, she fell to her knees, her head swinging back and forth as if she were in a drunken stupor. She knew the driver was speaking to her, but she couldn't understand a word. *What had happened?* she asked herself. *Had a grenade gone off next to her?*

She felt the driver's breath on her cheek, and she lifted her head.

"I told you. Kata," the driver whispered in her head. "My name is Kata Romanovna Hemakova."

Slowly, her blurred vision cleared. The world around her righted itself. She rose to her feet but not without having to grasp the top of the open door for support.

"If you're going to kill me"—Kobalt's voice was a thick rasp—"just do it now and get it over with."

"Oh, it will come," Kata said, "but first you'll try to escape, just like in the American movies. But I will bring you back, and shortly after that you'll tell me everything I want to know. By that time you'll be screaming for your daddy."

"I don't have a daddy. I never did."

Kata's eyes narrowed and she stepped closer to Kobalt. "Everyone has a daddy and a mommy."

Kobalt's grin was sardonic. "You're making such a huge fucking mistake."

"Am I?" Kata cocked her head. "Well, before we go any further . . ." The cattle prod jabbed out, the end connecting with Kobalt's kneecap. Kobalt grunted as her right leg collapsed. But she kept hold of the car door, her torso tilted away from it, as if she were a flag battered by the wind.

"Let's see how much running you do on one leg."

Kata grabbed her by the back of her collar. A brief tug-of-war ensued, which, inevitably, Kobalt lost, her handhold on the door slipping away inch by grudging inch. Blood welled where a nail was ripped off. Kata, grunting with the effort, hauled Kobalt behind her as she made her way across the pavement.

They passed through the mouth of the derelict building, the door hanging by a single rusted hinge.

The dim interior stank of age, mold, and desperation. Here and there the remnants of cooking odors seeped out of the walls, as did the acrid stench of cheap tobacco smoke. Precise squares of light from the blown-out windows checkered the filthy floorboards.

Kata hauled Kobalt into the center of the space, which long ago in a forgotten past had been cleared of interior walls. To the left, a pockmarked concrete staircase rose upward. Beside it, an elevator shaft; the elevator itself was missing.

"What's your beef with me, anyway?" Kobalt said in a dry, cracked voice.

Kata stood over her. She pulled Kobalt to her feet, thrust her face forward. "What? What did you say?"

Kobalt tried to isolate the pain in a corner of her mind, to lacquer it over with what needed to be done in order for her to survive. "Why are you doing this? Who's ordering you around like a puppet?"

Kata laughed. "Ah, here's where you keep me talking. The longer we converse the further you put off the pain."

"I'm already in pain," Kobalt pointed out.

"You think so?"

In response, Kobalt raked the HVAC grille she had managed to pull out of its socket in the car's rear console down Kata's face. Blood exploded from her forehead to her eyelids, her nose, her lips, and chin. She staggered back and Kobalt stepped forward, raking the grille again and again.

But they were so close together Kata didn't need her sight to jam the end of the cattle prod into Kobalt's side. Kobalt screamed, dropped the grille, and closed her fingers tight around Kata's wrist, pulling the cattle prod away.

Off-balance, the two women tumbled to the floor, rolling through the filthy detritus, disturbing the hunting of every rat on the ground floor. First one was on top, then the other. Their concentration was centered on the prod, nothing else mattered. Slowly but surely, Kobalt started to gain control, swinging the end in a shallow arc toward Kata's chest. Suddenly, Kata's right hand released and Kobalt felt the surge of victory. She almost had full control of the prod, but then a blur slashed across her vision. She jerked her head back just in time to avoid losing an eye, but the leading facet of Kata's emerald took a chunk out of the bridge of her nose. They were both bloody now.

Kata slammed the side of the prod against Kobalt's ribs. Pain shot through Kobalt's entire body and for a moment she felt as if she was going to lose, that this person whom she didn't even know was going to get the better of her, batter her into submission, extract what she wanted from Kobalt, and then kill her.

But that black moment passed, and she gathered her strength around her like chainmail armor. She buried her elbow in Kata's solar plexus, drove her right knee into Kata's groin. They both screamed in pain, and Kobalt lost all feeling in her right leg from the knee down. Her right foot seemed to hang in the air, as if it was connected to her by only a thin bit of tissue.

Kata regained control of the prod. "You fucking bitch," she managed through her grinding teeth.

But Kobalt had wrapped both hands around Kata's fist, and she drove the faceted emerald into the soft flesh of Kata's throat. The emerald tore through skin and fascia, crushing her cricoid. Air rushed out and Kata began to gasp, her inhales a horrific rail, gurgling and bloody.

Kobalt unwound her fingers, stiff with how tightly she'd held onto Kata's fist. Of a sudden, Kata's left arm reached up, her fingers clutching Kobalt's throat. Her face a death mask, she squeezed and squeezed with an unholy strength.

For a second, Kobalt was sure she blacked out, that for a second time within moments she could see the specter of death coming for her. Then she whipped the prod out of Kata's fingers and jammed it down her throat. Kata's eyes opened wide, her limbs drummed a spastic tattoo against the floor. This went on a seemingly endless time, though in reality it couldn't have been more than ten or so seconds, before her eyes rolled up into her head, one leg gave a last galvanic kick, and she lay dead beneath Kobalt's panting torso.

Kobalt was crying now, both out of terror and relief. She stared down at the bloody face of her erstwhile adversary with not an iota of remorse. After some time, her breathing returning to normal, she sat up, wrenched the emerald ring off Kata's finger, wiped it off, slipped it onto her own.

"Fucking bitch," she whispered hoarsely. "You got that right."

She scrabbled in the blood, found the key fob for the SUV, to which a set of keys were attached. She searched for Kata's mobile phone but couldn't find it. With no little difficulty she rose, her breathing painful and stertorous, and limping badly, moved toward the dim rectangle of the doorway.

With each step the cattle prod dripped a line of blood behind her.

51

ANA

THEY'RE COMING.

Ana stared down at her mobile's screen, checked the text was from Leonard Pine's dedicated phone number. **How many?** She texted back.

three, he replied.

that's all? she only brought two people with her?
kobalt seems supremely sure of herself
I'll disabuse her of that mindset shortly
b careful she's a nasty piece of wk

Ana thought about how it would be to confront her older sister face-to-face. It was something she'd longed for for some time. A sister who had children, the only one possibly who could conceive, as she and her twin could not. And now Kobalt was coming to get her children back.

She was about to sever the connection when Leonard Pine texted her again.

How is Hel?

And she thought, *Oh, for God's sake.*

same as she ever was, and immediately pressed END.

★★★

Swinging around, she saw Hel striding toward her down one of the citadel's labyrinthine corridors, a small, compact figure, well-toned, sunbaked body, with a ready smile that didn't conceal its caginess. Both her hair, cut short as a man's, and her eyes, were dark as iron. She was dressed in deepest blue leggings and fitted sleeveless shirt. Her boots were rugged but lightweight. Their soles made no sound on the stone floor. Bandoliers crisscrossed over her chest and back. The gold cross on its chain she never took off glinted softly in the light. A handgun was holstered at her right hip, a scabbarded throwing knife at her left hip. Paired smaller throwing knives lived inside the tops of her boots.

Watching her approach, Ana considered once again how everything and everyone had its place. To her, there was no difference between the things and people, though each had its assigned place in her hyper-analytical mind. If either was of no use to her, she had ignored it. And if it did have a use, that use was, by definition, finite. Be it a day, week, or year there was always a sell-by date, when she would inevitably discard that thing or person, move on to the next useful item. Even Hel, whose fighting prowess and tactical mind she held in the highest regard, was just another station in her journey to the salvation of the world.

"Have the children been fed?" she asked.

Hel looked up at her. "Fed and asleep, Mother."

Ana's eyes narrowed. "How deeply asleep?"

"They are beyond dreams, Mother."

"Yes." Ana smiled, almost wistfully. "What child doesn't love hot cocoa?"

"They won't awake until it's time," Hel assured her.

She nodded. She trusted Hel, but not as much as Hel trusted her. That was, of course, by design. She took Hel by the elbow, guiding her back along the corridor. "Kobalt will be here soon with two of her cohort, but I seriously doubt that the three of them will show up at the same time in the same place." She glanced meaningfully at her companion.

"I understand, Mother," and, breaking off at a branching of the corridor, Hel strode purposefully away. "We will be ready," she said over her shoulder.

When Hel had disappeared around a corner, Ana headed off to the children's new sleeping quarters, the state-of-the-art operating theater hidden behind the stone wall of the Chapel of the Burning Sword of God.

52

MOSCOW, RUSSIAN FEDERATION

Kobalt stood in Kata's shower, wincing as the hot water cascaded over her wounds. Strings of blood slithered down her torso and legs, turning into pink rivulets as they snaked their way into the drain. Her eyes were closed, her face turned up to the spray, despite the pain spreading out from the wound on the bridge of her nose. A bruise of many colors bloomed across her throat, but at least the imprints of Kata's powerful fingers were but a memory.

Every few moments, an involuntary shiver ran down her entire body, and a chill swept through her despite the steamy water. She could feel her right foot now, but the knee above it throbbed with every pulse of blood that ran through its veins under the cartilage.

It had taken all her willpower not to vomit on the way to the SUV, but in the end, she managed not to puke her guts up. Still, she leaned against the vehicle, trying to gather herself. Part of her knew she was in shock, but another part had forgotten where she was or how she had arrived here in this altogether unfamiliar section of Moscow.

The SUV. Of course. Sighing, she opened the driver's side door and, wincing with pain, hauled herself inside. She sat for a moment, head against the seatback, her hands gripping the wheel with all her might as if willing the strength back into her weakened body.

After an indeterminate amount of time, she picked her head up, noticed her surroundings, saw at once Kata's mobile lying on the passenger's seat. Bringing it out of sleep, she activated the GPS, found Kata's home address.

On the way there she passed by Zherov's building. The front was cordoned off, there was blood on the concrete steps, but no chalk outline, no sign of the medical examiner's vehicle or, indeed, a forensic team. In fact, only one police was standing guard, and he seemed there only to allow residents in and out of the building. As was the case in Moscow, there was no crowd. Pedestrians on the sidewalk hurried by, heads either down or averted. No one wanted trouble, or God forbid even be stopped and questioned.

Gritting her teeth, she turned off the hot water. As the shower slowly cooled then, abruptly, turned cold, she took a series of deep, cleansing breaths, clearing her mind. The cold water felt good on her nose and knees, but the spray felt like needles on the round bruise just above her left breast where Kata had first struck her with the cattle prod.

Stepping out of the shower, she wrapped herself in a luxurious bath sheet. She kept the water on, the sound of the spray calming her. She had looked for and found a professional doctor's first aid kit in the cabinet under the sink. Now she stood in front of the mirror, tending to the torn bridge of her nose. It took five stitches—the dissolving kind—to repair the damage, and studying it before she applied the liquid skin, she doubted her nose would ever look the same. Not that she cared overly; she welcomed this reminder of the fragile line between life and death.

When she was done with her nose, she walked gingerly into Kata's bedroom, opening the mirrored sliding door to a closet larger than most apartments in downtown Moscow, selected a silk dressing gown to replace the damp bath sheet.

Sitting on the end of Kata's enormous bed, she retrieved her phone from her bloody clothes, punched in the speed-dial number for Dima's private mobile line.

"*Moya malen'kaya osa!*" Dima cried when he heard her voice. *My little wasp!* "I have been beside myself. As soon as I heard Zherov was taken to the hospital my thoughts turned to you. Are you unhurt?"

"I'm fine," Kobalt said. "Where is Zherov? I dropped him off in front of his building."

"Shot," Dima said. "In the back."

"Is he alive?"

"For the moment, anyway," Dima said. "He's in surgery."

She felt a surge of relief.

"Your remit?" Dima asked.

Of course he would ask this, but she was prepared. "Omega has been neutralized."

"Congratulations. And your children?"

"Safe."

"That must be a relief." When she said nothing, he changed tack. "Who shot Zherov?"

"Unknown. I didn't see anyone. Whoever it was must have waited until I drove off."

A short silence. "Motive?"

"There could be so many."

Dima grunted an agreement. "My office tomorrow at nine sharp for your formal debriefing."

In the kitchen she made herself an ice pack with cubes wrapped in a dishtowel, fetched a bottle of vodka from the freezer, and sat at the oval table, leg up on another chair, and applied the ice pack.

She felt no remorse about lying to Dima about Omega. She hoped Lyudmila had neutralized it or would soon. If she failed, there would be no future for anyone. Not for the first time she felt the stirring of regret about leaving her to come back here. But as Lyudmila pointed out Moscow was her future. Besides, Lyudmila was right, Omega was expecting her. No point in trying to evade the trap they had set and making the infiltration more difficult than it already was. Still, it rankled her not being involved. Lyudmila had asked for her trust, not an easy thing for Kobalt to accept. But if there was one person she was apt to trust it was Lyudmila, who had brought her closure on the enigma of her birth parents. She thought about them, recalled standing in front of their graves, sensing a closeness she had never felt before. She owed Lyudmila.

Turning her mind to more immediate matters, she went to work on the vodka, straight from the bottle. Ice and fire slid down her throat, settling in her stomach, spreading warmth and a lessening of the pain. From where she sat, she could see into the living room and, craning her neck a bit, a sliver of the den. Whoever the hell Kata Romanovna Hemakova was, she thought, the bitch sure had herself a sweet deal, because there was no way Kata Romanovna could afford this atrociously furnished palace on her own dime. And so . . . The very first name and number she found scrolling through Kata's mobile was that of the SVR's Director General Stanislav Budimirovich Baev's mobile. Which meant one of two things. Either Kata was Baev's mistress or he had sent Kata to terminate her. Or both, judging by the three texts for a sitrep he had sent her. Who knew with these people?

Then, as she kept digging in Kata's phone, she came across the set of nude selfies Kata had sent to Baev. Well, what do you know. Lyudmila was right about the men in this snake pit. She needed to take control. She had her leverage against Dima safe and sound. Now she had a perfect method of meeting with Baev out of his office. She took another deep swig of vodka and admired Kata's body. *Funny how life works*, she thought. *My encounter with Kata is turning out to be one of the most fortunate ones since I crossed over the breach.*

She stood, ignoring the ice pack as it spilled onto the tiled floor. Time to get ready.

It had been a long, trying day for Director General Baev: a blizzard of administrative matters to attend to that would usually be handled by his adjutant, Ilya Ivanovich Gurin, now dead and forgotten. The increasingly contentious back-and-forth with Darko Kusnetsov. According to his boss, the head of FSB, Evan Ryder was still very much alive. *Why hadn't Kata dealt with her yet?* he had asked himself. *Why hadn't she answered his texts?* Then the afternoon was inundated by intel and sitrep updates, none from Kata. But then the remit she was on would never show up on normal FSB channels, or anywhere else for that matter.

The text came from Kata just as he was leaving the office. He stared down at the screen of his private mobile, read the single line.

surprise tonight! im waiting

Finally, he thought, *good news.* And felt a concomitant stirring between his legs.

Darkness had drowned Moscow by the time Baev drew up into Kata's driveway. As always, he gave the street a cursory look. It was the same, a couple of vehicles parked, including a black SUV farther down the block.

Using the key she had given him, he let himself in. At once, he smelled the perfume she always wore for him. His nostrils dilated, her scent leading him from the entryway, down the hall, and into her living room.

And there she was, sprawled on the curving purple velvet sofa, looking at him, an enigmatic smile on her beautiful face. Only it wasn't Kata's face. He stopped in his tracks, staring at her bandaged nose, then at the rest of her, dressed in Kata's clothes—specifically her black vinyl dress.

His face darkened and he scowled. "Where's Kata?" he said sharply. "Who the hell are you?"

Kobalt lifted her right hand to show him the huge square-cut emerald glistening on her middle finger. "You want to know who I am, Director General Baev? I'm Kata Romanovna Hemakova."

His laugh was singularly uneasy. "Don't be absurd."

"I'm the new Kata Romanovna Hemakova."

His frown deepened. "Come on now. Where is Kata?"

"Kata is dead," Kobalt said. "I killed her." She lifted the cattle prod with her other hand. "I shoved this down her throat."

Baev stared at her for the longest time, then he produced the small handgun he always carried with him. But before he could aim it at her, she was up. The prod touched his chest, and he winced.

"Don't make me do it, Director. I honestly don't want to hurt you." She never took her eyes off his face. "But believe me I will if you give me no choice."

He had started to hyperventilate. "I . . ."

"You know I wouldn't be here now in her house you paid for, wearing her clothes you paid for, unless she was dead."

His hyperventilating would not stop. "I . . . I believe you."

She took the gun from his unresisting fingers.

"As to who I really am I'm surprised you don't recognize me. Five days ago Dima was scheduled to take me to see you."

For a moment, a quizzical look, then as recognition dawned, he whispered, "Kobalt? You're Kobalt."

"Not anymore. Kobalt is dead. You're going to make sure that from tomorrow on my name is Kata Romanovna Hemakova."

"But you . . ." He started to feel faint. "How did you—"

"How did I kill Kata? My dear Stanislav Budimirovich—or should I call you Slava? Actually I like that better. My dear Slava, you made the fatal error of sending Kata to terminate me."

"I . . ." He shook his head emphatically. "But I didn't."

"She came after me." She cocked her head. "How d'you explain that, Slava?"

He ran his fingers through his sweat-damp hair.

"You can't. Because you're lying." She shrugged. "But even if by the slightest chance you're telling the truth it doesn't really matter because here we are, you and I."

He opened his hands wide. "No, no, I am not lying. Just let me think for a moment . . ." He put his head in his hands and went still.

The expression in his eyes led her to believe him. She waited and watched, could practically see his quick mind putting together the pieces of a puzzle.

After a moment his head came up. "This is the truth, Kobalt. I sent my adjutant, Ilya Ivanovich Gurin, to Kata with a remit to kill Evan Ryder. And for Kata to kill him, which she did, for I believed he was about to overstep himself." He gave her a piercing look. "Now I'm thinking he already had. It had to have been Gurin who betrayed you to Omega. He had the means, and the motive. And he assigned Kata to kill you, not Ryder, behind my back."

She gave him a skeptical look. "And had me attacked in Istanbul? Why would Gurin concern himself with me to this ultimate extent?"

"Istanbul?" He looked perplexed, but then waved away his confusion with a swipe of his hand. "You're here, that's all. He failed. As to why . . . jealousy is a strong motivator, especially in those who are overly ambitious. He knew I coveted you as an agent. He knew I was planning to take you away from Dima."

She cocked her head. "I'm listening." Because now what he was saying made perfect sense.

Baev nodded. "Gurin was terrified that I was going to replace him. He assumed once I had you there would be no place for him. And he was right."

"You said he was your adjutant."

"That's correct."

"A desk jockey I am not."

Baev snorted. He was regaining his equilibrium. "I'm through being interrogated. What is this all in aid of?"

She showed him what she had discovered at Ermi's office. "I'm sure your boss will be interested in what a loose ship you've been running. What Dima has been doing right under your nose."

Baev blanched as he looked through the Turkish lawyer's damning ledgers. Then he thought of Kusnetsov's bloody cleaver: steel, flesh, bone. *Whack!* "This . . . this," he spluttered, clearly knocked off his pins again. His eyes were wild when he looked back up at her. "What is this, blackmail?"

"Only in a way," she said. "It's not what I plan to do to you, Slava." Her smile was predatory. "It's what I plan to do *for* you."

He was still in shock at Dima's treachery; the blatant murders of his people, the crushing of so many remits . . . A shudder went right through him. "And in return," he said hoarsely, "what do you want?"

53

CITADEL I

The four horsemen of death for a stealth mission were to be avoided at any and all cost: Do not go in fast. Do not go in heavy. Do not go in without backup. Do not go in without an exit strategy. Ben knew, after the fact of course, that many was the time that Evan courted two, sometimes three of the horsemen, and had emerged not only alive but victorious. He, however, had never courted any when they were in the field together. If he was to be perfectly honest with himself, stealth was not his forte. Evan knew that, and yet she had sent him to infiltrate the Omega citadel at its backside. He supposed that she had no other choice. That didn't stop him from being terrified out of his skin. This situation was so far out of his expertise he felt like a bull in a munitions manufactory. As he crawled through the thick underbrush, he could only hope that Lyudmila was better at stealth than he was.

They were using old-school pin lights because LEDs carried too far. They came out of Lyudmila's capacious backpack, which appeared to be stocked with just about everything they needed. They were within a hundred or so yards from where the storm drain was supposed to be when the black sky lowered and rain began to beat down on them in sheets. Visibility instantly collapsed to near zero. On the plus side, the foliage foamed up steam around them, obscuring them as efficiently as thick fog. But by the time they reached the outlet, water was rushing out of it, inundating the surrounding area, causing them to slip and slide. More than once the steep slope necessitated one of them anchoring themselves by wrapping their hand around the trunk of a sapling while pulling the other up to safety. But that safety was relative as the saplings bent precariously under the weight of the two of them. One actually uprooted, causing them to backslide a couple of yards.

Eventually, however, they made it to the concrete lip of the outlet and for a moment stood to one side, catching their breath, watching the water cascading out and down the slope.

"Well?" Ben yelled in Lyudmila's ear to make himself heard above the twin roars. It was like being trapped behind a waterfall.

Lyudmila turned her head, yelled back. "We're already drenched to the bone."

So saying, she turned and, pressing her hands against the low arch of the drain, began to haul herself through. Immediately her legs were underwater up to just below her knees. Ben followed her. Using the same technique they slowly made their way through the channel. One good thing, Ben thought, was that the ferocity of the downpour had washed all the muck out, so the footing here was better than it was on the slope outside. However, the channel got progressively narrower, as if it wasn't a cylinder but a funnel. At the end, they were obliged to continue on hands and knees, the water periodically breaking over their heads, making it difficult to breathe.

They at last made it through. They had to grip the brick surround first with their hands and then with their boot soles in order to free themselves from the tumbling flow. But now they were in deeper water, and they pushed themselves up to the surface. Gasping and choking, they hauled themselves out of what they soon realized was one of three connected cisterns— water collection receptacles that served the citadel above.

Exhausted, they lay on the floor for what seemed long minutes, regaining their breath and equilibrium. Then suddenly, unheard in their approach, there were three armed figures looming above them.

A small, compact woman with coal-dark eyes and a feral grin bent down, her gold cross swinging, and ripped Lyudmila's backpack off, threw it into a corner. "My name is Hel. Welcome to the cita—"

Lyudmila scissored her legs around Hel's ankles so violently she took Hel off her feet. She was up and into the second figure, elbows and knees flashing, while beside her Ben took on the third. She had disarmed the fallen man when she saw Hel's throwing knife at her hip and slid it out. Hel kicked her in the side and she staggered back. Hel was drawing her sidearm when Lyudmila grabbed Ben and ran.

Behind them, one of the figures was up on one knee, aiming at their fast disappearing backs. She was about to fire when she felt Hel's hand on her shoulder.

"Stand down," Hel ordered, squeezing her shoulder.

The soldier under her command immediate complied but looked up at her questioningly.

"Now we have what we want." Hel grinned at the other two. Both had regained their feet. "It's the hunt we all love, isn't it?"

And together, silent as stalking tigers, they set off after their prey.

54

SUPPER AT TURANDOT

Dima received the text from Director General Baev as he was about to close up shop for the evening. Slightly miffed, he grabbed his overcoat and passed through the door to his office. He had big plans for this evening. It was the three-month anniversary of his affair with Nadya. Three months was some kind of modern-day record for him, or for her, whichever way you wanted to look at it. Dima chuckled to himself. He had to admit, there was something special about Nadya, a *je ne sais quoi* that caused a certain frisson so powerful that it negated his thwarted hots for Kobalt. Maybe it was the way she lifted her legs just before she orgasmed or how hard her nipples grew during sex, or the way she moaned that sent shivers through his groin. Whatever is was, he thought he was crazy about her, that he might just install her as a permanent part of his life, because lately, he couldn't imagine life without her musky scent and hot body.

Baev was waiting for him in the lobby. Whatever it was, Dima mused, it had better be short. He had booked a premium box at the Bolshoi, followed by supper at the opulent fin de siècle–style restaurant, Turandot. As if that wasn't enough, he had hired a boat for the night, to cruise them along the Moskva while they twined in the captain's cabin until the sun came up.

It had taken him fully three days to make sure every element was aligned. Now the evening was upon him and, instead of hurrying home to change into formal attire for the ballet, he was hot on the heels of his boss as their footsteps echoed through the entryway, and out the door.

A sleek black armored Escalade sat at the curb, its huge engine thrumming. Sergey, one of Baev's cohort of driver-bodyguards, opened the rear door for them. Baev slid in and Dima followed. The door thunked closed. The Escalade moved off as soon as Sergey was behind the wheel.

"What a week I've had," Baev said in his most conversational tone. "Entirely bracing." He opened a built-in humidor on his side of the SUV, handed a cigar to Dima, bit off the end of his own, and lit up. When he had it going to his satisfaction, he handed over the chunky silver lighter with the FSB seal engraved on it, and Dima got his own cigar going.

"Kusnetsov's recent purge put the fear of God into everyone." Baev blew smoke up toward the ceiling, creating a man-made cloud. Watching it slowly form, he said, "Every once in a while, even we, the guardians of the State, require a maximal lesson in the wages of the deepest moral corruption—the selling of secrets, exploitation of one's position, betrayal of your fellow operatives." Abruptly, he turned to Dima, "Don't you agree, Dima Nikolaevich?"

"I . . . I do indeed, Director." Dima's head bobbed up and down like one of those American bobbleheads that somehow made their way into Russian teenagers' lives.

"We are lucky, you and I, to have staked out our claim to the moral high ground. I cannot tell you, Dima Nikolaevich, how much pleasure that gives me day in and day out as we navigate the cesspool of national crime and international espionage."

Dima cleared his throat, "Director, may I ask where we're going?"

"What's the matter, Dima, don't you like surprises?"

"As well as the next man," Dima said, not at all sure he meant it. "It's just that I have been planning this evening for almost a week."

Baev was now wreathed in smoke. "Ah, yes, the lubricious Nadya."

"An anniversary celebration," Dima said laconically.

"Then congratulations are in order, my friend!" Baev nodded. "And a celebration, of course! Most warranted." He sighed. "You know, in many ways I envy you, Dima. You have it all: no wife, no children, a girl toy of inestimable value. You are, what? Six, seven years younger than me?"

"Seven, Director."

"Mm." Baev nodded. "Life is good, yes?"

"It is," Dima agreed.

For the next several minutes, the two men enjoyed their cigars in companionable silence.

"By the way," Baev said, seemingly apropos of nothing, "have you heard from Kobalt?"

"As a matter of fact I have," Dima replied, relieved to be talking business. "She has returned to Moscow. I will be debriefing her tomorrow morning."

"And the limpet you set on her?"

"Zherov. Yes, well, he was shot as he walked toward his apartment."

Baev's head swiveled toward Dima, his expression dark. "Here, in Moscow? Have you found his assassin?"

"Not yet. Kobalt didn't see anything when she dropped him off." He found it interesting that his boss didn't ask if Zherov was alive or dead, merely assumed the worst. "Zherov is still alive, Director, safely out of surgery. As soon as he's lucid I'll debrief him myself."

"Excellent." Baev visibly relaxed. "We cannot countenance one of our own being attacked, especially not inside the borders of the Federation."

The SUV had pulled out of the traffic flow, slowed as it pulled into the curb.

"Well, here we are, Dima Nikolaevich." The rear door swung open. "I promised you a surprise and a surprise you shall have."

The aqueous blue-green, the humidity-heavy, the mineral-laden air struck Dima like a physical blow. Immediately, he shrugged off his overcoat, slung it over his left arm. He wondered what in the world they were doing in the Moscow aquarium. It was after hours, the place devoid of visitors. Only a skeleton work crew was in evidence. None of them paid Baev and Dima any mind, as if they were used to escorted VIP visitors at this time of the evening. The man who had met them just inside the side door clearly knew Baev well. He smiled thinly when Baev introduced Dima. "Good evening," their escort said in response. "Colleagues of Stanislav Budimirovich are always welcome to our small island sanctuary." His smile widened. "Amid the busy bustle of the city we offer an oasis of calm and repose."

And indeed the atmosphere was slow-paced and serene, Dima thought, as their escort ushered them down aisles with tanks of all kind of sea creatures, some familiar, some Dima had never set eyes on before. Everything under the sea was a mystery to him, and slightly scary.

They took a hard left, where darkness and shadow prevailed. Only small reddish lights dimly illuminated the way. Their escort began to climb a vertical metal ladder. Baev courteously waved Dima forward and followed behind them both. As they ascended, the mineral odor became stronger, mixed with a definite fishy smell.

At length, they reached the top, and the escort helped him the last little way.

"Careful here," he said. "The boardwalk across the tank can seem rather narrow to anyone not used to being up here."

Dima frowned. "Where are we?"

"Oh, you're in for a rare treat," the escort exclaimed enthusiastically. "The sharks haven't been fed today. It's a sight to behold, let me tell you."

He felt Baev behind him now, as they moved out along the boardwalk. "Is this the surprise?" he said over his shoulder. The moment the words escaped his mouth he felt foolish. Of course this was the surprise! What else could it be?

The escort paused at the center of the tank. "Stanislav Budimirovich, I have much to attend to. I will leave you here." He moved off. Stepping at what Dima thought an alarmingly swift pace. But then he must be used to being up here.

Just before he vanished into the darkness, Dima saw him sidestep another figure that was heading their way.

"Well, Dima," Baev said, close at hand, "what d'you think of the view from up here."

Dima, who had studiously avoiding looking down did so now with no little reluctance. The vista was vertiginous. He saw some sharks, not too big, really. But then, well below them, a few shadows, terrifyingly huge, glided in the gloom.

"Bull sharks," Baev said. He pointed. "And that's Ongendus. He's the largest, the king of the shark tank." He lifted his gaze. "What d'you think of him, Dima?"

Dima had no words. Possibly Baev had anticipated this. "Oh, now, look who has graced us with her presence," he said without a pause.

Dima looked up, recognizing the figure approaching as it moved out of the deep shadows, into the ruddy illumination of one of the lights.

"Kobalt." His eyes opened wide. "What are you doing here?"

"Tonight, Dima, I'm a messenger." Coming up to him, she handed him a packet.

"What's this?"

"Open it." Baev's voice from behind him caused him to start.

He hesitated. Something deep inside him screamed at him not to open the packet, that the moment he did everything would change for him. And yet, moving of their own accord, his fingers opened the flag, pulled out the ledger. Opened it to proof of his first betrayal of FSB field personnel.

"What . . . what?" His voice was no more than a squeak. His knees had turned to aspic. "Lies . . . all lies!" Humiliatingly, his hands trembled visibly. "Where did you—?"

Kobalt smirked. "I discovered this ledger hidden in your conduit's Istanbul office. You had quite a horrific side business going—profiting from your comrades' demise."

He continued his protest in a strangled voice, but Baev cut him dead. "Don't, Dima. Don't humiliate yourself further by lying to us."

Dima, panicked, looked from Baev to Kobalt and back again. "What . . . what d'you mean to do?"

"Dima," Kobalt said, snatching the ledger from him, "I told you tonight I was a messenger. But I have been given a special privilege. At this very moment I am also Kali, goddess of death."

Her arm blurred out. The corner of her emerald ring sliced into the side of his neck. Even as Dima clapped a hand to the wound, his blood flowing out between his fingers, he dropped his coat, revealing a push dagger in his free hand. But before he could use it Kobalt jammed the electric cattle prod into his kidney. Dima screamed. Again. His arms flung out. And again. He torqued off the edge of the boardwalk, plunged into the shark tank

"Now," Minister Kusnetsov said, emerging from the shadows, "let us see who takes the first bite, Slava, my cohort of tiger sharks or Ongendus."

"Ten thousand to the winner," Baev offered.

"Done," Kusnetsov said, clearly in a festive frame of mind.

And they—all three of them with varying amounts of avidity—watched the hungry sharks shoot toward the flailing body, the scent of blood already upon them. Soon enough, the water was churning, the interior of the tank clouding, but not before the two men had settled their bet.

"Ongendus it is!" Baev crowed.

"Well done, Slava." Kusnetsov turned to face Kobalt. "And well done to you, Kata Romanovna." For that was who Bobbi was now. Kobalt was officially dead. Baev personally had wiped her name, dossier, and what few references remained from the relevant sector of the FSB servers, backups, and redundancies, overwriting the entire sector ten times on every one, leaving no electronic trace, no possible way to retrieve the original entries.

"Slava was right about you all along." His smile broadened. "He has nominated you as the new head of Zaslon, which you will inhabit for a trial period of one year, overseen by Slava, of course." He sniffed the air, as if sensing the blood below them. "After that time, I will make a final determination."

He took her hand in his for a moment, and when she felt the immense power flowing from him to her, she thought immediately of the feeding sharks far below her boot soles.

"Your first remit is to purge the entire directorate. Slava will have the personnel files sent over to Dima's—to your office. You can evaluate each one."

"Unnecessary." Kobalt returned the cattle prod to safety beneath her long black coat. "They all go. Full purge of Zaslon."

"Is that so?" Kusnetsov cocked his head, as if seeing her in a new light.

"It is."

He shot Baev a glance. "If that is your decision."

"It's made," she said with finality.

Baev cleared his throat. "What about Zherov?"

"Zherov's a special case. Besides, he'll be in no shape to return to duty."

Kusnetsov let out a barking laugh. "I like this one, Slava. I do indeed." There was silence for a moment, save for the sloshing of the salt water. Then he pursed his lips. "By the way, I understand the millions Ermi stashed away for Dima have vanished." His hand swept outward. "Completely gone."

"With Ermi and Dima both dead," Baev said, "we'll never know what happened."

Kusnetsov shrugged. "The spoils of war," he opined. Then, with a glance at Kobalt. "So, Slava, is this one supremely smart or supremely dangerous?"

"Could be I'm both," she said before Baev opened his mouth.

Kusnetsov laughed again. "Yes, I believe you just might be. So . . ." His tone changed, warmed. "It seems tonight we have much to celebrate." He turned. "Slava?"

"Ah, yes." Baev rubbed his hands together. "I do believe we have a reservation at Turandot, the finest restaurant in all of the Federation!"

55

CITADEL II

Evan stood in the pouring rain, waiting for her sister to open the door of the citadel. She felt a prickling at the nape of her neck and a serpent uncoiling in her lower belly, where her inner strength originated. This was not good, and she knew it. She would need every last ounce of strength in the coming hours, of this she had no doubt. She would be taxed to the limit and beyond. There was a distinct possibility she wouldn't make it out of the citadel alive. Ben knew that, too, which was why he'd initiated their short convo back at the airfield in Graz.

The door—thick wooden slabs bound by massive iron bars— slowly swung back, revealing a slender woman, beautiful, deep-blue-eyed, impossibly tall. From her asylum, she regarded Evan with a steady, penetrating gaze.

"So. Robin. You've come such a long way to fetch your children." Her words pierced even the downpour, honeyed, spinning a mesmeric web.

Evan was fascinated. Even so, her parents had prepared her. "Something like that."

Ana smirked. "Spoken like a true mother."

Evan cocked her head slightly. "But my dear sister, how on earth would you know?"

You must strive to wrongfoot her at every turn, her father had said during their briefing. *That is your only path in.*

A flicker of Ana's eyelids someone less astute would attribute to a raindrop confirmed Evan had hit home.

The smirk was back, one side of Ana's mouth jerking up. "How does it feel, my dear sister, to be standing out in the rain, while I'm as dry as a bone."

"Dry as a bone inside as well as out," Evan shot back.

If she feels, even for an instant, that she's gotten the best of you, her father warned her, *it's too late. She'll eat you for supper.*

That flicker of Ana's lids again, like a flame momentarily knocked sideways by the wind.

Evan took a step forward, spoke again before her sister could reply—and how strange it was, confronting a sister she'd never known she had! "I'm not even sure the Reveshvilis are my parents," she said. "I don't look anything like them." Another step forward; now there was scarcely six feet between them. "But you . . . you're the spitting image of your mother."

This was a barb her father predicted would sink deep, and immediately she saw that he was right. Ana huffed out a breath.

"I'm nothing like her," she spat out.

Evan could almost feel her venom as well as hear it. There was a toxicity to her that made Evan's blood run cold. Watching her sister now she had cause to wonder at the extreme dichotomy of her thinking. She was a biologist dependent on the scientific method, but she was also a would-be messiah, requiring the stealthy application of psychology.

"I understand completely why you'd think that," Evan said. "But from an objective point of view, the two of you are frighteningly alike."

"What would you know about it?" Ana sneered.

Evan ignored her question. "You're the dark side of her, Ana."

"She's as insane as a mad hatter."

"You're the child who should never have been born."

Ana's eyes narrowed. "Fuck you."

"Mama was right." Evan leaned in. "There's a shadow on you, the mark of evil."

Ana laughed but all her muscles tensed up. "I am the Light." The cords on the sides of her neck stood out like steel bands. "I am the living embodiment of God."

"What you are is a charlatan—a butcher posing as a scientist. You think you're unique? There were plenty of you in the Third Reich. What they did to prisoners, to children is unspeakable. And now you're following in their footsteps."

Ana shook her head. "You could not be more wrong. We are prayer warriors here. We are one."

"But it was you who decided to experiment on the 'prayer warriors' who came to their senses, who refused to follow you any longer."

A resolute urgency constricted Ana's frame, a coiled energy, as of a viper about to strike. She lifted an arm, her hand spattered now by raindrops. "You see this land? This place? This is my kingdom—the forest between worlds."

Her face was a mask, half in light, half in shadow. "You're a stranger here. You know nothing of my world."

"I know you think you've exalted yourself in God's sight just as Noah did. And like Noah you believe you're God's instrument in remaking the human race. That's what your experiments on human reproductive organs are all about, aren't they?"

There was no answer Ana could have made, just as there was no answer Evan could have heard. She slapped a palm to the side of her neck as she felt a pinprick like a mosquito bite. But it was no mosquito. Moments later she felt the world begin to swim around her. The last image she had was of Ana's grinning face, large as a harvest moon, before she plunged into unconsciousness.

She awoke as groggy as if she had been on a three-day alcohol bender. The headache behind her eyes was pretty much the same, too, but the stinging on the side of her neck was decidedly not. Her body felt impossibly heavy, and it was an effort to raise her head. She could not have been out long; she was still sopping wet.

When her vision sufficiently cleared, she saw she was in a spacious room filled with polished chrome and low pebbled glass partitions—a far cry from what she imagined the interior of the citadel would look like. She was tied hands and ankles to a stainless-steel table. All around her machinery winked and clicked and clucked like hens about to give birth. Her nostrils flared to sharp scents, to the chill air-conditioned air. She knew a sterilized room when she smelled it.

"Ah, there you are, Robin."

Ana entered her field of vision. That grin so wide it looked distorted.

"Now we can continue our talk in comfort." She reacted to Evan's involuntary shiver. "Chilled, are we? I'm not surprised. All right, then, let's warm you up." She reached to her left, spread a blanket over Evan's body.

"Better now? Yes." Ana leaned in, her face bare inches from Evan's. "Regarding the beginning of our conversation, I didn't believe a word you said. Why should I? You can hardly know the Reveshvilis." She spoke their name as if she was unrelated. In her mind, Evan supposed, she was. "I can't fathom why you'd want to, Robin. They abandoned you and your sister. Rebecca bore you and then gave you away to strangers—strangers!—in a strange land. What could they possibly mean to you? Nothing. Less than that when you think about it."

She withdrew her head like an adder changing its mind. "And yet here you are, speaking to me as they would speak to me. Parroting their criminally distorted view."

Evan was disappointed in herself. Here she had thought she was winning the psychological war with Ana when in reality her sister had been playing her, keeping her attention riveted so, along with the noise of the rain and wind, she wouldn't hear the prayer warrior coming up behind her. What a fool she had been. Her father had warned her, but she had come here smug, too sure of herself. Her only hope was that through her own sleight of hand Ben and Lyudmila had found their way inside the citadel undetected.

They split up. At a T in the corridor Ben went one way, Lyudmila the other. Neither of them knew where the corridors would take them, but at the moment that was a secondary issue. Staying alive was primary.

Ben had no weapon. So far as he knew, everything they needed was in Lyudmila's backpack. There was only one way to rectify that. He slowed his pace, listening carefully for oncoming footsteps. When, inevitably he heard them approaching, he stood his ground. The moment the Omega man came into view he rushed him. That was the last thing this man expected, and the moment's lag between his brain and his brawn was too long.

Ben barreled into him—a large square man with a military brush cut. The man was all muscle; Ben's rush sent him back only one step, but Ben hooked a leg behind his ankle and sweeping inward with the leg sent Brush Cut crashing onto his back. At once, Ben was on top of him, but Brush Cut smashed a fist into Ben's sternum. Ben's vision went white, then black. By the time it returned to him, he'd lost his advantage.

Brush Cut grabbed him by his shirtfront, hauled him up, sent him rocketing into the stone wall. All the breath left him, pain flared from the epicenter of the first strike. The balled fist came straight at his aching sternum, aiming for a killing blow, but Ben just managed to knock it aside with an edge-kite to the inside of his wrist. This gave him the opening he needed. The leading edge of his massed fingertips slammed into the side of Brush Cut's neck with the effect of a two-by-four. Brush Cut's head swung like a pendulum. His eyes were unfocused, like a heavyweight who was out on his feet.

Ben stepped in. It was a mistake. Brush Cut was feigning helplessness. He covered Ben's punch with his hand, twisted, then again threw Ben against the wall. He followed that up with . . . But at the last second Ben twisted away, absorbing only a third of the blow that might otherwise have rocked him off his feet. He'd had about enough of this sonofabitch. He stayed against the wall, allowed Brush Cut to come to him. He ducked a roundhouse, struck two quick jabs to his kidneys, then jammed his knee into his crotch. As Brush Cut's body folded reflexively, Ben grabbed his head and twisted it violently, hearing the neck vertebrae snap, crackle, and pop.

Brush Cut collapsed. Bending over, Ben took possession of his weapons—a compact Beretta Model 12 machine gun and a Czech-made CZ 75 semi-auto handgun. Dizzied, he slid down the wall. He hurt all over and he had trouble breathing. He had to pull himself together. He went into prana—slow deep breathing, returning oxygen to his lower belly, where the root of his strength lay.

Got to get going, he thought as he rose, and shakily set off down the corridor, his strength returning to him like a series of little gifts with each step he took.

56

CITADEL III

Lyudmila got caught trying to circle back to retrieve her backpack. But perhaps that was her plan all along. A man and a woman stood in front of her, grinning, the man gesturing with the barrel of a submachine pistol, the woman with a wicked-looking knife. Obediently, she raised her hands.

"Let's talk about this," she said in Russian. Their baffled expressions confirmed they didn't speak the language. "What are you dick-faces doing here being lorded over by Tsarina Ana? She's a bitch-psycho, you know that, don't you."

As she spoke to them, she stepped closer, unthreateningly, without giving them a reason to fire the weapons they had leveled at her.

"Listen, I've got a whole box of candy bars in that backpack, and I'm dying for one. I'm happy to share." She took another step closer. "You like candy bars, right. I mean, who doesn't?"

No reaction. She kept coming, a tiny bit at a time, so as not to alarm them.

"Wait, wait, you'll like this one." Another step closer. "This is exciting, I promise! Vladimir Putin just announced a brand-new plan for the economy. The goal? Make people rich and happy. List of people attached." She grinned. "No? Nothing?" She shook her head. "You people, I swear!" And promptly grabbed the short barrel of the man's submachine pistol, smacked him hard on the point of his nose with the heel of her hand.

Blood spurted, he gave a cry of surprised pain, and she snatched the pistol away from him, used it to parry the knife stab the woman directed at her. Lifting her right leg, she smashed it down on the side of the woman's left knee. Her leg immediately buckled and Lyudmila raked the barrel of the pistol along her temple, scoring a deep gash that welled blood. She took her weapons as well, then used the tip of her boot to send the man with the smashed nose into unconsciousness.

"Well done!"

She turned to see Hel, the compact warrior with the gold cross chained around her neck.

"But now, sadly, your journey is at an end."

"You don't get to do that," Ana said. "You don't get to claim them as your parents."

"What do you care?" Evan replied. "You and your sister Luzida have renounced them."

"Irrelevant." Ana leaned forward again, chin jutting out, eyes glimmering. "You're an interloper, a trespasser. A fucking alien to everyone." The corner of her mouth twisted up. "And for your information my sister's name is Lucinda, not that ugly version Konstantin gave her."

"I don't care how many times you change your names, Ana, you're both still batshit crazy."

Ana struck her across the cheek, a backhanded blow that made Evan's head spin. *She's strong*, Evan thought. *Stronger than she looks*. That backhander wasn't an attack; it was retaliation. Finally, she had gotten under her sister's skin. Kostya and Rebecca said she was crazy, and they weren't wrong. *Everyone has a weakness*, she thought, *including me*. She had to pray she could work Ana's to get herself out of here before her sister found her own.

Ana pressed a button, tilted the slab Evan was tied to into a diagonal angle. "I want to show you something." She lifted her shirt above her navel, pushed her trousers down, exposing herself while Evan looked on in fascinated horror.

"Contrary to the received wisdom of my family history I wasn't born barren."

Evan found her gaze riveted to the ziggurat of scars crisscrossing her sister's lower belly. First, a vertical scar from the center of her pubis to halfway to her navel. A shorter horizontal scar slashed across it just above her pubic mound, making an upside-down cross. On each side smaller, angular scars made up the ziggurat.

Evan shook her head, part of her disbelieving. When she spoke, her voice emerged as a husky whisper. "Ana, you experimented on yourself."

"While I was at the clinic. Jon Pine assisted me like a good little major domo. I was the boss's daughter, after all." She covered herself up, then stepped forward, delivered another backhand slap. "You're pitying me? Every scientist on the verge of a major breakthrough experiments on herself first. I wanted to create a new kind of baby—a better child, one born without Original Sin, with no relationship to Adam and Eve."

Evan licked her lips. "How is that even possible?" She was appalled. Just the fact that she asked this rational question was evidence that she was falling further and further down Ana's demented rabbit hole.

"Gene manipulation. With the CRISPR Cas9 technique I am editing the human genome, taking out all undesirable traits, adding new ones, creating the perfect human without any of the seven deadly sins, which over and over again have caused one catastrophe after another, one worse than the next."

"You're not a geneticist."

"How naïve you are." Ana's tongue against her palate made a disapproving sound, like the clicking of nocturnal insects. "Konstantin and Rebecca don't know I'm a geneticist. If Konstantin had he'd never have given me a position at the clinic. That's not their field at all. But I needed a safe place to experiment with my preliminary findings."

She pressed another button and the head end of the slab rose high enough for Evan to see beyond the low pebble-glass barrier to the left of the bay she was trapped in. She gave an involuntary indrawn breath. "Wendy . . . Michael," she whispered, seeing them lying side by side on surgeon's tables, seeing her worst nightmare for them a reality.

"So lovely, don't you think?"

"Whatever you're planning to do to them, I beg you not to." Evan squirmed under the blanket, her fingers working, working the tiny edge weapon she had secreted, hidden from view.

"Let me tell you something, there's nothing worse than knowing you've been abandoned. First it seeps into you, then it burrows its way into the very core of you, and when it sinks its claws into you it never lets go.

"That's what happened to me, Robin. Rebecca rejected me. My first memory is of her turning away from me, while a nurse picked me up, cradled me. Neither of them ever held me, fed me, soothed me when I was ill, when the nightmares began, even when the roller coaster of elation and despair sickened me beyond all understanding. They just shoved drugs at me."

Ana lowered the slab, and the children disappeared behind the pebbled glass partition.

Evan was on the point of breaking in two, of being slammed

from one family revelation to another. She felt bruised and exhausted. Still, there was no other choice but to go on. "Use me, Ana. Just let them go."

"Mm, no." She stepped closer so she could look down on Evan. "Here's what's going to happen, sister dearest. I'm going to work on them. That should take a good five or six hours and, lucky you, you'll have the perfect view to watch the procedures."

"No, no, no."

"And then, after a short break of stretching and a snack, I'll start on you." She smirked. "That should be most interesting, us being sisters and all."

The blade had cut through the leather strap, freeing her right hand. It wasn't enough. Like it or not she would be forced to wait until Ana went into the next bay to prep for her experiments on Wendy and Michael. By then it might be too late. She felt despair welling up. She could not help feeling like a swimmer out of breath and stamina, about to go down for the last time. She fought to banish the hopelessness lest it overwhelm her.

Where the hell were Ben and Lyudmila?

While Ben was stalking and being stalked, Lyudmila had her hands full.

"Fight like a human being," she said with no particular inflection, and certainly no edge, to her voice. Vocal nuances were important, she had learned, especially at the beginning. It was animal instinct, the lizard brain seizing control. The situation could get out of hand before it had a chance to begin. "Not like a man."

Hel regarded her with night-dark eyes. She seemed dark all over, as if she were composed of shadow. Except for the glint of gold on her tiny cross. Lyudmila knew there was something worth doing here when Hel set down her PB semi-automatic without ever taking her eyes off Lyudmila.

"All right, let's take the more painful road." Hel shrugged. "It's your funeral."

There was no space between that last word and her leap at Lyudmila. That was okay. She stood her ground, feet planted beneath her, unmoving. Time slowed down, as it always did for her in these situations. The last thing you wanted was to act precipitously. She waited until the last moment, when Hel's charge had reached maximum velocity, one leg striding forward, the other behind, balancing her. From absolute stillness to a blur of motion, grasping Hel's wrist, swinging her hips, then her torso into the direction she was pulling her arm, using Hel's own momentum against her, dragging her around and down onto the ground. She heard the snap as the back of Hel's head hit the floor, but she felt no gratification. Too soon for that feeling—for any feeling. She had emptied her mind; her body was all momentum.

She stamped on Hel's chest—a mistake. Hel grabbed onto her ankle and twisted so violently that Lyudmila was taken off her feet. She rolled, but Hel, on her feet now, kept hold of Lyudmila's ankle, kept twisting it. Lyudmila swung her body around, absorbing a vicious kick to her thigh. For a moment, her leg went numb. Hel was expecting this, for she had aimed at the main nerve running along the outside of the bone. She grinned, smelling victory.

Which was just what Lyudmila wanted. Locking her hands behind Hel's knee, she brought her crashing down, the impact causing her to release her hold. On her knees, Lyudmila punched Hel in the face, then again and again and again, until it was unrecognizable through the bloody pulp.

Scrambling to her feet, she swept up the PB, took one last look at Hel's unmoving form, hesitating for just a moment. No time to go back for the backpack now. She and Ben had been ambushed. They had taken too long getting past the guards. Evan needed them, assuming Ben was still alive and in one piece.

She whirled, hearing stealthy footsteps, and prepared herself. Then she saw Ben, bleeding, noticeably the worse for wear. They stopped eight feet apart, took each other in with their professional gazes. Then, as one, they grinned.

"The meat-grinder," Lyudmila said.

"And yet here we are." Ben looked down at the body sprawled on the floor. He went over, couldn't tell from the face, a bloody mess, but he recognized the bandoliers crisscrossed over Hel's chest and, between them, the glimmer of gold. Crouching down, he thought of Leonard Pine, thought of his desperate request. Reaching out, he jerked the thin chain and its pendant from around Hel's neck and pocketed it.

He groaned as he rose to his feet.

"All good?" Lyudmila asked, a hand on his shoulder.

Ben swept his arm out. "This way."

When he turned, she saw the bruises and lacerations on his back through his ripped jacket and shirt.

57

INSIDE

"She's afraid of you."

Ana had been about to step away, to head over one bay to where the children slept, all unknowing. "What?" Now she turned back to stare at Evan.

"That's right," Evan said, thinking this was her only hope of digging into her sister deep enough to alter the outcome of this night. "Terrified, even." She shook her head. "It's not that she never loved you, Ana. She was scared of what would happen to her if she did."

"I don't believe you." But the look in her eyes, the sudden cloudiness, told Evan that she did.

"Believe what you want," Evan told her. "That's what you've always done, isn't it."

Ana's eyes narrowed. "How dare you assume you know me!"

There it was again, the verbal blow, and her use of "How dare you!" That outrage, raw, full of the pain only a child deprived of love could feel. "You don't know me at all."

"Oh, but I do. D'you think you're the first person who longed to be held and never was?"

Ana extended her head again, adderlike, her face within inches of Evan's. "For nine months I was a part of her. For nine months I had to share her, even while I was inside her. Then she split open like a melon, and where was I then? Who was I ever to her?"

Evan's right hand snaked from under the blanket, the edged weapon she had hidden flashed like a bolt of lightning. A moment later blood welled from Ana's sliced cheek. Ana gasped, staggered back, hands to her face. Evan sawed through the strap restraining her left hand, but she was still glued to the table by her feet. As she sat up to reach for the right strap, Ana twisted Evan's wrist. The knife clattered to the floor. Ana's hands, bloody, clawed, wrapped around her neck, thumbs against her windpipe, pressing inward. Soon enough Ana would throttle her to death. Seconds left, under a minute surely.

And so even as the oxygen in her lungs guttered, even as her wildly beating heart began to shriek its warning, she understood that her intent was correct, her aim was true: she had slipped through the one chink in Ana's psychological armor, reaching in and holding on to her vulnerable spot.

"Do you think you're special?" Her voice like gravel in a cement mixer. "Do you think that you're different from everyone else?"

"Of course. Mother made it so."

In her desperation, Ana had slipped mightily.

Black spots winked in and out of Evan's field of vision. "Mother, as we both know, is insane, Ana," she lied, but lies were all she had left. "Just like you." Lies feeding into everything Ana had been telling herself. Then a sharp veer away, to play on Ana's deepest fear. "The two of you are insane in exactly the same way. You're both monsters."

Ana's scream was bloodcurdling. Her agitation reached

its apex. Taking one hand from Evan's throat, she drew her arm back to deliver yet another backhand slap. Evan used the opening, slashing the edge of her hand down into the junction of her sister's neck and collarbone.

A snap like a dry twig trod on in the middle of the forest.

Then the gunfire began, short rapid bursts like the dread tattoo of soldiers beating on war drums.

Three down, thought Ben

And Lyudmila thought, *How many more?*

There were six, as it turned out, but Ben and Lyudmila had already been through the Omega meat-grinder and were still standing. Besides, they were weaponized now, and they used the PBs to good effect, backing each other up, splitting up and coming at the enemy from two sides in a pincer maneuver. That ploy was only useful once, then they had to go on to the next: an enfilade where Lyudmila stood her ground in a vaulted room with a sword and concrete cross at one end with three Omegas arrayed against her. Ben, entering through a doorway on their left, raked them with three bursts of fire.

Through the smoking remains, Lyudmila said, "Where the hell are they?"

Ben, stalking down the line of bodies, found one woman still alive. Crouching down beside her, he said, "Where are they?"

The woman looked up at him with bloodshot eyes. He had shot her in the chest. Blood drooled from the corner of her mouth. She licked her dry lips, tasted her own blood. "Fuck you."

Ben understood how much effort she put into those two words and knew he didn't have much time left with her.

"My name is Ben. Tell me yours."

"W . . . why?"

"Because . . ." He bent closer. "You deserve to be called to God by your name."

"Jo . . . Johanna," she whispered.

"So Johanna, I need to make you understand. I'm looking for the children. The children, d'you understand. I'm their uncle. They're my family. Your Mother Suspiria is going to operate on them, murder them. Is that what you want? Two innocents killed?"

Johanna blinked and tears welled up, overflowed her eyes, leaving tracks down her cheeks. She shivered. "I'm cold . . . so cold."

Ben took off his ripped jacket, spread it over her. "There you go, better now." He smiled down at her. "Johanna, please, tell me where they are."

Johanna's eyes were glazing over, her breaths became harsh rales. "They're . . ." She spasmed, coughed violently, vomiting up a gush of blood.

"Johanna, stay with me."

"Ben." Lyudmila stood over his left shoulder. "More of them are coming. I can hear them."

He ignored her, gripped Johanna's shoulders. "Just . . . please tell me where to find them."

Her eyelids fluttered. Her bone-deep shudders ran up his arms, through his hands, on the verge of blacking out. He felt the approach of her death as if it were his own. His body trembled.

He bent closer, his ear almost against her blood-slick lips. "In . . . in the operating theater."

"Ben, for the love of God!" Lyudmila was pulling at him. "They're almost on top of us!"

Still ignoring her, fully concentrating on what he had to do. "Where?" His voice had taken on a terrible urgency. He was so close; he couldn't lose her now. "Johanna, where?"

"Beyond . . ." A great sigh: she was going. "Beyond the cross." A soft hiss, as of a membrane punctured. She convulsed once. Her heels beat against the floor. Her left leg twitched, but she might already have been gone.

She would not give up. The human body, so frail in many ways, vulnerable to disease, radiation, poison, was in other ways difficult to kill. The body, all instinct, fought to stay alive through all manner of abuse.

Despite a broken clavicle, Ana seemed only to gain in strength. And Evan, hampered as she was by being pinned by her ankles, was at a disadvantage, even though Ana's left arm was greatly weakened and she could not raise it up to shoulder height.

"You may be insane," Evan said with a weak cough, "but you're not stupid."

Ana, concentrating on pressing her right thumb into her sister's windpipe, seemed oblivious to anything else. Evan was gasping, choking. She grasped Ana's wrist, trying to wrest it away, but her lack of oxygen had robbed her of strength. She felt as weak as a day-old foal.

"The gunfire means my people are close. They sneaked in through the storm drain."

A gleam in Ana's eye. "I had prayer warriors waiting for them. Guess who told me?"

Evan had a good idea who had betrayed them, but that was a matter for later. If there was a later. "And yet here they are," she said, "coming closer and closer."

"But not quickly enough to save you, sister dearest." Ana bore down on Evan's windpipe. "I'm going to squeeze the life out of you."

More bursts of gunfire, louder, nearer.

"And . . ." Evan coughed, tried to catch her breath, but her windpipe was now completely cut off. She was underwater without an air tank or hope of surfacing. Her sister was holding her in place. She thought of her recurring dream of Bobbi climbing on her in the river, holding her under the water. "And you think of me as an enemy." Her voice was thin, strained.

"The only enemy is yourself. Look in the mirror, Ana. What d'you see? Not yourself, no. You see your madness. You see your mother. That's the way you'll go. That's your fate, locked inside your own insanity."

Ana shrieked, her eyes opened so wide Evan could see the whites all around. Then she jerked forward, slamming into Evan, and her grip dropped away.

Evan had no idea what happened until blood spurted out of Ana's mouth.

"No!" she cried. "No! Ana!"

And there was Ben, the CZ 75 he had taken from Brush Cut aimed squarely at where Ana had stood. Evan smelled the cordite of the discharge. She wrapped her arms around her sister, taking great, shuddering breaths. "No more! For the love of God, Ben, leave her be."

But it was too late. The bullet had punctured Ana's heart, and she lay heavy against Evan, unmoving, unbreathing. Lifeless as a marionette whose strings have been cut.

58

EXIT STRATEGY

Wendy and Michael lay on adjacent operating tables, still, pale as effigies. But they were alive and, as far as Evan could tell, unharmed. They looked so peaceful, like a sleeping princess and prince. Evan, rushing to them, extended a hand. She could not help touching them, as if to make sure they were real, not a figment of her imagination. Then she bent, kissing each on their forehead, inhaling their sweet exhalations.

"They're sedated," she said to Ben, who stood just off her right shoulder. Lyudmila stood in the doorway, all her senses alert to any sign of movement near them.

"That's a mercy," Ben said, looking at the rolling cart laden with scalpels, forceps, scissors, clamps, retractors, needles, sutures, and a gleaming fleet of strange-looking implements he had never seen before—in short, a horrifyingly large suite of surgical instruments laid out with the utmost precision.

Evan's eyes filled with tears as she said, "My dear ones. How beautiful they are, Ben. How innocent."

"Possibly not as innocent as they once were."

She shrugged away his words, not allowing her thoughts to

head in that direction yet. "Let's get them out of here. I don't want them waking up in the surgery."

She carried Wendy, and Ben, stoically ignoring the pain it caused him, lifted Michael into his arms. The three adults were all too aware of what they'd suffered since they'd entered the citadel, but by unspoken agreement no one asked or offered one word about their injuries. They were hyper-focused on the children, what they might have gone through, as well as getting them out of this stone labyrinth as quickly as they could.

"Ben," she said, as they moved through the corridors.

"We dealt with the immediate threat," he replied, correctly reading her thoughts. "There were, I think, ten, and how many more are still here neither of us can even guess. All we know is that since the last attack we haven't seen anyone still alive."

The rooms were large as ballrooms, as ornate as the corridors were stark—fireplaces massive enough to roast a pair of boars or an adult deer, sculpted mantels, corbelled ceilings, cornices depicting various hunting scenes, above which were painted, incongruously, angels, cherubs, and seraphim cavorting in pink and pale-blue skies.

Lyudmila led the way, having memorized the paths through which she and Ben, after a number of wrong turns, had at last made their way to Evan. They encountered no one; the place was eerily silent. When they approached the entryway beyond which was the massive front door they understood why.

"At least a dozen of them," Lyudmila whispered, shrinking back around the corner where the others stood. "Maybe more."

"We'll never make it past them," Ben husked.

"O ye of little faith." Lyudmila palmed her mobile. Glancing up at Evan, she said, "Ready?" When Evan nodded, she input three numbers on the keypad. "Sixty seconds," she said, pocketing her mobile.

"Prepare yourself, protect Michael at all costs," she said to Ben, her voice hoarse and strained from her near strangling at her sister's hands. Her neck felt terribly abraded, swollen. "In fifty seconds all hell is going to break loose."

"What's going to happen?" he asked.

Lyudmila grinned. "Our exit strategy."

"Countdown," Evan said. "Forty seconds."

Lyudmila briefly turned back to her. "The children?"

"Golden slumbers," she murmured, and kissed the top of Wendy's head.

Precisely thirty-five seconds later, the packets of C-4 in Lyudmila's backpack, lying abandoned but not forgotten in the corridors below where they stood, exploded with a titanic series of blasts that shook the entire citadel from its very foundations. The prayer warriors blocking their way scattered like fish frightened by an oncoming orca.

"Move!" Lyudmila cried. "Now!"

Around the corner they ran, Lyudmila spraying whoever was foolish enough to remain.

As she hauled open the heavy wooden door a fantastic *whoosh!* billowed up through the citadel. As the fire ate through the C-4 containers, the heat that radiated from the thermite Lyudmila had added to the explosive was like a blast furnace, even at this distance. Walls shook, then crumbled as the thermite fire ate through everything.

They were out the door, running as fast as they could through the pattering of the rain, the distant rumble of thunder moving off to the west, through the courtyard and past the walls, for the cover of the thick underbrush, beyond which was the sanctuary of the forest. Behind them fireballs ripped through the various roofs of the citadel, exposing the fire to even more oxygen, feeding it incessantly. Nothing and no one inside could possibly survive such a conflagration. The ground shook beneath them to the deep rumblings of ceilings collapsing, walls blowing out, massive timbers cracking, turning orange-red, then white as a blank sheet of paper.

"Down!" Evan cried in her cracked voice.

Just in time. The force of the blast-furnace wall of air rushed over their bent backs as they crouched. The thickets around them flattened, then blackened, dying on the spot. The sky was crimson and charcoal. The air stank of twisted metal, disintegrated mortar, ash, and cinders. Then the sickly-sweet stench of incinerated human flesh befouled the superheated air, making them gag. A sleet of ash, charred wooden fragments turned missiles, white-hot metal spikes, tore the night apart.

Evan was in the lead, then Ben, with Lyudmila as rear guard, though there seemed little need. With a thunderous roar, another fireball rose, igniting the night sky, showering another load of flaming debris several hundred feet into the air. The wet ground shifted under them, loose rocks tumbling under their running feet, sliding away. Ben stumbled, fell to his knees, cradling Michael to keep his head from hitting the dirt.

He crouched there, trying to catch his breath as rain and flaming debris fell on all of them. His head throbbed and his lacerated back was blistered with agonizing pain. Ahead, unaware, Evan was sending a text to the clinic's helicopter. But Lyudmila ran, helped Ben back on his feet.

"Maybe I should take him," she offered.

He was about to answer her when he heard a sharp crack. A moment of shock when he felt nothing, then a blinding pain engulfed his left hip. He went down, turned to see Hel framed in the wide opening of the high ivied courtyard walls, her face a bloody mess, aiming another shot at him. But Lyudmila was too quick for her. She squeezed off a fusillade from her machine gun and Hel was blown backward onto the courtyard's cobbled center, vanishing into the inferno billowing from the castle's blown-out door.

"Evan!" Lyudmila, kneeling beside Ben, called. "Evan!" She had taken Michael from him. He was flat on his back. Blood seeped from the wound in his hip.

Evan rushed up, gently moved Wendy so she was slung securely over her left shoulder, and then lowered herself to one knee by Ben's side. She gently palpated the area of the wound. Ben groaned through gritted teeth. "I think the pelvic bone is shattered."

"The copter will be here within minutes. There's a stretcher on board."

Lyudmila nodded, her hand on Ben shoulder. "Hang in there," she said to him.

Evan, so many emotions chasing each other through her mind, felt all coherent thought abandon her. *Ben.* Her eyes locked on his and when she smiled, he returned it.

59

AFTERMATH I
SCHNELLER PSYCHIATRIC CLINIC, GERMANY

The copter pilot radioed ahead to the clinic as soon as they were all inside. Evan and Lyudmila got Ben settled and, raiding the copter's well-provisioned first aid kit, did what they could to make him safe and comfortable for the long trip back to Germany. By that time, Wendy and Michael were awake, though still groggy. They clung to Evan like limpets, refusing to let her go, even for an instant.

"Aunt Evan, is it really you?" they cried, as if waking from a disturbing and deeply felt nightmare. "You sound different."

Evan touched her throat, still tender. The working over Ana had given her had affected her vocal cords, perhaps permanently. Her voice was a bit lower, rich and smoky. Her sister's mark on her.

Kostya was ready for them. He quickly tended to Ben's back, then left him in the care of the orthopedic surgeon who had driven from Köln the moment Kostya had called him. Then he gave the children thorough physical exams, and pronounced them unharmed and in good health. Which was all Evan cared about. And Ben. Of course, Ben. Then the children were put to bed, and finally Kostya turned his doctor's skills to Evan's injuries.

Evan had asked the grandparents not to introduce themselves—as far as Wendy and Michael were concerned the doctor who examined them was just that: a doctor. This was hardest on Rebecca who was anxious to see them, talk to them, hold them, but as Evan rightly pointed out they needed time to adjust to being freed, to being with her—to just being. But Rebecca's anxiety needed an object, and so she had hovered like a wraith over Kostya's shoulder as he fussed over Evan's wounds, making sure there was no serious physical damage to her neck and throat. As he had gently spread salve on her wrists and ankles.

"She actually had you strapped to an operating table?" Rebecca said, after Evan had recounted in detail everything that happened at the Omega citadel.

Evan could see that Rebecca was trying hard to hold it together, but her terror over the thought of Evan being in such grave danger, a nightmare scenario she must have played out in her mind ever since the three of them had taken off in the clinic's copter, still danced behind her eyes like hobgoblins. When Evan finally told them that Ana was dead, Kostya had no discernable reaction; Rebecca sighed with relief and the hobgoblins began to still.

"Death. Death is all I see," had been her prediction, Evan thought. She hadn't been wrong.

"I wasn't scared at all! I knew you would come!" Michael said the next morning. "You're like a superhero!"

"Wonder Woman," Wendy said.

"Batman!" Michael cried.

Wendy rolled her eyes. "Batman's a guy, silly."

Evan laughed. "It's just me, Aunt Evan."

"Superhero enough for us!" they shouted in tandem.

They were in Kostya's study, Evan, Lyudmila, and the children. Ben was being prepped for surgery later in the afternoon. The study was a cozy room full of books and oversized furniture, with drinks and all manner of food on a low table in front of the long sofa, served by Leonard Pine.

Wendy had gone silent while Michael continued to rabbit on excitedly, and now she abruptly burst into tears. After holding her emotions in check for the entire time of their incarceration in order to be strong for her brother, finally understanding that their ordeal was over, that everything would, indeed, be okay, the dam burst and the terror, anxiety, and the rage spilled out in a torrent.

Michael saw his sister break down and, of course, he began to cry, too, his reasons more confused and amorphous.

Evan gathered them into her arms, held them as they sobbed and sobbed. Over their heads, she glanced at Lyudmila, shook her head sadly. After what the children had been through, these extreme mood swings were to be expected, Kostya had told her. Perfectly normal. The point was to react normally to them.

"Now, listen, my darlings," she said as she held them at arm's length and looked into their tear-streaked faces, "I would so like to have something to eat—I'm starving! You must be too. So let's eat." She grinned like a loon, teasing laughter out of them. "And later some Coke, as a special treat, yeah?"

"Yay!" They nodded enthusiastically.

Evan gestured. "And this is Lyudmila. She was with us on the helicopter, remember?"

At this, Wendy wiped her eyes, staring. "Lyudmila," she said. "Does that mean you're Russian?"

"It does, indeed." Though Lyudmila smiled at both of them, Wendy cringed away, burying her head in Evan's side. She'd overheard enough stories about what her Aunt Evan did and who was the enemy to be scared all over again.

Lyudmila, intuiting Wendy's distress, said, "But I'm a *White* Russian, isn't that so, Aunt Evan?"

Evan nodded. "Indeed it is." She turned Wendy around to face Lyudmila. "Lyudmila is my friend. My very good friend. She helped me and Ben rescue you. Remember?"

Wendy knuckled her eyes for a moment, then opened them wide. Lyudmila was sitting cross-legged on the carpet, feeding Michael, oblivious to his sister's angst, bits of food, which he devoured like a tiny trencherman.

Now Lyudmila turned again to Wendy, her smile as broad as the room. "Wendy, will you allow me to tell you a joke? It's a Russian joke, but I think you'll like it."

When Wendy nodded after a brief hesitation, Lyudmila said, "Okay, ready? Why do Russian spies always walk around in threes?" When Wendy shrugged, she said, "One can read, one can write, and the third keeps an eye on the two intellectuals." It took a moment, but then Wendy burst out laughing, and Evan saw Bobbi as she had been when they were children, before the hatred, the betrayal, the pain.

60

AFTERMATH II
MOSCOW, RUSSIAN FEDERATION

"Prognosis?" The newly anointed Kata Romanovna, director of Zaslon, said. Kobalt was getting used to her new name, responded to it without a hitch or hesitation.

"He's making good progress," said the attending physician, a pulmonologist. He was a blond man with the face like a ship's prow. Kata thought he was lucky to spend most of his working days behind a mask. "The good news is the bullet missed his spine. He was shot in the upper-right quadrant. The bullet fractured his scapula and went right on into chest muscle, which was dense enough to stop the bullet." He shrugged. "We had a hell of a time repairing his scapula and when we went in, we found a collapsed lung." He checked his pager. "Rehab will be a long, painful process, but on the bright side he's in exceptionally good shape." He checked his pager again. "I'm sorry, I've got to go."

Kata had been speaking to the doctor outside the door to Zherov's room. The corridor was like any other hospital corridor, filled with the susurrus of lowered voices, the squeaking of nurses' shoes against linoleum, the hushed *click-clack* of carts and gurneys passing by. All these she ignored. It was the smell that got her—the sickly-sweet miasma of antiseptic, anxiety, sickness, and death.

Without another thought she pushed through the door. A single room befitting his rank. The hospital bed was against the right-hand wall, near the window that looked out on the vast car park. Zherov was under the covers, lying on his left side, hooked up to a series of beeping machines checking heart rate, blood pressure, oxygen level, and the like. Tubes ran from hanging plastic sacks into the backs of his hands. Painkillers, probably.

"Hey, you," she said, approaching him with a smile.

"Hey yourself." His smile was brighter than hers, but then he'd had nothing to smile about since he was shot. "What's new?"

He was thinner than the last time she had seen him, paler. "Your beard, for one thing."

"I think it makes me look distinguished." He winced as he tried to move himself up on the pillow.

"You in a lot of pain?"

"Define a lot."

As she went to the closet, ripped plastic film off a pillow, he said, "Omega?"

"Defunct, according to reports. Their headquarters in the Carpathians went up in a series of fireballs visible for miles around." Which meant that Lyudmila had made good on her promise. She had expected nothing less. But since they'd parted in Romania, she hadn't heard from her. She didn't know whether to be angry or worried.

"All right then." He frowned. "You find out who shot me?"

"She's dead," Kata grinned. "I shoved a cattle prod down her gullet."

"Ingenious."

She laughed lightly. "I took it off her."

"Fly on the wall," he said wistfully.

She nodded. "You would have liked what you saw."

"I bet."

"Anton." Her demeanor grew serious as she drew a chair up beside him. She offered the pillow, but he shook his head, so she kept it on her lap as she sat. "Turns out Baev's adjutant was the one who ratted me out to Omega."

"Stands to reason he's the one who got to Ermi, too."

"Uh-huh."

"And what happened to him?" he asked. "The adjutant, I mean."

"Ilya Gurin?" She shrugged. "He came to a bad end. Had his throat slit."

"Oh."

She stood up, placed the pillow on the chair seat, and went to stand by the window. Through the blinds she could see the sun spinning dizzily off the windshields of the vehicles.

"There's only one thing wrong with the theory that Gurin ratted me out."

"Oh?"

"Sure. Gurin didn't have access to the Kobalt dossier. He couldn't have known about my Omega remit, let alone how to contact them in Odessa." She waited a beat, but when he didn't say anything she continued. "Another thing. Gurin had no idea we were in Istanbul. How could he? Even Dima didn't know."

She turned. "But you did, Zherov. You were with me when we met Ermi, and you yourself told me you had seen the Kobalt dossier, so you knew all about my Omega remit."

"Me? But . . . but why would I do such a thing?"

"You just threw Gurin under the bus, didn't you?" She stepped toward him. "You had him do your dirty work, then set him up to be your fall guy if things went sideways."

Zherov turned his head away. "Come on, Bobbi. We

concluded someone with a grudge blackmailed Ermi into giving up the address."

"But we know that's not true." She paused to allow that truth to sink in before continuing. "You might as well tell me. I'll be easier on you than the FSB inquisitors I'll have to call in." She gripped the back of the chair. "Your life is already sufficiently fucked up. I can make the aftermath infinitely easier for you. But if I walk out of this room . . ."

A terrible silence ensued, not for her but for him. "Okay." Zherov sighed. "The truth."

"And nothing but."

He did not return her smile. "So Ilya was in love with me. Madly in love. He did everything I asked him to do, unquestioningly."

"And did you love him?"

"I loved his usefulness," Zherov admitted.

Kata's knuckles turned white on the chairback. "Go on."

"So, okay, I wanted to get rid of you. Nothing personal. But you were a rising star. Dima knew it, Baev knew it, and so did I. You were standing in the way of my ambitions. I couldn't get where I wanted to go with you ahead of me. Zaslon wasn't big enough for the both of us. I'd bitch about it to Ilya and he completely took on my point of view. Now you became an obstacle to *him*. That was him all over."

She tried to ignore the contempt in his voice. "And the knife shop in Istanbul?"

"Well, of course I knew what was coming. Ilya found me an ex-con, and I called the thug when I went to pay the breakfast bill. I gave him Ermi's address. But I have to admit that bastard was more of a handful than I had expected. Still, it worked out, didn't it?"

"Really? I was still alive."

"Somewhere between the time I called him and our arriving at the knife shop I realized you intrigued me too much to have you killed so quickly. Then, of course, it was too late to stop him."

"And you couldn't do it yourself."

"Not after you pulled me to shore on that sandspit off Istanbul."

"Very gallant." She came around from behind the chair. "Is that all?"

"Yes, that's all."

"Actually, it isn't. There's Ermi's murder." She rolled her shoulders to ease the tension that bunched her muscles. "The Omega death ritual—Ana's frightening reminder to her acolytes of the wages of betrayal—involved beheading and jamming a death gag into the victim's mouth. It stuck in my mind that only half the ritual was completed with Ermi—the part I had put in my debriefing report. Which you read. So you must have set up Ermi's murder. But how, I wondered. Your ex-con was busy at the shop, couldn't be in two places at once. That's when it hit me: you hired two of them, one to kill me at the knife shop, the second to go after Ermi." She stared at him. "That's right, isn't it?"

"Fuck you, Kobalt."

Without another word, she grabbed the pillow, smashed it down over his face. "I'm not Kobalt, you fucking fuck," she said through gritted teeth. "I'm Kata Romanovna Hemakova."

She kept the pillow in place until he stopped moving and the outputs flatlined.

"Kobalt is dead."

Throwing the pillow back onto the shelf of the closet, she opened the door, stepped outside. She was already down the corridor and around the corner by the time three nurses hurried into his room.

61

AFTERMATH III
SCHNELLER PSYCHIATRIC CLINIC, GERMANY

Evan found Leonard Pine in the kitchen, finishing a snack he had made for himself. It seemed any time of the day was right for tea, especially during stressful periods. As she stepped in, he poured her a cup of tea from a beautiful Meissen china teapot. Ben was still in surgery. There was nothing she could do for him, except pray. Not her strongest suit.

"Take a pew," Pine said. "I've been expecting you."

He was sitting at one of the work counters, staring out the window as night drew closer, the forest, plunged into pitch darkness, a mere silhouette. She drew up a stool and settled herself.

He gestured. "Milk? Sugar?"

"Let's cut the English butler act, shall we?" she said shortly. "It's confession time."

"As you wish."

He took a sip of his tea. His face betrayed nothing. He was dressed casually for him—gray wool slacks, a cream sweater over a sky-blue shirt with a regimental tie. His shoes, however, were his usual oxford wingtips, mirror shined.

She took the gold cross on its thin chain Ben had handed her and dropped it on the counter between them. The chain was dark with Hel's blood.

He picked it up, cradled it in his cupped palm. His fingertips ran over the cross. "She's dead. My poor sister."

Evan glared at him. "After putting a bullet in my friend's hip."

"I'm sorry about that."

Evan hit him then. He flew off his stool, knocking it over. He sat on the floor but did not touch his jaw, which was already roughened and red from the blow.

"You're sorry about that?" She looked down at him in disgust. "Are you also sorry you betrayed us to Ana?"

He made to get up, but she said, "Stay right there," and he subsided back onto the floor.

"I had no choice," he said. "Ana said she'd kill Hel if I didn't do what she asked." He held out a hand. "At least I didn't give you away. I didn't tell her you weren't Robin."

That was true enough. "Your action still could have gotten all of us killed." When he made no reply, she went on, "You were the perfect mole. You saw and heard everything around here." When he remained silent, she added, "Get up already."

She waited until he was back on his stool, had straightened his shirt and tie, before she said, "Okay, Herr Mole, what do you have for me?"

He took a sip of his tea. He shook so badly he had to hold on to the cup with both hands.

He cleared his throat. "Give me a moment, will you?"

"Sure, take your time." Evan's tone dripped contempt. "You have ten seconds."

He gave her a furtive look, or maybe he was simply abashed. "Are you going to tell the Reveshvilis?"

"No, you are."

He digested this news for several moments before nodding

in acquiescence. Then he took a tremulous breath and began. "One night, probably just after midnight, I was outside taking a breath of fresh air. From around the corner I heard Ana's voice. She was speaking on her mobile."

"When was this?"

"Shortly before the Herr *Doktor* ordered her to leave."

"Go on."

"When I crept close, I heard her in conversation with her sister. 'Listen, Lucinda, you've got to find a way,' she said."

And Evan heard again the echo of Ana's strident voice, "*And for your information my sister's name is Lucinda, not that ugly version Konstantin gave her.*"

"What else did you hear?"

"They were talking about millions of dollars."

"Millions?" The short hairs at the back of Evan's neck stood up.

Leonard nodded. "That's right."

Evan shook her head. "But millions of dollars? Where would Ana's sister get that kind of money?"

"That's precisely what Ana asked her, though not as nicely."

"And what did her sister say to that?"

"I couldn't hear that, of course. But Ana listened, then replied. 'When?' And then, 'How rich did you say he was?'"

Leonard sighed. "It turns out Luzida also changed her name when she moved to Slovenia and established citizenship." He winced. His jaw was beginning to swell.

For the rest of the evening, through dinner and then story time, Evan arranged to be alone with the children. For the most part they seemed happy, thrilled to spend time with her, but there were pockets of silence when they clung to her, and she rocked them wordlessly. She did not ask them about their abduction or their incarceration inside the citadel, trusting that they would tell her in their own time, at their own pace. As for her, she felt her heart must burst at the giddiness of being with them no matter what they were doing or saying. An emotional flickering pulsed through her. Sometimes, she felt unbearably close to them, as if they were her own. Strange, very strange.

At story time, they asked her for Peter Pan. She had read them the book so often she had memorized the bones and some of the muscle of the story. What details she could not remember, she pulled from the Disney film. They asked her to repeat the flying sequence, when Peter took them to Neverland. They fought sleep, but finally, it took them over and their eyes closed, their breathing turned slow and regular, two precious bodies in one big bed, wrapped around each other. They had asked that the lamps stay on, calling them "nightlights," as their namesakes in the story called the streetlights outside the Darlings' London townhome.

For some time after they fell asleep, Evan sat by their bedside, watching over them, wishing them sweet dreams, sending all the love she had to them in an endless flow. Nevertheless, she could not stop herself wondering how deeply they had been scarred by their ordeal. They had already suffered the loss of their parents. They would need psychological help to work through their fear, helplessness, and anger, she knew that with a certainty. She could not think of anyone better to provide this support than Kostya. And, in any case, she would be here to help guide them for as long as Ben was recovering and rehabbing. After that, it was their choice whether to remain here with their grandparents or to return to the States. Until that time, when, inevitably, they acted out, she would be here to hold them; when, inevitably, they broke down in tears, she would be here to hold them, and when they laughed, she would laugh with them, urging them on toward happiness.

Happiness.

At what point something inside her changed she could not

afterward have said, but somewhere along the line looking at them was like looking inside herself. It occurred to her then that going after them, finding them, bringing them to safety, even at the possible cost of her own life or that of Ben's and Lyudmila's, was the most important remit she'd ever undertaken. It seemed odd, at first blush, but saving the world was abstract. Saving Wendy and Michael was real, visceral. She felt it down to her bones. They were part of her; she was part of them. And she knew Bobbi lived on inside them. Her sister was dead, but sadly Evan had discovered that death did not assuage hatred or the feeling of betrayal. And yet, the more time she spent with them, the more her hatred faded, the more forgiveness became a real possibility.

Happiness. For her it wasn't easy.

She continued her silent vigil, thinking, *They're here, they're healthy, they're safe.* She thought about them the night of their escape, on the copter's unfurled ladder, firelight sparking one side of their brave faces as they climbed up to where the mechanical Peter Pan hovered, ready to whisk them off to Neverland.

"It's not on any chart," she sang softly. "You can find it in your heart . . ." Were those the exact words? It didn't matter. She sang the refrain again.

Tears came, then. She made no attempt to stop them.

"How's the boy?" Evan said when she stepped into the clinic's post-op suite.

Ben smiled. "Feeling no pain. For now, anyway." His face darkened. "Prognosis?"

"You look like shit."

"Fuck you very much."

She laughed. She had said it as a joke, of course, but she was appalled at how pale and drawn he looked, lines etched deep into his face she had never noticed before. Had they even been there, or had he been marked as she had by this field assignment?

"I meant the kids," he said.

"They'll be fine, Ben. I just introduced them to their grandparents; they're having breakfast together. Already Rebecca is a different person, animated, smiling, delighted at everything the children say or do. Wendy repeated the joke about the Russian spies Lyudmila told her."

Ben smiled. "I know that one."

"When she hit the punch line, Kostya laughed so hard tears came to his eyes."

"That's good for all of them." He was clearly pleased, the news taking him out of himself for the moment. "I spoke with Zoe. She misses both of us, but she's having a ball with her friends."

"It's wonderful she's adjusted so well to you being away for long periods." The moment she said it she knew it was a mistake.

He frowned. "Yeah, well . . ."

"I miss her too," she said hastily. "I'll call her later today."

"She'll love that."

Evan cleared her throat. "I just spoke to the surgeon. Nice guy. Handsome, too."

"Oh, for God's sake!"

"The latest tests are all good. It's early days yet but pretty much certain you'll regain your ability to walk."

Ben closed his eyes for a moment.

"So how d'you feel about canes?" she said in a brightened voice. He grimaced and in return she gave him her widest grin. "I'm going to find you the best damn one available. Maybe I'll even have it made to order. What's your preference, ebony, blackthorn, Malacca? I think a sculpted lion's head on top would suit you. King of the jungle, what d'you think?"

"So . . ." He sighed. "My field days are over."

She was quiet for a moment. "Listen, Ben. Maybe it's for the b—"

"Help me understand, dammit," he barked.

He had every reason to be angry. "The truth is you're better as control than as a field agent."

"Ouch."

She held up a hand. "Wait. Hear me out. I'm so concentrated on working out there, handling the endless stream of problems in the field, I often lose sight of the big picture. As an example, I was more fixated on rescuing Wendy and Michael than on dealing with Omega. That's what you and Lyudmila were doing." She smiled. "Ben, my Ben, you're the one who always sees and reacts to the macro elements. That's your thing; it's what you're best at. That's why you're able to move pieces around the board so successfully."

He regarded her with both anger and gratitude.

"We're a team, you and I. The best team I've ever been on. That's not going to change one iota. I sure as hell won't let you put yourself out to pasture."

A silence arose, just the metronome beeping of the monitors that could depress even a kid as Christmastime.

Just as his gaze was turning inward, she piped up. "So. Back to business. Turns out . . ." She approached his bed. "You'll never guess who Ana's twin sister turns out to be."

"Madonna," he said facetiously. "Who?"

"She changed her name just like Ana did, but she went several steps further. She's Lucinda Horvat now."

Ben almost did a double take. "What? Samuel Wainwright Wells's wife?"

"None other." She leaned closer. "And, get this, the two sisters were in touch. Leonard Pine overheard Ana asking Lucinda for money—millions."

"But this was . . . when?"

"Two, three years ago. Which means . . ."

Despite his dark mood, a bright spark lit up Ben's eyes and his breath quickened. "Which means that Lucinda Horvat seduced Wells and married him so she could siphon his money to her sister and Omega."

Evan nodded. "And that by now Lucinda Wells is the head of Omega in the States."

"She's likely the one who ordered you abducted and both of us dead," Ben said.

He pursed his lips. Then, crisply, "Hand me my mobile." When she did, he punched in a speed dial number. "We need a sponsor we can trust, who's independent of the government and who has deep pockets."

She knew precisely who he meant, and while he spoke to Isobel Lowe, she stepped away in order both to afford them privacy and to reassure Ben that she trusted him. But in her heart of hearts she wondered whether she trusted his longtime friend, trusted that their relationship was strictly business as Ben had repeatedly assured her it was.

But those fears were for another time, another place. For now, she saw the wisdom in getting her backing. Frankly, as General Aristides had told Ben in no uncertain terms, there was no longer a place for them within any of the government's clandestine agencies. And besides, she didn't want to be there. Neither, she was sure, did Ben.

"It's done." Ben handed the mobile back to her. "As soon as I go through rehab here and get my strength back, one of her jets will be waiting for us in Köln."

Evan nodded, put a hand on his shoulder. She grinned. "Then you'd better get through rehab ASAP, Ben. We have more work to do."

Notes on the Novel

As in all my books I try to be as true to life as possible. There purportedly is an ultrasecret division of the Russian SVR, known as Zaslon, all protestations of the Russian government to the contrary. Zaslon differs from *spetsnaz*, for instance, which is more or less equivalent to the American Special Forces, because it is not involved in military actions, but in high-stealth ops, of which the SVR can safely deny all knowledge. Nonetheless, it is true that the SVR has taken to hiring ex-cons who ran murder-for-hire operations inside their prisons for its most unseemly and politically delicate wet work. The boatyards in Odessa are as depicted in the novel.

However, I am at heart a novelist, not a journalist, so inventions will creep in here and there. Some examples: though I am aware that Reveshvili is a Georgian name, the fact is Kostya's great-grandfather emigrated to Russia, but did not, as some émigrés did, Russify his name. Rebecca's family hails from St. Petersburg.

There is a clinic in the Bergisch Gladbach area outside Cologne, but it bears no resemblance whatsoever to Reveshvili's clinic. Nice area of Germany, though. Picturesque, which is why I chose it. Kostya's theory regarding twins, interesting though it may be, is his alone. To my knowledge, it does not exist in real life.

Acknowledgments

Grateful thanks to my amazing team:

Victoria Schochet Lustbader—the empress of editors

Linda Quinton—my alter ego and fiercest advocate at Forge Books, a better publishing maestro I cannot imagine

Eileen Lawrence, Jennifer McClelland-Smith, and the entire marketing team for your ideas and endless resourcefulness

Patrick Canfield—my in-house conscience

Lani Meyer—my wonderful copy editor

Alexis Saarela—my tireless publicist

Robert Allen, Steve Wagner, and Emily Dyer at Macmillan Audio

Lauren Fortgang—the strong voice of Evan and *The Nemesis Manifesto*

Mitch Hoffman—my agent. I don't know how you do what you do, buddy, but you do it so well!

A very special Thank You, as always, to Tom Doherty—mentor and friend